Under the Same Stars

Tim Lott

W F HOWES LTD

This large print edition published in 2012 by
W F Howes Ltd
Unit 4, Rearsby Business Park, Gaddesby Lane,
Rearsby, Leicester LE7 4YH

1 3 5 7 9 10 8 6 4 2

First published in the United Kingdom in 2011
by Simon & Schuster

A CIP catalogue record for this book is available
from the British Library

ISBN 978 1 47120 008 3

Typeset by Palimpsest Book Production Limited,
Falkirk, Stirlingshire
Printed and bound in Great Britain
by MPG Books Ltd, Bodmin, Cornwall

Dedicated to Jeff Lott, a dear friend and brother

Those are the same stars, and that is the same moon, that look down upon your brothers and sisters, and which they see as they look up to them, though they are ever so far away from us, and each other.

– Sojourner Truth, 1797–1893,
abolitionist and former slave

CHAPTER 1

SUNDAY, 31 AUGUST 2008, TOKYNGTON, LONDON

Salinger Nash pressed his eyelids together, trying to keep at bay the fantail of light that spread through the gap separating the heavy purple velvet curtains from the window frame. He knew that his goal of remaining in darkness was hopeless, but he could never be sure of the most obvious of facts when he first awoke.

He became aware of a familiar, raw sensation, something like an emotion, located around the wall of his sternum. It was close to being anger, but more passive, facing inward as well as outward. It was a nexus of heat, and of hurt, and of friction – as if the lining of his innermost self, long wounded, had been poorly cauterised leaving an ever-tender scar. The scar was stitched with guilt – a guilt unattached to any sin that he could remember committing.

The light seemed to be brightening behind the pink screens of his eyelids. He became conscious of standing back and watching himself from within, trying to pin labels onto his own mental states. It was futile, but he could not escape the compulsion. The problem of how he felt when he first awoke was the first of a series of mysteries that he was driven towards grappling with every day. The sensation of not knowing, of not knowing anything for certain, lay deep, a space beneath the rawness, an unsettling blankness that never abated.

The rude snorting of a rubbish truck grew louder and louder as it approached, pig-like, along the street outside. Combined with the light, it took a jemmy to his consciousness. Salinger pushed his eyes open, and focused resentfully on the gap in the curtains. He had spent a lot of money on thick, plush cloth, only to find that the original purpose – to render the room dark, even in bright sunlight – was subverted by this unconsidered, albeit obvious, detail.

So much that was obvious, Salinger thought, went unnoticed.

Tiane – Christiane Wilson, his partner for almost three years now – began snoring, unconsciously echoing the truck. Salinger stared at her, mildly offended. There was a space between the two of them of some nine inches. It was about average, he supposed. After an argument it could stretch to twelve or even fifteen inches. On a good day, they would wake up lightly touching.

He reached over and pinched Tiane's nose to stop the noise, harder than necessary. Her arms flailed up in self-defence, pushing him away. She muttered something obscene and turned on her side.

Salinger considered how he felt about Tiane that particular morning. He examined her cropped, dyed-black hair, the slender line of her neck, her slowly slackening chin.

He remembered that he loved her. Sometimes – too often – he forgot this, but today the knowledge was immanent, secure. He felt the sense of how much he owed her. A golden chain of light, projected from the curtain top to the sheets, linked them. He made shadows on the luminescence with his fingers. A dog, a rabbit, a monster.

He needed to rise from the bed and give his soft jumbled thoughts – and the chaotic emotions that rippled in their wake – a vigorous shake. He needed to be put into order. Life – once it was up and running – tricked him into feeling relatively normal.

He stood up, naked. His thoughts swung towards the uncomplicated desire for sex. He moved around to Tiane's side of the bed. His semi-erect cock was level with her open mouth. He stepped forward, closing the distance, so that it almost touched her lips.

Tiane began snoring again. Salinger noticed a bubble of spit forming, breaking, then pooling at the corner of her lips. His incipient lust gave way to a faint distaste. He turned away and reached up to a plastic hook on the back of the bedroom door and took down his pale-blue waffle-cotton dressing gown. The front was stained with egg yolk from the previous day's breakfast. He wrapped it round his torso and secured the belt with an unstable knot which immediately began to unravel.

He looked for his slippers. Unable to find them, he gave up and went barefoot, stubbing his toe immediately on an inch of coir carpet that had for several months protruded between the landing and the bathroom. He cursed the material and tried, as he had dozens of times before, to press it into place with his foot. It sprang back slowly into position as usual, with practised insolence.

In the bathroom he stopped to splash his face with cold water, and searched the mirror for the remnants of the crust of sleep at the corners of his eyes. The small scar just in front of his right ear where he had fallen and banged his head on the edge of a glass coffee table as a child remained faintly visible. His hair looked greasy and thin. His skin, once olive, was becoming sallow. His eyes showed alarm, his brows were reaching out to one another to meet in the middle. He stuck out his tongue. It was as grey and furred as the hindquarters of a stray moggy.

He felt perfectly neutral about these observations. He disliked looking in mirrors much less than he once had. Now that he was forty, he reasoned, everyone looked as bad as everyone else. The competitive element of this part of life at least had receded.

He reached up to the bathroom cabinet and took out his clandestine supply of Prozac, which was concealed inside an empty aspirin box. Tiane believed herself to be allergic to aspirin so she had no reason to look inside.

He did not wish Tiane to know that he was medicated. It was one of the few secrets that he kept from her. She believed that antidepressants chemically generated an inauthentic self. It was when he had heard her casually refer to them as *happy pills* to a friend that he decided that he could not trust her with the knowledge. They were not happy pills. They did not make him happy. They rendered his life supportable. They fended off madness by reconfiguring synapses.

Salinger had given years over to therapy, counselling and psychoanalysis. When these had proved ineffective, he had consumed self-help books, practised kundalini yoga and feasted on St John's wort. Still his moods came in storms, and the sensation that he was tumbling down a cliff leading to a vertiginous precipice never quite left him.

It was only the Prozac that worked – except that nowadays it didn't. The violent mood swings he remembered from his teenage years – during the decade after his father, Henry, had abandoned his mother and left the country for good – were beginning to reassert themselves, despite the serotonin jag that the pills were designed to provide. Whether his depression arose out of that desertion, or from some trauma arising from the leukemia he had been born with – and eventually, as an infant, cured of – was another impenetrable conundrum.

He swallowed the green-and-white capsule anyway and replaced the punctured foil-and-cellophane pouch. He made his way downstairs. In the hall, the newspapers were spread on the doormat – a left-wing broadsheet for him and a middle-England tabloid for Tiane.

He glanced at the papers as he carried them into the kitchen. The headlines were routinely dispiriting. He could hardly distinguish one day's information from the next. The country was failing. The world economic system was about to collapse. The sub-prime crisis was reaching its prime. The golem Bush loomed and lurched within the benighted bunker of the White House.

His putative successor, John McCain, had the previous day chosen a running mate, Sarah something. She was a hyper-hygienic soccer mom with a chipmunk demeanour and a patriotic ignorance. McCain clearly believed she would seal the presidential deal for him by appealing to the moron vote. Salinger thought it was probably a good strategy. It would only take a slight push to secure another Republican victory. Americans would be loath to elect a black leader, even one as pasty and as distant from the ghetto as Barack Obama. In fact, now that Salinger thought of it, it was unimaginable.

He sat down at the table and read on. Anglicans were still divided over homosexuality. Northern

6

Rock was cutting two thousand jobs. The economy was at a sixty-year low. Everyone hated Gordon Brown, just as much as everyone had once hated Tony Blair. Switching jockeys as the horse faltered had been worse than pointless.

Everything was unravelling. It had been the same story for as long as he could remember, even in the boom years, where instead of optimism there had been a spreading stain of greed and an anxious suspicion of hubris. The hubristic part of the equation was turning out to be particularly acute. One story informed him that house prices were down 8 per cent for the month of July alone on the year earlier. At this rate, in a year's time, the modest maisonette that he shared with Tiane in Tokyngton, north-west London would be worth less than his mortgage.

The headlines made him feel oddly cheerful. It was the comforting predictability of the English mind, he supposed – the habit of expecting the worst and being vaguely reassured when it transpired.

Salinger made himself toast and coffee, splattering the black liquid onto the marble work surface, nudging crumbs carelessly onto the floor. A bright blur of pleasure coalesced inside him. Simple things had the capacity to make him joyful. He tasted the Marmite on his tongue, the dark warm kick of the coffee. The bread was good, expensive, sourdough. He believed in splashing out on the basics. Unsalted butter, French.

Full-cream milk from a farmers' market. Tiane was happy with Kingsmill and Anchor and found his extravagance mystifying. They could barely make the gas bill nowadays.

He ploughed through the leader articles of his newspaper as he chewed and swallowed the brittle bread. We were failing our young people, our old people, our poor people. We were letting black people down so badly they were stabbing and shooting one another on a daily basis. We were failing every test spectacularly. Another ice cap had melted, another polar bear had expired from sunstroke. Worrying about global warming was compulsory. Doing something about it was an ethical requirement.

There were so many moral demands. Once Salinger had thought life was simply about earning a living, not breaking the law and protecting yourself and those close to you. Now there was an endlessly elongating queue of matters of conscience, all apparently valid. They each demanded some kind of commitment and required immediate action.

Failure to take appropriate steps would result in the death of a donkey, the starvation of a child, the increase, at a geometrical rate, of typhoid in the Niger or wherever the shit was hitting the fan that week. This novel requirement on the Western conscience felt oddly inhuman to him. People weren't that good.

He lit a cigarette, enjoying both the nicotine kick and the feeling of mild transgression. He glanced at Tiane's newspaper. It told much the same story as the broadsheet, albeit from a different angle. Our young people were failing us, black people were letting us down, gay, lesbian and transsexual people were making a fuss about nothing. Everyone was fat, or prematurely pregnant or smoked and drank in colossal quantities. The tabloid was in accord with the broadsheet that dissolution had reached epic proportions.

He stopped to stare out of the window at a bird that was perched on a bough. He wasn't sure what kind of bird it was – he was poor at naming things. Whatever it was, there was a simple pleasure in just watching the bird being bird-like, birdish, birdy. It was trilling wildly in celebration of nothing in particular. That was the proper attitude to life, he decided – hymns to guiltless, joyful meaning-lessness. He felt that the cheerfulness of birds must have something to do with their absolute lack of conscience, combined with the inestimable advan-tage of extreme stupidity.

The bird flew off, leaving behind it a small white gobbet of mess on the windowsill. Salinger studied the mess for a moment, hoping that it might be symbolic of something or other, then gave up and went back to skimming the newspaper. He allowed himself to drift in a comforting soup of prejudice and received opinion. It wasn't until he reached the headline on page 31 that his attention narrowed and focused.

New Orleans braced for chaos as hurricane looms
Police patrol streets with bullhorns urging people to
flee in face of storm that has already killed 70

The hurricane this time was called Gustav. Salinger wondered about the genealogy of hurricanes. Why were some male and some female? Could some be said to be related? Was Gustav born of the same meteorological womb as Katrina, that witch-monster of weather systems?

Another windy day in Louisiana. New Orleans was a cursed city, reflected Salinger. He often wondered how Carson could bear to live there. He had visited his brother there on only one occasion, ten years previously. He found the city unbearably hot, edgy with crime and top-heavy with an inflated idea of its own importance.

The last time he had spoken to his brother was shortly after Katrina had moved past, leaving the levees to buckle under the weight of water. Then, watching the devastation and isolation of those left behind, Salinger had found himself filled with an intense anger.

He had jumped up in his chair and thrown his cigarette packet at the screen in frustration when, five days into the crisis, a woman holding a crying, hungry, desperately thirsty child complained that still, even now, no one had come to help, as military helicopters overhead dived and swooped and threatened, watching for looters. Her wheelchair-bound father had succumbed to the flood. Her

10

eighty-year-old mother was missing. No relief had arrived.

The government's indifference to the city, while the old drowned in their roof spaces and black corpses drifted down Canal Street, had shocked him the way an earthquake in the Sichuan province or a mining disaster in Peru simply couldn't. They were Americans dying down there. He watched their TV programmes, listened to their music, ate their food, attired himself in their fashions. The English were their recent ancestors, practically their relatives. Such callousness seemed medieval. Or perhaps it was perfectly modern, perfectly American.

In order to properly enjoy the rare satisfaction of venting his moral outrage, he had phoned Carson. It had been the first time they had spoken for a number of years. Carson, who, like most of the white population, had evacuated before Katrina had struck, was unworried, unoffended, imperturbable and infuriatingly emollient.

His refusal to blame the government, or anyone in particular, frustrated Salinger. Since Carson had become a born-again Christian, after marrying a church-going massage therapist from New Mexico, his natural equanimity had evolved, or possibly regressed, into an impenetrably amiable fatalism.

Salinger had cut the telephone call short, without bothering to make an excuse. They had not spoken again until Carson travelled to England for their mother's funeral.

Salinger moved beyond the hurricane story and

started working his way through the television previews with a pencil, marking the programmes he wanted to record. The phone began to ring. He ignored it.

Salinger circled another highly rated American TV drama series that he would record but never find the time or the determination to watch. The plots required too much concentration. The dumb Yanks got smart when nobody was looking.

The phone rang off, then started to trill once more. Salinger looked at the clock. It was seven thirty. It then occurred to Salinger that the only people who rang persistently early on a Sunday morning were those bearing news of bereavement. He picked up the receiver trying to imagine candidates for imminent fatality.

'Salinger?'

He recognized the voice, softened though it was from its original suburban London flatness into a syrupy American drawl which Salinger could never quite stop thinking of as phoney.

'Carson.'

'Sorry if I woke you.'

'You didn't wake me. I was just thinking of you, actually. What time is it there?'

'About one in the morning.'

'How are you? This is a surprise.'

'I'm good.'

Salinger waited for an explanation for the phone call, but there was only a silence at the other end of the line.

'Are you calling about the hurricane? I was just reading about it.'

'Gustav? That's all going to be fine. We're all moved out. We're in Jackson, Mississippi this time. It will pass us by. No, I'm not calling about Gustav.'

Salinger picked a crumb of toast out of his teeth, and felt surprise at how entirely unsurprised he was to be hearing from his brother for the first time in two years.

'Thing is, Dad's not well, Salinger.'

Salinger nodded. He looked at the clock on the wall again. The time was the same as when last he looked. He wondered if the clock was broken or whether it was just one of those days when time moved more slowly than he expected.

'How is he ill?'

'I'm not sure. I got a letter.'

'He's still not on the phone? Or the Net?'

'It's not actually a letter from him personally. It's from that woman, Ladybird.'

Salinger became aware of a faint griping sensation in his stomach. He felt through the fold of his dressing gown and rubbed his abdomen. He noticed that he had Marmite on his fingertips and had stained the front of the gown again with the stuff.

'Do you want me to read it to you?'

Salinger could hear a slight fumbling and rustling at the other end of the phone, then Carson coughing, then a short silence.

'There's no address,' said Carson. 'There's not much of it. It says,

> 'Dear Carson,
>   Your father promised to keep in touch as to his movements. Well, since we have stayed put in Provincetown for the last twenty years, there has been nothing to tell. But now we have moved back to Las Cruces because your father is unwell and the health care is better there. Please also inform your brother, Salinger. Henry sends his regards.
>   Yours sincerely,
>   Ladybird Keillor.'

Salinger rubbed his stomach harder. The gripe was worsening, as if he had swallowed gravel or glass.

'Salinger? Are you still there?'

'I'm trying to imagine how I should react.'

'You expected he'd get back in touch again one day – didn't you?'

'I haven't really thought about it.'

'I understand that you're upset.'

'I'm not upset.'

'Salinger . . .'

'What kind of letter is that? After nothing for twenty years. He doesn't even say where he is. He doesn't even say what's wrong with him.'

'Do you want me to call you back later? When you've had time to digest things a little? I'm not going to go to bed for a while yet.'

Salinger put the phone back on its cradle. As it clicked into place, Tiane appeared at the kitchen door. She was wearing crumpled white-flannel pyjamas and a pair of black-cotton Chinese slippers which, slightly too big, flip-flopped as she walked.

She approached him silently, and covered the back of his hand with her palm. It occurred to Salinger that her skin felt slightly papery. He wondered if it was age, or if he simply hadn't noticed before.

'What's the matter, Sal?'

Salinger squeezed her hand, then started rubbing his knees with his palms in small circular movements. It was a nervous habit he had developed in childhood and never quite shaken off.

'What makes you think anything is the matter?'

'You're crying.'

He touched his face and felt the moisture there. He tore off a sheet of kitchen roll and dabbed at his cheeks. He looked up at Tiane. She was the same age as Salinger but looked five years younger. She didn't worry about things. It was good for the complexion.

'Are you having an episode?'

Salinger always referred to his bouts of depression as *episodes*. He didn't reply. He looked up at her, taking in the slight roughness of her skin, the way her shoulders drooped slightly as if in permanently amused resignation. Her eyes searched for his, but he couldn't meet them. The

15

honesty that Tiane sometimes asked for frightened him.

Sometimes, when he was brave, they had long conversations with their eyes. They lay on their pillows, an inch apart, stared at one another, deep into one another, for minutes at a stretch. Light refracted back and forth, like two mirrors facing, in infinite regression. Behind the light, something more.

But today, somehow, the cost seemed too great. The prospect of his own nakedness under the glare of her gaze pulled his eyes down to the floor.

'Salinger?'

'It's my father.'

'Is he all right?'

'He's ill. He's left the East Coast and moved to New Mexico because the health care is cheaper.'

Tiane said nothing, then moved over to the kitchen top and poured herself a cup of coffee from the cafetière. She always drank from the same cup, a big old mug she had bought from a flea market. It had Cornish-blue stripes on a cream background. On the radio, someone was talking to the presenter about her three wonderful children, one of whom suffered from severe autism. Apparently the listener's parental love had not been impaired as a result of his disability, despite the fact that he showed no emotions other than anger or fear.

Salinger found himself doubting that this was true. People contrived to believe what they wished they felt.

Tiane sat on the chair opposite Salinger and sipped at the rim of her mug, then blew on the surface of the coffee to cool it.

'Are you worried, Sal?'

'I'm weary.'

Salinger slowly tore the sheet of kitchen roll in half.

'Why can't he just be a normal old man? Living out his life in some bungalow on the south coast.'

'With your mother.'

'That wouldn't be much fun. What with the two years she's just spent in the ground.'

Tiane was chewing on multigrain toast which she had foraged from the refuse pile of a local supermarket. She hated waste. The radio chattered. She wasn't listening to it. She just liked the noise.

Salinger looked at the window. The light was brightening the street, raising curtains, illuminating exits and entrances.

'Why don't you go and see him?'

'The same reason I didn't go and see him before.'

'You can't forgive him.'

'I just don't like him. I don't like America, either.'

'Why not? You've only been there once. How can you know?'

'I just don't like it.'

'You're not taking it personally, then.'

'What personally?'

'That he chose America.'

'Who? Henry or Carson? Anyway, as far as I'm concerned it's welcome to them.'

'Where is Henry exactly?'

'The letter didn't bother to say. Or what was wrong with him.'

Tiane sipped at the coffee, making a loud slurping noise.

'You sound like water down a plughole.'

Tiane slurped louder, then put the mug down.

'Maybe it's time you made an effort to try and reach out to your father.'

'"Reach out"?'

'Re-establish contact. Make a gesture. However you want to put it.'

'Any "reaching out" needs to come from him. He's the one who fucked off.'

Salinger felt his sense of weariness intensify.

'I've got to go soon. I've got to be at the studio.'

'It's Sunday. You don't *have* to go to the studio.'

'You think my work can be indefinitely postponed. It can't. I need to make a change. I can't wait any longer.'

Salinger looked again at the window. The light would never leave you alone, particle or wave, wave or particle, indeterminate.

Carson rang Salinger back just as he was about to leave the house. This time, he urged Salinger to come to America.

'I don't know, Carson,' said Salinger. 'I'm pretty busy. What's the point?'

'I'll pick up the fare. We've been too long apart.'

'We saw one another at Mum's funeral.'

'That was nearly two years ago. For a total forty-eight hours.'

'That was down to you.'

'Let's not get into the blame game.'

Carson had arrived the day before the funeral, checked into a hotel, turned up at the church late, spent thirty minutes at the wake, then flown back to America the next day. Salinger hadn't seen him shed a tear.

The reason for the brevity of the visit, he had told Salinger then, was that LouLou, his wife, was pregnant with what they hoped would be their first child. She lost the baby six weeks after the funeral, as she had lost others before. Salinger had forgotten how many.

'We could make it a road trip, American-style. I'll show you around the city for a few days, once the storm's blown out, then we'll hire an old Chevy or something and drive out to see Dad. Stay in some funky hotels, the sort that you like. Give Henry a surprise. I'm pretty sure he'd like to see us.'

'I don't know why you're so sure. He went to a considerable effort to get away from us.'

'He just fell in love with someone. It happens. Don't take it personally. It happened to me too. You don't choose who you fall in love with.'

'We don't know where he is.'

'I'll make further enquiries. I'll locate him.'

'I have an exhibition to prepare.'

'An exhibition?'

19

'Of paintings. Possibly an installation. I don't know.'

Carson said nothing. Salinger suddenly felt the need to justify himself well up inside him.

'I'm trying to move on from the cartoons and the illustrations and the greetings cards and all that schlock.'

'I like your cartoons. And the greetings cards. LouLou loves the one with the bear. It's funny.'

'It's just a living. I'm trying to do something more. I've booked a space. I've got a gallery interested.'

'Can't you put it off?'

'Sure. Why not? It's not like my proper job. I do bears, right?'

'I didn't mean that. It's just that Lou and I would love to see you. Dad being ill – it brings it home to you.'

'What does it bring home?'

'*Family*, Salinger. Will you think it over?'

'I don't know.'

'I've got something else to tell you. I've been putting it off because, well, it's not gone so well before. But listen. LouLou is pregnant again.'

'Congratulations.'

Salinger scanned the sports pages of his newspaper. Real Madrid were asking £33 million for Robinho.

'I've got a feeling this time. It's going to be OK. I'm going to be a dad, Salinger.'

'How far gone is she?'

'Five months. It's looking good, really good, the

doctors say. It's a boy. I've seen the scan. It's incredible. Perfect. We've already named him. We're calling him Henry.'

'Henry?'

Salinger bit back his incredulity.

'Henry. That's great. Another Henry.'

'Thanks. *Thanks*. So will you come?'

Salinger turned to the book section. There was a review of a book about the *Carry On* films. Salinger started reading it. The reviewer described it as tawdry and dull. He had a sudden vision of Sid James' face, enormous, leering at him, cackling like a knowing idiot.

'Salinger?'

'Let me have a think about it.'

'You will? You'll think it over?'

'We'll speak later in the week. OK? Listen, I'm late. I have to go.'

'Salinger, can I ask you something? A favour? LouLou's got this thing about Henry Jnr's English heritage. Roots, family tree – that sort of thing. I wonder if you have any old photos of when we were kids. Of grandparents, of Henry and Evelyn. I don't have anything here. So . . .'

'I don't have much either.'

'Was there anything among Mum's stuff?'

Salinger had cleared out his mother's house after the funeral. Most of the stuff he had thrown away – the dumpy high-street clothes, the cheap crockery, the worthless figurines and mementoes of holidays in the Mediterranean. There were a couple

21

of old biscuit tins he'd kept and briefly glanced through. The contents seemed to comprise largely old railway tickets, postcards and Christmas cards but there were a few photographs.

The tins were in the loft where they had been left untouched since being rescued from Evelyn's small flat in Twickenham. Salinger had borne the responsibility of looking after his mother through the last lonely decade of her life, while her former husband and elder son lived out their lives, oblivious, three thousand miles away.

He had loved his mother, although her life had been a burden to him. Her death had left him stricken. He felt that he was the only one who had grieved for Evelyn. Henry hadn't even acknowledged the letter that Carson sent informing him of her passing. Carson had at least gone through the motions of filial distress – he had looked suitably dour on the day of the funeral – but otherwise had appeared to take the loss entirely in his stride.

'There might be some photographs somewhere.'

'Can you take a look? You could bring them with you.'

'Like I say – I'm kind of busy. Maybe I could send them.'

Salinger put down the phone, once again without saying goodbye. Tiane, who had gone upstairs in order to dress, walked into the room wearing stiff new denim APC jeans, a white T-shirt and no shoes or socks. She carried a ream of paper under her arm.

'Preparation for the new term,' she said.

'Is it tomorrow?'

'Tuesday. There's three hours' worth of it. At least. I'll tear into it while you're at the studio.'

Tiane worked as a maths teacher at a comprehensive school in Wembley, several miles from Tokyngton. Unaccountably to Salinger, she enjoyed her work, despite her frequent complaints that the children were unruly and dismissive of the subject that she taught. Her head was full of mathematical certainties, and she was mysteriously enthusiastic about passing them on to the teenage hoodies, tarts and thugs that populated the sink school she taught in.

Salinger had no understanding of how mathematics was useful to the bulk of the population, but the fact that it *was* important was a matter of faith for Tiane. Numbers, and the relationship between them, she found beautiful. She applied numerical principles to her life, living her days according to probabilities and deductive reasoning. She thought her life through with the meticulousness of a planning application.

Numbers did not speak to Salinger. They were symbols with meanings, but they were meanings he could not begin to understand or find himself drawn to. They were cold abstractions, juiceless. Life, he felt, had a shape that was deeper than statistics, indifferent to probability.

'Carson wants me to go to America on a trip to go and see Dad.'

'You said the letter doesn't make it clear where he is.'

'Carson wants us to go and look for him.'

'Can you afford it?'

Tiane's mind compulsively tended towards the practical.

'He's offered to pay.'

'Perfect. So when are you leaving?'

'Right. Have Carson tell me how golden his life with Jesus is? Take me to visit the sainted father in a journey across his sacred country? Put up with LouLou again. Listen to his self-justifications, his self-satisfied boasting, his born-again . . . *slurry*, his awful, positive, upbeat-American-bullshit take on everything?'

'You sound a little jealous.'

'Why would I be jealous?'

'Because you think he's happy.'

'I'm not happy?'

'Are you?'

Salinger started to consider this fresh mystery.

'What does the question even mean?'

Tiane yawned and fidgeted with her ballpoint pen, which had left a blue stain on the tip of her finger.

'I want to get started on this work. You should go to the States. You should see your father and brother.'

'Why?'

'It might make you feel better.'

The studio complex was often busy on Sundays. Sculptors, painters, photographers and others,

24

thirty-three total in residence, were as likely to turn up at weekends as on a weekday.

The receptionist at the front desk had been there only a few days. She insisted on Salinger showing identification despite the fact she'd let him in once before. He showed his security pass. The photograph made him look like Pacino in *Donnie Brasco* – wrung-out, seedy.

'Your name is Nash Salinger?'

'Flip it.'

'Salinger Nash? Like J.D. Salinger?'

'That's it.'

She handed the security pass back to him. He turned to walk towards his studio.

'Were your parents fans?'

'My father was. Not just of Salinger. He loved all American writers. In fact, he liked one woman American writer so much he called my brother after her.'

'He called your brother a girl's name?'

'Carson. After Carson McCullers. He thought no one would notice.'

There was a pause. Salinger pondered how many times he had been through a version of this conversation before.

'McCullers? Never heard of him,' said the receptionist, taking out her mobile phone and beginning to text. 'But I liked J.D. Salinger. We did him at school. I've got a cousin called Zoe. She's in the same boat as you and your brother.'

'The Salinger character was called Zooey.'

25

'I don't think so. There's no such name as Zooey.'

The receptionist did not look up from her mobile phone. Salinger made his way along the plain, windowless corridor towards his studio.

He pulled open the ugly white-glossed chipboard door marked *15*. On the other side was a twenty-foot by twenty-foot room with a ten-foot ceiling and two skylights. It housed a jumble of paintings, sculptures and drawings.

Since leaving school, he had made a living from two primary sources – illustrations for magazines and newspapers, and greetings cards. He had a natural flair for the latter. Manufacturers paid him a lump sum for his designs for every occasion from party invitations to children's birthdays. He could get several thousand pounds for what was no more than a day's work. His most popular piece was of a brown lachrymose bear. The card was simply entitled 'Sorry'.

Illustrating had provided him with a living, but lately he had grown bored with the work. His political caricatures remained in demand – his Gordon Brown, based on the greetings card bear, sullen, dour and desperately trying to be cuddly, was particularly popular with the commissioning editors of the political pages of magazines and the weekly journals. But he found the work dull and repetitive, and furthermore, he was losing interest in politics.

He had spent the last two years trying to develop his skill as a painter. He started off doing portraits of celebrities – of soap stars, models and TV personalities – taken from photographs he'd seen in magazines rather than sittings, and executed in a variety of historical styles. Coleen McLaughlin in a Francis Bacon triptych, his Bruce Forsyth in a Stanley Spencer churchyard scene, and *Portrait de Thérèse* by Balthus featuring Geri Halliwell instead of Thérèse. He also tried doing sculptures on degradable materials – a figure of Kerry Katona in untreated iron that rusted almost immediately, a figure of Paris Hilton carved from frozen meat that began to rot as soon as it thawed.

None of the results pleased him. The paintings and sculptures were intended as a satire, or more precisely, a joke. They were simply a new aspect of his cartoonist's knack of capturing the essence of a face in a few lines.

He wanted to do more than just jokes, representations, caricatures. In one corner of the room was a selection of eyes preserved in formaldehyde. There were eyes of animals, eyes of humans, eyes of flowers. There was a digitally enhanced video installation of the interior of an eye. There was a representation of a giant eye from the *Big Brother* reality programme. There was a giant papier mâché representation of a human eyeball.

Salinger stood still for a moment and stared at the elements of his now-abandoned eye project. Tiane had mused – tritely, as far as Salinger was concerned – that perhaps they weren't eyes at all, but 'I's. She speculated that Salinger's self-confessed narcissism, his unhealthy obsession with the contents of his own head, had finally spilled over into an obsessive Freudian slip, a tic that converted the ungraspable into something crudely tangible. The death of his mother – she speculated – had resulted in this fanatical attempt to reassert the fact of his own existence.

Not a bad guess for a maths teacher, thought Salinger, at the same time mildly reproving himself for patronizing her. But it nevertheless seemed a far-fetched interpretation. Whatever the truth, his repetition of the image of the eye wasn't getting him any further into the understanding of the nature of seeing.

As an artist, Salinger was aware that he was didactic and unoriginal, which he had previously thought did not disqualify him as an artist but made him interesting. He did not favour the obscure statements and references held inside the secret language of art. Everything he did was obvious. He thought the point of art was to be obvious, and that since you couldn't escape parodying or copying someone or other you might as well be straight-forward about it.

It was all derivative, which was fine. Except that it wasn't. The rationalization was wearing thin. He had decided that being deliberately unoriginal was not original at all. It wasn't even funny. The eye project may or may not have been original, but it at least wasn't consciously referential. He had made an attempt to explain it to Tiane. He told her it was about the way that the mind put the conceptual world together, that it resembled the manner in which the eye put the visual world together – out of clues, cues and memories, rather than direct experience. He wasn't sure, however, of his own interpretation. He feared that he was simply being pretentious.

Then there were the other paintings. These were so personal, so naked, he was scared to put them on show – scared even to paint them, much of the time. They reminded him of *art brut*, paintings by untrained artists, often confined to mental hospitals. They were full of anger, fear and loathing.

There were sexualized images of pre-teen girls floating on wings through blasted desert landscapes, black vortexes sucking in delicately drawn natural landscapes of flowers and trees, healthy faces of pin-up girls disfigured by weeping lesions. There were fat people, poor people, old people being joyfully mowed down by the artist in a spray of machine-gun fire. There was a depiction of a Southern lynching done in the style of a Norman Rockwell painting.

The paintings, he knew, were direct outcrops of his bouts of mental illness. They embarrassed him. He thought they were melodramatic. Worse, they tested the idea that art no longer had anything to do with ethics. Because these paintings – in Salinger's view – were fundamentally shameful. What kind of a monster would paint such visions?

29

However, Franklin De Freitas, the gallery owner who had approached him, was only interested in these paintings, however hard Salinger tried to convince him to accept that the jokey celebrity parodies or some development of the eye installations had equal or superior worth. Salinger had reluctantly agreed to De Freitas' offer, but he was beginning to have second thoughts. The exhibition, he felt sure, would be condemned as a repulsive failure. But still he compulsively worked on the paintings, drawing on his memories of madness, half dreading their completion.

When Salinger returned home that evening, he pulled down the loft ladder and retrieved the two biscuit tins that were his sole inheritance from Evelyn. He emptied out the first one, which had a picture of two grey-white, cheerful Scotty dogs decorating it. The tin had once contained shortbread. Now it was chipped, faded, peeled. He looked at all the marks and wondered how each had come about. Were they all the result of small, forgotten collisions, or did the passage of time itself somehow generate decay, peeling, chipping?

He started rifling through the contents. As he had expected, he started to cry again – Salinger was unusually lachrymose – but it was a pleasant kind of grief, largely recreational. The material, though, was not especially emotional. Most of the contents were receipts for electrical and household goods. There were expired insurance policies and archaic documents for Evelyn's small, ancient Fiat Panda, there were a couple of stamps, some empty envelopes and three blank postcards from Ventnor on the Isle of Wight. There was a skein of thread, a plastic thimble, and a couple of paper clips.

He turned to the second tin. He flipped it open. The lid was barely attached to the body any more, and hung loosely off the hinge. Salinger emptied out the contents. Along with the postcards, tickets and Christmas cards, there were newspaper clippings and recipes, unfilled tax returns, used airline check-in seat stubs, and a few counterfoils from the West End musicals that Evelyn would treat herself to once in a while. There were also photographs – maybe twenty in all. He laid them out in a grid of four by five.

They were disappointing. He doubted that there was anything here that LouLou could derive any ancestral pride from. Most of them were badly composed or out-of-focus snaps of him and Carson as children. At random he picked one off the floor. Carson was sitting in a small red-metal trolley and Salinger was pulling it by means of an extended metal handle. Salinger's face was red with the effort, and creased in a frown. Carson was reclining on the trolley, wearing shorts and a slightly torn T-shirt with a print of Captain Marvel on the front. Captain Marvel wore a shiny red one-piece suit with gold boots and a pearl-white cape. There was a gold flash of lightning across his chest and a gold sash around his waist. Carson himself was laughing, hanging his black-plimsolled feet over the edge.

Salinger couldn't remember the scene at all, but he remembered Carson's T-shirt. Carson had loved it and Salinger had coveted it. His father had picked it up at an auction of Americana. Henry loved American comics, just as he loved American literature, and for a while had collected them. But he had never allowed Carson and Salinger to read them in case they damaged them. The T-shirt had been a form of apology. Carson had worn it almost every day, even in winter, until it became too shabby to wear.

There were five other photographs of Salinger and Carson, always together, both roughly at the same ages, Carson around ten years old, Salinger maybe five or six. In every picture, Carson wore the Captain Marvel T-shirt.

There was another, later picture of him and Carson when they were about nine and thirteen years old respectively, just before Henry had left for America, Salinger imagined. They were facing each other and smiling. Their fists were raised as if they were about to start a boxing match. The image was a kind of joke – Carson and Salinger had never got along.

Salinger turned to a photo of Evelyn and Henry. He held it up to the light. It was black-and-white. From the fashions, it looked like it was taken some time in the mid-1960s. They were in a back garden somewhere. Henry was wearing a narrow-lapelled suit, a thin knitted tie with a squared-off end and a pair of spectacles with broad black plastic rims. He was squinting at the sun. Evelyn looked oddly middle-aged. The tightly gathered waistband of her short floral dress – which although not quite a mini was probably daring for its day and place – gave her an artificial spare tyre across her middle. Her hair was styled to look like Dusty Springfield's, and although the photograph was black-and-white, Salinger felt sure that her lipstick was pink.

There were a few other shots that he would send to Carson – their paternal grandparents, Molly and Albert, on their wedding day, a shot of Evelyn's father standing on a beach with a beach ball and his stomach pulled in, a few snaps of Evelyn and Henry's wedding day.

Replacing the remainder of the contents of the tin, he noticed a plain cream-coloured envelope that had gone undetected amongst the newspaper clippings and recipes. It was sealed with yellowed Sellotape and unmarked.

He peeled off the Sellotape, which had retained a surprising amount of its stickiness, and opened the flap. Upending the envelope, a small square of what appeared to be laminated paper, or plastic, fell out. It was buckled and creased. It took him a few seconds to realize that it was the blank side of a photograph.

He turned the picture over. He couldn't make it out. It was black-and-white, badly faded. It was almost a ghost image. From the distinctive shape of the white border, he guessed that it had come from an old Polaroid Land camera.

Once he had identified an eye and a chin he was able to put together what appeared to be the image of a face around these visual anchors. The picture had been taken very close up. It filled the frame entirely. The face appeared to be that of a child – maybe four or five years old. Salinger did not recognize the face, either because of the fading of the print or because he did not know the subject. There were blotches on the face and random lines. He put these effects down to age and discoloration.

As he inspected the faint image more closely, it occurred to him that he was possibly mistaken about what he had taken to be the effects of time. Another interpretation was possible.

The warping and blackening of the left eye of the child could just as well be an injury. The upper lip, which he had originally thought was simply full, might be distended and swollen. That dark patch on the cheek could be bruising. The right eye might not be squinting in the light. It was – perhaps – almost completely closed and puffy. The more he looked at it, the more the dark line spreading from the nose resembled a line of blood.

He held the photo up to the light that penetrated weakly through the trapdoor from the landing below. The lines became clearer. Gradually, Salinger became convinced that the photograph was of a child who had been beaten, or damaged in some kind of accident.

The image began to press in on him. There was a look of incomprehension in the child's eyes, mixed with a strange gratitude. As if the child had felt they deserved this punishment, and was thankful that it was now over.

He realized that he was now holding the image at arm's length, as if wanting to distance himself from it. He returned the photograph to the envelope. Along with the twenty photographs from the tin, he placed it in a transparent A4 plastic sleeve which he had brought up with him for this purpose.

Downstairs, in the front room, Tiane was still working on the preparation for the new term. Salinger removed the photograph from the plastic sleeve and the envelope.

'What do you make of this?'

He passed her the photograph. She put on her reading glasses, and inspected it carefully.

'I don't know. What is it?'

'Look at it again. Look at it closely.'

He watched her face. After a few seconds, her expression altered from puzzlement to recognition to concern and finally, revulsion.

'Is this what I think it is?'

'What do you think it is?' said Salinger.

'I don't know what to think. It's some kid, isn't it? Some poor kid. Where the hell did you find it?'

'Among my mother's things. I was going through them in the attic.'

Tiane screwed up her eyes and brought the photograph closer.

'Is it your mother? It looks a little like her.'

'I'm not even sure if it's a girl. It could be a boy.'

She handed the photo back as if it carried a curse.

'Maybe your father knows something about it.'

'I'm not going. So I guess I'll never know who it is. Or how they got to be in a mess like that.'

'You could send it to Carson.'

'That's just too weird. He asks for photographs of his family and I send him a Polaroid of an anonymous battered child. If that's what it is. Is it what it is?'

'I'm pretty sure. What else could it be?'

'The mind makes patterns. It's very faded. It's hard to tell.'

'It's a child with its face bashed in. That's what it is.'

'What the hell is it doing among Mum's stuff?'

'Does it matter? You should get rid of it.'

'Get rid of it? Don't you think that it's interesting?'

'Your curiosity.' She grimaced. 'Aren't there limits?'

'To curiosity?'

'That thing is ugly and it's horrible. Even looking at it is like looking at – I don't know – pornography. It's child pornography.'

'It's just an old photograph.'

'Your family has enough problems to be getting along with. Brush this one under the carpet. If it's

36

anything to do with you at all – which it probably isn't – it's history now.'

'That's good advice.'

'Are you going to take it?'

Tiane looked up at him. This time Salinger met her eyes. They were tender and solicitous, but milky, hooded. She ran her finger down the line of his cheekbone and smiled.

'Be careful, Salinger. Be careful not to hurt yourself.'

Salinger touched her finger with the tip of his and smiled in return.

'Why change the habit of a lifetime?'

A look of sadness flickered, then faded like dusk across her face.

'Because it hurts me too.'

Salinger nodded, momentarily stroked the back of her hand, then replaced the photograph in the envelope. He tried to seal the envelope with the yellowed Sellotape, but now the adhesive appeared to have suddenly exhausted itself. The flap obstinately jinked open every time he tried to press it down.

CHAPTER 2

MONDAY, 15 SEPTEMBER 2008

Salinger and Tiane journeyed to the airport in silence. Salinger was aware of some particular quality to the silence that suggested something other than tranquil reflection or the focused concentration of a conscientious motorist.

If she was angry about something, he couldn't imagine that it was to do with their imminent separation. After all, it was only for a couple of weeks. And it was her that had encouraged him to go to America in the first place.

He cast his mind back to try and find the root of her displeasure, which seemed to stretch back to the beginning of the month. Did it start at the moment when he had backed out of the exhibition with De Freitas, afraid of the public exposure of the inner workings of his private self? Did she think he had failed the most fundamental artistic test – that of courage? Or perhaps, more simply, she now believed she had hitched her wagon to a failure.

Salinger's decision to go to America – he supposed – came out of a need for a break during which he could try and overcome his sense of disappointment in himself. There was also the hope of new inspiration – some fresh way forward. He had no particular wish to see Carson, or to find Henry. He simply wanted a free passage out of the country, an emergency exit from his own sense of underachievement.

Carson had booked him on a flight, business class. In the hour before he and Tiane had departed for the airport, Salinger had packed his single nylon carryall with a sense of growing anxiety, even panic. Carson had bought him an open ticket, so he had the reassurance that he could return whenever he wanted. But he didn't like flying and he was unsure that what awaited him on the other side of the Atlantic might not simply be a provocation rather than a balm for his state of mind.

It was uncharacteristic for Tiane's mood to be so sour for so long. As a rule, she was almost unnaturally good-natured. The ridges and potholes that had appeared in the normally smooth landscape of her temperament seemed to point to something beyond everyday tension. She was brittle, skittish, given to unpredictable outbursts of rage and tears. She was quite unlike herself.

Now she sat behind the wheel trying to find a way into the lane at Chiswick roundabout that would carry her onto the M4. Salinger had several times seen what had appeared to be opportunities to cut into sufficient space, but he had managed to muster the self-control to say nothing.

Things unsaid. What defined the nature of a relationship – any relationship – more precisely than that? But what was it that Tiane was not saying? He imagined a pistol being slowly loaded. Her gaze was unbendingly fixed on the road ahead. When she spoke, which was hardly at all, he got the impression she was carefully self-editing.

He stole a gaze at her as she finally found a lacuna in the traffic flow and darted the car into the space. The slight tightness of the muscles around the eyes and lips added weight to his theory of imminent announcement. She wore no make-up. Tiane didn't really do cosmetics. On the very few occasions that she had tried, she displayed a plasterer's subtlety combined with an infant's sense of colour. This, too, Salinger loved about her. Not the fact that she wore no make-up, but her failure to know how to apply it properly. It was touching, like a misspelt shopping list.

Tiane momentarily caught his eye but her expression remained unchanged. Then she returned her gaze to the traffic. Salinger felt the silence thicken, then, and deepen. He decided to switch on the radio to relieve his discomfort. It was tuned, as usual, to Magic FM.

In an hour or two he'd be on the way to America and all the interior shards of glass, the tripwires, no-go zones, graveyards of memory and barely visible red, yellow and green lights would be forgotten and irrelevant. He would become a fresh person – at least for a while. After all, wasn't that the point of America? Wasn't that the central idea?

'Wonder if Carson had anything to do with the

sub-prime crisis?' ventured Salinger, unable to bear the silence any more.

'Meaning?'

'Maybe Carson helped bring down Lehman. He sells houses. People selling houses to people who couldn't afford it is why the economy is up shit creek. He's at the coalface.'

'Does shit creek have a coalface?'

'You're missing the point.'

Salinger had watched the bankers walk out of the Lehman Brothers building with their little cardboard boxes that very day on the news. The world was unravelling. They'd be stockpiling food soon. A return to barter. Salinger found that he was looking forward to some chaos, a taste of authentic decline. The previous ten years of bingeing, of luxury and excess had left him with a longing for austerity, something that would brace and clarify and renew the world.

'Yes. Of course it was Carson. Carson's always to blame.'

Tiane fell back into silence. Out of the window, Salinger watched English suburbia ribboning past. Line after line of terraced houses, trampolines in back gardens, uPVC windows, unattractive sofas bought in new year sales, gazebos, outdoor heaters. Light-industrial warehouses announced by violently ugly plastic signs plugged the gaps between these small theatres of pebbledash and half-timber. There were curry cottages, Chinese restaurants, kebab shops.

Salinger liked it. A life lived close together, however tawdry, was better than a life lived spread apart, as in America. Lack of space was a boon. It conferred intimacy.

She took the slip road signposted for Terminals One, Two and Three. Salinger felt in the inside pocket of his jacket for the envelope containing the photograph that he had taken from the loft. He rubbed it between his fingers and thumb, feeling the fresh vellum. He didn't want to pack it in case the luggage was lost. Somehow he felt that the picture was important, but he didn't know how.

He would show it to Carson, and to Henry if they found him. One of them might be able to provide a clue to its origin or its meaning. He had studied the image over and over again, but could still make no sense of it. As the days passed, new questions incubated. Why had his mother kept it? Who had held the camera? Why was it folded and creased, as if someone had tried to destroy it?

Salinger decided it was time to risk speaking to Tiane once more.

'Are you OK?'

'Why wouldn't I be?'

That appeared to be the end of the matter. Tiane took the ramp up to the car park and slid the car into a parking spot annoyingly and unnecessarily distant from the entrance to the terminal. She pressed the button that released the boot catch and slid out of her seat. Salinger was worried that she intended to accompany him to the departure lounge. He had hoped the offer of a lift to the airport had been no more than that – a courtesy defined roughly along the parameters of a minicab service.

Salinger wheeled his luggage towards the signs marked *Departures*. Tiane, still wordlessly, trotted along next to him, her feet saddled in a pair of tired trainers. Clearly she intended to stay with him until the last possible moment.

Salinger found himself feeling vaguely disappointed. He enjoyed the airport promise of neutral space. It felt like a pleasant anteroom within which to acclimatize himself to American air – sparkly clean, efficient, anonymous. Tiane's presence kept him tethered.

He checked in his luggage while Tiane stood to one side. The woman behind the desk informed him that the flight was delayed by an hour.

'Well, I guess there isn't much point in you . . .' said Salinger.

'Maybe a drink?' said Tiane.

Salinger understood that this was not a question.

'A coffee?'

'I fancy a proper drink.'

Tiane steered them towards a fake English-style pub which was low-lit, dingy and dark. The clientele seemed to largely comprise fat people eating crisps. Salinger sat down at a dirty table, imprinted with rings from previous drained glasses, while Tiane went to the bar and ordered. She came back with what appeared to be a gin and tonic for herself, going by the slice of lemon and the bubbles, and carried a bottle of lager for him. She hadn't asked him what he had wanted. He took a sip of it. Tiane sank the theoretical gin and tonic with a single gulp. She smacked her lips, tapped the glass once with her fingernail and sat back in her padded vinyl seat.

'Are you looking forward to seeing Carson?'

Salinger started to wonder now if he had imagined the Imminent Statement. Tiane now seemed relaxed, verging on the cheerful. She had bought a bag of chilli crackers that she had upended on the soiled table. She was picking at the small orange salty wheels with her unadorned fingernails.

'Not especially.'

Tiane bit into one of the crackers. He watched her mouth work as she masticated it into an ochre gloop.

'Then why did you agree to go?' She brushed a grain of cracker from her cheek with her finger.

'I don't know the reason why I do half the things I do.'

Tiane's expression indicated that this answer wasn't sufficient.

'It's not costing me anything. I might find out something I didn't know. I might even have a nice time. Maybe Carson has changed.'

'Maybe you've changed.'

'Everybody changes.'

'Are you going because you want to see your father?'

'I'm a little curious. Carson, me and Henry haven't been together in the same room for thirty years.'

'Maybe you won't be. Henry doesn't know for sure that you're coming. Are you sure that he'll welcome you? Are you sure that he'll even be there?'

'So what? What are you saying? I'll still have had a free trip to America. I'll have had a break.'

'What is it you need a break from?'

'Everyday life. England. Painting. Franklin De Freitas.'

'Do you feel you need a break from me?'

Salinger, who had been distracted by a man two tables along arguing with his wife – he was now prodding her on her tattooed arm with his small fat finger – nevertheless responded immediately.

'Of course not.'

'Tiane stared down into her empty glass.

'You want another drink?'

'Vodka tonic, large.'

'Aren't you driving?'

'Are you my fucking father?'

Salinger got up from the sticky, plasticky seat and ordered a single vodka from the bar, with a double tonic. He hoped that Tiane wouldn't notice the dilution. He checked his watch. The departure time was still too remote for him to escape to the other side of the security gates. He sat back down and offered the drink to Tiane, who was grazing on the crumbs of the crackers. She knocked it back in one.

'That was a single.'

'I'm concerned about pedestrians.'

'You're treating me like a child.'

'Why are you trying to pick a fight?'

'Will you miss me?'

'Oh, come on, Tea . . .'

'You, won't. Will you?'

'Do you really need me to make those kind of gestures? We're grown-ups, aren't we? That doesn't mean I don't . . .'

'You don't what?'

'That I don't love you. I do. Of course.'

Tiane stood up and swayed on her feet slightly. She started nodding as if she had suddenly understood something that had been previously obscure.

'Do you want a coffee or something?' said Salinger. 'They do them at the bar.'

'I should go now.'

'Sit down. Please. What's the matter?'

'I have to go.'

She bent down and kissed Salinger on the cheek. Then she looked at him, directly, hard, in the eyes. Salinger tried to work out what it was that was being communicated.

'*What*, Tiane? What's the *matter*?'

She hesitated. Salinger felt himself losing his patience.

'*What?*'

Tiane pursed her lips and sat unsteadily down again.

'I don't know.'

'We shouldn't part like this.'

'What's the point of having a long conversation? You'll be gone in a few minutes.'

'The plane won't check in for half an hour.'

Tiane bit her lip, then looked past him towards the man with the tattooed arm.

'Don't go, then.'

Salinger stared at her uncomprehendingly.

'Don't go where?'

'Don't go to America.'

Tiane's face had hardened. She returned her gaze to Salinger. Her body had stiffened. She sat up ramrod straight in her chair.

'It was you that insisted I go in the first place.'

'I know that.'

'So why have you suddenly changed your mind?'

'I can't explain. I just want you to trust me.'

'You want me to cancel the trip without even giving me a reason.'

'I'll pay back the money for the ticket. I'll talk to Carson about it. I'll explain that it was all my fault. I'm just asking you to do something for me on *trust*. On trust, Salinger. Come home with me.'

'Why do you keep saying the word "trust"? Is this about trust?'

Salinger stared at Tiane, trying to figure out the equation. He hadn't even wanted to go to America, but now he had told Carson that he was

47

going. Carson would be waiting at the airport. Knowing Carson, he would have made all sorts of arrangements, designed schedules, booked hotels, purchased tickets for this or that attraction.

'God knows what trouble Carson has gone to. And we're going to visit my father. My sick father.'

'But you don't even want to go. You told me. You couldn't care less about Henry.'

'It's a bit late now. I'm committed.'

Tiane's face contorted into a mercurial, some-times gargoylish series of expressions. Salinger found himself unable to read any of them for certain. There seemed to be anger there, and confusion. Momentarily, he saw regret. Finally, her features settled into a blank, tired mask. Her eyelids flickered as if she was suddenly falling asleep.

'I know you would be letting Carson down. I'm not even going to pretend that it makes sense, or that it's fair. I simply want to tell you, here and now, that I need you to stay here in London with me.'

Salinger's confusion deepened. Tiane hardly ever showed need. She was and always had been profoundly independent. She had never pressed him for children, or for 'commitment' – whatever that meant – or for anything much at all. She appeared entirely satisfied with his continuing presence, his enduring respect, his heartfelt admiration.

He looked at the check-in pass in his hand. He

fanned his face with it. It produced a light breeze. The pass seemed to make the journey official, fixed, entirely unavoidable. He looked at Tiane again.

Tiane scanned his face, briefly seeking something that apparently she was unable to locate. Her expression altered. For the first time that day, she smiled, a genuine, open, generous smile.

'I understand, Salinger. It was a stupid idea. I was being selfish. I don't know what's wrong with me. Stress, probably. I'm under a lot of pressure. The Ofsted inspection. Go and see your brother and your father. I know that you need to. You're right, I told you to. Don't worry about it. Go. Please.'

Tiane stood again. Taking his cue from her, Salinger rose too. He reached out towards her. The gesture felt feeble and inauthentic.

'Tiane . . .'

For a moment he thought of doing it, of just throwing the boarding pass away and walking back to the car with Tiane. But it made no sense. Everything was *arranged*.

He drew her to him and hugged her. She was uncharacteristically stiff at first. Then she went limp, then she hugged him back, desperately, as if he was leaving on a hazardous journey and she might never hold him again. Salinger noticed other customers in the pub staring at them and found himself feeling self-conscious.

After a few more seconds coiled round one

another, Tiane disentangled herself, gave one final – brave? – glance and then simply started to walk briskly away. Salinger made no move to stop her. He watched her as she pushed her way through the crowd towards the exit.

Tiane turned and waved. She was smiling in a way that he could see was meant to be reassuring but that was, in fact, frightening. For a moment, every cell and corpuscle of Salinger's body pressed him to follow her, to take her home, to mine her secret, the secret that she didn't even seem to have access to herself. But then he felt as if his body was collapsing inwards. It felt too heavy to move with his feeble legs. He felt the pressure of time at his back like a gale. The announcements on the departure board called to him like Christmas lights. The PA announcements were sirens, calling him to the ocean. He turned and walked determinedly in the direction of passport control.

The passenger lounge on the airside of the security gates was busier than a street market. Loud pop music issued from speakers above his head. Salinger found one of the few empty seats and settled down to eat the sandwich and coffee which he had bought from a chain-store concession. The coffee was too hot, the sandwich was too cold. He put them both down on the moulded plastic table attached to the seat, and waited for physics and mathematics to make the necessary adjustments, for the power of bell curve to reassert itself, for the principle of entropy to work. All energy lost dynamism; all phenomena tended towards the mean, the tepid, the mediocre.

He looked in his shoulder bag for the book that he was sure that he'd packed. Only he'd forgotten to pack it. Now he was going to have to go and get some shitty best-seller from the airport book-shop. Salinger couldn't remember the last time he'd read a novel less than twenty years old, and the terminal concession was unlikely to stock anything that had been out for longer than six weeks.

He slumped back in the chair deciding that he couldn't be bothered. He considered his feelings instead. For once he was absolutely clear about what they were. He was afraid. He was afraid of seeing his brother and afraid of seeing his father. But he had no idea why he was afraid.

Salinger suddenly wondered where he had found the impetus for taking a road trip from New Orleans across the one thousand three hundred miles that it would take to reach the place where their father supposedly was suffering an illness somewhere along the spectrum from a serious cold to terminal cancer. He found that he had no idea what he had been thinking of in accepting the offer. Sharing a car for days on end with a brother he hardly knew any more – who he had never known well in the first place – struck him now as an agonizing prospect, fraught with difficulty and the possibility of conflict.

Salinger tried to clear his mind by scanning his newspaper. Several spreads told the story of the fall of Lehman – how Barclays had pulled out of a last-minute takeover bid and left the bank to hang in the wind. One article explained that we still needed bankers 'even though many were horrible people'.

Another columnist was worrying that voters historically shifted their vote away from black candidates at the last moment. He concluded, once again, that Barack Obama had little chance of election to the presidency. John McCain had made the statement that 'the fundamentals of the economy were sound'.

Yet another hurricane, this time christened 'Ike', was hammering Texas and Louisiana. In central Houston, most of the windows on one side of the state's tallest building, the thousand-foot JP Morgan Chase Tower, blew out. Salinger liked this fact. He had a weakness for prophetic symbols. At the same time, he hoped that the aftermath of the storm wasn't going to make their drive to Las Cruces from New Orleans any more uncomfortable than it was already liable to be.

His flight had begun boarding. Salinger yawned and threw the newspaper into a bin. He headed for the book concession. He needed to find something that would see him through the eight-hour flight. He could never enjoy watching movies airborne. The people were too small.

He headed straight for a section at the back of the

shop marked *Modern Classics*. After scanning the few small shelves briefly, two books caught his eye. The first was *Zen and the Art of Motorcycle Maintenance* by Robert M. Pirsig. Salinger remembered that when Carson was in his late teens, he had told Salinger that it was his favourite book. Salinger remembered how unlikely that seemed, considering that Carson had always seemed to him to lack the capacity for both reflection and curiosity. Perhaps his apparently lumpish lack of emotional responsiveness was in fact a kind of satori.

He had never read the book himself. Maybe it would give him an insight into Carson's personal psychology, an area that he had always found entirely inaccessible.

The other volume was Steinbeck's *East of Eden*. This was one of his father's favourites. In Henry's personal canon there was first, Hemingway, secondly, Salinger, and thirdly, Steinbeck. This was a nice edition, hardback, well designed. He decided on impulse to buy it for Henry – just in case they found him. It was a heavy book. He could either give it to him as an ironic comment on his parenting abilities, or, failing that, club him round the head with it.

East of Eden, he remembered now, vaguely, was where Cain had been exiled after the murder of his brother. So if they didn't find Henry, Salinger reasoned, it would do for Carson just as well.

CHAPTER 3

LONDON – NEW ORLEANS

The flight was uninteresting. All flights were uninteresting, unless they were unpleasant. Then they were frightening.

Salinger passed some of the time trying to remember his childhood so that he could at least establish the rudiments of some common ground with Carson. The details in his mind remained stubbornly vague.

Salinger had spent countless hours in analysis and therapy, but had never come up with any incontrovertible reason for his fragile mental health. Some therapists made the unchallenging suggestion that it was connected to the fact that his father deserted the family, never to return, when Salinger was ten years old. Others said that it was because Salinger had suffered leukaemia when he was born, returning home after months of hospital treatment followed by a long, and doubtless uncomfortable, convalescence.

His childhood illness had presumably intensified the normal sibling rivalry, another potential source of his damage. But Salinger had little memory of

54

any particular conflict with Carson. Carson had simply been punishingly indifferent.

The occasional vision of Carson's face as a child floated into Salinger's mind as the hostesses bustled past and the clouds outside his window formed towering black and gold-tipped mountains. The face was curiously bland. He couldn't even see anger there. Why would there be? After all, there was no one for Carson to be angry with. There was only an absence, an erasure with a name and a title – Salinger, the Great Dethroner.

After Carson himself left home to go and study business at college in Surrey, Salinger had almost completely lost touch with him. His later emigration to America, following in the footsteps of their father, had barely been a wrench. It had been the straight-forward extension of a long-established tendency.

It was all history now, Salinger supposed. Years of analysis had done nothing to convince him that the past was as powerful a force on the present as the army of shrinks and mind doctors insisted. He didn't miss his brother, and neither did he resent him. He was a piece of a jigsaw that had long been lost. The puzzle that his life now constituted contained neither a Carson-shaped piece nor a Carson-shaped hole.

Salinger had tried to pass the rest of the time on the journey by reading *Zen and the Art of Motorcycle Maintenance*. He had found most of it dull and impenetrable. Much of it was an abstruse attempt to untangle various strands of classical philosophy. He was surprised that Carson had found such enthusiasm for it – if that enthusiasm was actually genuine and not simply a pose, as he suspected.

One phrase stuck in Salinger's mind before he put the book to one side and switched on a movie. The protagonist, Phaedrus, he read, was 'waiting for the missing seed crystal of thought that would suddenly solidify everything'.

The idea of the seed crystal triggered a connection in his mind – the idea of 'Ice Nine' in Kurt Vonnegut's *Cat's Cradle*. It was one of Salinger's – and Henry's – favourite books, a fantasy in which Felix Hoenikker, an atomic scientist, discovered the seed crystal for turning water to ice at room temperature. The crystallization of what was designed to be fluid had, in that novel, led to the end of the world.

He was just beginning to wonder if Pirsig had read the Vonnegut book when a steward offered him a preprandial drink. He knocked back two miniatures of brandy, and bolted his three-course meal. Then he promptly fell asleep.

On landing at Houston, Salinger was awoken by an offensively cheerful voice instructing him to 'de-plane'. He joined the jumbled, irritable worm heading for immigration.

Inching forward in the queue, he found himself rehearsing his long-standing prejudices towards

America, the place his father had so idolized, which had hypnotized him, captured him and spirited him away from his family. America had been the surgeon's knife with which Henry had cut his ties to his past.

He remained bewildered as to why both his father and his brother had chosen to settle there. A country which executed criminals, which had virtually no socialized health care, in which fabulous wealth coexisted alongside barbaric poverty made no sense to him. It was the kingdom of the bland, it was the moronic inferno.

Henry's exodus at least – unlike Carson's – made some sort of rough sense. Henry had grown up in the golden years, when America was a titan, and stood without blemish. His father's head as he had grown up had been filled with visions of skyscrapers and tailfins, Superman and Sinatra and California Girls and – later – Hendrix and Muhammad Ali. He had fallen in love with America in the innocence days. He once told Salinger that it all dated from seeing the James Dean movie *Giant* at the Gaumont State Cinema, Kilburn, when he was ten years old. He fell in love with the landscape and the sky, and it was a passion that had never paled, only deepened as he grew older.

Carson's move to America was harder to understand. Carson couldn't have experienced America as Henry had. Nothing truly inspiring had happened in America since Woodstock. It had all been decline – born-agains and preventive wars and race riots and assassinations and minimum wages. McJobs on the main street, blow jobs in the White House. Ugly clothes and plastic surgery, artificially whitened teeth, terrible haircuts.

As far as Salinger could make out, there was only one thing that had driven Carson to America – the determination to honour, consciously or not, his lifelong fixation with his father. Everyone, Salinger supposed, needed a myth. Henry's was America. Carson's was Henry.

As Salinger inched his way forward towards immigration, he noticed that most people in the queue were looking up at a point some ten feet above the processing desks. He followed their gaze. Television screens were suspended above the queue at regular intervals. They showed a digital loop of what appeared to be an advertisement for the USA – smiling children, multicultural faces, cowboys, skyscapes, landscapes and cityscapes. The raised eyes in the queues below seemed to drink in the promise, baby birds with mouths open for insects.

As he approached the immigration desk he caught sight of a prominent sign. It read *Any inappropriate jokes may result in your arrest.*

There it was, in black and white, in a brutal sanserif typeface – the scaly corium that lay underneath the smooth, visible epidermis. When all was said and done, insisted Salinger to himself, they were fascists with iPods, white trash lowbrow bullies with fat thighs and stupid wives.

Salinger's private tirade was interrupted as he was beckoned forward across the red line to the passport-control desk. The official, a small man with a crimson face, brightly polished cheeks and a nose like a gobbet of purple Play-Doh looked at him with intense suspicion, as if he could tele-pathically sniff out Salinger's hostility.

The immigration officer examined his passport slowly and with what seemed to be unnecessary and pedantic meticulousness. After what seemed to be several minutes, he finally looked up at Salinger, and for the first time made eye contact. His gaze seemed completely mechanical. When he spoke, the voice was coarse, almost guttural, something like Salinger imagined a Bronx accent might be.

'You an attist?'

'What?'

'An *attist*.'

Salinger felt it imperative to divine what the mind behind the small, penetrating eyes was trying to articulate. He sensed that he would be summarily removed to some inhospitable holding tank if he was unable to solve the riddle – the Homeland Security Service had a global reput-ation for capricious incarceration.

Salinger blinked several times, suspiciously, he imagined, before he worked out what it was that the official was trying to say.

'An artist?'

'That's what you wrote.'

Salinger now remembered that in an act of hopeful vanity he had described his profession as 'artist' on his recently renewed passport. Previously he had contented himself with the more humble 'illustrator'.

'Right. Yes, I'm an artist.'

The official considered this carefully as if it was, in itself, grounds for detention.

'You make a buck out of it?'

Salinger was uncertain what the least provocative response might be.

'Sort of.'

The man, who, Salinger noted from reading his badge, was called Dexter M. DiSoto, nodded as if trying to assess the verisimilitude of his reply.

'What kind of *at*? Pitchers?'

'Paintings, yes. Also conceptual stuff. Installations, that kind of thing.'

The man furrowed his brow. Clearly he had no idea what Salinger was talking about.

Salinger tried to muster an encouraging, open smile that he imagined would go down well in America, but what came out, he suspected, was furtive and snide. The customs officer looked at him again, unsmilingly.

'Y'like that guy wid da big fish?'

Salinger blinked.

'Hirst, is that the guy? Yeah, I know. He's a little overrated, right? But I like that stuff about decay, y'know, death. The whole cycle thing.'

The man stamped the passport and closed it gently.

'I like that chick that did the inside-out house, too, you know, like all the space was, you know, on the outside. I liked that. What was that broad's name?'

'Rachel Whiteread?'

'Is that her name? Yeah, that's her. I like her. You know her?'

'Personally?'

'No I don't mean *personally*. What you think, I think because you're an attist you're going to know every other attist in England, right? No, I mean, do you know her *stuff*?'

'Yes. I do. Of course.'

'You like it?'

'Yes.'

'She's pretty good.'

'Yes.'

The official rolled his eyeballs skyward as if searching for something. Eventually, he uttered a small grunt of satisfaction, then looked back at Salinger.

'Like the hieroglyphs on Egyptian tombs. Right?'

'What?'

'That's what it said on Wikipedia. I read that sometimes so I can learn something. I like to keep up a bit. I paint a bit myself.'

'Do you?'

'You know de Kooning? I try to paint like him. I make a mess, but I like trying.'

'I like de Kooning.'

'You got good taste. But what the hell do I know?

I'm the immigration guy. Have a good visit to America, Salinger.'

He passed the passport back to Salinger and waved him on. Salinger stared at him briefly. Then he moved through towards the luggage concourse, clutching the passport.

There were American flags everywhere – on the mall concourses, on the magazine covers. He wondered how the Americans managed to remain patriotic as the new century showed them in such a sour light. Anyway, how could you love something as abstract as a country? It was like loving an equation, or a rune.

The flight to New Orleans from Houston took forty-five minutes. Salinger went through the arrival formalities and then stood waiting at the baggage claim. At Louis Armstrong Airport, those greeting arrivals could enter the carousel area.

A tall, middle-aged man with a pleasant face wearing a New Orleans Saints baseball cap said 'Hey' to him. He was reminded simultaneously how friendly Americans were to strangers and how they ate up the language like lazy vultures – the word 'hello' now having been replaced over the last decade with 'hey'.

His instinct was to bury his nose in a book or to pretend not to have heard him. But the man seemed undeterred. Now, improbably, he started to recite Salinger's name.

'Salinger! Sally!'

He took a second look at the man and, feeling foolish, realized that it was Carson. He had been tricked by the baseball cap, the tentative moustache and the all-American outfit of billowy zip jacket, pressed but poor-quality jeans, polo shirt and dumpy trainers. He looked different from how he remembered him at the funeral, when he had been clean-shaven and worn a black suit with a white open-neck shirt.

Salinger took a step back. Carson was grinning broadly. Salinger felt a jab of unexpected, and vaguely unwelcome, affection. He thought he had shaken off any residual feelings for his brother long ago.

His big brother. *Carzy*. Six feet tall, blond hair fading at the temples, hairline partially concealed by the cap. Wide shoulders. A little flab around the waist but not much. The polo shirt had a faded imprint of the New Orleans fleur-de-lys. A good-looking man, an improvement on Salinger, who was four inches shorter, yellowish-grey in complexion and – to his own mind – weaselly.

Carson closed the space between himself and Salinger in a stride. He enveloped Salinger in his powerful arms. Salinger felt embarrassed by the openness of the gesture. All the same, he joined in the pantomime with an answering embrace.

'My little brother,' muttered Carson into his shoulder. 'Sally boy.'

'Carson,' said Salinger.

'Thank the Lord you've come,' Carson said,

whispering, as if talking to himself, or praying. Salinger extricated himself from the bear hug, took a step back again and smiled neutrally.

'It's good to see you, Carson. You look good.'

'Thanks. You too.'

'You look American.'

It was true – there was an openness to his stance, a lack of English guardedness in his very physical presence. On his visit to England for the funeral, in contrast, he had seemed tense and anxious without at any time obviously manifesting grief.

'That a bad thing?'

Carson picked up Salinger's holdall. They moved out into the street. Although it was late afternoon, the heat nearly floored Salinger, even out of the reach of the murky sunshine. He could feel a coat of dank sweat filming his skin.

He wondered, once again, why he had come, and was grateful, in the same moment, that he had.

'So, I guess this is our Chautauqua,' said Carson, easing the car out of the airport parking lot and nodding towards the Pirsig book, the spine of which protruded from Salinger's shoulder bag.

He had read about the Chautauqua during the flight. It was a Native American expression meaning – according to Pirsig – 'journey of the soul'. The unnamed narrator, a fictionalized version of Pirsig himself, worked the narrative back and forth between the Chautauqua that he was taking with his teenage son, Chris, and the mental breakdown of Phaedrus who had driven himself insane trying to find the meaning of the Greek concept of *arete* or 'quality'. Phaedrus, the fictional narrator and Pirsig all appeared to be the same person.

'You still a fan of the book?' said Salinger.

'Absolutely. Great wisdom in those pages.'

'I'm not really getting it.'

'Stick at it. All makes sense in the end.'

'You can be Zen and a Christian?'

'It's all just labels, so . . .'

Carson guided his Lexus along the main expressway that connected the airport to the centre of New Orleans. The engine barely made a sound. Carson had bought it, brand new, the previous month. There was still plastic covering on the rear seats. He had instructed Salinger to remove his shoes when he got into it.

Salinger had noticed two bumper stickers on the back. *Know Jesus, Know Peace – No Jesus, No Peace* and *Prayer: The World's Greatest Wireless Connection.*

'What happened to the old Chevy you were talking about?'

'In the end, I thought this would be more practical. You can't imagine how hot it might get across West Texas and New Mexico – even in September. You like it?'

'It's fine.'

'You're not disappointed?'

'Not at all,' Salinger lied. 'It's a Lexus, right?'

Sleek, air-conditioned efficiency, the monster that was gently, comfortably destroying the globe.

65

The outside world of heat, noise and odour seemed remote and irrelevant.

'RX400H. Silver grey. Great car. It's got poke, it's got torque, it corners like a bitch. Man, I love this wagon. Hocked myself up to the butt to get it. Like steering a cloud.'

Carson explained to Salinger that the car was one of a new generation of petrol/electric hybrids. It had air suspension, apparently, whatever that was. Carson pointed proudly at the wood trim and the peach-coloured leather upholstery. He pressed a button to adjust the electric seats. He seemed particularly excited by the small video screen set into the dash. A miniature camera mounted on the back of the car beamed a digital image to the screen. Salinger could not work out how this was an improvement on a simple mirror.

'0–62 in 7.62 seconds. But when you're doozying round town, petrol engine shuts off completely. Quiet as a bicycle. 4 x 4 if we want to go off road. Electric motor that powers the back wheels as well as the front if you want to engage it. Three engines in all, one internal combustion, two electric. The IC powers the electric.'

Salinger had no interest in cars. He would have preferred the Chevy.

'Makes me giddy as a cheerleader when I get into this car. Real luxurious. Sit back. Feel that leather. Go on. Stroke it. Go ahead.'

Salinger dutifully ran his finger over the surface of the seat. It just felt like leather.

'Isn't that nice?'

'It is nice, Carson.'

Having taken him through the price of the vehicle and the loan plan and the outstanding low-interest deal that he got on it through a friend with a dealership, Carson insisted that, before they drove back to the house to meet LouLou, they went and took chicory coffee and beignets at the Café du Monde on Jackson Square. This was how they had commenced Salinger's brief and unsatisfactory visit a decade previously. Carson apparently intended to establish it as some sort of tradition.

As they approached the city, they glided past an array of low-level commercial developments which seemed merely to act as support structures for the offerings of the billboards that loomed above, for steaks, seafood, TV programmes, sex, money, gambling, Internet dating. Salinger had been to India a few years previously and had preferred the functional advertising that he saw there, for concrete, steel, ball bearings, tarmac. He liked the honesty of it. Now the DNA of advertising had been altered, generating the unnatural dream worlds of brand building, creating carefully designed romances for inert material, for water and bread and clothes and saucepans.

The Louisiana Superdome jammed up the view on the righthand side. As it drew closer, its vastness oppressed Salinger. He tried to imagine all the people huddled in it after Katrina, thirty

67

thousand of them. Was it true what happened in there? People dying in rivers of piss and shit, snipers having a field day, rapists picking their victims at leisure, whole families begging for help that never came, while George Bush shot a five over par.

He remembered someone telling him – was it Carson? – that the stories had all been fabricated, a product of mass hysteria. Someone committed suicide, that was for sure, jumping off one of the balconies. Armed guards prevented the desperate population leaving, in case they started looting. It was pure Hieronymus Bosch. The National Guard didn't turn up for a week.

The Superdome now dominated their field of vision. Salinger stayed silent. Opening that particular window into the heart of American life would provoke Carson. Carson didn't do darkness. He did light, hope, stability, optimism, God.

'Is the city putting itself back into shape, Carson?'

'Whaddya mean, shape?'

'After Katrina, I mean. It looks pretty normal down there to me.'

Over the edge of the raised freeway Salinger could see the grid of the French Quarter.

'Place always survives. It's a city of survivors. City should never be there in the first place. Built on a swamp. Crazy. It'll be OK. Maybe more Hispanic than black in the long term. Lot of those guys in the Ninth Ward ain't coming back in a hurry. Still in trailers, most of them, in Houston or gosh knows where. But you adapt. We adapt. Things are good. We're doing a lot of good work down here.'

'Who is we?'

'The community. The Church. Had volunteers come from all over the country to help rebuild. Just in case you think Christians are all too busy bombing abortion clinics and hunting queers with sniper rifles.'

Carson laughed lazily. The sound was liquid and rich. When he lived in England, Carson's laugh had been more like a non-infectious cough, dry, chesty, struggling to take in oxygen.

The Lexus took the ramp off the freeway. They descended to Canal Street. Along the central reservation, flanked by lamp posts and palm trees, ran the streetcar line supported by a ravelling spider's web of electric wires.

Salinger's mind flashed back to the TV pictures from Canal Street after Katrina – the corpses in the doorways, the National Guard brandishing rifles at people trying to find food in the abandoned shops, the wash of dirty liquid reaching up to the first-floor windows. The white ghost clouds of rain, the traffic signals changing without purpose, their colours reflected in the surface of the water. The trembling iron balconies, the desperate faces of the people, most of them black, all of them poor, wading through the toxic slurry. Diabetics without medicine, the elderly without shelter or food or water. Dead people in wheelchairs. No relief. A man walking down the wide avenue holding a white flag in surrender. To whom? Elsewhere houses on cars, cars on houses, pointless helicopters swooping like threats.

It was madness, chaos, neglect on a colossal scale. He saw in his mind the face of a woman in labour who swam for thirty minutes through sewage and chemical-filled water, searching for dry land where she could have her baby, leaving her nine-year-old to fend for himself.

It was hard to recognize it now as a disaster area. You could see a tidemark where the waters had gone down, but otherwise it was more or less as he remembered it from ten years before. An old neighbourhood department store had become a chain hotel, but the Popeye's Chicken concession, Harrah's Casino, the Walgreens drugstore – all the landmarks he remembered – remained intact.

'Can I open the window? It doesn't look the same through glass.'

Carson slid down the electric windows. The heat blasted Salinger in the face along with a half-remembered smell of rotting vegetation, rising damp, petroleum and deep-fried chicken grease. He tried to identify the fabled magnolia blossom in the mix, but failed. The dirty hot rottenness was a smell as distinctive to New Orleans as that odd bready staleness of the Paris Metro.

They drove past the Canal Place mall where Salinger had gone to the movies and browsed for gifts last time he had visited. There was a swimming pool on the top of the tower which he had used, looking down on the buildings warping and distorting in the heat below. There was a car park a few hundred feet beyond the mall and twenty yards from the banks of the Mississippi. Carson guided the Lexus in and found a place immediately. Salinger would say this for America – it never ran out of space.

They left the car. Carson briefly inspected it and wiped a splash of mud off the wheel arch with a chamois. Then they began to walk parallel with the river towards Jackson Square, past the old Jax beer brewery, now yet another mall, largely targeting tourists.

CHAPTER 4

VIEUX CARRÉ

The clothes that Salinger had worn for the plane, a thin poplin shirt and taupe linen trousers, clung to him like the scalding flannels they handed out on the plane. He could feel a headache beginning to incubate. Carson slung a heavy arm around Salinger's shoulders.

'The Big Easy, Salinger. The Crescent City. The Land of Dreams. Here we are. Me and my kid brother. At long last.'

'It's great, Carzy. A real buzz being here.'

Salinger watched, fifty yards in front of them, the jazzmen performing outside the green-and-white awning of the Café du Monde. It was corny stuff, but all right. Banjos, a cornet, a trombone. The tourists were tipping, getting their photos taken. Mercifully, Carson removed his arm from Salinger's shoulders. Salinger could feel the bloom of sweat on his face. Underneath his arms, dark islands were forming and spreading like mildew.

'Hot enough?'

'Murder.'

'Not usually this hot in September. It's a bad

patch. You get used to it. Come on, look, there's no line. Table right over there.'

He indicated a spot a few feet away from the musicians. One started playing 'Summertime'. An old white woman who had bought a tourist parasol from a gift shop began half dancing on the pavement, clumsy and out of time, trying to distract herself from a life of button-downs, pastel shades and painkiller rush.

'You lagged?'

'I slept a while on the plane.'

Raising his arm weakly, Salinger tried to hail a waiter. They ignored him.

'What do you want?' said Carson.

'You order for me.'

'Nothing on the menu except beignet, chicory coffee and orange juice.'

'Give me the works.'

One of the swarming waiters manifested, summoned by a slight nod of the head from Carson. He was dressed all in white with a black dicky bow and a dinky white starched-cotton hat folded artfully like a napkin. Salinger decided the place was OK, despite the congregation of babbling tourists. Huge fans rotated slowly, suspended from the canopy above their heads. The jazz band switched to 'Down by the Riverside'. In the background, calliope music drifted across from the paddle steamers.

'Two orders of beignets, two café au lait and two orange juice.'

'Mmh hmmh.'

The order arrived within a minute. Salinger found that he was fiercely hungry and went at the beignets tigerishly. In seconds, his face and clothes were comprehensively dusted with icing sugar.

'If you're greedy in the Café du Monde, it turns you into a ghost right off,' said Carson.

Salinger didn't answer. His mouth was full of beignet, sweet hot clouds of dough. He washed them down with some of the chicory coffee. He felt his looming headache recede slightly. Carson swung back in his chair, eating his own beignets with a precise delicacy. Not a spot of icing sugar marked his tidy jeans or neat brown polo shirt. He slipped a small digital camera out of his pocket and took a snap of Salinger, who was by now surrounded by crumpled napkins with which he was vainly trying to remove the sugar from his clothes. He was only succeeding in spreading it further. There were several small piles of white dust in front of him mixing with beignet crumbs.

'That's one for the album. Man, you haven't changed. You always were messy as a pig. But it's really something to see you, brother. *Really* something.'

'How are you, Carson? How's everything? How's LouLou?'

'Lou's great. *Great.* It's going to happen this time. We're real excited.'

'You're looking forward to being a father.'

74

'What can I say? Every time we tried before, it didn't work out . . . so . . .'

'This time you're sure though.'

'LouLou went through the mill. Three times she's miscarried. I don't even like to think about it. What that woman went through. This is the first time we crossed that fence to the second trimester. We're not up the mountain yet, but it feels like a mighty river has been crossed.'

'A river and a fence and a mountain. Quite an obstacle course.'

'I can't wait. I *cannot*. I think about it all the time. To wake up, Sally, and have a son. Imagine it. To have such a blessing. It blows your mind.'

'Let's hope he does better than the original.'

'Bygones and bygones, Sal. Dad is going to be knocked for a loop when he finds out.'

Salinger found that he wasn't listening. He was concentrating on the sound of Carson's voice rather than the content. He seemed to have transformed himself from lower-middle-class north London suburbanite into a 1970s pirate-radio DJ.

'I can't believe this is what you really sound like.'

'I don't get what you mean.'

'Are you putting that voice on for my benefit? I can't get a trace of who you were. You used to sound like . . . well, just like me. Even when you came over to Mum's funeral – you sort of sounded a bit like the old Carzy. But there's nothing left of London in you.'

'You think I'm faking my voice?'

'It just feels unfamiliar.'

'This is who I am now.'

'Of course. I'm tired. So Louise is good?'

'Hold on a minute.'

Carson beckoned for the bill. Immediately, a waiter handed him a chit. Salinger reached in his pocket for some money, but before he could negotiate his way through the receipts, sticks of gum and small English coins Carson had thrown a ten-dollar note on the table. The waiter removed the money. A rapt, slightly prayerful expression appeared on Carson's face.

'That woman turned my life around. She's full of moxy. You know what moxy is, Salinger? Spirit. *Wherewithal.* Get up and go. I was so lucky to meet her. I didn't have any sure course until I met LouLou. You know what? Let me tell you something.'

There was a long pause. Carson fixed Salinger with a man-to-man-let-me-tell-you-exactly-how-it-is stare. Salinger awaited the forthcoming revelation.

'If I hadn't met her, I wouldn't be the man I am.'

Carson, it seemed, hadn't merely grafted on an American accent. He had adopted the American *form* of language, marching sentences dramatically up a hill only to drop them in a ditch of understatement. He had become a willing vassal of the empire of anticlimax.

'That's nice.'

'And Chrissy? How is she?'

'Who?'

'Chrissy. Christiane. That's her name, right?'

'Oh – *Tiane.*'

'Tiane? That what you call her?'

'We rub along. Two sheets of sandpaper.'

Carson nodded. Salinger thought he could detect disappointment in Carson's expression. Had he expected more? *Listen, Carson. Let me be completely straight with you. I wouldn't be the man I am if I hadn't met Tiane.* But that wasn't true – Salinger would have been exactly the man he was if he hadn't met Tiane. Tiane was his girlfriend, not an agency of self-improvement.

But they saw things differently here. Everything here was meant to make you better or worse. The reality from where he stood was that nobody much changed, nothing had much effect and everything inside your head just got more muddled up as time went on.

'Yeah, I know where you're coming from. Marriage can be tough, I guess.'

'We're not married.'

'You know what I mean. A girlfriend, partner, squeeze, whatever you want to call it.'

Salinger swallowed his last mouthful of beignet.

'Could I get some more of those?'

'Damn fat hog. Have what's left of mine.'

Carson handed his one and a half remaining pieces of beignet over to Salinger. Salinger dispensed another cloud of sugar onto his trousers, and stuffed the warm sticky roll into his mouth.

'You like it?'

Salinger put a thumb up.

'Good eating. This is a food city, Salinger. *The* food city. There's nothing like it in the world. It's a place bent on enjoying itself, come what may. It has this indestructible spirit. It celebrates life. No room for pessimism. No place for doubt.'

Salinger was grateful for the fact that Carson had not yet urged him to accept Jesus as his new best friend. However, the memory of Carson's tendency to evangelize New Orleans was beginning to return. The devastation that the hurricane had wrought had apparently only intensified Carson's faith that he had settled in the greatest city in the greatest country in the world.

The last time he had visited, Carson had relentlessly peddled him the charms of the Vieux Carré, of Magazine Street, of Audubon Park, of the uptown restaurants and bars, of the popcorn chicken and the andouille sausage and the po boys and the jambalaya and the crawfish boils, of the Zulu kings and the jazz funerals and the romantic, wide, rolling Mississippi River.

Privately, Salinger felt New Orleans had a bigger opinion of itself than it deserved. The myth of New Orleans magnified and glorified everything caught in its glare. When you stripped away all the theming and tat and fakery and tourist garbage, it was just a very small city with a great deal of crime, a lot of nice restaurants and some good music bars.

'You got your muffaletta sandwiches right over there on Decatur at the Central Grocery. Or would you like a shrimp po boy? I know just the place to get a great po boy, with the Tabasco and all. Mothers Restaurant up in the business district. Meatballs are good. It's known for its jambalaya.'

The heat and jetlag were beginning to worm at Salinger. He finished the coffee and the beignet.

'I'm not hungry, and I'm pretty weary.'

'Let's take a quick walk around the quarter, then I'll drive you home and maybe you could have a little lie-down.'

'A walk?'

'Ten, fifteen minutes. There's just so much great stuff here.'

Carson was rising from his chair. Salinger could not summon the resolution to protest. The beignets sat in his stomach. He felt that they were somehow gathering mass rather than digesting.

The light was heavy, thick and slightly brown, like builder's tea or sewage. They exited the café into Jackson Square, the white Catholic cathedral dominating the space. The buskers here were better than outside the café. Two black teenagers in ripped jeans were tearing up 'St James Infirmary Blues' with a steel guitar and a mouth organ. Salinger, finally having separated some American currency from the detritus in his pocket, flung a quarter into their hat. The guitar player stopped halfway through a phrase to ask if he wanted any change. Salinger grimaced in embarrassment, searched for a dollar bill, but could only find a five. He threw it into the hat, then immediately regretted it.

He felt the sun hacking at his neck. There was a man selling ironic Katrina T-shirts which read *FEMA PLAN – Run, Bitch, Run*. There were face painters, fortune tellers, mimes, magicians, musicians, inept bird-conjurors, hectoring tap dancers.

Another black man, wearing a Jazz Fest T-shirt and cargo shorts, popped out of a doorway and blocked Salinger's path.

'Hey, man, five bucks says I can tell you where you got those shoes.'

Salinger looked down at his shoes. He had bought them at a bespoke shoe shop near Brick Lane. Salinger looked the hustler up and down. He was flyblown, ragged, spindly-legged. There was no possibility that he had even heard of Brick Lane, let alone Rathbone and Clark.

'You're going to lose that bet,' said Salinger.

'No, man. I got the second sight. I got the third eye. I'm a seventh son. I can tell you where you got those shoes. Five dollars says I can.'

The man started waving a five spot in front of Salinger's face. Carson smiled.

'It's a scam,' he said mildly.

'There's no way he can know.'

'You're going to lose,' said Carson. 'I don't know how, but you're going to lose.'

'I'll take the bet. OK, tell me where I got these shoes.'

'You want me to tell you where you got those shoes? For five bucks?'

'Sure, go ahead. For five bucks.'

'Shake on it?'

'Shake on it.'

Salinger shook the man's hand. It was warm, calloused, clammy and unpleasant.

'OK, man. You got those shoes on your feet, man. All right.'

He gave a broad smile. Salinger grinned foolishly back.

'Fuck.'

He hesitated, looking momentarily for a way to escape the contract, then reached in his pocket for another five-dollar bill and handed it over. Business concluded, the man flicked off his smile and went in search of the next mark.

'Sucker,' said Carson.

'You got that right,' said Salinger.

He noticed a small sheet of glossy paper flapping on top of a fleur-de-lys sewer cap and on impulse picked it up. It was a tourist flyer with a headline that read *America's Worst Catastrophe! An eyewitness account of events surrounding the most devastating disaster on American soil! . . . Souvenir Hurricane Katrina Tour available for purchase!*

The tour included the wrecked Ninth Ward which took the brunt of the damage when the levees split. People dying in filthy waters, slowly starving on the rooftops. Later, the apocalyptic crosses on the doors, marking the coming of the government ranks, too late. Salinger imagined the coachloads of tourists disgorging from the maw of a shiny coach, swarming over the archaeological remains of human misery.

Carson led him on. The fifteen minutes stretched into forty-five. Carson bought a muffaletta sandwich at the Central Grocery, while Salinger stared at the novelty delicacies displayed in the window – bumblebees in soy sauce, chocolate-covered grasshoppers. The vast sandwich, stuffed with provolone cheese, salami and olive salad, was to take back for LouLou, who was, according to Carson, 'eating like a heifer, but still looking like a gazelle'.

Neither description chimed with Salinger. As he recalled, she was more reminiscent of lemur or minx, with a trace of adder. They wandered past the fruit-and-vegetable market, then up through Ursulines to an exhausted Bourbon Street, all tourist shops and hollow promises. Carson insisted it would be wild after nightfall, even though it was only Monday night.

The shops sold penis-shaped pasta and obscene T-shirts. One read *Fuck You, You Fucking Fuck.* Men broad as rhinos wore shorts with loaded, bulging pockets and smoked ridiculously large cigars while sucking on paper buckets of brightly dyed cocktails.

There was a weenie cart in the shape of a hot dog. Salinger remembered his father pressing John Kennedy Toole's *A Confederacy of Dunces* on him as a ten-year-old. All he could remember about it was that the main character worked on a New Orleans weenie cart and wore a stupid hat.

They passed a small brass band of six or seven teenage boys who funked up a marching tune with bop and swing and hard-rock rhythm. Salinger stood and watched, gradually allowing himself to move his feet in time. A policeman arrived. Salinger expected the beefy, grim-faced cop to move them along, as they were blocking the sidewalk completely. Instead, his grimace smoothed out, he did a little dance and threw a buck into the hat.

Passing a Visitor Information stand, he picked up some more tourist flyers. There were glossy brochures advertising crocodile tours, bayou tours, zoo tours, park tours, aquarium tours. The pavements reflected the heat, swirling the dirty light in carpets of dust. The French-style wrought-iron balconies were as striking and beautiful as Salinger remembered, but he couldn't respond to them. He was too tired. His eyes began to lose focus. For a moment he thought he might faint. Carson, heedless, led him on.

They ate an ice snowball with strawberry syrup from a stand, then carried on past Marie Laveau's House of Voodoo, Hooters restaurant, an array of five-and-dime stores with dark, faintly sinister interiors. They passed the Praline Connection soul-food shack in Faubourg Marigny, the Mona Lisa pizza house, decorated with hundreds of different reproductions of the unaccountably popular icon. Salinger remembered eating there on his last visit, the heavenly cocktail of salt and fat. Nobody did junk food like New Orleans.

At different times he picked up scents that Carson informed him were sweet olive, ligustrum, and Confederate jasmine. They walked past the Audubon Hotel where, Carson sententiously informed him, James Audubon compiled *Birds of America* and Tennessee Williams wrote *A Streetcar Named Desire*. Salinger had never heard of Audubon and didn't like Williams – or at least, not *Streetcar* – but he was reluctant to say anything to deflate Carson's still-expanding bubble. He had resolved to be on his best behaviour for the visit. He had come to the conclusion that he couldn't afford to fall out with someone who he was going to spend an undefined amount of time with in a confined space.

They continued towards the flea market shops on Decatur. None of them seemed to have sold a single item since he last visited. He remembered the same 1950s neon clock, the giant Native American headdress, the chrome bumper from a Chevy Impala, the fans and masks and torn lace veils. They were cathedrals of tat – old signs, clothes, dolls, magnifying glasses, china animals, posters, wigs.

They finally made their way back to the car park, past the House of Blues, where, on his last visit to the city, he had made a pilgrimage to see the Neville Brothers. Once again, Carson inspected the chassis to make sure that no damage had befallen the Lexus since he had left it. Satisfied, he hauled himself into the car with a satisfied grunt.

They headed towards the house in the Garden District. Salinger felt a rush of annoyance with Carson for dragging him round the French Quarter when all he wanted to do was lie down. Ten years of separation and the tension was already coalescing.

He was probably irritating Carson too, though there was no way of being sure. Salinger knew Carson well enough to know that all conflict would be expressed between the lines, hairline cracks in toughened concrete. In his mind, this made Carson a typical American, those global masters of passive aggression, smiling perkily while they water-boarded, clusterbombed, drone-decimated.

They drove towards St Charles Avenue, a block from Lee Circle. Salinger noted the beautifully named streets – Euterpe, Melpomene, Terpsichore. He vaguely remembered they were all Greek muses of one kind or another.

As they made their way up St Charles, Salinger began to notice the white crosses still painted on many of the doors begin to multiply. The crosses indicated that the house had been searched and was clear of corpses.

Joggers flopped brightly round the park, engaged on the great American project of postponing death. Salinger remembered the zoo in Audubon. They had a pearly white alligator there, an albino. He liked the zoo. He liked all zoos and aquariums, preferred them to the discomfort of safaris and fishing trips. Nature was better when properly packaged.

They hit a pothole. The roads were pitted with them, some the size of truck wheels. The Lexus absorbed the shock without difficulty.

'This is where the air suspension comes into its own. They just don't fix this shit up,' said Carson. 'No tax money, so . . .'

The lushness of the tropical greenery increased as they followed the streetcar line. One carriage came towards them, dinky, occupied largely by what looked like commuters rather than tourists. Air blew through the open windows, setting the hair of the passengers into flurries and whirls. Salinger had to admit, despite all the things that he thought tedious about New Orleans, he was a fan of the streetcar. It was just a great way to travel – slowly through the moist heat, natural wind in your face, the clack and clunk of the steel wheels on the road underneath you. He mourned the fact that a lot of the buses in London no longer had windows you could open. Same with most hotels nowadays, everywhere. Why were people so against air when it was one of the few things we weren't running out of?

Salinger saw at least a dozen signs announcing the foreclosure of properties. The sub-prime crisis was ripping at the country, tearing at the world.

The Lexus pulled into a wide, deserted road. The sign read *Annunciation*. Salinger was still feeling irritable, but he knew he had to open up a second front of politeness for LouLou. They hadn't got on the last time. The niceness broke him in the end, the endless American commitment to middle-class manners, the neurotic politeness. *Would you step out of the car, please, sir. Would you adopt the position, please, sir. Would you stand still while I pistol whip your black face, you nigger piece of shit, sir.*

They pulled into the front yard of a large wooden house, painted bright blue. There was a Kawasaki motorcycle outside, black and silver.

'This is it,' said Carson, surveying his patch of territory proudly.

The façade of the house was slatted and painted white. There were four white pillars supporting a portico. In front of a picket fence, there were stairs leading up to a deck, where there was a lounger suspended on hinges. It rocked in the breeze. The light was fading. There was a lamp hanging above the doorway. The door itself was panelled and highly glossed, painted an iridescent dark green. Strands of Mardi Gras beads hung over the wrought-iron facing of the stoop. There were three high sash windows, wooden-framed.

'It's nice.'

'Long way from Brent. Those depressing terraces. Six houses in a row, pebbledash, bay windows, hydrangea.'

'I live in a terrace. I like it.'

'Well, some are nice, I guess.'

'Is that your motorbike?'

'The Kawasaki Ninja? ZZR600, goes like a road-runner with a rocket up its butt. Six piston brakes, 4 into 2 into 1 exhaust. It's Lou's. She used to do all that stuff, the biker-chick thing. I joined in as a hobby for her sake, for about six months, but it's kind of unsafe as far as I'm concerned. Now she's pregnant, she's said goodbye to all that. Well, I nagged at her till she did, I guess. We're putting it on sale. Got the Lexus instead. Safest car on the damn road according to *Consumer Reports*.'

Carson slid out of the driver's seat and began to haul Salinger's luggage out of the boot. As Salinger exited, the front door of the house opened.

A compact woman appeared, somehow tightly confined, as if there were something within her that her skin could barely contain. The words *packed, stacked and jacked* came into Salinger's mind. She was forty-six years old, but she was jumping in the air like a teenager, her short blonde hair springing horizontally out of her skull with each levitation. She held her arms out and forward, advancing swiftly towards Salinger. The sight reminded Salinger of a pointer dog he had seen once while accompanying a radical girlfriend on a hunt sabotage in Wiltshire.

'Uncle Sal!'

She enveloped Salinger in her toned, bony arms, administered a brief hug, then immediately released him as if she had had seconds thoughts about her initial enthusiasm.

'Not quite an uncle yet.'

'But you are! Little Henry's already *there*.'

She rubbed her stomach and looked down, admiring the pronounced bump.

'How are you, LouLou?'

'I'm *great*. How are *you*?'

'Pretty much OK.'

'Mmh *hmmh*. You look *great*. How was the flight?'

Salinger wondered why people always insisted on asking that stupid question.

'Long, uncomfortable, dull.'

LouLou rustled up a dry laugh.

'I think I may have deep-vein thrombosis,' continued Salinger. 'An hour to live, max.'

Carson appeared from behind them, hauling the luggage.

'Hey, hon.'

'Hey, darlin'.'

She smiled showing a fine set of American teeth. The three of them stood there, each fixed to the spot. Then, silently, they moved inside, and LouLou set about making Salinger another cup of chicory coffee while Carson put his bags in the upstairs room that they had prepared for him.

Salinger flopped gratefully down into an angular, unyielding armchair, upholstered with what looked like deck-chair canvas. He stretched his neck and took in his surroundings. The interior was frighteningly tidy. Not a single item appeared to be out of place.

Magazines on the coffee table – *Time* and *Vanity*

Fair – were arranged at precise right angles to the long edge of the polished glass surface. Large-format books, all of which appeared to be on the subject of design and house improvement, stretched along properly mounted shelves on faultlessly painted walls. There was a book called *The Purpose-driven Life* on top of a fireplace sill.

There were one or two tasteful prints on the wall – a rubbing of a New Orleans manhole cover with the distinctive fleur-de-lys and the five stars and a poster for the 1995 Jazz Fest. An iPod dock was connected to two small white speakers. No wires were visible. On the polished wooden floor there were two deep-red rugs which looked as if they were of Native or South American origin. On the wall, facing the street, there was a lurid, large folkart representation of the Virgin Mary with an elaborately carved frame. There were gauzy rust-coloured curtains with draws and a pelmet. The window at the landing on the stairs was modern stained glass.

'You take sugar, Sal?'

Carson had taken off his shoes, and was now throwing meaningful glances at Salinger's, which he had replaced on his feet at the end of the car journey. Dutifully, he slipped them off again. Carson picked them up and carried them over to the mat by the front door.

'Just milk,' called Salinger after him.

The degree of order in the house made Salinger uneasy. Where was the human mess? He turned from inspecting a faux-Victorian glass light fitting on the wall to find both Carson and LouLou seated on the geometric cream leather sofa opposite, gazing at him eagerly. A cup of coffee had been placed in front of him on a small coaster. The words *Laissez Les Bons Temps Rouler* were inscribed on the mug. There was a plate of flat, brown, sticky pralines to the side of it.

'So, *Salinger*. Tell us *everything*. How's you and your girlfriend? How's work?'

LouLou, a small bird in carefully tailored jeans with an elasticated waistband and a white peasant blouse, perched on the front edge of the sofa, apparently determined to be entranced by every detail of Salinger's life and thoughts. Sitting back beside her Carson conspiratorially rolled his eyes at Salinger.

'England. Cold. Relationship. OK. Art. Struggling. Money. Likewise. That's about it.'

LouLou seemed momentarily delighted with the reply. Her eyes were commercial-bright. She seemed unsure what to say next. Salinger felt a sudden desire to accidentally knock his cup of coffee on the carpet. Carson stood up and went and put his crushed beer can into a recycling bin.

'How's the massage business?' said Salinger.

'The great thing about it is, the more stressed people get, the more they come and see me,' said LouLou.

'You have a speciality?'

'She's just started doing Christian massage,' said Carson.

'It's a little more modest than the usual offerings,' said LouLou. 'I incorporate prayer and some Bible reading. People seem to like it.'

'What's not to like?' said Salinger, stuck for a response. LouLou examined his face for traces of sarcasm, and finding none visible, smiled and patted her stomach.

'Are you looking forward to being an uncle?' said LouLou, still looking down at her abdomen.

'Oh yes. Absolutely.'

'Do you like children?'

'They're fantastic, of course.'

'Well I hope you're going to come to the christening.'

'I only just got here this time.'

'It really is great to see you.'

'It's great to see you, too.'

'Family is so important.'

'Oh yes. Completely.'

There was another brief pause during which, once again, nobody seemed to have anything to say. It was Salinger who eventually broke the silence.

'Have you heard any more from Dad, Carson? Have you let him know that we're coming to see him?'

Carson took his seat again, and scratched the back of his neck, a habit Salinger remembered from childhood. Carson always did it when he was addressing an especially knotty problem.

'Tell you the truth, I don't know how to tell him that we're coming. I'm still not sure where he is.'

Salinger flinched.

'We're going on a road trip to see Dad, but we don't know where he is? I thought you were going to make further enquiries. I assumed you knew where we were heading.'

Salinger was aware that a note of irritation had slipped into his voice, but he felt powerless to stop it. The coffee had put an edge on his tiredness, and LouLou's bright, beady eyes were making him nervous.

'Don't worry, we'll find him.'

'I can't believe I came all this way and we don't even know if Dad wants to see us.'

'Of course he wants to see us.'

'Then why hasn't he given us an address? Why hasn't he phoned?'

'Maybe he doesn't know my phone number. You know. It's just Dad.'

'"It's just Dad." Why does that let him off the *hook*? Like the way he is, he has no choice about.'

Salinger became aware that his voice was increasing in volume. Carson shifted uncomfortably in his chair and scratched the back of his neck again. Salinger reined himself back in.

'Sorry, Carson. I'm just jet-lagged.'

LouLou picked a tiny speck of dust from the arm of the sofa. She stared at the carpet, then excused herself to go to the bathroom. Carson rose, and took another beer from the fridge.

'Look, Salinger. He's in Las Cruces, we know that much. He's sixty-four, so he's not going to be hopping about the country like some kind of gypsy. There will be about three cafés where arty types hang. Half a dozen, max. We'll find news of him in one of them. And he's ill, so he's probably not, you know, too *ambulatory.*

'I figured that even if we don't find Dad – and we *will* – then we'll have had a trip, an experience that will always be valuable to us, that we can find growth through, perhaps even some kind of closure.'

'Closure of what?'

'Maybe that's the wrong word. I don't know. We're not so close to one another nowadays, Salinger. This journey will be good for us. It'll be more than that. It'll be *fun.* That's why I wanted you to come here as my guest.'

There it was, slapped down on the table like an affidavit. Carson had paid for his air ticket. Carson had booked the hotels and paid for them in advance. Salinger had accepted. Carson had purchased the right to his goodwill. Salinger knew he had no choice but to keep up his side of the bargain.

'You're right. I'm sorry. I'm looking forward to it.'

'So am *I.*'

Carson grinned again, rose and clapped Salinger on the back. Salinger felt discomfited by the gesture. Carson had never been a back-slapper or an arm-puncher. In fact while they were growing up he couldn't remember that Carson had ever touched him, or their mother.

'Listen, I'm sorry if I messed up, bro. I should have found his address somehow. I'm a bit dumb sometimes, but I didn't mean any harm. Shake on it?'

Carson held out his big beefy hand. Reluctantly, Salinger offered his in return. Carson's fist closed over Salinger's fingers, enveloped them and pressed hard enough, almost, to hurt.

They were planning to leave around lunchtime the next day. Carson had a few tasks to finish first. It would be an eight-hour drive to Austin, Texas. Salinger, Carson and LouLou sat down to a late dinner. The table had been carefully laid with cream-coloured china and thick, heavy glass goblets.

LouLou and Carson had so far made no attempt to press their religious convictions on Salinger. Other than the conspicuous lack of swearing, which Salinger found peculiar, there was no obvious sign of what Carson called his 'faith position'. Salinger hadn't even seen a Bible.

LouLou had prepared red beans and rice. Apparently it was a New Orleans tradition to eat red beans and rice on a Monday, something to do with fishermen not working on Sundays. As Salinger reached for the bottle of Gallo wine he noticed that both Carson and LouLou were bowing their heads. He cocked his head back from the wine, then, suddenly comprehending, bounced it forward in unison.

Carson began to speak in a low, half-whispered tone.

'Lord, thank you for this gift of food and drink. Thank you for the gift of family, and thank you for bringing our brother, Salinger, across the ocean safely. Grant us the grace of gratitude, and may the Lord protect us on our long journey together across the American soil. May we grow closer as a consequence of that journey, and may old wounds now be healed.'

Carson looked up at the ceiling, then directly at Salinger, his lips pursed, his eyes wide. Salinger found himself unaccountably moved. He avoided Carson's eye, and reached again for the wine. He found his arm rising to raise the glass.

'To little Henry.'

Carson and LouLou immediately raised their glasses as well.

'Little Henry.'

'And big Henry,' said Carson.

Salinger put his glass down. The table fell silent. LouLou began to dish out some collard greens.

'So you like motorcycling, LouLou?'

'Not any more. Sold the Kawasaki last week. They're coming to take it tomorrow. End of youth. Well. Maybe that was years ago.'

'You going to miss it?'

'Good riddance. I'm desperate to be a mom. Baby buggy goes as fast as I want.'

Salinger turned his gaze on the folk-art painting of the Madonna.

'This is a Catholic city, right? But you're both Protestants?'

'We're Baptists, yes,' answered LouLou. She was now doling out spoonfuls of the gooey red beans.

'So what's that about? Why didn't you just convert to Catholicism?'

He could see LouLou's frame flex within its skin slightly as she continued to dispense the food. Steam from the plate diffused the light.

'Well, I was rebirthed as a Baptist, Salinger. So I guess I didn't have much choice in the matter.'

'And Carson here just came along for the ride?'

'It wasn't like that, Sal,' said Carson. 'LouLou showed me what I'd been missing. She opened my eyes to . . . I don't know. Things I didn't understand.'

'This looks great,' said Salinger, aiming a fork vaguely at the red beans and rice. His hand wavered. He wasn't sure which he liked the look of less.

'How come you're not staying in N'awlins for a few days? We could give you a real nice tour.'

'I did the full tour last time, I guess. And I'm eager to get on the road with Carzy here.'

'So,' said LouLou, her voice bright and determined. 'When y'all leaving? What's the route?'

'Don't know,' said Salinger. 'Carson has it all planned out.'

'He likes to plan,' said LouLou. She took

Carson's hand and squeezed it. Carson leaned over and kissed her on the cheek, leaving a tiny canola-oil smear.

'I do,' said Carson. 'I like to make sure things are under control.'

He helped himself to some more beans. He had consumed the first helping in six bolted scoops.

'So this is the tour. The first part of the run is long and boring. All the way from here to Austin, Texas. Nothing to see, nowhere to go. Then Crawford. Then to Dallas. We'll go to the Kennedy Museum.'

'Why Crawford?'

'Hometown of George W.'

'Why would we want to go there?'

'Curiosity. Fact that it's on the way. Pay tribute to a great American leader.'

'I'm not rising to it, Carzy.'

'Didn't think you would, Sally. But I still think it would be interesting and it's not out of the way. Then, Amarillo, Tucumcari, Albuquerque, Sky City, Las Cruces. Then we find Henry.'

'And what then?'

Carson looked surprised at the question.

'We say "Hey,"' he said, finishing the last of his tremendous meal, sitting back, and patting himself on his sleek American potbelly.

CHAPTER 5

LAKESIDE

In the morning, after finishing his shave, Salinger resentfully inspected the small green-and-white pill that he had once considered his salvation from mood swings, blackened memories and angry outbursts. When he had first started taking it he had assumed that it would damage his imagination, limit his personality and anaesthetize his soul. But it had so far proved entirely benevolent.

Sometimes he considered giving it up, just to make proof of his own self-sufficiency, but he had never been able to find the courage. It seemed to graft an extra layer of skin with which to protect himself against the world. He feared that, without it, he would relapse into the mental turmoil he had suffered as a teenager, some years after his father had left home.

Then, like Phaedrus in Pirsig's book, he had lost all sense of himself, all purchase on the world. He had been in a perpetual state of waiting, like Phaedrus, for the seed crystal that would make sense of everything. It wasn't until after he recovered that he accepted that no such crystal existed. There was only flux and

99

dissolution, which somehow had to be rendered supportable.

Medication didn't resolve the puzzle, but it moderated the painful effect of understanding that the puzzle was insoluble, that the forces of randomness made any solution impossible. It was like standing in a spinning whirlpool in a moving river and being asked to precisely describe the river.

He popped the capsule in his mouth and swallowed it without water. He had already showered. LouLou had left for work. He had resisted the temptation to enquire further into her techniques for Christian massage therapy in case he failed to resist mocking her.

Carson had gone downtown for some last-minute provisions. He also needed to buy some new trousers and get a haircut. Salinger had two hours before he returned and then Carson had some church business to complete before they left. The two of them intended to depart early afternoon and make Austin come the evening.

He dressed, finished packing and made himself breakfast and coffee. There was wheat bread, and, noticing that the Marmite that Salinger had brought over for Carson as a gift had been opened – it was apparently impossible to get in Louisiana – he made himself some toast and smeared the tarlike goo onto a slice.

He picked up the local newspaper, the *New Orleans Times Picayune*, and started flicking through it. The newspaper was slick, more sober than an English tabloid but less authoritative than a broadsheet. There were a few national stories – *Central Banks Pump Billions Into System Desperate for Cash* – but the overwhelming bulk of the stories were parochial – accusations of cronyism in St Tammany Parish, a triple murder in the St Bernard housing project, pothole crisis in Metairie. There was a lot of print still devoted to the Katrina rebuilding. It was going slowly. The population of New Orleans was down 40 per cent while crime was rising to pre-Katrina levels.

Salinger found most of the stories uninteresting, only becoming really engaged when he reached the obituary pages. The first part of the section was taken up with photos of old white people who had died in this or that 'retirement facility' or 'peacefully at home'. Punctuating these tributes were the obituaries of young black men. Not just one, or two, but at least a dozen. They had all died of gunshot wounds. Postage-stamp-sized photographs marked their passing. Most looked to be about twenty or younger.

The images stared up at him. He felt unable to turn the page. The scale of it. Black kids were slaughtering each other while white people died in their beds. A dozen dead kids, in one small city, in a week. He remembered talking to Carson about it last time he had visited, when Salinger had mentioned the high level of crime in New Orleans. Carson had shrugged as if nothing could be more unremarkable.

'Mostly black-on-black stuff. It's just what they do. If you're white and live in a good area you're pretty safe.'

He tossed the newspaper to one side. He decided he should check his emails, hoping that there might be something from Tiane. He still hadn't worked out why she had been so urgent about persuading him to stay in London. The more he thought about it, the more it disturbed him. Was it some kind of veiled threat?

He eventually located a laptop computer, in Carson's den, where he kept box files on the household finances, his own personal flat-screen TV, a table-soccer game and an acoustic guitar.

He booted the Mac up; it requested a password. He tried all the usual possibilities – Carson's birth date, his wife's name, the word 'password' – without success. He typed in the word 'Henrynash'. The screen flared up into a screen saver featuring multiple digital images of Leonardo da Vinci's *Last Supper*.

He typed in his server address and accessed his email account. There was nothing there other than some random spam. Viagra, penis enlargement, another campaign to reduce world poverty. He had hoped for some kind of explanatory note from Tiane, or an apology, or a few words telling him there was nothing to worry about.

He didn't feel unduly concerned. Salinger often travelled away from London and Tiane never seemed remotely troubled by the prospect of his absence. She lacked the neediness from which Salinger so manifestly suffered. Her self-sufficiency, while welcome, also unsettled him. He liked to be needed when he felt like it.

Still feeling a mild frisson of annoyance for her thoughtless degree of independence, Salinger composed an email.

Tea

Arrived safely at the House of Christ in the 'City of Sin' – as it likes to imagine itself.

No arguments as yet, but have had to bite my tongue on several occasions to prevent myself from being inappropriately rude/English. The house is tidy to a creepy extent, soup cans alphabetized, pillow- cases bleached, pressed and folded. But it's nice enough if you are anally retentive to a morbid degree.

LouLou is just as I remembered her – frighteningly friendly, disconcerting, stretched like canvas over a slightly over- sized frame. I am sure that she is hiding some immense and terrible secret. But in all honesty, they have been very welcoming. I have simply been my usual curmudgeonly self. Or possibly I have been having, as you call it, an 'episode'.

We are setting off this afternoon. Somewhat to my own surprise, I am looking forward to it. I don't get to ride in a Chevy, though, unfortunately. Carson has bought a brand new Lexus instead. I've never seen anyone in love with a car so much, other than my dad and that stupid Coup de Ville he once bought when we lived in that house by the graveyard. He wipes it down with a cloth every time he drives it and makes me take my fucking shoes off so I won't soil the carpet.

Red beans and rice for dinner last night. Slop, but since tradition demanded that you eat it on Monday Carson ate about a gallon, LouLou, maybe a spoonful. Somehow this fitted their personalities.

LouLou, by the way, is now offering 'Christian massage therapy' at her spa. That sounds like a party for your head. They haven't been too much in my face about the God stuff, but we did say a prayer before eating. It felt very odd. I distracted myself during the prayer by thinking of you bent over the table naked with your legs spread apart and your finger up your cunt.

That probably gets me another ten thousand years in hell.

But – that way madness lies. For the next two weeks I don't even have the opportunity for auto-erotic activity, since I'll be sharing a room with Carzy and I'm sure that he will be vigilant against all forms of sinfulness.

I think I had better go now. I am using Carson's computer without his permission. And we are leaving in a few hours.

Look – what was that all about at the airport? Are you OK? I'm sorry I had to go, but you understand, don't you? Do you? Don't you?

Email me soon.

Love

Sally from the Alley

He pressed 'Send', then closed the email server and took the cursor to the 'Start' button so he could close the computer down. Then he hesitated. There were secrets on everybody's computer. Unaccountably, urgently, he found himself wanting to know what Carson's were.

Salinger checked his watch. Carson wouldn't be back for another hour at least. LouLou was at the spa. Instead of hitting the 'Turn Off' button, he went back to the email server and started scrolling through the browsing history.

What was there was boringly quotidian. There were incomprehensible work sites to do with real estate, eBay, eight or nine links that seemed to be to do with money saving, some Christian access pages, airline deals, links to Internet shopping home sites. Salinger felt disappointed. Even if Christ had cleansed Carson's soul of transgression, there must still be a record of it on his computer. Sins always left a trace.

He started browsing the folders, looking for anything that might have an ambiguous or suggestive, or even unusually dull, name. He looked in accounts, in 'My Pictures', in financial projections. Nothing. He was just about to log off when he remembered one last strategy. He instructed the computer to 'Show Hidden Files and Folders'.

The desktop immediately displayed four folders. They were named Private 1, Private 2 and Private 3. The last one was a little more specific. It was called Tom (Finland) – Private 4.

He right-clicked on the first one and went to Properties. It contained video files. He did the same with the rest. All video files, except the last one which was JPEG.

His finger hovered over the mouse. He stared at the folders. Private. Private. Private.

Suddenly he felt ashamed, and then relieved to be ashamed. Perhaps, he reflected, he wasn't such a bad person after all.

He went to the 'Start' menu and closed the computer down.

Carson returned with a conventionally slapdash and inappropriately neat American haircut – floppy, graceless, rounded, side-parted. He moved around the house in short, brisk, purposeful bursts of activity. He showed off his new bargain jeans to Salinger – which, he informed Salinger, were 60 per cent off the list price. They were identical to the pair he was already wearing.

'OK, I got one last thing to do before we head off, bro. I'll be maybe two hours, then we can get right off.'

'What last thing?'

'It's a church project. Out in Lakeview. Helping rebuild the communities after Katrina. Something I'm committed to. I don't really want to let them down. People have put a lot of effort in. Come a long way. I'm sort of project manager. If I don't turn up, then why should they? Sorry if it delays us. It's in a good cause, believe me.'

'There's still rebuilding going on? After three years? Why hasn't the government sorted things out?'

'It don't work like that here, Salinger. In England, when things go wrong, you go to the government. Here, the government is the problem, not the solution. The enemy, some might say.'

Carson went out into the yard and took a shovel and bucket out of a small wooden shed. He started to load them in the back of the Lexus. Salinger followed him listlessly, trying to figure out the logic behind Carson's last remark.

'How is the government the enemy?'

'You're English. You wouldn't understand.'

'Try me. You're English and you understood.'

'We just don't expect it to act like our *protector*. We like to keep it out of our face. Saps the strength. This here is more of a volunteer culture, you might say. We help one another out, because sure as sugar is sweet the government isn't going to do jack. They're there to keep the peace and punish the criminal. Or that's what they should be doing. Keeping it minimal.'

'I don't get it. Why, after Katrina, didn't you all get pitchforks and march on the White House?'

'I wasn't angry.'

'How could you not be angry?'

'No one was to blame. They never had a situation like this before. No one knew how to deal with it. It was just human error.'

'Maybe God was to blame.'

Carson gently closed the boot of the Lexus, and wiped a smear of dead bug from the paintwork with his fingertip.

'I don't know about that. One thing's sure, we cleaned the place out.'

'What does that mean?'

'It was kind of weird that it hit the Ninth Ward worst of all. Don't you think?'

'Are you saying what I think you're saying?'

'I'm just stating a fact, bro. These old neighbourhoods, they're breeding grounds of poverty and crime. Now they ain't there. Seems to me that everything happens for a purpose.'

'Is that right? So God came after the blacks and gave them what they had coming.'

'I didn't say that. Not at *all*. But you know. What goes around comes around.'

'That's a meaningless phrase. It's just something stupid people *say*.'

Carson wiped the dead bug from his finger onto the front lawn.

'I guess we're not going to see eye to eye on this one.'

'But, Carzy . . .'

Carson interrupted him, holding up his hand like a stop sign.

'Look at me, Sal. I'm nothing special. I'm not clever like you. Yeah, I guess you're right, I'm pretty dumb. But I have a wonderful wife and a child on the way, and a good job and enough money. Heck – I'm happy.'

'God has favoured you?'

'I think so.'

'You've been lucky.'

'I've kept the faith.'

'Meaning?'

'Maybe God rewards the faithful.'

'Katrina was a punishment for the unfaithful?'

'The Lord sends all sorts of tests to all kinds of people.'

'You don't seriously think it happened to them because they didn't believe in God?'

'Maybe they believed, maybe they didn't. Maybe they just didn't live righteous enough lives. Hey, don't ask me. Like I say, I'm just a dumb Yank. You brought it up, not me. I didn't ask to have this conversation. But if you're asking me, do the faithful have their reward? I say, yes they do. And not only in heaven.'

'So let me get this straight. Let me pin it down. Did the Holocaust happen because the Jews didn't believe in Jesus?'

Carson swung himself up into the driver's-side seat, but kept talking through the open window.

'Come on, Sal. I can't answer questions like that. That was a work of man, not God. As for Katrina – the weak have moved on. The hurricane was – I don't know – nature's test of commitment, if you will. Anyway, it wasn't only the blacks that were hit. You'll see. Listen, I got to go and do this thing. Why don't you come with?'

They drove out to Lakeside, a white area to the north of the city, a suburb of Metairie. Like the Ninth Ward, it had been razed to the ground when the levees broke. Most of the houses by now had been repaired and rebuilt, but there were a dozen or so lots that were still primarily wreckage.

Carson parked outside a white clapboard house with the front yard in a disarray of broken machinery, wheelbarrows, an abandoned child's bicycle. Outside five people, all in their teens or twenties, were milling around wearing reflective yellow tabards. As Carson exited the Lexus, they collectively raised their hands in greeting, chorusing 'Hey's, 'Hi's and 'Hello's. They all carried shovels, or hoes, or pitchforks. Salinger followed Carson, and found himself caught up in a roundabout of introductions.

'Carrie, this is my little brother, Salinger. Randy, this is Salinger. DeShawn, Sissy, Steve – Salinger.'

'Hey.'

'Hey, Salinger.'

'Nice to meet you.'

'Great to have you here,' said DeShawn, a burly young black man with cropped hair and vast shoulders. 'You here to do some voluntourism?'

They were all smiling at him. They wore identical T-shirts which read *Fulfilling the Gospel Mission in Lakeside*.

'Voluntourism?'

'We're all voluntourists,' smiled Carrie, brandishing her pitchfork. 'Came down to see what we can do.'

'Sissy here is from Baton Rouge. You too, right, Carol? Steve and DeShawn are from Detroit. Randy from Ann Arbor. They all came down to do their thing.'

'Praise Jesus,' said Steve. Their smiles were steady, unremitting.

'We should all get back to work,' said the young man called Randy, who had a ponytail and weighed around twenty stone. His trousers had worked their way down his hips to reveal an inch of buttock crease.

'OK, guys. Let's go to work,' said Carson.

One by one, the Christians turned away and began to walk through the house to start digging and clearing the debris in the back yard. Carson removed his denim jacket to reveal his own *Fulfilling the Gospel Mission* T-shirt.

'Inspiring, dontcha think? There are about thirty such projects like this. In this area alone. Conventioneers make days to come out here, tourists come, faith groups come. They clear yards, hack at trees. This is how we do it in America. This is what I'm talking about.'

Carson beckoned Salinger to follow him through to the back of the house.

'This is how you do it in the white suburbs. Who used to live here? Some banker?'

'An eighty-four-year-old Afro-American lady, who is presently living in a trailer park in Houston. In about four weeks she'll have her house back, thanks to people like this. You imagine that happening in England? Everyone would be sitting on their butts waiting for the man with the clipboard to come down and sort it all out for them. You guys are still subjects of the jolly old Queen. Here we have citizens.'

They came out into the back yard. The six smiling teenagers were working steadily. Carson picked up a shovel and offered it to Salinger.

'That old stump needs digging out. You going to do some work for THE LAWD, brother?'

Carson was smiling, mocking him. Salinger took the shovel. One of the volunteers threw him a T-shirt. He ripped off his shirt and put it on.

'You can keep that,' said Carson, who was now helping three others to remove a collapsed tree. 'Looks good on you.'

Salinger nodded and began to work at the stump. It was going to take a lot of effort to dig the roots out. But the energy of the Christians was eerily infectious. He cut at the earth, steel meeting wood. He worked till his hands were raw.

Two hours later, they were back at the house. They showered, then loaded the car. Salinger checked

112

his shoulder bag. He couldn't locate his wallet. He didn't want to tell Carson. His shame at losing things was intense. But he had scanned all the rooms he had been in, burrowed down the bottom of his bags, checked every unlikely place that the wallet could be. He was sure it was in the house somewhere, but where exactly he had left it was a blank.

He put the search to the back of his mind and went downstairs. Carson was in the kitchen, filling a water bottle for the journey. His face was still red from the effort of working at the house. Salinger felt tired, but oddly elated by the visit to Lakeside. He had chatted to the voluntourists while he worked. Most of them were ordinary kids working their way through college. They were doing it for free, apparently out of pure goodwill.

It was a very different place from Europe all right, thought Salinger, as he spooned down some of the hot biscuits and hominy grits that Carson had prepared for him.

'Howdja like them grits?' shouted Carson. He was now loading a cooler with juice and soft drinks.

'Not much,' said Salinger. 'I like the biscuits. Rather like scones.'

'You don't like grits? That's good soul food.'

'Carson, you're from Willesden. You don't have to like everything just because it comes from New Orleans. Grits are fucking horrible. Like wallpaper paste.'

113

'I like grits,' said Carson cheerfully. 'Are you ready? It's getting a little late. We need to get on the move.'

Salinger saw that he had no choice.

'I can't find my wallet, Carson.'

'That's on the dresser behind the TV, you dope.'

Salinger imagined that Carson was delighted by this reassertion of their traditional roles – the pragmatist and the flake. Carson zipped the cooler bag and started carrying it towards the Lexus. Salinger cleaned his plate, washed his hands and doused his face with water.

He noticed a pinboard suspended above the toaster, occupied with recipes, quotations from the Bible, a cardboard cut-out of what appeared to be an angel, and a picture of a unicorn. Dominating the pinboard was a list it appeared that LouLou had written on her computer and printed out.

Principles of Self-mastery
Be who you are
See the illusion
Allow what is to be
Live in the now

He heard the car horn sound. When he went outside, Carson was holding the door open. The Lexus stood gleaming, spotless in the driveway.

He was smiling again. Carson was nearly always smiling.

'Salinger. This is awesome. Isn't this *awesome?*'

Salinger had to admit to himself that he was excited. Outside of his one previous visit to New Orleans, he had never done the America thing. He had never travelled from coast to coast on a Greyhound bus, never visited the canyons of Fifth Avenue, never taken a photograph in front of the Hollywood sign. His vision of America was almost entirely constructed out of ideas taken from newspapers and movies and the stories that Henry used to tell him as a child.

Spending a week – at least – in a moving steel cage with a brother he barely knew any more and didn't particularly like was not the way that he might have chosen, ideally, to undertake the journey. All the same the trip stretched ahead of him in his imagination like a river of mercury, shape-shifting, unpredictable, potentially toxic.

The Lexus set off in the direction of the suburbs of Metairie and Kenner, making its way to the I–10 which stretched westward towards the Louisiana capital, Baton Rouge, then Lafayette, Lake Charles and eventually Austin. Carson had warned Salinger that the ride would be featureless and dull until they began to penetrate into the heart of Texas. Then, he remarked drily, it would still be dull, but on a grander scale.

Salinger felt the weariness grow on him again. Depression could be a lot like fatigue. Or perhaps he was simply jet-lagged, or maybe the work in the yard had drained him. He had barely spoken since leaving the house.

Carson was ramping up the music on the car system. Salinger had been fed a steady diet of New Orleans classics since they pulled out of the driveway.

'Daniel Lanois. You know Lanois? He has a house in the French Quarter on Esplanade Ave. Produced all the big ones. U2. Dylan. Willie Nelson. Emmylou. All of 'em. He's *Québécois*. That's where the New Orleans Cajuns came from in the first place, Quebec, Acadia. There's an affinity. It's a hodge-podge here, a gumbo if you will.'

Salinger tuned out, and fixed his eyes on the skyline. He wished that the Prozac was more effective. Perhaps he should increase the dose. The black mood that had settled on him at Heathrow had lightened but not shifted. Even while he was working at the mission, he hadn't been able to entirely shake it off.

Even doing God's work was no solution. Virtue solved nothing at all. Maybe there wasn't a solution. Maybe his crime was too great, even though he didn't have the least idea what it might be or when he had committed it.

CHAPTER 6

NEW ORLEANS – AUSTIN

Seventy miles out of New Orleans, passing Baton Rouge, Salinger spotted the yellow Louisiana State Penitentiary bus. Inside, around twenty convicts in black-and-white striped uniforms, like characters in an archaic cartoon, were clearly visible through the barred windows, looking sullen or blank. Their wrists were cuffed. Two prison guards at the front of the bus watched them intently.

Salinger had seen a documentary on the place once, years before. It had never left him. They called it Angola, or the Farm. Shards of detail had got stuck in his memory. He saw in his mind the image of an eighteen-year-old boy brought in to the Penitentiary yard for the first time and being shown the prison cemetery where he would be buried, maybe seventy years later.

Other faces floated into his mind, the faces of men who were plainly innocent but who had suffered incompetent and underpaid defence lawyers. A stubborn, mulishly intractable justice system would not allow them right to appeal. Some had been convicted on the 'three strikes and you're out' policy, and were spending the rest of their lives in jail for lifting a pack of cigarettes from a supermarket.

He saw again in his mind the old lags being interviewed by the TV crew – grey-haired and beaten down but somehow impressive and dignified, explaining to the newcomers – teenage kids for the most part, gang bangers and low-level drug pushers – that they were entirely alone now. Their family, their friends, their wives, would all sooner or later give up on them. The Farm was now their entire world for ever. This was something they needed to accept or their time would go hard.

One last image pressed into his mind – the look in the eyes of one of the eighteen-year-old boys at the moment when this knowledge of his perpetual abandonment took hold. He had never imagined that a human face could contain such desolation.

'I feel sorry for them,' said Salinger.

Carson glanced down at the prison bus. One of the guards lifted his gaze at the same time. Carson raised a hand in greeting. The guard nodded slightly, then returned his gaze to the prisoners.

'Don't feel too sorry for them. They're probably on the way to practise for the rodeo next month.'

'They have a prison rodeo?'

'Yeah, it's like a fricking holiday camp in there. Arts and crafts, entertainment, food, what have you. The horse riding, of course. Shame you won't be here then. I could take you for a day out.'

'It's open to the public?'

'Sure. Seven, eight thousand people go there. Big deal around here.'

The car was still level with the bus. The prisoners didn't look like they were looking forward to anything much.

'It's still sad, though.'

'It *is* sad. Poor devils. They should just have put some of them out of their misery in the first place,' said Carson.

Salinger felt himself flinch slightly.

'You mean kill them?'

He turned to Carson to examine his expression. He saw no sign there that he was joking. Salinger got the impression that his eyes were slightly unfocused, as if contemplating something far in the distance.

'In certain circumstances it's justified, I believe, yes I do. Some of these guys have done very bad things. Maybe if you were related to the victims you might drop all this bleeding-heart liberal bullcrap.'

It was the first time since he had arrived in America that Salinger had heard Carson shift his tone from one of unremitting mildness.

'See, I've worked with some of the relatives of victims, Sal. As part of my church work. I've seen dozens of them. People destroyed by the loss of their loved ones. Lives ruined by some act of pure evil. It's the devil's work. I'm telling you straight.'

'The little guy with the pitchfork?'

'You can laugh. I've seen what these people do. The devil's not a little guy with a pitchfork. The devil's a feeling. It's a lust for the empty, for everything that's negative. For power instead of love. It's the death wish. It's in all of us. Some of us let it ride. They . . .'

He nodded down towards the bus.

'They let it ride. Some people enjoy hurting others. Some people feel no repentance for what they do. Not ever.'

'But what's the point? I mean, of revenge? It's hollow. It's all too late.'

'The point is, Sally, that it helps people.'

'Who does it help? It's futile.'

'The bereaved, the relatives and friends of the victims. That's the *point*. I've met these people. When that needle goes into the vein of that miscreant who stole their most precious thing away from them, when justice is done, when an eye is given in return for an eye, those people who lost their loved ones can begin to heal. I've seen it myself. I'll tell you something, Salinger. In all seriousness. Revenge is a kind of grace.'

'Oh come on, that's just . . .'

'If you met the father of some ten-year-old who had been sodomized, tortured, killed like a dog and thrown in the back of a dumpster like a piece of trash, you might feel differently. I've met that father, Sally. I've met that mother. I know that retribution helped that mother and that father to put their lives back together again. Who are *you* to say, I won't help that poor mother, I won't help that father, I won't help that brother and sister?'

Sal looked ahead of him at the bright air then shifted his gaze down to the wing mirror. Far in the distance he could see the receding figure of the bus through the heat haze.

He closed his eyes and tried to fall asleep. Minutes later, he was dreaming of God and prisons and churning oceans of grits and anal sex with LouLou, spreadeagled face forward on her Christian massage bed, under forks of yellow lightning stretching across vast purple skies.

While Salinger thrust and trembled, completing, as he climaxed, his final humiliation of Carson, he waited for his punishment. The executioner would bear the mild, stoic expression of his brother as he ended all things, for ever.

The barbecue shack was a large shed with a sloping corrugated-metal roof. It stood at the crossroads of a small town that appeared to comprise nothing more than the crossroads itself, a gas station and the diner.

Inside, three black women and two black men, all in blue hairnets, were lined up behind a long steel counter. A queue of a dozen or so people stretched out in front of the counter. Arranged behind Plexiglas were great haunches of meat, and in the compartment next to them soft white rolls and loaves of bread with the consistency of cotton wool. There was a range of gravy boats and a display of sickly-looking, overcoloured desserts. Salinger and Carson took up their places in the queue.

'Texas is beef country,' said Carson. 'The smoked-brisket roll is the best you can get this side of Big Bend.'

'Let me pay.'

'It's on me.'

'I've got it.'

'Sure, if you say so, Sally.'

'Your name's Sally? Ain't that a girl's name? It short for Salvatore? You don't look like no Italian.'

The woman at the cash till, a grossly overweight black woman with her hair dyed orange, fixed Salinger with a deadpan glare. Her eyes made him think of whelks. She went back to totting up some figures on a scrap of paper. Her name tag announced her name was Gloria.

'It's short for Salinger,' he said, conscious of the prissiness of his voice in contrast to the rasping self-confidence of the server.

Gloria continued totting up the figures without looking up.

'Ain't *that* a girl's name too?'

She caught the eye of the chef who was preparing the brisket. He gave a grin, showing slabs of broken brownish tooth. Salinger ordered the brisket roll and a huge side of BBQ ribs for Carson, along with a tub of Coke from a spigot for himself and a peach ice tea for Carson. The food arrived in less than a minute and the woman behind the till called out Salinger's name. He put the food and drink on a tray and started to take it outside.

'You wanna *pay* for that food, Sally?'

'Sorry. Yes. Of course.'

Salinger put down the tray on the counter and fumbled for the notes and coins he had in his pocket. He haltingly tried to count them out. There wasn't enough to pay for the meal. The woman at the cashier's desk didn't take her gaze from him.

'You OK there, Sally? I ain't rushin' you, am I, sister? Even girls got to pay.'

She cast a glance over to one of the other counter workers, who raised a mocking eyebrow.

'No, no, not at all. I'm sorry, I'll just . . .'

Salinger dropped the money on the floor. He fell to his knees and gathered up his notes and coins, blushing. By the time he stood up, Carson had settled the bill and was carrying the tray outside.

He clutched the money in his hand and hurriedly followed Carson out of the diner. The woman whooped and shouted after him.

'See you again, Sally. Come back soon. We like comedians here. You're a real funny girl.'

He pushed the door open, nearly tripping on the edge of the floor as it gave way to a step. Carson had laid out the food neatly on a plain wooden table. He placed a large paper cup of Coke on Salinger's side and a bottle of peach ice tea on his. He was calmly unwrapping a paper napkin. Salinger tried to push the handful of money at Carson.

'It's fine, Sal. Worth it for the stand-up.'

Salinger put the money back in his pocket. He felt five years old.

'That was embarrassing,' said Salinger. He sat down on the bench opposite Carson.

'They were yanking your chain. They're pretty nice guys.'

Salinger sucked on the straw that protruded from his Coke bucket and frowned as he tasted the sour smack of chlorine which they used to clean out the soda fountains. He took a bite of the brisket roll to eliminate the taste. He imagined it teeming with artificial hormones, e-numbers, genetically modified muscle.

Carson gnawed violently at his hunk of ribs, dispatching them before Salinger was halfway through his roll. After a minute of satisfied silence, during which he let out a theatrical belch, he pushed the plate to one side and took out a pack of low-tar cigarettes.

'Wanna burn one?'

'LouLou know about this?'

'She pretends that she doesn't know. You smoke, right?'

'Sometimes.'

'All artists smoke, right? Come on. Keep me company.'

Salinger hesitated, then took one. He pulled off the filter, lit the cigarette and took a drag. The nicotine rush made him pleasantly giddy.

'Remember when we used to smoke behind the gym at school?' said Carson.

Salinger shook his head.

'Come on, you *must* remember. You and me and Tog. You used to steal the cigarettes for us. We'd pretend to be having a fight, and when Mrs Benson came and pulled us apart you'd slip behind the counter and trouser a packet. You were a good thief. I taught you to smoke.'

'No, I don't remember that. Or anyone called Tog. I don't think I ever stole anything. I was far too young to hang around with you and your friends.'

'Of course you remember. We went to the sweet shop just on the corner of that road that led up to the park. You stole sweets too. Spearmint chews for me, Black Jacks for you, Beech Nut gum for Tog. Then we would go and smoke the cigarettes together behind the gym. We got caught once and Dad stopped our pocket money for a month.'

'You must be mixing me up with someone else.'

'Those were good days. We had a lot of fun at that place.'

Salinger was sure he hadn't smoked his first cigarette until he was eighteen. School had simply been a trial, a force-feeding of information that he would excrete as soon as he swallowed it.

'What else do you remember about our childhood?' said Salinger.

The elephantine woman with the orange hair emerged from the restaurant and began clearing up the paper plates. She rolled from side to side like a plastic toy Salinger remembered from childhood, a Weeble. The phrase *Weebles wobble but they don't fall down* surfaced from some misplaced chamber in his memory. Salinger nodded in her direction and thanked her. She inclined her head slightly, but said nothing.

'It was pretty average,' said Carson. 'Dad worked all the time. Mum cooked and cleaned. Standard suburban English childhood. Boring, uneventful, safe.'

'You finished this, honey?'

The woman was shaking Salinger's Coke bucket. As she shook it, her tremendous breasts jiggled, slightly out of sync.

'Sorry, yes, thank you very much,' said Salinger, trying to conceal his fascination with the immensity of her torso.

'Sorry, what the hell you sorry about?' said the woman.

'It's just something English people say,' said Carson, tipping the woman a dollar. 'He's not really sorry. Or at least he's not sorry about anything in particular.'

'What he sorry 'bout then?'

'Just for generally taking up space.'

'Ain't nothing to be sorry about,' said the woman, retreating like a cruising battleship in a choppy sea.

'Thanks, Gloria,' said Carson. 'You have a good day.'

'Mmh hmmh.'

Salinger watched her go. He felt sorry that he had said sorry.

'What else do you remember?'

'We walked to school, walked over the cemetery.'

'It was kind of weird living in a house overlooking a graveyard. I used to think the ghost of Granddad was going to come out and get us. You could see his stone from my window.'

'You were morbid even then, I guess.'

'Anything else?'

'I don't know. We watched TV, did the football pools. You read books, drew pictures, I listened to records and made Airfix models. It wasn't very exciting. I guess that's why Dad felt the need to get the heck out,' said Carson.

'You ever feel angry with the old man?'

Carson looked surprised.

'Angry? For what?'

'Come on, Carson. Henry abandoned us.'

'No point in getting angry. It was sad, but I admired him. Still do. He had the courage to do what so few people do. To follow his dream. Be who he wanted to be.'

'That's just another way of saying that he was entirely selfish.'

'Everyone's selfish. Everybody does what they got to do. The ones that don't are just too scared to do what they want. But he was always good to us when he was there. When he went, he left us well provided for. And we were teenagers by the time he went.'

'I was ten years old.'

'We could look after ourselves pretty well.

Mum and Dad just weren't well matched, were they? Anyone could see that. In those days, you didn't have too much choice. You got married young, put up with the consequences. He married the first pretty girl that would have him, got himself a job and worked. In the end, it was killing him. I don't blame him for upping sticks and moving here when he saw his chance. He had guts.'

'Henry could fuck a dog and steal his collar and you'd call him an animal lover.'

'That's not fair. You shouldn't talk about Dad like that.'

'Do you remember much about me as a child?' said Salinger.

Carson stared at the sky as if for inspiration.

'I remember the cigarette shed.'

'Is that all?'

Carson looked puzzled.

'Oddly enough, I don't remember very much.'

'Do you remember trying to suffocate me?'

'You kidding?'

Carson fanned himself in the heat with his still-unused paper napkin. Salinger, his throat dry again, wished he hadn't let what was left of the bucket of Coke go.

'You sat on the covers over my head. You sat on them until I nearly passed out.'

'I did?'

'Thought I was going to die.'

Carson stubbed out his cigarette indifferently.

128

Salinger caught his breath. He struggled to expand his lungs.

'No, I don't remember that,' said Carson. He stopped fanning himself, and carefully wiped a particle of mayonnaise from the corner of his mouth. 'You always dramatize things so much. I guess artists have pretty lively imaginations.'

'You must remember,' said Salinger.

'Listen, Sal, I can't even remember what we had for breakfast yesterday. You finished that roll? We need to get back on the road.'

Without asking, Salinger reached over to Carson's peach ice tea, and gulped back the dregs. Gradually, willing himself to be calm, he found his breathing returning to normal.

For the remainder of the journey to Austin, Carson kept strictly to the speed limit, despite the fact that there were no speed cameras and no other cars in sight.

As Carson drove, Salinger took an A4 notepad from the back seat and began to sketch his face. He traced the slightly squinty eyes – so much like Henry's – and the softening cheekbones, once angular and sharp but now blunted by time, muffalettas from the Central Grocery and fried-shrimp po boys. He shaded in the few long, light wrinkles on the forehead, like wide seagulls in the distance, the thin, straight lips that undermined the generous width of his mouth.

'Stealing my soul,' said Carson, swerving slightly

to avoid an empty beer bottle that had rolled onto the road.

'That's photographs.'

'Can you make me look sexy?'

'I'm not a plastic surgeon.'

Carson slipped the car into cruise control. He glanced down again at the sketch.

'You should be an artist.'

'There's no money in it.'

Salinger sketched the slight blueness of Carson's stubble, the tiny nick on his cheek that he left when he shaved that morning. He saw the beginnings of crow's feet at the edge of the eyes, and long, maverick strands of hair that protruded from the light rough of his eyebrows. There was a small silver crucifix on a chain round his neck.

He tried to imagine the expression that Carson would wear if he was unguarded, then he wondered if there was any such thing. Even if you weren't editing yourself to the watching world, you never stopped editing yourself.

The face, decided Salinger, told you nothing at all. It was just a screen onto which the seer projected their own fantasies – if they could be bothered to project at all. Most were too busy looking at themselves to see anyone else. It was an impenetrable secret, wherever you stood – in front of a mirror or face to face.

Salinger put the pencil aside and abandoned the drawing. It was hopeless – like trying to depict the soul of America with the meridians and symbols of a map.

Carson glanced down once more.

'That's really good, Sal.'

'You think so? You can have it.'

'Really? You mean it?'

'Sure. Honestly. I haven't even started it anyway. It's worthless.'

'It's not worthless. I couldn't do anything like that if I spent the rest of my life. I'm honoured.'

'Think of it as me giving you back your soul.'

'Well, I appreciate that, but Jesus did that for me already.'

Salinger tore the picture out of the sketch pad and put it onto the back seat. After a few more minutes' cruising, Carson pulled into a side road.

'Five o'clock. I got to call LouLou.'

'You can't wait till we get to Austin? We should be there inside an hour.'

'No, I call her at five o'clock. That's the arrangement.'

Later, they drove past intermittent oil rigs like drowsy woodpeckers. There were rows of velvet mesquite trees, their yellow flowers long ago scattered. Salinger had been dozing again. He became aware of Carson's voice drifting through his sleep haze.

'Makes the sweetest honey.'

'What?'

'Those mesquite flowers. When they blossom.

They make good honey. You can use the pods to make flour, too.'

Salinger stretched and yawned.

'We in Austin now?'

'People think Texas is all rednecks and rodeos. Austin is different.' Carson pulled into the centre of the road to make a right turn. An immense American truck, its flat chrome face gleaming cockily, sounded its air horn, making Salinger start. The driver waved amiably at Salinger and Carson from his cabin loft. Carson waved back.

'It's a university town for a start. Main campus of the University of Texas is here so there are professors, students, what have you. And it's the capital, so there are politicians, lobbyists, journalists. Lot of high-tech companies. Also musicians. Lot of musicians. Calls itself the Live Music Capital of the World. I been here a coupla times. It's a pretty whacked-out territory.'

As the Lexus drifted down South Congress Avenue Salinger noted several stickers on doors and lamp posts that bore the legend *Keep Austin Weird*. The bulk of the city was built on one of those ubiquitous, functional American grid systems. Here, just outside the centre, there were music bars, restaurants and retro junk stores, selling folk art and antiques.

'They call this Soco. The boho zone, so-called. Thought you would like it. Me, I woulda checked into the Holiday Inn. There it is, right there, the Hotel San José. Got this out of the *Rough Guide*.'

It was running eight o'clock now. Most of the retail units on the strip looked closed, and the clubs and restaurants and bars were beginning to open. The natural light had almost gone and neon and street lamps were pushing back the darkness.

Carson steered the Lexus into the hotel parking lot. The car came to a halt. Salinger pulled himself out of the air-conditioned pod onto the tarmac. It was springy from the heat. As in New Orleans, Salinger immediately felt his skin filming with sweat.

He and Carson walked towards the low, open passageway that led to the entrance. It was a converted 1950s bungalow-style motor hotel hidden behind stucco walls. There was a Scandinavian feel to it – minimalist and simple with clean, low lines. There were courtyards, and cacti on the windowsills.

Salinger and Carson collected their key from a young woman wearing a tight, sleeveless T-shirt through which her nipples poked like lugs, then made their way to their room. A typed poem was pinned to the door on a scrap of paper.

> *Often we are sad animals,*
> *Bored dogs, monkeys,*
> *Getting rained on.*
> *– Robert Haas*

The room was airy and fresh, plain walls, white-washed, low ceilings, white linen. There was a bedspread patterned like a Native American rug.

'The bed's a double,' said Carson. 'I asked for a twin.'

'I don't mind if you don't,' said Salinger, hoping that Carson would mind enough to change the room.

'I move around a lot. I'm like a fricking weevil with heebie-jeebies. I'd kick you out of the bed at 3 a.m.'

They went back to the lobby, and tried to get themselves switched to another room. There was nothing else available. Salinger hid his disappointment.

Outside in the courtyard, Salinger had ordered some cheese and red wine, Carson a bottle of Lone Star beer and a bag of potato chips. The balconies that enclosed the yard gave the space a European elegance. The pool reflected yellow electric light in wavering liquid patterns on the surface.

'It was kind of you to take the trouble to find this place,' said Salinger. 'I know it's not your style.'

'You're my brother, Sal.'

Salinger, for no reason he could understand, suddenly wanted to weep. He pushed his napkin onto the floor, and wiped his eye with it as he picked it up.

'Most hotels in England are still chintz, horse brasses and nylon sheets,' said Salinger,

Carson sucked down his beer, closing his eyes. Salinger watched his Adam's apple bob back and forth as the beer went down.

'Is there anything you miss about the old country, Carzy?'

Carson put down the beer carefully dead centre in the middle of a circular coaster and wiped his mouth with a napkin.

'A decent cup of tea. Fish and chips, the real kind, done with beef dripping. Blackberry and apple crumble. Custard. Apart from that nothing much.'

'I like the change of the seasons,' said Salinger. 'The colour of autumn. That week when spring pushes through.'

'Particularly not the weather. The light is grey. Like an old flannel.'

As soon as they got back to the bedroom, Salinger began to undress. Carson, apparently unwilling to let Salinger see him without his clothes on, retreated to the bathroom. Salinger remembered that he had been the same when they were children – careful of exposure, fierce in the maintenance of his privacy.

Salinger found the room stuffy. He didn't like air conditioning, so opened the window. The movement of air pulled the bathroom door slightly ajar. Through the crack, Salinger could see Carson, now in blue-drill pyjamas, neatly folding and putting away his day's dirty clothes, even though, presumably, they would not be worn again until after they were laundered.

Salinger let his shorts, pants and T-shirt fall in

a pile at the bottom of the bed. He continued to watch as Carson took a rolled sheet of paper out of the jacket pocket that he had hung on a wall hook.

He unfurled it carefully. Salinger realized that it was the portrait he had drawn in the car. Carson stared at it intently. An odd expression crossed his face, as if he was searching for something in the picture that he remembered being there but could no longer locate.

A floodlight came on outside the bathroom window. It illuminated Carson's features, erasing the years. He was suddenly Carson again, *Carzy*, the odd, self-censoring boy he had shared a room with – a life with – for the first fourteen years of his existence.

Seeming suddenly to become aware of Salinger, Carson looked sharply up towards the door. His eyes met Salinger's. Salinger held his gaze. He thought, momentarily, that he could see something there like fury. Then Carson's face softened so completely, Salinger dismissed the thought.

'It's a great picture, Sally. Thank you.'

'It was a doodle. I can do better.'

'I like this one. I really do. It captures something. I don't know.'

Carson emerged from the bathroom and carefully placed the sketch in a stiff plastic folder, which he then put in a tan-leather briefcase. Salinger had no idea why Carson had brought a briefcase with him. It was a very Carsonesque thing to do.

'I guess I'll sleep on the sofa,' said Carson.

'Don't be ridiculous. The bed's big enough for both of us. The sofa is too small and it's like a rock.'

Carson switched out the light. In the quiet of the dark, Salinger crawled into the double bed on the left-hand side. He felt Carson carefully sliding onto the other side. He suddenly felt an unaccountable terror of touching his brother, and wished that he hadn't dissuaded him from sleeping on the sofa.

After a while had passed and Salinger could hear Carson breathing slowly and evenly, he turned on his side and examined Carson's profile through the half-light, careful to keep his eyes open only an undetecable slit. Carson lay on his back, his eyes closed.

He wondered what it was his brother wanted from this journey. He wondered what he himself wanted.

He had the fleeting intuition that neither of them could fulfil their wishes, whatever they were, without doing the other harm.

CHAPTER 7

AUSTIN – CRAWFORD – DALLAS

Salinger awoke with a burning sensation squatting under the base of his throat. The familiar morning rawness had ramped itself up into anger. It was a chafing knot, a ball of hot metal. It had no source or target that Salinger could name. It was just *there*, inescapable, along with the meaningless, free-floating guilt that attached itself to it.

Salinger wanted to lay the world to waste, to scour pitted landscapes with the strafe of gunfire. To destroy all that was good and green and flourishing. He squirmed in his bed, as if movement could dislodge the slow thrum, the primal pulse of his pointless, incurable fury. He wished he could find a way out of his own skin.

He knew the sensation would dissolve, or at least sink underground, once he had risen from the bed. Carson slept on, a faint burr of snoring issuing from his pillow. His face was a white billboard advertising peace. A yellow grain of sleep crusted the edge of his eye like a dusting of pollen.

Salinger rose from the bed and stumbled into the bathroom. Illuminated only from outside, the walls of the room seemed pale blue, numinous. He flicked the light switch and fumbled for his bath bag. He found the Prozac and bolted it.

He hid the pill sleeve. He did not want Carson to know, any more than he wanted Tiane to know. His depression shamed him. He was somewhat mad, somewhat weak, somewhat damaged. He was out of tune, he was not normal, he was the object of his own ridicule.

Carson's good looks, his happy marriage, his untroubled temperament, his simple love of his own life, his moronic faith – they felt like both an accusation and an affront.

The thrum and throb of his anger continued under the cage of his chest. There was no reason for any of it. The contents of his head were chaotic and toxic. There was nowhere to go, except the refuge of sleep. He lay down and closed his eyes and gratefully gave in to the pull of his own weariness.

When he woke again, an hour later, Carson was out of bed and humming tunelessly to himself as he shaved in front of the magnifying mirror. He was now wearing navy-blue boxer shorts and a white T-shirt. Salinger could see the colours of his face in the distant distorting shaving mirror, like flesh melted, fat and liquid. He watched him as he drew the razor down the line of his chin. There was a slight smile on the side of his mouth. Even shaving seemed to be capable of putting Carson into a condition of mindless satisfaction.

Carson noticed Salinger watching him, finished the last stroke of his razor, and wiped away the foam with a clean white towel.

'Sleep OK, Sally?'

'I don't know. I was asleep.'

Carson started humming 'Born to Run' and made his way back into the main room. He began dressing. The clothes he had selected for his day's outfit were geometrically pressed and laid out on top of the bed in a straight line. There was a plain white button-down shirt, a pair of buff-coloured socks and a pair of jeans that were identical to the ones he had worn the previous day. They were badly cut, shapeless and unflattering.

Salinger showered and dressed. He wore tailored shorts and an expensive white Italian short-sleeved shirt embroidered with yellow flowers that Tiane had bought him for his last birthday. In London it was everyday wear. Here, he felt self-conscious.

They loaded the Lexus. Carson wanted to leave immediately, so that they could be sure of arriving at the Kennedy Museum in Dallas in plenty of time before it closed, but Salinger insisted they take a walk down South Congress Avenue first.

The parade of shops displayed folk art, paintings, clothes, old signs, cowboy shirts, second-hand knick-knacks. Salinger bought a twenty-five-dollar milagro cross for Tiane. It was a small wooden crucifix with pewter charms – milagros – nailed to it, flaming hearts, birds, fish, angels, flowers.

One shop displayed a huge painted triptych of

New Orleans during Katrina across one wall. Corpses lay scattered in the water. The city was depicted as being consumed by flames and wind. In the main part of the triptych, the ghost of a young girl hovered. Blown-up newspaper headlines were plastered over the other two panels. They read *Horror, Despair, A City in Ruins, Chaos, Death, Crisis, Sea of Sorrow.*

Carson was looking at his watch, as he had done repeatedly since leaving the hotel.

'We should probably be making a move soon, so . . .'

'What do you think of this, Carzy?'

He waved towards the triptych. Carson took no notice.

'What I think is that we should get going or we're not going to have time to take in all that we want to today.'

'You're not looking at it.'

Carson glanced at the triptych.

'It's kind of melodramatic is what I think. Now can we get going?'

By the time they made it back to the hotel parking lot, it was approaching noon. Carson, who had not once broken the speed limit since they had left New Orleans, began to let out the throttle on the Lexus, at one point even riding a red light.

They took the I-35 towards Crawford. Salinger adjusted the seat back to a recline position while Carson chewed metronomically on a wad of gum. He was still playing a pure diet of New Orleans music – a live Neville Brothers album had just finished and a Cajun compilation was starting up with 'Jolie Blon' by Nathan Abshire and his Pinegrove Boys.

Salinger settled his mind into the waltz time of the music. He felt pleasantly blank. They turned off the Interstate and made their way west past Lake Waco towards Crawford. The road narrowed down into two wide lanes.

In front of them, about a hundred yards away, Salinger noticed a nervous, wretched-looking mongrel dog on the road shoulder, trembling as if stricken by cold, or heat. Salinger glanced at the speedometer. Carson was travelling maybe 5 mph over the limit, trying to make up the time that had been lost on the shopping trip. The car closed the distance towards the dog. Salinger automatically put a restraining hand onto Carson's arm.

The dog staggered sharply into their path. There was a sound like a mallet striking a pillow and then a more brittle series of bumps. The mongrel had disappeared under the wheels. Salinger momentarily heard a noise like dry wood cracking.

Salinger turned to his left and examined Carson's face. He had stopped chewing the gum. His face had tightened slightly. Salinger looked ahead and then in the wing mirror. There were no other vehicles in sight.

'You hit the dog. You hit the dog, Carson.'

'I know. I know I did.'

'You should slow down. You were driving too fast.'

Carson raised his foot slowly from the gas pedal. Salinger felt the gravity as the speed decreased. He was still staring at Carson's face. It didn't look as if he had a plan. The car continued decelerating.

'Did you kill it?'

'I don't know.'

Carson checked the digital screen that displayed the view from the rear-mounted camera. It only showed empty road. He started to swing the car around in a loop. The Lexus made it back towards where they thought Carson hit the dog. There was no sign of it. The car came to a stop.

'It's not here. Maybe you didn't hit it after all,' said Salinger hopefully.

'I hit it.'

Carson pulled the car off the road and killed the engine. He opened the door and left the car. Salinger saw him inspecting the fender. He put his head back in the car, took a cloth out of the side pocket of the door, and wiped something from the front of the chassis. He returned the cloth to the car. Salinger saw that it was stained red and grey.

Salinger watched in silence as Carson closed the car door again and made his way ten feet off to the side of the road. Salinger felt unable to leave the car, but after a minute had passed, he reluctantly opened his own door.

Salinger immediately became aware of a faint whimpering sound. He climbed down from the car and walked over to where Carson was standing.

The land beyond the edge of the road was dirt, rubble, boulders, grit. There were no buildings in sight. A foot and a half from Carson's right leg, the dog was spreadeagled in a puddle of water. It reminded Salinger of a small beanbag that someone heavy had recently sat upon.

Salinger couldn't work out why there would be a puddle there. It was perfectly dry with the temperature in the low 80s. The puddle was stained dirty and red. Blood was flowing from a wound in the dog's side. Its eyes were open. It was panting furiously. It looked immensely sad. It looked as if it wanted something so desperately. The stream of blood, now widening, was about a foot long. It stretched out towards Carson's shoe. Carson moved his foot backwards slightly to avoid getting it soiled.

'Should we call for a vet?'

Carson didn't answer. Salinger looked up at his brother's face. It was raised to the sky. The sun caught it full on. Carson's eyes were closed. His lips were moving slightly.

'Carzy? Can you hear me?'

Salinger was surprised by the strident note of panic in his own voice. Carson slowly opened his eyes. He looked profoundly calm. He gazed down at Salinger and touched him on the arm. His voice was low and soft, as if he was just emerging from a refreshing sleep.

'It's OK, Sally.'

'No. I don't think it's OK. The dog is dying. It's really hurting. Look at its eyes.'

'It's OK. You don't have to worry.'

Carson closed his eyes again and stood completely still, his hands clasping one another.

'What the fuck are you doing, Carzy?'

Carson's eyes flicked open again, quickly this time. Suddenly, urgently, he started to move. There was a large rock a few feet away that looked like it weighed maybe five pounds. Carson picked it up.

'Go back to the car.'

Salinger grabbed hold of Carson by the arm. He felt muscle ripple under the fat and the cloth.

'We can call for a doctor or something, we can.'

Carson pulled away from Salinger and brought the rock down on the dog's head, about an inch behind the eyes. The dog screamed. Its eyes stayed open, bloodshot, the eyeballs rolling back into its head.

Carson raised the rock again. There was a bloom of blood on his white shirt. Carson noticed it and his face registered annoyance. Carson brought the rock down again. The eyes of the dog continued to register a faint light. The rock came down a third time. The dog raised its spine once an inch or two into the air, then collapsed back onto the ground and stopped moving altogether.

Salinger watched a red ant move slowly across the ground. He became vividly aware of a universe of living creatures beneath his feet. Beetles, maggots, flies, larvae, tiny scorpions. Beneath them, the dead, layer upon layer upon layer.

His head was ringing. He remained absolutely still as Carson returned to the car and brought back an old, clean blanket that he kept in the trunk. Carson wrapped the dog's body in it, then picked it up and cradled it as if it were a newborn.

When Salinger spoke again, his voice seemed too dry. His words were croaky and sparse, leaf skeletons spinning hopelessly in the air.

'What are you doing, Carson?'

'We need to bury him.'

Carson found a hardware store in a town eight miles down the road. The journey passed in silence. Carson went in and bought a shovel. Through the plate-glass window, Salinger noticed him searching for the one that was the best value.

Before they drove on, Carson took a fresh shirt out of his luggage and changed into it, leaving the bloodstained one in a nylon laundry bag that he kept packed separately.

After a mile, Carson pulled over. He left Salinger in the car while he started to dig, ten yards from the edge of the road. Salinger didn't look. He just sat in the car staring out of the front window at the perfectly straight road which disappeared into a grey-blue horizon. He thought he could smell the remains of the dog from the boot, a damp, cold, old-penny odour. He wasn't sure – the air conditioning seemed to remove all real smells, just as the plate glass of the windows rendered the outside world anodyne.

After five minutes Carson returned and opened the boot. Salinger was aware that the dog was being lifted. No longer able to stand apart, Salinger got out of the car. Taking the few strides to the roadside plot, he saw that Carson had laid the dog, blanket and all, in a hole maybe three feet deep. He was filling it with earth. Flies buzzed around the dog's snout.

'It's OK,' said Carson, softly once more.

He didn't seem to be speaking to anyone in particular. Salinger clasped his hands in front of him as if he was protecting his softest parts.

The hole was filled in a few minutes. Then Carson came and stood by Salinger's side. Salinger stared down at the small pile of dirt. He felt the touch of Carson's fingers on his arm.

'You killed the dog,' said Salinger quietly. 'You killed it twice. With the car and with the rock.'

Carson's hand was still on his shoulder. He was rubbing in small circles the size of a tea plate on the surface of his shirt.

'It's OK, it's OK, Sally, it's OK.'

They drove on in silence towards Crawford. Salinger glanced at Carson's face. He appeared to be entirely at peace with himself. Salinger flicked his glance away before Carson had a chance to catch his eye. He had a feeling of urgent hunger.

After a while, the road fell away to a crossroads. Salinger dimly registered a sign announcing that they were entering Crawford, Texas. Carson slowed the car.

They reached a second crossroads. On one corner stood a gift shop. It was called the Yellow Rose. There was a huge poster stretched across the façade. It read *Evil Prevails When Good Men Do Nothing.*

There were five American flags, then a number of smaller banners – *Our Heroes* and *Support Our Troops*. Opposite, five huge steel grain-silos blindingly reflected sunlight.

Carson stopped the car outside what appeared to be the only diner in Crawford, Spano's Coffee Station. Four gas pumps stood to attention outside. Carson and Salinger left the car and headed towards the shadowy interior.

'You a little nervous?' said Carson.

It was the first time either of them had spoken for an hour.

'Why should I be nervous?'

'Wearing that fag shirt.'

Salinger looked down at his Italian floral shirt.

'Have you ever heard of Glasscock County?' said Carson.

'No.'

'It's near here. Maybe a hundred miles. Recorded the highest Republican vote in the US in the last election. *93 per cent.* Can you scan that? Man, around here, they *believe.* And those kind of Republicans don't hold with no floral shirts. Not on anyone without a pair of hooters anyhow.'

They entered the diner. There was a line of four fat, bearded men sitting on stools at a long bar, each nursing a sweating glass of beer. Two were wearing baseball caps, and two of them cowboy hats. They turned to look, unsmilingly, at Salinger and Carson.

Salinger became acutely conscious not only of his shirt, but his tailored shorts. He looked towards Carson, who seemed unperturbed. Carson nodded towards the men at the bar.

'Hey.'

None of them moved or spoke. Carson caught the eye of a waitress who had her hair oiled into black ringlets and skin like scree. She was white, overweight and around seventeen years old. Her name badge read *Lori*.

'Hey, Lori. How are you?'

'I'm good.'

'You think you could find us a table for two?'

'I guess.'

Salinger walked carefully behind Carson away from the bar into the main dining room. There were about twenty tables, all empty, adorned with plastic tablecloths in a gingham design. There were two large wall-mounted TVs showing the same sports channel.

Salinger, now shivering in the grip of the fierce air conditioning, examined the decor, while Carson inspected the menu. On the wall behind their heads there was a mocked-up film poster that announced *The Last of the Clintons*. There were George W. Bush key rings for sale at the till counter and framed photos of Bush with Colin Powell eating in the diner.

'He actually come in here?' said Carson to Lori, who had arrived to take their order. 'The chief?'

'Sometimes,' said Lori. 'Not often, I guess. I never seen him.'

Carson turned to Salinger and said loudly, 'You think those guys next door think you're a fag?'

'Probably.'

'You do look kinda queer.'

'I know.'

Carson looked up at Lori.

'Could you tell those gentlemen next door that this man, despite his flamboyant shirt, is not a homosexual. And he and I are not partnered in an ungodly same-sex relationship. We are, in fact, blood brothers. I should also say that I am a devout Christian. My brother is English which is why he is dressed inappropriately.'

'Mmh hmmh.'

Lori looked blank and chewed her lip. Carson grinned, and checked the menu one more time.

'I'll have the cheeseburger and the deep-fried jalapeños.'

'Same for me,' said Salinger.

'And a Diet Coke. And my brother here would like a small glass of Bassin de Vichy water served at room temperature with a slice of lemon.'

'A glass of *wha*?'

'Just kidding you there, Lori. Something from the spigot is fine.'

Lori retreated. Salinger looked at Carson. To his surprise, Carson started to laugh, a low hoarse giggle. Salinger gave him a hard look and hugged his arms around himself to fend off the chill.

'Lighten up, Sal. Ain't this a situation?'

Lori flicked a switch behind the counter. Music burst out at a deafening volume.

'Who's this one by, Lori?' yelled Carson.

'Billy Ray.'

'Billy Ray Cyrus?'

'I love Billy Ray the most.'

'Who doesn't? What's this one called?'

'Called "Ain't Your Dog No More".'

When Lori brought the soft drinks over, tainted once more with chlorine, Salinger and Carson were laughing together. Salinger was bent double and wheezing.

'What's so funny?' said Lori.

'Nothing. Nothing's funny,' said Salinger, bringing himself under control, straightening up and reaching for his drink.

'We're just a little bit upset is all,' said Carson.

'You guys are crazy,' said Lori as she laid out the cutlery.

The weather, which had been gauzily overcast, was changing. A vast frightening sky unravelled, which threatened to reach down and consume the fragile landscape.

151

The CD player was on shuffle, which had broken the New Orleans greatest hits monopoly. Now Carson was roaring out in tuneless harmony with Springsteen.

'"Godda wifeankids in Baltimore JACK, I wen' out for a ride an' I never went BACK."'

Salinger felt his spirits buoyant for the first time since he had landed. The image of the dog's eyes rolling back in its head kept flashing back to him. But instead of depressing him, the spectacle of violence had liberated something.

'Hungry Heart' ended. Carson punched the air with the final chord. A moment later, the opening chords of Sandy Denny's 'Who Knows Where The Time Goes' floated from the speakers.

All across the sky all the birds are leaving
But how can they know it's time for them to go?

'I just love English miserablism,' said Carson.

'I don't,' said Salinger. 'It makes us miserable.'

They listened to the remainder of the song in silence. When it finished, Salinger pressed the 'Off' button on the console.

'How could you do it, Carson?'

'You talking about the dog?'

'It was cold-hearted.'

'It was the best thing.'

'I could never do that.'

'I had a friend to help me.'

'What friend?'

'I asked Jesus for advice. He gave me his strength.'

Carson reached to switch the music back on. Salinger turned it off again.

'Just give me a moment. We can listen to music for days.'

'Why be morbid? What's done is done.'

'I just want you to tell me. Do you not feel bad, at all?'

'An accident happened and I did what I could to address the situation.'

'Don't you feel responsible?'

'Not really. Everything has a purpose.'

'What was the purpose of killing that dog with your car?'

'It isn't given to us to know such things, Salinger.'

'But don't you feel bad?'

'Dog's don't have souls,' said Carson simply.

The skyline of Dallas loomed out of the desert in the distance. Killing and burying the dog had put them behind schedule. It was gone three. The museum closed at six.

Salinger was not as bored as he had expected to be during the journey. Driving through the Texas landscape had an odd effect on his perception of time. It had ceased to tug at him, demanding this or that like an imploring child.

He noticed Carson again checking his watch.

'We've got plenty of time, Carson.'

'I don't know. The traffic gets pretty bad on the outskirts.'

'You want me to do some driving?'

'Yeah, right.'

'I can drive, you know. You move the wheel. You press the gas pedal. You use the brake when you want to go slower.'

'Thanks – but no thanks.'

'You hungry? I've got some Fritos somewhere.'

'No thanks.'

'You spoken to LouLou today?'

'I'll call her at five o'clock.'

'Carson. What are we going to say to Dad? If we even find him.'

'We'll find him.'

'So what's on your mind? What do you want to say to Henry?'

Carson didn't answer. Salinger dug the packet of Fritos out of his bag and tore it open with his teeth.

'Don't mess the carpet,' said Carson.

'Do you know what a profound fear of mess means in psychoanalytic theory?'

'Just don't mess the carpet.'

'When was the last time you saw Henry?'

'Some twenty years since, I guess.'

'Odd that you've not been more in touch.'

'You just put crumbs down the seat, Salinger.'

Salinger lazily dug them out with his fingers, then licked the remnants off.

'It's not my doing that we've not been in touch. Henry hates telephones and the Internet. Letters only, that's the rule. Moved to Provincetown within six months of me coming to live here, so I couldn't exactly drop in on the off-chance. Two thousand miles between us. He sent me an address, but his handwriting is so bad I could never quite make it out. I wrote at first, but never got a response. Don't know if the letters even got to him.'

'Think he ignored them?'

'I'm sure it was just a mistake.'

'Sounds to me like he was avoiding you.'

'Maybe. Can you not put that packet in the side pocket? In case you haven't noticed, there's a dedicated space for litter.'

'If he was avoiding you – I mean, doesn't it upset you?'

'Dad did what he had to. I'd have liked to have seen more of him. But he chose his path. That path didn't include us.'

Out of the window, Salinger could see a dust devil rise. In the distance, walking rain, a shower that evaporated before it reached the scorching ground. The land was absolutely flat. The outer fringes of the Dallas suburbs were beginning to eat up the empty space.

'How do *you* feel about Dad?' said Carson, looking momentarily away from the road towards Salinger.

'I feel nothing. Like with you and the dog.'

'How can you feel nothing? He's your father. You have to forgive him, Salinger.'

'I told you – I don't feel anything.'

'It's for your sake you have to forgive him, not for his.'

'I don't *care* about Henry. That suits me just fine.'

'He loves you, Salinger.'

Salinger felt the desire to laugh, but managed to modify his expression to a thoughtful grimace at the last moment.

'How do you know?'

'He's our father.'

'Did he say it?'

'I know it all the same.'

'What if he doesn't want to see us?'

'He must want it somewhat or he wouldn't have sent the letter.'

'Without an address on it.'

A red traffic light brought the Lexus to a halt. Carson turned in his seat and from the back of the leather upholstery picked up a few crumbs that Salinger had missed.

'Listen, Salinger. I don't want my child to be born into a family that is broken. We need to try and do some healing. I want my son to meet his grandfather, if only once – perhaps only so Henry can say he doesn't want anything to do with him. But I have to give that child the chance.'

'So you don't want to see Henry for your own sake?'

'Last time I saw him – when he was living in Cruces – he was straightforward about wanting to maintain distance. I sensed that he wasn't over-joyed that I'd become a Christian.'

'He's not really in a position to make a moral judgement.'

'He doesn't have to be in a position. He's our father.'

A horn started sounding behind them.

'The lights have changed, Carson.'

'I know that, Salinger.'

It was another half an hour before they reached the centre of Dallas. This time they were checked into a Holiday Inn. Salinger had assumed that this was a matter of economy, but just as they entered the traffic-choked street in which the hotel was sited, Carson insisted that he preferred chain hotels anyway.

'Are you just trying to get a rise out of me?'

'Sure I like chain hotels. Tell you something, Salinger. The Holiday Inn chain was an invention of a genius. Kemmons Wilson, 1951. Unsung hero. Man who changed the face of the world.'

'With cattle sheds for businessmen?'

'You know, you think you're such an independent thinker, Salinger, but everything you believe is straight out of the book.'

'What book?'

'The book of liberal bullcrap. Thing is, he changed the face of the world with an *idea*. Let me tell you about Kemmons Wilson. He used to travel all the time for his business. One time in '51 – he was a builder then – he drove with his family from Memphis to Washington. First holiday they ever took. Because that man worked like a dog. On that trip he found out first hand how unreliable all the private little motels were. They ripped you off – surcharges, a dollar extra for a TV and so forth, poor quality. Most were fleapits. Those little Mom and Pop joints that everyone looks back on with such affection, they were mostly run by conmen and chancers.

'On that trip he had the idea of building a brand of hotel that, wherever you went, you could be guaranteed – *guaranteed* – the same quality at a reasonable price. A place you could trust. And he made that idea come true – by sheer force of will, Salinger, by simply believing that it could be so. He started with zip a de do da – his mother worked as a dental nurse. Time he retired in '79, it was the largest chain in the world.

'One guy, one idea. In that, the beginnings of modern America. The beginnings of the *world* as much of it looks now. Taking outlets that are poor quality, trashy, unpredictable and making them *safe* for a traveller to go to at a reasonable price. What is wrong with that? All this bitching about globalization, standardization, homogenization. Think what England was like before it arrived. What was there before Starbucks? Second-rate greasy spoons where the tea was stewed and the coffee tasted like mud. What was there before McDonald's? Wimpy Bars. What was there before Gap? Burton. And you're telling me we're screwing up the world?'

The Lexus came to a halt. The Holiday Inn

sign flickered high at the end of the street. A static jigsaw of traffic held them in its grip.

'1951. That was the golden year. Coming of the malls. Victor Gruen, the first modern mall in Seattle. Model taken up all over the world. Clean, quiet, dry, temperature-controlled. What did we have in Willesden? The high street. What was in the high street? Bakers selling soggy rolls. Butchers selling sausages filled with cardboard and toenails. Fishmongers with three varieties of fish. The Cosy Nook café, the Copper Kettle, the Buttery. The consumer didn't count. And all this happened in the pouring rain in the freezing cold. Americanization isn't ruining the world. It's been saving the fricking place for the last fifty years. Not counting the fact that it saved the Brits in two World Wars before that. How many died so that people like you could spend their lives complaining about Cheese Strings and Disneyworld? By the way, ask any kid what they think about Disneyworld.'

'But . . .' said Salinger.

'We're here.'

Salinger felt irritated, unfairly outmanoeuvred. Carson pulled the car into the hotel driveway and slid down the electric windows. A bellhop in livery and a peaked cap approached.

'Valet or self-park?' said the bellhop.

'How much is the valet?'

'Ten dollars.'

'Plus your tip. We'll take it in,' said Carson.

The bellhop looked sour, but waved them in the direction of the car ramp. The Lexus descended to the underground lot. They found a space immediately and Carson did his ritual walk around the car, checking for scratches and dirt. He went through the interior, cleaning it with a cloth and removing all traces of litter.

They made their way up to the lobby. Carson checked them in and they hurried to the room to drop their bags off. Despite the fact that there were only ninety minutes left before the museum closed, Carson insisted on unpacking his case and hanging up his clothes so that the creases had a chance to fall out.

It was a short taxi ride away. When they reached the building, Carson and Salinger stopped outside to stare at the underpass where Kennedy had his movie-star smile eradicated by Oswald. Neither of them was born at the time of the assassination, but Salinger had watched the Zapruder footage countless times. The sun reflecting off the chrome grille of the open-top limo, the presidential smile and wave, the occlusion behind the signpost, his hands coming up to his face. Jackie leaning over to gently ask why. The crimson halo throwing him backwards. The head dissolving. Jackie climbing onto the trunk of the car, obscenely displaying, like her husband, her inescapable mere humanity. The limo accelerating into the tunnel, the world sucked after it into the dark.

They went and stood on the famous grassy knoll,

situated behind a wooden picket fence. This was where the second shooter – according to the conspiracy theorists – positioned himself to deliver the *coup de grâce*.

A middle-aged black man approached them, brandishing a black-and-white picture of a twelve-year-old boy, his head circled with a red pen. The boy stood among the crowds on what the man said was The Day. He said the boy was himself. The man was offering to sell them his memory.

'I was there, brother, I was there on that day. I remember it like it was yesterday. You see this picture, brother? I saw Jack Kennedy shot. I saw it happen. See me here? I saw the running man, I saw the man with the umbrella. Ten bucks I'll tell you the story. See those white crosses?'

He indicated two crosses painted onto the road that entered the underpass.

'First one was where the first bullet struck. Second one was where the second bullet struck. They didn't mark a spot for the other bullets. From the second shooter, my brother, for shooter number deux.'

Carson and Salinger walked briskly away in the direction of the museum, but a second man, white this time, who was selling a magazine about the shooting now approached them and started to deliver another garbled pitch about the man with the umbrella, the man in black leather and some other man whose name Salinger couldn't quite make out, Jim Braden or Borden or Boden.

The weird, nerdy guy – untidy kinked hair stuffed

under a hunting cap, combat trousers, military boots – clearly delivered this pitch countless times a day. Salinger bought the magazine just to make him go away, and put it in his bag without reading it.

They made their way to the entrance of the Book Depository. The queue was short, ten people or so. To the left of the ticket counter, there was a five-foot-high blow-up of Kennedy and Jackie being driven from Love Field. Salinger passed the waiting time by counting Kennedy's teeth.

They journeyed through the museum, tracked along a marked pathway of photographs, models and exhibits, J.F.K.'s progress moment by moment towards the underpass. Salinger watched the Zapruder footage once again. It never lost its power. It had more purchase on his imagination even than the planes and the towers, which, like everyone else, he had watched in real time. It was so particular, so personal, so achingly private somehow.

Henry had once told him that, when it happened, he had gone to bed and pulled the covers over his head. He always used to drone on like an old man, like a hack newsreader, about it being 'the end of innocence'. But what was innocence? Simply a lack of knowledge.

It was knowledge that was obvious, even banal. Nothing could completely insure you, even if you were President, even if you were drinking a skinny latte in an air-conditioned rooftop restaurant, from the malice of nonentities, from the distant swarming of tiny, fanatic lives. How could you not notice

162

threat? Because not noticing helped you survive, just as noticing did.

He stared long and hard at the glassed-in exhibit barricading the space where Oswald had propped himself up beside two piles of books, and with extreme skill, loosed off the bullets. Salinger thought there must have been another shooter. Otherwise why did Kennedy go first forward, then backwards? It was common sense.

The speakers announced the closing of the museum in ten minutes. Salinger made his way towards the exit feeling both drained and vaguely elated. Carson had gone to the rest room. While he waited, Salinger took the magazine that the conspiracy theorist had thrust into his hands and flicked through the pages. He winced, catching sight of the pictures on the centrefold – J.F.K. stretched out on a gurney, his brains slopping out of what was left of his head.

They returned to their room at the Holiday Inn. While Carson channel-grazed, Salinger flicked through some of the sketches he'd made to pass the time on the journey.

The dead dog he'd drawn from memory. The vision of the animal in the puddle still chafed, but the cadaver with its bashed-in skull no longer stood in accusation of Carson. In his mind it merged with the pictures he had seen in the magazine of Kennedy with his brains splattered across the gurney.

Salinger's attention wandered to the TV screen.

Carson was still flicking between ads for over-the-counter medicines, lawyers, sanitary pads, car-price reductions, eyelash thickener.

The news channel was reporting that people were scared, that the game was up, that money itself was dying. AIG was holding on to fluidity thanks to getting itself nationalized by the American government, though nobody used the word. It was simply being taken 'into control'.

An ad promoting a device that would convert photographs into 3D images that were then fixed within a Perspex cube appeared. Carson put down the control and turned to Salinger.

'That reminds me. Did you bring those photographs out with you?'

'Photographs?'

'For LouLou. Of the family. You said there might be some among Mum's stuff.'

Carson went to his bag of dirty clothing, took out the white shirt that bore the stain from the dead dog and started dabbing at it with some kind of proprietary stick.

'Does it say on the packet?' said Salinger.

'What?'

'This product removes ink, oil, paint, dog's blood, guilt?'

Carson held the shirt up to the light and examined the material critically. He rubbed the smear from the stick with his finger into the stain.

'Yeah, it's pretty all-purpose. Did you bring the photographs, Sal?'

Salinger reached down into the depths of his bag and rummaged. Although the envelope that held the photographs was a largish Jiffy bag, he couldn't find it. He began to unpack the entire holdall.

'Hell, Salinger. You still spread more manure than a cattle truck wherever you go.'

Salinger found the Jiffy bag, lodged in the corner of the holdall under a large thick sweatshirt, which, given the temperature, he had no idea why he had brought. He pulled open the seal and spread the photos on the bed.

Carson scrutinized the small array of pictures. Some were face down. Salinger started flipping them to reveal the images.

'I remember that! Look at that, Sal! Our old cart. You remember we used to pull each other up and down the hill?'

Carson was indicating the snap of Salinger pulling Carson on the red-metal trolley.

'That Captain Marvel T-shirt,' said Salinger. 'You wouldn't take it off. You wore it every day till it fell to pieces.'

'Always loved the Cap'n. That lightning stripe was sort of my trademark. I put it on my exercise books, scrawled it on the back of my hand. Drew it on my chest once with a ballpoint pen. Mum went nuts, scrubbed it off with a Brillo pad. Hurt like hell.'

'I've forgotten. What was his party trick?'

'Just had to say the word "Shazam" and he got a bunch of superpowers. One for each letter.

Wisdom of Solomon, strength of Hercules, stamina of Atlas, Z . . . Z . . . what the hell was Z?'

'Zip? Zeal?'

'Zeus. The power of Zeus. Courage of Achilles. Speed of Mercury.'

Salinger touched the picture with the tip of his finger.

'I remember I always used to pull you even though you were bigger. Some superhero.'

'I used to pull you too.'

'I wouldn't let you. Not after you let go of me and I smashed into the tree.'

'What tree?'

'At the bottom of the hill. You were pulling me down and at the last minute you let go. I whacked into the tree and cut my face open. After that I didn't let you pull me again.'

'Don't remember that.'

Carson was now picking between his teeth with a bow of dental floss. Every part of him remained both immaculately well pressed and sanitary. His teeth reflected the too-bright overhead spots. Salinger returned to examining the photos.

'I like this one.'

He held up the black-and-white photo of Evelyn and Henry, Evelyn's hair styled like Dusty Spring-field's, piled into a stack the size of a honeydew melon.

'Neither of them looks very happy,' said Salinger.

'Those days, people didn't always smile when

166

you stuck a camera in their face. Wasn't so much the done thing,' said Carson.

'It's all so disconnected. Look at the way the washing line dissects the space between them. Look at the fact that their hands are not quite touching. There's a tiny space between them. Look at those dark clouds in the sky. It's like a painting of a bad beginning.'

Carson threw his flossing wand into a litter bin.

'You're always seeing things that aren't there, Sal. They were happy for a while. A lot of couples are happy and then they're not. They lasted fifteen years. It's not such a tragedy. Not many nowadays make it through that many laps.'

Salinger and Carson worked their way through the rest of the photographs. Carson looked faintly disappointed.

'Sorry. I know they're nothing special. It's all Mum had.'

'We'll make do. That one of Mum and Dad is good. There was nothing else at all?'

'There was one more. Yes.'

Carson was now sitting on the bed, next to Salinger, putting the photos carefully – it seemed to Salinger that he had already sorted them chronologically – back into the bag. Salinger got up and went to his shoulder bag. He pulled the envelope from the zip side pocket, drew out the Polaroid and tossed it onto the bed next to the other photographs.

Carson's eyes fell on the print. He squinted at it, trying to make it out.

'What in heaven's name *is* that?'

He picked it up, inverted it, held it up to the light. Then he held it back towards Salinger.

'I can't make it out.'

'Look again. It's a face. Look, there's the nose. That's an ear and that's the hairline.'

Carson looked again.

'OK. Maybe. Yeah, I can see it now. What about it? Who is it? It's all discoloured.'

'It's not discoloration. It's bruising.'

Carson brought the photo up close to his face, then recoiled.

'Shit!'

Carson dropped the photograph onto the bed. It fell face up. He reached and flipped it so only the back was visible.

'I don't know what it was doing in Mum's tin. I don't know who it is,' said Salinger. 'I brought it out here to show Henry. I thought he might be able to explain it.'

Carson cautiously flipped the photo again, glanced at it swiftly, then put it back face down.

'No need to wait that long. It's Henry. It's a photo of Dad when he was a kid.'

Salinger took the photo from the bed and examined it again.

'Are you sure? It doesn't look like Henry.'

'Yeah, well, you don't look much like you did thirty-five years ago, let alone fifty. It stands to reason.'

'What does? How do you know it's Henry?'

'Maybe Dad never told you. He was beaten by

Granddad Albert. Used to go after him with a poker.'

'Dad told you that?'

'Sure he told me about it. Just before he went to America. I've never seen the old man so upset. He only told me because he was drunk, or feeling guilty or something, and I was feeling sorry for myself. I think he slapped my leg or something and felt bad about it. Thing is, Albert used to hit him in the face. Used to use anything – cups, keys, a metal toy even.'

'You just said it was a poker.'

'He was pretty versatile, according to Dad. Henry cried, Salinger. In front of me. I had never ever seen him cry before.'

'Really? That really doesn't sound like Dad. Pouring his heart out to a fourteen-year-old kid.'

'It's him, Salinger. Who else could it be? And it does look like Dad. Look at his eyes. Something about the squint.'

'It's not a squint. His eyes are puffed up from the bruising.'

Salinger wasn't convinced. Although the face was blackened and bruised and anonymous, he felt sure he would recognize his own father.

'Albert was a thug, Sal. Come on – put two and two together. Mum has an old photo of a beaten child. Dad was beaten by his father as a child. What else do you think it could be?'

'There were Polaroid photos when Dad was this young? Anyway, why would Evelyn have it?'

'Polaroid company started in the '50s, I think, maybe late '40s. Could be. And maybe it was Henry's. He left a lot of old stuff behind.'

'But why would there be a photo? It doesn't make sense.'

'Maybe it's not Dad, then. I don't know. But you should leave it alone. You really think he wants to see this photo? Whether it's him or not him. Albert beat him bad. You're going to show this to a sick old man? Come on, Salinger. Burn the damn photo. Get rid of it. Don't do this to Henry. However much you might resent him for leaving us – and I know you do, I'm sure you do and I understand that you do – don't torment him with that.'

Salinger fingered the picture. He looked up. Carson was holding out his hand for the photo.

'*You* don't resent him?' said Salinger.

'No, I don't resent him. Give me the photo, Sal. I'll get rid of it.'

'I don't think so.'

Carson let his hand drop.

'Keep it then. Just don't give into your over-developed sense of melodrama.'

'You think I would show it to Dad just for effect?'

'Why did you just show it to me?'

Salinger felt a sudden sting of shame.

'The way you flung it on the bed. Like you were in a scene out of a play.'

Carson was looking at him with an unreadable expression on his face. He expected reproach, but it could have been pity, or anger. For a moment he thought it was fear, but that made no sense.

'Promise me, Salinger. Promise me you won't do it.'

Salinger put the photo back in the envelope and into his shoulder bag.

'OK. I promise.'

'Will you swear?'

'Swear on what?'

Carson looked grave. When he spoke his voice was lowered.

'On the life of Henry Jnr.'

'What?'

'You heard me. On the most precious thing I have.'

Salinger rubbed his hand on the outside of the bag, imagining momentarily that he could feel heat coming from it.

'OK, I'll swear on whatever you like.'

'Thank you.'

'Now, why don't we go down and have some supper? Change the air.'

'Say it then.'

'Now *you're* being melodramatic.'

'I'm asking you.'

Salinger sighed. He felt suddenly ridiculous. He regretted showing Carson the picture in the first place.

'I swear on the life of Henry Jnr.'

CHAPTER 8

THE BIG TEXAN

The following morning, Salinger and Carson headed off early in the direction of Albuquerque en route to the Native American pueblo, Sky City. Carson was pre-selling the experience as he guided the Lexus through another string of nowhere towns – Henrietta, Bellevue, Jolly, Wichita Falls, Electra.

'It's one of the oldest continuously inhabited areas of the United States. Acomas have been there since the twelfth century.'

'Until the Spanish came and messed them up. Evangelical Christianity in a nutshell,' said Salinger.

It would be pleasant, he reflected, if he could arrive at one of the destinations without expectations, but as ever, Carson was determined to play the part of tour guide.

'Catholics. Different beast. Yeah, they played havoc with those Indians. Got them to build a mission there, Sant Esteban del Rey. Hundreds of them died building a church there. Took away their culture, made them into Pope dopes. But we're paying 'em back today all right. Those Acomas, they are raking it. The government fobbed them off with what they thought was worthless land. But then the Indians started setting up casinos, because they had the legal power to make that decision. Those days, gambling most places outside Nevada was illegal. Casinos sucked in the money. Karma in action for you. Acomas have more money than they know what to do with.'

'So we're going all this way to see some casinos?'

'No casinos. We're going to one of the most spiritual sites in the United States.'

Salinger returned to reading his book. He had abandoned *Zen and the Art of Motorcycle Maintenance* the previous day, none the wiser, leaving Phaedrus still searching for the meaning of 'Quality'. It seemed to Salinger that he was having a hell of a time working it out. Now he had started *East of Eden*.

'You liking that?'

'Not sure yet,' said Salinger.

'You ever see the film with Jimmy Dean?'

'Nope.'

'Me either.'

Salinger brought the book up closer to his face hoping that Carson might take the hint and leave him in silence, but Carson was in an unusually garrulous mood.

'You know that Dean was number one for Henry? He thought Dean was the greatest. Don't know why. I thought he was pretty fake myself. Second-rate Brad Pitt. Pitt is the better actor. Bigger range. James Dean just did one thing. He just looked cool. And then he died. So he got to be the icon. But Pitt has more talent.'

Salinger wearily put down the book. It was apparent that reading was not an option.

'You're not just saying that because Brad Pitt lives in New Orleans? Anyway, this isn't the film, it's the book. Steinbeck is a greater American than Dean or Pitt.'

'So what's it about? What's the story?'

'It's based on Cain and Abel.'

'I get it. Me and you, right? That's what made you buy it.'

'I had the crazy idea of giving it to Henry. I don't know why. I've dog-eared it now.'

Carson reached over for the CD changer. Crosby, Stills, Nash and Young's 'Carry On' burst out of the speakers. Carson started to rock gently back and forth in his seat. With a surprisingly in-tune high and tremulous voice, he joined in the a cappella chorus.

'Carry on . . .
Love is coming . . .
Love is coming to us all . . .'

Carson seemed to know all the words by heart. Salinger felt a faint, surprising urge to sing along but it felt too oddly intimate. He stared out of the windscreen silently. Out of the corner of his eye, he could see Carson jogging on the seat, mouth open, eyelids narrowed in a sort of ecstasy.

174

The final chorus began. Carson looked across at Salinger.

'Come on, Sal! Join in! You do low, I'll do high.' He slapped Salinger's leg.

'You're being jocular. Jocularity makes me uncomfortable.'

Salinger remained silent as Carson picked up the chorus again.

> *'Carry on . . .*
> *Love is coming . . .*
> *Love is coming to us all . . .'*

The song finished in a fade-out of wah-wah guitar. Carson tapped off the CD player.

'Mum used to sing that song to you.'

'That's something else you remember about our childhood. That's three things in all.'

'I've forgotten the other two already.'

'The Captain Marvel T-shirt and the cigarette stealing. So-called . . .'

'And behind the gym with Tog. It's all coming back, Sal. The floodgates are opening.'

'What else?'

'OK, I'm exaggerating. That's all I can think of for the moment. Her putting you to bed. Singing that old Crosby, Stills, Nash and Young song.'

'She sing you to sleep too?'

'Not that I recall. But then, you always were special. Still are, right?'

'Yeah, I'm pretty special.'

Salinger found that he had the trace of a tear in his eye, thinking of Evelyn singing the song, even though he couldn't remember it. Carson noticed before he could wipe it away.

'You *crying*, Sal? Man, you're such a fricking girl.'

He laughed.

'There's a sign for somewhere called Kickapoo. Whoever would name a town Kickapoo?'

'You never cry, Carson?'

'Don't think so.'

'Not even as a child?'

'Not that I can remember. Which, it turns out, don't mean much.'

'I don't remember you ever crying either. Not as a kid or an adult.'

'Does that mean something? Aren't you meant to grow out of that sort of thing anyway? Anyhow, I just remembered. I *did* cry. Few months ago. When LouLou told me she was pregnant. I started, and I couldn't stop. Like all the tears I never cried were in there too. She got scared so I made myself stop.'

Carson didn't seem affected by the memory. His face remained set in what Salinger had come to see as its default mode – amiable, unconcerned.

'Think that's it with me and crying, though. Think we're through now.'

After five hours' solid driving, without so much as a bathroom stop, Carson took a detour onto the I–40 freeway just outside Amarillo. He had decided that they were going to eat at the Big Texan Steak Ranch and Opry, a 'must see' according to Carson.

'Jesus Christ,' said Salinger, as they pulled into the parking lot. 'No offence intended.'

The ranch was painted bright yellow, with a vast blue sign on the first storey announcing *World-famous Steaks*. There was a life-size papier mâché cow, a wooden cut-out cowboy mounted on stilts ten feet above the ground and a cowboy boot higher than a man. Six Texan flags waved in the wind on flagpoles towering above the roof. There was a large steel windmill, and three white stretch Cadillac limos with giant cow horns mounted on the bonnet parked outside in the lot.

'No point in hiding your light under a bushel, I guess,' said Salinger.

One sign outside the restaurant advertised that it was the *Home of the 72 oz Free Steak Challenge* while another, rather superfluously, informed visitors that *The Public Is Invited*. It appeared that it wasn't merely a place to eat – a further sign listed a number of supplementary functions, including motel and 'horse hotel'.

There was a parking spot right in front of the entrance. They pulled into it, then, as usual, Carson inspected the Lexus for marks. Finding none, he walked with Salinger into the restaurant out of the heat. There was hardly any natural light inside. The dark was kept at bay with spots and table lamps. There was a slaughterhouse on the wall of elk deer, bears, vultures, buffalo, and wild boar. Maybe a hundred heads in all. The restaurant was huge, it seemed half the size of a football pitch.

'What is the "Steak Challenge" exactly?' said Salinger, as Carson hailed a waitress.

'You have to eat a four-pound steak, a baked potato, a bread roll, three jumbo shrimp and a side of coleslaw in an hour.'

'It's a race?'

'Got to beat the clock. Much more difficult than you might imagine. Very few people manage it. You'd be amazed how many people believe they are capable, though.'

A table was mounted on a small stage and a short, broad-shouldered man – Salinger guessed he might be Korean – was working his way through an immense plate of food. A waiter stood by holding a watch.

'People sometimes barf,' said Carson. He pointed to an iron bucket by the side of the stage.

The Korean, if that's what he was, chewed grimly on. Salinger watched him intently as they were led towards their table by a young waitress in a white ten-gallon hat and a blue-denim shirt. She wore a large pink paper flower tucked into the hat band.

The dishes included oddities that Salinger assumed very few people ordered except out of bravado. There were mountain oysters – which, Carson gleefully informed him, were bulls' testicles – and rattlesnake meat (*very little meat, lots of bones*, according to the laminated-plastic menu).

Salinger found it hard to take his mind off the Korean, who was by now flagging. The gap between his mouthfuls was becoming more and more extended. He looked at the floor in desperation. From time to time, diners would walk up to the stage to urge him on. He would never speak, but give a faint smile and nod, and then turn and stare down at his meal, narrowing his eyes in concentration.

Salinger decided to reward himself for the five-hour drive by ordering some red wine with his BBQ platter and cowboy beans. Carson chose the eight-ounce prime rib *au jus rare* with home-made horseradish sauce, Texas rice and fried okra. While they waited for the food, Salinger took a stroll up to the challenge stage to take a closer look at the Korean's progress. The man regarded him palely but amiably. He seemed unable to focus.

'How's it going?'

The Korean performed the faint smile and the nod with which he fended off conversation.

'Why are you doing it?'

Smile, nod.

'Does it hurt?'

The Korean defiantly picked up a fork, hacking off a piece of baked potato to force into his maw.

'Why don't you just stop?' said Salinger. 'It's

like you've put yourself in a freak show. It's humiliating.'

The Korean looked blank, then suddenly angry. Momentarily, Salinger thought he was going to leap out of his chair and punch him. An attendant who policed the table at all times glared icily at Salinger, and tilted his head to one side, prompting Salinger back to his cubicle.

Salinger returned to the booth, poured a large glass of wine from the half-bottle of California Shiraz and sank it in one. He felt suddenly depressed. His platter, predictably enormous, arrived. He picked at it listlessly. Carson was mechanically devouring his steak in great, red, rag-edged chunks.

'Fun place.'

'A riot,' said Salinger. He rearranged some of the beans on his plate and sank another glass of wine. He felt slightly giddy.

The Korean abandoned his bid after twenty more minutes. There was a faint round of disappointed applause, and the Korean waved weakly. He staggered back to the table where a group that Salinger presumed were his family were sitting – a dumpy, grey-faced wife and two hyperactive infant boys who were throwing a bread roll back and forth, unreprimanded.

Salinger stared up at the severed animal heads on the walls. They were interspersed with a dozen different kinds of handguns and rifles. The wine was making his head swim. He felt nauseous.

He experienced a sudden, intense craving for a cigarette.

'Want to burn one, Carzy?'

'Maybe after I've had a coffee. You want one?'

'I need to get outside anyway.'

'They're in the car, in the glove compartment.'

Carson threw Salinger the keys to the Lexus. Salinger made his way outside, weaving slightly. When he got inside the car, he found the pack empty. His head felt like a balloon, as if it had expanded to a size larger than normal. Away to the left, maybe a hundred yards, he could see a small grocery store that looked like it might sell cigarettes. He locked the car doors and walked towards it.

It was further away than he thought. When he got there, he saw that it was down at heel and a little grimy. The people inside looked faintly dangerous, he thought, then dismissed the thought as ridiculous. He was being paranoid because they were poor and Hispanic.

He walked up to the counter, placed the keys on it while he reached for his wallet and asked for a pack of Lucky Strikes. The man behind the counter was fat, ugly and about fifty years old. He reminded Salinger of Orson Welles as Hank Quinlan in *A Touch of Evil*. He didn't look up from his newspaper. Instead, he reached behind him and, without turning his head, pulled out the pack. Salinger took out a five-dollar bill. The ugly man, still not looking up, threw a few coins of change across the counter.

181

Out of the corner of his eye, Salinger could see two other customers. Except that they didn't seem like customers. Since he had come into the store they had just stood in the aisles without inspecting anything on the shelves. They both had ragged jeans, dirty denim jackets and cartoon moustaches. One of them had a cowboy hat that had a small hole in the brim. He tipped the brim of the hat at Salinger, but in a way that seemed more hostile than friendly.

Salinger nodded back. His eyes focused past the man in the hat and beyond the dirty plate-glass window to the open desert.

Outside, Salinger could see the Korean woman and the two unruly children. As he watched, the Korean man stumbled and fell to the ground. He had apparently fainted. The children started crying and the woman looked around helplessly.

'Slope-eye down,' said the man with the hat. There was no trace of a Mexican accent. He shot Salinger an unpleasant grin. The two Mexicans – if that was what they were – instead of going to help, were enjoying the spectacle and laughing.

Salinger had done some first-aid training. He ran out to the scene, stuffing the cigarettes and wallet in his pocket. The woman looked at him. The children continued screaming. The heat was like a giant hand squeezing his head.

Salinger gently turned the inert man on his front. Immediately he opened his eyes, and smiled gently up at Salinger. Then he sat up straight. The children stopped crying. The woman smiled and touched Salinger's arm.

'Thank you. Thank you. You save him. Thank you.'

Salinger smiled vaguely in return. He wasn't quite sure what to do next, so he nodded a few times, waved and then walked back towards the restaurant. He sat on the porch and smoked a cigarette, feeling proud of himself, although he had done nothing. The cigarette tasted dry and flaky in his mouth, the smoke aggravated his windpipe, but he smoked it down to the stub all the same.

He went back inside and watched while Carson dispatched a vast plate of apple pie and ice cream. A new challenger was up on the platform and was gorging at a steady rate. He was vast, maybe two hundred pounds. It looked as if he would have no trouble finishing the tiny plate in front of him.

The waitress brought two coffees. The man on the platform suddenly vomited in the bucket. Diners turned away, laughing. Salinger and Carson drank their coffee. Salinger insisted on picking up the bill. Carson suggested that his 10 per cent tip was a little on the modest side, and threw in an extra five dollars. Salinger was still feeling a glow from his good Samaritan moment. They stood up and headed for the exit.

'Pass me the keys, Sally.'

Salinger felt in his pockets.

'The keys, Sally.'

Salinger felt his stomach tighten. He searched his bag, then emptied it out onto the floor.

The keys weren't there.

'I think I might have left them at the tobacconist's.'

'The what?'

'The general store. The supermarket. Whatever you call it.'

'What store? Where?'

'See, this Korean, the guy onstage, he fell down and . . .'

But Carson was already running towards the exit. Salinger followed him, trying to keep up. He called after him.

'Sorry, Carson. I'm sorry.'

He followed Carson out to the parking lot. Carson was not, to Salinger's surprise, stamping his way full speed over to the general store. Instead, he was staring at the parking lot outside the front entrance.

Salinger followed his gaze. Where the Lexus had been parked, between a battered Japanese saloon and a red flat-bed truck, a fourth white stretch limo was parked. The Lexus had gone.

Carson broke into a run towards the general store. Salinger followed him, not wanting to catch him. The nausea inside him expanded. The wine worked in his blood, the sun pulsed on his head. He felt grit in his throat.

When he made it to the storefront he could see

Carson hammering on the door. A wire grille had been secured over the front. A sign, written badly in felt-tip pen, hung from a spike in the wire netting. It read *Close back soon.*

Carson sat down slowly on the ground and put his head in his hands. Salinger sat down next to him. Carson took one of the hands away and scratched the back of his neck fiercely. Salinger could see a faint red welt at the spot.

Carson lowered his hands and turned to Salinger. 'You know what?'

His accent had faded. His voice was London again, suburban.

'What, Carson?'

But Carson didn't seem to have anything further to say. Once again he simply scratched fiercely at the back of his neck.

'It's insured, right?' said Salinger.

Salinger tentatively placed a hand on Carson's shoulder. Carson responded by suddenly pushing his face up to within an inch of Salinger's. Salinger noticed, at the bottom of his field of vision, a slight fleck of drool on Carson's lip. In his eyes he saw something that he could not name but that he remembered.

Then Carson stood up. He remained stock still for a couple of seconds, and breathed deeply and rapidly, as if relishing the fresh air. Then he turned and walked briskly away into the empty Texas plain.

Salinger remained sitting where he was. He now had no clothes other than those he stood up in, no cell phone. He had his shoulder bag with his iPod in, a sketch pad and some pencils, but his wallet was empty of cash.

He turned to see where Carson had gone, but he had disappeared from view.

CHAPTER 9

AMARILLO

Salinger sat outside the Big Texan for an hour, smoking cigarettes, one straight after the other. He had no idea what else to do. The pack of cigarettes slowly emptied. He kicked at the earth, and watched the sun until he became aware that it had shifted position slightly under his gaze.

He took out the pencil and pad that he always kept in his shoulder bag and began to draw some of the people who had been coming and going to and from the restaurant. They seemed straightforward and happy. He avoided all taint of satire as he sketched the open smiles, the good-natured eyes, the rounded bodies bred by leisure-saturated lives and simple, Manichean constructions of the world. Or so he imagined.

Salinger had begun contemplating spending the night in the open range as penalty for his stupidity, when he felt a light pressure on his shoulder. He turned and saw Carson. Carson was also smoking a cigarette, which he assumed he must have either bought somewhere or bummed off someone.

Salinger stared guiltily at the Lucky Strike pack. It had cost him $4.25 and a Lexus.

Carson sat down next to Salinger. He made a clicking noise at the back of his throat, and laced his fingers together in front of him.

'You're back,' said Salinger.

'That's right,' said Carson.

Carson stretched his legs out in front of him, and poked at a stone with the ball of his foot.

'Look, Salinger. I just wanted to say that I'm sorry.'

'You're sorry.'

'Do you forgive me?'

'Do I forgive you?'

'Are you going to carry on repeating everything I say?'

Carson looked mild and blank and far away.

'I got your car stolen with everything in it. You want me to forgive you.'

'That's right.'

Salinger nodded.

'Where did you go?'

'Nowhere special. Needed to think. Needed to pray.'

Salinger was unable to meet Carson's eyes. He felt it was neither simple to speak nor simple to remain silent.

'I'm an idiot, Carzy. I always have been. Something wrong with my fucking head.'

'I walked away like an infant, Sally, and I'm a grown man.'

188

Carson offered a cigarette to Salinger. Salinger took it and tore off the filter, but didn't light it.

'Will you shake hands with me?' said Carson.

Carson reached out his hand. Awkwardly, Salinger took it. In a slick, irresistible movement Carson enveloped him in a bear hug.

'I'm an unreliable, incompetent fool,' said Salinger over his shoulder. 'I can't be trusted. My mind always lets me down. I reprimand it. I scold it. I rage at it. I threaten it with torments. It takes no notice of me.'

'I know what you are. But it's you. It's you, Sally.'

They stayed like that until Salinger started to feel awkward. His eyes remained open. He gazed at the blurred horizon.

After thirty seconds, Carson's phone began to ring. He peeled himself away from Salinger, and clicked the green answer button. He listened, responding with nothing other than the occasional murmur. Finally he spoke.

'We're right in front of the restaurant. Two of us. You can't miss us. Underneath the Big Texan sign. Just next to that huge great whatever it is. Cowboy boot. In front of the parking lot. OK, thank you.'

He clicked off.

'The police. They're just a few minutes away.'

'The police,' repeated Salinger blankly. He realized that he hadn't yet fully considered what the implications of the loss of the Lexus were.

'They said they'll give us a lift into town if we want.'

'That's good.'

They fell into silence again.

'You loved that car – didn't you?' said Salinger.

'It was just a car.'

'I'm really so very . . .'

'Don't say that you're sorry again.'

They scanned the horizon for the police cruiser. In the distance, they could see a black-and-white Ford Mustang approaching.

'What are we going to do?'

'Rent another car. Buy some clothes.'

'We're still going to look for Henry?'

'Of course.'

The numbness Salinger had felt in his body and brain since the Lexus had gone began to recede. His mind felt oddly sharpened.

'Have you rung LouLou and told her?'

Carson ruefully shook his head.

'Can't do that. Don't want to upset her. A pregnant woman doesn't need the stress.'

'She'll get the stress sooner or later. When you tell her about the car, I mean.'

'But I won't be there to support her through it. Also, she's got another test to do. She's had so many damn tests. It's stressful enough.'

'What kind of test?'

'Routine stuff. She'll be fine, she's strong. It took her a long time to conceive, but now it's happened the doctors say she's got as much chance as any normal pregnancy. Phoning her up and telling her that the car's been stolen isn't going to help a single thing.

'I'll get the insurance process into train. They should get me a temporary replacement. I might even be able to get a permanent replacement by the time we're due back. That's if they don't consider the loss of the car being due to extreme negligence. Hell, LouLou might not even notice. In any case, getting a new car by the time I break the news will considerably ease the passage, so . . .'

Salinger could now see the police car pulling into the lot. It stopped directly in front of them. A brawny man emerged, chewing a toothpick. He wore a fawn wide-brimmed hat and khaki uniform with blue epaulettes, a blue tie and a wide black-leather belt. His eyes, mouth and nose, noted Salinger, were all pushed towards the centre of his face, as if tugged there by a tiny gravitational black hole. The eyes were bulbous and hooded like a bullfrog's. There was a broad expanse of empty skin forming a border to his hairline which was cropped a good four inches from the base of the neck. He removed his hat, revealing an expanse of stubble on top of his head. Carson rose to greet him.

'You got here quickly. We're . . .'

The patrolman held his hand up and Carson fell silent. He flicked his eyes from Salinger to Carson then back again. He sniffed once, and stretched his neck. He took a notepad and pen from his belt.

'Which one's the idiot?'

191

'I beg your pardon?' said Carson.

'The idiot who left the keys on the counter of the Mexicany shit shop.'

'That would be me,' said Salinger, conscious of his voice sounding weak and apologetic. The patrolman's eyelids flickered slightly when he heard the accent. He nodded and turned his gaze on Salinger. He chewed lazily on the toothpick.

'Australian?'

'English.'

'English, huh? That explains a great deal. Yeah.'

He turned to Carson, opened his notebook, stared into it and squinted.

'Bear with me. Bear with me. Can't always read my own damn writing. You Garson Mash? The guy who phoned?'

'Carson,' said Carson. 'Carson Nash.'

'The idiot is your brother? That's tough, having an idiot brother. Got one myself. Real Grade A retard.'

The policeman cocked one leg up on the low wall and spat the toothpick onto the ground. His eyes strayed up to the restaurant sign.

'Always meant to eat here. Never got round to it. Don't know why. You two have some chow?'

Salinger and Carson both nodded.

'How the hell was it?'

'Pretty good,' answered Salinger.

'Not interested in your opinion. English don't know squat about good food. English leave keys on the counter where lowlife Mexicanos chew

192

polecat Tacos and brew up plans to steal shit. Must have been like Christmas Day in Chihuahua.'

He stared at Salinger curiously.

'How come your brother ain't English too? Something damn fishy there right off.'

'I've lived here for twenty years,' said Carson.

'An honorary American.' He pronounced the word 'honorary' with a hard 'h'. 'Guess you at least sound like you know how to talk normal. That's something. What's the food in the Big Texan like, Garson?'

'Carson. It's good if you like meat.'

'Who don't like meat? You like meat, idiot?'

He turned back to Salinger and regarded him through narrowed eyes.

'I like meat, yes,' said Salinger.

The patrolman seemed somewhat mollified by this response, but still not convinced.

'What kind of meat?'

'I don't know. Most really. Beef. Lamb. Pork.'

The patrolman nodded, and returned his gaze to the sign.

'I should pay a visit. Always meant to try that Steak Challenge.'

'Tougher than it looks,' said Carson. 'Some guy was puking his gizzard up in there.'

'I got a pretty healthy appetite.'

The patrolman patted his stomach with both hands, then took his leg off the low wall and ostentatiously scratched his balls. Carson waited until he had finished before speaking again.

'Can you – would you mind very much – just telling us what the chances are of getting the car back?'

'The chances? Let me see now . . .'

The cop feigned performing some complex mental calculation. He scribbled furiously in his notebook as if working out odds.

'Yeah. That would be about right.'

He held up the notebook so that Salinger and Carson could see it. The word 'ZIP' was written in plain black capitals.

'Those are the chances, according to the onboard computer.'

'But surely,' began Salinger.

'This is the way it is. It ain't like the TV. Your wheels is gone across the border and they ain't coming back. Or maybe that car is in some lock-up garage by now, somewhere within a fifty-mile radius. There's a lot of lock-up garages in a fifty-mile radius. We can't bust 'em all. You know we have other stuff to deal with here in the US of A, English. Murderers, rapists, gang bangers, beltway politicians, serial killers, what have you. We could be chasin' 'em now if it weren't for you giving your damn car away to some lowlife.'

'Witnesses?' ventured Salinger. 'Mightn't someone have seen the car?'

'Stop trying to think so hard. You'll hurt yourself, English old boy. Nobody notices nothing around here, even if they got a reason to notice, and nobody does got a reason to notice. So no witnesses. The car is gone. That Lexus is headed for Mexus. You been a bad brother. If I was your big bro I would spank you soundly and send you to bed without your supper.'

'I would deserve it, I expect.'

'Damn straight you would deserve it, huh, Carson old boy?'

Carson nodded.

'Good. So this is what we're going to do, brothers. Because I'm a nice guy and because I don't hold no grudges 'bout Boston Harbour, I'm going to give you two Limeys a lift back into town. Then you can complete the paperwork and make your insurance claim, though if they got an exemption clause in case of idiot brothers, I wouldn't be surprised what – so – ever. Anyhow, that would be your problem on top of your other problems like not having a car and having an idiot gene in the blood. You still got some plastic?'

'We both got our wallets.'

'Yeah, well, listen, Carson, get the kid to check you both into a hotel, making sure the bill is on him. Then get him to buy you a stiff drink. Then you rent a car, and then you get out of my town and stop messing up my crime-fighting schedule. Let's get this signed and sealed. I usually take high tea with muffins and strawberry jam around this time. And sugar lumps. That's my routine and now it's all messed up. I don't like my routine messed up. OK?'

'OK.'

'OK then.'

The policeman nodded, then paused and turned towards his car. Then he looked back.

'Hey, idiot.'

'Yes, sir.'

'What did you have to eat at the Big Texan?'

'BBQ platter with cowboy beans.'

'No mountain oysters? No rattlesnake?'

'Just the BBQ.'

'You watch those beans in my car, boy. Don't you reek the place out. What about you, big guy? What did you eat?'

'Prime rib, rice, fried okra.'

'You should be safe. Cowboy beans, shit. Get in the car. I'll show you the way to Amarillo. I'll show you why they was hugging their pillow there, you Limey faggots.'

The paperwork at the small police station took less than an hour. The patrolman, whose name, it transpired, was Wendell Valentine, then dropped them at the nearest Holiday Inn. He threw them an idle wave as he drove off and tipped his hat. It was mid-afternoon. They were dirty. Their clothes were stiff with sweat.

'We got to buy some new threads,' said Carson.

'I can finally get you into a decent wardrobe,' said Salinger.

'Is there something wrong with the way that I dress?'

'Except that you dress like a hick, no.'

'You're going to dress me up like a girly boy?'

'It wouldn't do you any harm.'

'The insurance company are going to drop a Ford Taurus round at the hotel in a couple of hours. In the meantime we can take a stroll downtown. We can go on a nice little faggot shopping trip.'

There was no point in taking a shower as the only clothes they had were caked with dust. Instead, they headed directly off towards what few shops there were within walking distance.

At five o'clock exactly Carson called LouLou. After he rang off, Salinger asked him again if he'd told her about the Lexus.

'Yeah, right.'

'Meaning?'

'Meaning no fricking way.'

'Would she have been angry with you?'

Carson rolled his eyes upwards.

'What do you think?'

'It wasn't your fault.'

Carson adjusted his shirt slightly. It had worked its way partially out of his belt. There was a tiny stain on the cuff where he had tried to remove a splash of steak jus with a napkin soaked in soda water.

'Sally, you've got a girlfriend, right? Well, having a girlfriend is very similar to having a wife.'

'In what regard?'

'In regard of the fact that it not being my fault makes no – difference – what – so – fricking – ever.'

As they continued walking, Salinger found

himself surprised at how high his spirits seemed to be. The shops were standard issue. A grocery store, a gift shop, a bar, a supermarket, a motorcycle store, Häagen-Dazs concession. Salinger stopped to stare in the window of a funeral parlour. Displayed at the front was a small black pyramid with an enamel plate of a brown teddy bear mounted on it. The bear was smiling cheerfully and carrying three balloons, red, blue and yellow. He studied the printed card lying flat beside it.

The Pyramid Infant Cremation Urn is crafted from black Cambrian granite, a semi-precious agate noted for its distinct veining patterns and deep translucence. Evokes the history and mystique of the Great Pyramids of Egypt. Bottom-opening threaded stopper. $850.

There were no clothes shops. They did a U-turn to explore a road that Salinger had glanced down as they strolled along the main street, passing the same shops once again. Salinger stumbled at one point, and *Zen* fell out of his bag. He stooped to pick it up. As he straightened up, he found himself staring into the motorcycle store. There were rows of gleaming bikes. A sign next to the door read *Rentals Available*.

Salinger blinked once, and looked up at Carson. 'Cancel the car.'

Carson was fumbling in his pocket for cigarettes. 'What?'

But Salinger had already disappeared into the motorcycle store.

Carson wasn't easy to convince. Although he possessed a motorcycle licence – because it had been one of LouLou's hobbies which he had reluctantly fallen in with – he hated the exposure to risk that riding a motorbike involved. Salinger, however, was insistent that the omens favoured it.

'Think about it, Carzy. Riding across the Texas fields on a big shining hog. Everything has a purpose, right? You said that, right?'

'Yeah but still . . .'

'Don't you think someone, somewhere is talking to us? We lost the Lexus. Just before we take the delivery of the rental car, we walk past a motorcycle shop. Then on the sidewalk OUTSIDE THE SHOP, I drop a copy of *Zen and the Art of Motorcycle Maintenance*. *Zen and the Art of Motorcycle Maintenance*, Carzy! A book about two family members finding themselves on a motorcycle road trip. If that isn't synchronicity, I don't know what is. The deliberate accident, Carzy. The planned coincidence. It's beautiful, you've got to admit it.'

'It's crazy. It's dangerous. What do you think I am, a teenager?'

Carson seemed resolute. Salinger dug into the back of his mind trying to find an argument that would convince him.

'Just think how Henry would feel. You know he always thought you were a bit of a stuffed shirt.'

199

Carson frowned.

'He did?'

'Of course he did. Why wouldn't he?'

'I guess I do have something of a cautious streak.'

'Just imagine turning up on Henry's doorstep on an 850 cc hog. Maybe he won't think you're such a stuffed shirt any more. And even if he doesn't, so what? Shit, Carson, imagine what fun it would be! You don't even have to wear a damn helmet in New Mexico! We're fifty miles from the state border. That's going to be a unique experience. And with you driving, I know one hundred per cent that we would be completely safe, because you are such a safety-obsessed, tight-arsed suburban English boy at heart.

'So why don't we do it? Come on, let's do it! Why not? I'll pay. It's on me. It's my gift to you. What do you say, Carson? For once in your life, stick your neck out and take a chance. You and me. I'll ride pillion. There's still three hundred and fifty miles between here and Las Cruces. We can take it slow, take in the scenery, check out the pueblo, have an adventure. It's all different when you take the windscreen away. It's real.'

The man behind the desk, who resembled a civil servant more than a motorcycle salesman, with grey hair, a healthy tan and a crisp white button-down shirt, looked at his watch.

'We have to close soon. You want a bike or not, gentlemen?'

Carson scratched the back of his neck anxiously.

'LouLou would kill me.'

'She's going to kill you anyway. Besides it was her that got you into motorcycle riding in the first place.'

'That was before I was going to be a father, Salinger. Don't you understand what that means?'

'Not really.'

'It means not just thinking about yourself. It's irresponsible, Salinger. What if something were to happen?'

'Something already *did* happen. The car got stolen. Nothing else is going to happen. We've used up our bad karma allowance. It's all credit from now on. And Dad will think it's great. Go on, Carson. Do something on impulse for once in your life.'

'I already did. I moved to America.'

'And that worked out for you – didn't it?'

The store owner started to usher the two of them towards the door.

'We're closing up. I'm sorry.'

'Carson. *Please*.'

Carson stood stock still. His lips were very firmly pursed, and his eyes narrowed. He gave a slight shake of the head, then turned to walk towards the exit.

'I'll text LouLou and tell her about the Lexus,' said Salinger.

Carson stopped walking.

'You wouldn't do that.'

'This is for your own good, Carson. Rent a bike.'

'It's not safe.'

Salinger took his phone from his bag and started to prod at the keys.

'Dear LouLou . . . we have had . . . some bad luck . . . I'm afraid . . . Your beautiful new car . . .'

'I know that's not what you're really texting.'

'But you can't be sure – can you?'

'You can't blackmail me, Salinger.'

'. . . has been stolen. We are stranded in the middle of . . .'

Carson made a sudden move to grab the phone out of Salinger's hand, but Salinger skipped backwards.

'Sal, this is childish.'

'. . . the middle of the desert. Carson gave me the keys and . . .'

Carson gave a loud exhalation of breath.

'OK, you damn infantile pest. But I'm wearing a helmet, and I suggest you do the same, and I'm not going a mile over 50. We only ride in daylight hours and we swap the bike for a car the moment we get to Las Cruces.'

Salinger punched his fist through the air and whooped, American-style.

They set off the following morning at 10 a.m. The road from Amarillo towards Sky City took them west along Route 66. They had chosen a Mulberry Red 2006 Triumph America, based on the original classic Triumph Bonneville. 790 cc twin cylinder engine, five-speed gearbox. Wide, raked-back handlebars, disc brakes, eighteen-inch front wheel. It was sold to them as being for riders 'of limited experience'. Carson liked it because he thought it was relatively safe, Salinger liked it because it looked cool as shit. He particularly liked the classic black-and-white Triumph tank badges. The forward-set highway pegs gave it a contour that suggested the Harleys in *Easy Rider*.

The engine was almost as silent as the Lexus while they forged along the blacktop. The roar of the passing air sang in Salinger's ears. In the two pillion bags, there were all the possessions they needed to last them until they found Henry. A few pairs of briefs, some shaving kit, an extra pair of jeans for each of them, three T-shirts each, one sweater each. All were bought in a bargain store at a strip mall just outside Amarillo. There were four sealed packs of Lucky Strike two lite, two full-strength.

Salinger had his arms around Carson's waist. Carson, despite his resolution to stick to 50 was travelling at 55 mph. His black motorcycle helmet with full face guard was carefully adjusted and strapped firmly on. Salinger's helmet was jammed into one of the pillions. His head was bare. The sun hammered down, the wind was warm. He felt himself to be fully within the landscape, absorbed like rain into the parched plains. In his mind, he rolled with the bowling dust devils.

This was a feeling he had never known – the electric frisson of pure freedom. His pulse beat evenly, he had the impression that his pupils were fully distended to take in the earth and sky. His buttocks were beginning to ache, but he didn't care.

Carson suddenly slowed, then pulled over by the side of the freeway.

'Something wrong?' said Salinger.

'Follow me.'

Carson kicked down the cycle support, racked the cycle up onto it, and dismounted. Salinger followed him, puzzled. They appeared to be in the middle of nowhere. Cars and vast blunt trucks careered past, the roar of their engines approaching like thunder, then receding. Out of the wind, the heat made itself felt more powerfully, sheets of energy pressing down like gravity.

'Where we going, Carzy?'

Carson reached into his bag and brought out a white plastic bag with something in it.

'What's in there?'

Instead of answering, Carson led him a few yards down towards a battered, graffitied fence. Salinger saw people, three hundred yards away maybe, outlined in the heat haze. There seemed to be a number of large objects, maybe ten feet high, sticking out of the ground at angles among the small, scattered crowd.

As they approached, the vision came into focus. There were ten parallel shapes pointing upwards to the sky. Salinger made out eventually that they were ten different models of American Cadillac, covered in graffiti, half buried in the Texas dust.

'The Cadillac Ranch,' said Carson, reaching into the white plastic bag and bringing out two cans of spray paint. 'Graffiti is encouraged. I bought these in town. So . . .'

'Who put this here?' asked Salinger, taking one of the paint cans and shaking it, listening to the ball bearing clacking inside.

'Some San Francisco art collective back in the '70s. I'm no artist but – it's neat, right?'

Framed against the wilderness of the sky and plains, the artwork was unsettling, witty, disorienting. As they closed in on it, Salinger noticed that, along with the Cadillacs, there was a cartoon-like bomb buried in the earth.

'Their little joke, I guess,' said Carson. 'A "post-apocalyptic vision" if you will.'

Nine or ten people were wandering among the cars, most of them brandishing spray cans. All the original paintwork had long been covered, then re-covered in layer after layer of graffiti, mostly banal – names, tags, stick men, squiggles, the occasional obscenity.

Salinger stood behind the roof of the nearest Cadillac, removed the top of his can, shook it, and started to spray.

'This will all be gone this time tomorrow,' said Carson, spelling out the names 'Carson', 'LouLou' and 'Henry Jnr' in gold paint on one of the bonnets.

'That's the beauty,' said Salinger, now scoping out his picture carefully. He had never really done any street art, but he had always seen the appeal.

No demand for quality, no critical reception to fear. There was nothing but the spontaneity and the cloud of self.

After five minutes' work he stood back and admired the result. Carson came and stood next to him, smiling approvingly.

'You can't sing, you give car keys to thieves, you dress like a bitch, but you do have something of a knack when it comes to a picture,' said Carson.

The depiction was of two figures, travelling down a highway on a motorbike. Neither was recognizable as Salinger or Carson, and yet something in the crudely sprayed expression suggested each one of them vividly – Carson careful, serene, a little uptight, focused on the road ahead, Salinger somehow nervous, flighty, excited. Using a few strokes of the paint and a slight blurring effect, he had suggested motion, and speed, and freedom all at once. Carson took out his cell phone and prepared to snap the artwork, but Salinger held up his hand to halt him.

'Let it be. It's there and it's gone. It's meant to be that way. Don't record it. Let it disappear.'

'You know what, Salinger?'

'What, Carson?'

'You're a pretentious, arty-crafty, pseudo-intellectual poseur.'

'Your point being?'

Carson put the phone away, but continued staring at the picture Salinger had made. Salinger watched his face carefully. A shadow momentarily passed across it.

'I look kind of unpleasant. Angry maybe. Something.'

'Maybe that's in your head rather than the picture.'

'Is that how you see me?'

'As "kind of unpleasant"? No.'

'Are you sure? Because I look a bit of a dick.'

Salinger examined the picture himself carefully. Already a small boy, about ten years old, was overwriting part of the lower half of the image with long random pink tentacles of spray paint.

'No. I'm not sure, come to think of it.'

'You don't like me?'

'I didn't think about it like that.'

Salinger briefly considered the possibility that Carson's feelings had been hurt. Salinger had always assumed that Carson was invulnerable, Captain Marvel incarnate.

Carson stared at the image on the bonnet for a few seconds longer, then turned back to the bike.

'Best get going,' said Carson. 'We've got a long way to go.'

He paced off briskly, alone, in the direction of the bike.

Salinger followed. He turned back to look at the Cadillac one last time, and could just make out that nearly all his painting had been eradicated by the boy with the pink spray paint.

CHAPTER 10

ALBUQUERQUE

It was a full day's drive to Sky City. Salinger and Carson decided to make an overnight stop in Albuquerque and spend the following morning at the pueblo.

The noise of the wind on the bike made communication difficult. Salinger was happy simply with the sensation of forward movement. He enjoyed the feel of his brother's stomach held lightly between his hands, not so much for safety but for reassurance. Carson drove carefully, never varying his speed, never taking the hint of a risk.

They stopped in Tucumcari, largely because Carson remembered a Lowell George song that he listened to as a child in England called 'Willin'', which referred to the town. He told Salinger that he had once imagined it a place of glittering lights, dusty cowpokes, slatternly women, lounging hoods, gamblers in wraparound sunglasses. In reality it amounted to no more than an extended strip mall, with Dairy Queen, McDonald's, Burger King.

They walked into Dairy Queen, but Salinger found both the surroundings and the menu so unappealing – DQ Dogs, Chicken Strip Baskets and Grillburgers – they decided the best they could do was a Big Mac. They sat beside the yellow arches at a plastic table and gazed at the charred, desolate landscape that bordered the town.

'Surely the most dismal of all American inventions,' said Salinger, sucking on his Diet Coke and picking at a bag of fries.

'Diet Coke?'

'The strip mall.'

'Do you know who buys the most McDonald's in Europe?' said Carson. 'The French.'

'Does that prove something?'

Carson considered this.

'Not really.'

'Any news from the police about the Lexus?'

'Yeah. They didn't find it again.'

'Can't you pray or something?'

'It doesn't work like that.'

'It says in the Bible that you can't pray for your car?'

'It's not like ordering a pizza.'

'What have you got to lose?'

'A little dignity, I guess.'

They finished the food and smoked a cigarette. Carson pointed out towards the edge of town.

'Route 66. Where all the dust bowlers came out in their tractors in the '30s. First real environmental disaster.'

'And all-American.'

'No one can say we don't innovate.'

Salinger threw his fries into a bin, stared around

him at the thin, sad forest of signs for motels and auto body shops, liquor stores and hamburger joints.

'Do you really love this country, Carson? Really like, as in, *love*?'

'Yes, I do.'

'What does that feel like?'

'I'll tell you how it feels. When they play "The Star-Spangled Banner" at a Saints football game, I stand up, I place my right hand across my chest and I feel pride in my heart.'

'What do you like about it *exactly*?'

He stared at the horizon, the rising dust, the louring sky.

'You're looking at the mall, and you're thinking that it's ugly. And it *is* ugly. But people like it. People like convenience. People like predictability. And look out beyond the town. Look out to the desert. Look at the light. It's different from anywhere else. Hard-edged. Brilliant. Gauzy in the eastern part, but here you are left with crystalline atmosphere. Cut and dried, hard light – there's a real beauty to that.'

'Anything you *don't* like about the damn place?'

'Yeah. Too many fricking tourists.'

They threw the paper containers into the trash, and returned to where the bike was standing. Carson kicked it off the stand, started the engine, let it roar. It was a hundred and seventy-five miles to Albuquerque.

★   ★   ★

The hotel in Albuquerque, once again, was a Holiday Inn. Carson started apologizing.

'Listen, the hotel in Cruces is a nice boutique-y one. The Hotel Encanto, the Enchanted Hotel. Like the enchanted mesa, right? That's what they call the Acoma pueblo.'

Now they had the motorbike, staying in Holiday Inns didn't bother Salinger so much. The bike conferred outsider status. He felt he could watch the homogeneity, the careful branding, the meticulous uniformity from a distance, not as a participant but as an observer. And after all, a bed was a bed was a bed.

They ordered room service while they sat watching the rolling news on TV. Salinger emptied out his pannier to look for his bath bag and, finding it, left the contents on the floor. On the screen, there was a report that someone at Lehman's had been seen urinating on his PC. 'It was like Bellevue in there,' said one worker. Tourists were turning up to take photos of the Lehman building.

The news item concluded by summing up the week. A ribbon ran along the foot of the screen describing the *Week of Catastrophe*. Merrill Lynch had gone into an emergency merger with Bank of America. The AIG bailout had cost the American voter $85 billion. Share prices had tumbled by 30–40 per cent each day since Lehman.

There was an interview with the former AIG head. He said that he had lost his 'entire net worth'. The reporter noted that he still managed to run his own private jet. The scroll across the bottom of the screen changed. It now read *AMERICAN CRASH – Never-ending nightmare on Wall Street – Financial giants implode, jobs shredded.*

'Your country's fucked,' said Salinger.

'Yours too,' said Carson without looking up from his maple pecan cheesecake.

'Holiday Inns, Dairy Queen and sub-prime mortgages. Quite a contribution to civilization.'

'Don't forget Pizza Hut.'

'You phoned LouLou today?'

'She's doing fine.'

'You mention the Lexus?'

'I didn't get round to it.'

After they had finished eating, Salinger went to the business centre and opened his email account. There were twelve emails. Four were spam, three were from his studio, another four were from friends. One was from a small art newspaper asking if they could have a telephone chat with him about his forthcoming exhibition. Clearly they hadn't heard the news of its cancellation.

There was nothing from Tiane. Salinger started to feel a touch of panic. He opened a screen.

Tiane

Carson ran over a fucking dog. Then he clubbed it to death with a rock.
   Do I have your attention?

How about this?

I got his Lexus stolen. I left the keys on the counter of a dodgy Mexican grocery store.

When Carson found out, he had this look in his eye. I think then I knew what that dog must have felt with Carson standing over him.

Then he prayed and got it all under control.

On his gravestone, I would inscribe those words: 'He got it all under control.'

Is your mind still wandering?

We just did the last two hundred miles on a 790 cc Triumph America. Me riding pillion, no helmet.

I didn't tell you, but my mood was midnight blue when I left London. It's lighter now. It's almost aquamarine.

Email me. I'll fill in the gaps.

Sal xx

Salinger returned to the room to find Carson still

awake, sitting on a hard chair and skimming through his copy of *East of Eden*.

'What do you think of it?'

'It's a pretty big book.'

'Yeah, that's what the reviews said.'

'You ever wonder why Cain hated Abel so much? After all, it wasn't such a big deal that God didn't like his offering.'

'What *was* his offering?'

'Bible doesn't say. It was "of the land". Some wheat or something, I guess,' said Carson.

'Cereal isn't much of a gift. Difficult to wrap. Low on visual appeal. No wonder God was pissed off.'

'Abel rocked up a sheep and stuff. Sure, there's a quality gap there. Still. Nothing much to kill a brother over.'

'Cain had issues,' said Salinger. 'That mark God put on him was like Hebraic electronic tagging.'

'Did you know that the mark of Cain was there to protect Cain? So that if anyone found out what Cain had done and tried to punish him for it, then they would risk God's wrath.'

'That's a little indulgent on God's part – wouldn't you say? I mean, for killing someone with a rock. Was it a rock?'

'Doesn't say. Cain did pretty well in fact. Headed off to the land of Nod and built the first city.'

'I guess God understood a thing or two about brothers,' said Salinger. 'Such as that they can be fucking annoying.'

'God understands everything,' said Carson,

and tossed the book onto the side table. 'He just doesn't always explain it too well. You email Christiane?'

Salinger didn't reply. He rifled around in his bath bag for his toothbrush.

'Everything OK, bro?'

'She's not emailing me.'

'Why don't you phone her?'

'It's just not something we do. We're grown-ups, we can live without speaking to one another for a few days.'

'You're not scared to call her, are you?'

'Not at all, no.'

'Maybe a little?'

Salinger found his toothbrush and began applying the paste.

'Listen, mate, it's fine.'

'How have things been between you two?'

Salinger raised the toothbrush to his mouth. Then he slowly lowered it again. He felt the overwhelming need to share his anxiety.

He sat on the bed and, as accurately as he could remember, related the scene at the airport. Carson listened in silence. His face lost its normal all-purpose amiability as Salinger spoke. By the time he had finished Carson was grave and pensive.

For a while he didn't say anything. Instead, he rose from the bed and started very carefully folding up the clothes that Salinger had earlier deposited in a heap on the floor.

'You don't have to do that,' said Salinger softly.

'I don't mind.'

Carson folded each item tenderly and precisely, layering them one by one in a geometric pile on the bedside table. He barely glanced at the clothing as he deftly straightened edges and smoothed down collars. He stroked the clothes, he caressed them into shape.

'So what do you think?' said Salinger.

'It's kind of disturbing, I guess.'

'It's uncharacteristic.'

'How have you been getting on generally? I don't really know her, so . . .'

'She'd been a little out of sorts for a week or two. But Tiane's great.'

'What kind of woman is she?'

'The kind that doesn't hide behind make-up. Or anything. There's a nakedness to her. Entirely trustworthy. Honest. Got your number but never uses that information against you. Most of my relationships have been wreckage, even before they actually turned into wreckage. She's the only one that . . .'

He struggled to think what it was about Tiane that drew him so powerfully to her.

'She's so completely herself. I can't put it more simply than that. She doesn't care what anybody thinks about what she likes. She has terrible taste in everything – music, art, books. A bit like you, I guess.'

Carson smiled.

'But she doesn't care in the slightest, she likes

what she likes. That's so unlike most of the people I mix with.'

'What kind of people do you mix with?'

'People who aren't like Tiane.'

'I don't mean to pry but – is your sex life OK?'

Salinger shifted uncomfortably on the bed, and crossed his legs.

'I don't feel entirely at ease talking about that.'

'Do you trust her completely?'

Carson finished folding, ran his fingers across the pile of Salinger's clothes as if comforting them, then joined Salinger on the bed. He lay down on one side. His feet were bare. Salinger could see him flexing his toes. The toenails were perfectly manicured.

'What do you mean?'

'You don't think there could be someone else that she might be involved with?'

The laugh that Salinger heard himself issue felt unnatural and forced.

'That's just not in Tiane. She would never be unfaithful. There isn't the smallest bit of deceit in her. And if she was unfaithful, she would be completely unable to hide it.'

'Maybe that's why she can't reply to the emails.'

'You're really not making me feel better about this.'

'So why do you think she didn't want you to go away?'

Salinger shivered. The air conditioning was too high. He went to the window in the hope that he might be able to open it. As in every other chain hotel he had ever stayed in, it was unaccountably and infuriatingly sealed. He crossed the room and tried to turn the air conditioning down but he couldn't work out how the electronic remote controls worked. He gave up and sat back on the bed next to Carson.

'Well? What's your theory?' said Carson.

'I don't have a clue, Carzy. She's not a remotely needy person. Or a mysterious one, for that matter. It makes no sense.'

'I'm sure it's nothing. You'll see. When you get back, it will be fine.'

'Spare me the soft soap.'

Carson sighed, and started to take out the pyjamas he had insisted on buying along with the pants and jeans and T-shirts. They appeared to have remained perfectly pressed despite spending the day rammed into the pannier.

'How old is she?'

'She's forty this year.'

'You ever asked her to marry you?'

'It's not about that.'

'She want a kid?'

'I don't know why I bothered telling you about it.'

'Well, you asked me what I thought.'

'It's not the Bible belt, Carson. It's London. People don't have to get married and have a family to love one another. We're fine as we are.'

'OK, well, then you're fine.'

'We are.'

'Excellent.'

This appeared to be the end of the conversation. Salinger felt no better for unpacking his worries. In fact, he felt worse.

He decided to listen to some music downloads on his iPod, but the iPod wasn't where he remembered leaving it.

While Salinger was searching for it – the iPod finally turned up on the floor behind a standing lamp – Carson managed to get undressed and into his pyjamas without Salinger noticing. It occurred to him that not once on the journey had he seen Carson naked, or even in his shorts.

As Salinger searched the iTunes library, he thought again of Tiane. Although what Carson was saying struck him as wildly off beam, he did sometimes wonder if he failed to tell Tiane often enough how much he loved her – of the unshakeable commitment he felt towards her, his fierce concern for her happiness. He thought he would do anything for her. But she rarely asked him to do anything, and he had never quite found the knack of projecting his mind into hers – of putting himself into her shoes. It was a typically male failing, he supposed.

It came upon him in the moment that all he wanted to do was get out of the hotel room, out of the state, out of the country and back to Tiane. But it was impossible. He had to finish his business first. He had to come face to face with his father.

His thoughts trailed away. He didn't have the

faintest clue what he was going to say to Henry, if they ever found him in the first place – which he doubted. Henry, it seemed to him, didn't much want to be found.

Perhaps it was for a good reason. Salinger found himself wondering, momentarily, if Henry was wiser, and perhaps more merciful, than he had hitherto imagined.

CHAPTER 11

ACOMA PUEBLO (SKY CITY)

They left immediately after breakfast the next morning. As they cruised at a steady 50 mph, closing down the miles towards the pueblo, Salinger felt restless and vaguely irritable. His head ached. He had slept badly – there had been a party going on in the room above that had continued till 3 a.m. Carson had slept through it all without a murmur.

Salinger tried to centre himself by concentrating on the landscape. The trees had died out and the flat greenness had been replaced by looming red mesas and earth the colour of Kia-Ora. An immensely long freight train sliced across the empty desert in the distance.

The air and light started to lift his mood. His headache faded. After just over an hour the pueblo came into sight, a rack of low-rise habitations carved out of the summit of a huge sandstone cliff. As they approached, the cliff grew more and more immense. Carson pulled the bike up to the base of the summit, where there was a visitor centre and a café.

They headed into the café for a cup of coffee

before taking the tourist bus up to the pueblo. The place was slick and modern, furnished mainly in coloured plastic and selling elk burgers and bison burgers, Navajo fry bread, Acoma baked bread, and cappuccino coffee.

'I came here once with LouLou,' said Carson, ordering two cups of coffee. 'It's kind of magical.'

They took the coffee outside and shared a cigarette. Six or seven other visitors were spread across the waiting area lumbering with pendulous cameras, clip-on hip bags and towelling ankle socks. Salinger clutched his sketch book. He left the stub of his pencil behind his ear.

A bus pulled up and a young woman stepped off. She was sweating under a bizarre costume. Salinger started to sketch it – a plain black sheath dress with a narrow red band around the chest adorned with an electric-blue cloak of some roughly knitted or crocheted material. She had what appeared to be a necklace of bone and, behind that, a circular symbol, also blue, that appeared to represent the sun. On her left shoulder was an epaulette of white feathers out of which sprang clusters of green-and-white string, held together by a rainbow made of what appeared to be felt.

Strangest of all was her headgear. From the forehead to the tip of her nose, she wore a curtain veil that appeared to be made of some sort of synthetic pink material, perhaps nylon or viscose. On the right of her head, just at the hairline, was an enormous red feather. On the other side, a single narrow grey feather. And attached to the rear of her head, like a corona, or a halo, was a large fan of more feathers, brown and white, spread out in a semicircle.

'Hey,' said the woman in a tired voice.

'Hey,' muttered the waiting throng.

'How are ya?'

'How are *you*?' answered a bald, half-witted-looking elderly man wearing a tam-o'-shanter and check pants, and grinning hugely.

'Tell you the truth, I'm sweating like a whatcha-callit in this thing.'

She lifted up her curtain veil to reveal a pair of yellowish eyes. Salinger sketched faster. The girl was beautiful, in her mid-twenties, with skin that looked more oriental than Native American.

'We don't usually do this get-up for the tours. It's an Acoma dancing costume. There's a festival coming up at the weekend, so the management in their wisdom thought it might be an idea to get me done up like an Acoma go-go girl. I hope you're enjoying it, because I sure as hell ain't.'

There was a ripple of laughter. The woman let her veil fall back, and told the crowd to follow her. Carson stubbed out the cigarette and they followed the small throng on board.

The woman collected their tickets, muttering to herself. The bus engine started, and it immediately began weaving its way up the side of the cliff towards the pueblo.

The woman introduced herself as Tahoma of the

Big Sun Clan. Mechanically, she explained that Acoma Indians still lived in the settlement, though they mostly lived in the village of Acoma, fifteen miles away. They called Sky City by the original Navajo name, Haak'ooh. It was three hundred and sixty-seven feet high and composed of sandstone. Acoma meant 'people of the white rock'. The settlement comprised four villages, Acomita, McCarty's, Anzac and Sky Line.

The settlement – she continued – was founded in 1150 and was taken over by missionaries in the seventeenth century. After the Battle of Acoma, only two hundred and fifty Indians were left out of two thousand. The children were sold into slavery. The surviving men had their right foot cut off after an order by the Conquistador Don Juan de Oñate.

Tahoma seemed tough and knowing. She clearly didn't like being a tour guide much. Nevertheless, she had picked on various members of the group to strike up a rapport with. It was probably recommended by the tour guides' handbook, thought Salinger. Her eyes lighted on Carson.

'Hi. What's your name?'

'Carson.' Carson turned towards Salinger. 'And this is my brother, Salinger.'

The rest of the members of the coach party turned their heads in his direction. Salinger felt oddly flustered.

'Salinger Nash,' said Salinger.

'Hey, Salinger,' said Tahoma.

'Hi.'

'Where you from?'

'A land far away and long ago.'

'What?'

'England.'

'OK, let's give a welcome to our Founding Fathers,' said Tahoma, giving a brilliant smile.

A few of the people on the bus clapped and laughed.

'Wouldn't that be "colonial oppressors"?' said Salinger.

'Hell, we don't bear a grudge. Do we, folks?' She adjusted her crown of feathers, which habitually fell lopsided.

Still smiling, Tahoma turned away to another member of the party.

'Where you from?'

'Idaho.'

'She's pretty hot behind all that Red Indian camouflage,' whispered Carson.

'You're a married Christian about to start a family. And they call them Native Americans nowadays.'

'I'm just saying. I can say, right?'

The bus laboured up the hill, finally coming to a stop in the middle of the settlement. As the group exited the bus, a light rain began to fall. Salinger heard Tahoma curse, and she tried to protect her head feathers with a glossy copy of a guidebook to the pueblo. All around them were what appeared to Salinger to be unattractive mud huts dotted with what Tahoma informed them were *kornos*, beehive-shaped ovens in which the Acomas baked pueblo bread. Fifty yards away they could see the roof of the Catholic church, the Mission of San Esteban del Rey.

Tahoma began to dutifully recite how the church was built on forced labour. The stone for the walls was dragged from Kaweshtima, Mount Tailor Mountain, thirty miles away. If one of the stones touched the ground, the Acoma had to drag it all the way back again, since it was considered to have been defiled.

Salinger was looking over the wall that led to the drop three hundred and fifty feet below. The landscape spread out and away into the distance, an orange emptiness. Salinger seemed to be aware of an electric hum in his ears. The rain clouds were penetrated by ladders of light which reached down to the ground from the thunderheads. Intermittent and distant lightning connected the sky and the ground.

Tahoma led them towards the graveyard that stood in front of the church. The cemetery was surrounded by sandstone walls that were decorated with grotesque clay masks.

'The bell was a gift from Charles II of Spain . . . the cemetery has five layers of graves, forty feet deep . . . There are facial features on raised bumps around the wall of the cemetery . . . To bury the dead the Acoma Indians who had been converted carried earth up the winding trail to be able to have a burial ground. This is barren rock so the earth had to be packed on top.

'There is a retaining wall that is nearly fifty feet high at the outer portion and makes a square measuring two hundred feet across.'

Salinger wondered why all tour guides were so obsessed with statistics. He'd never met anyone who was remotely interested in statistics, other than sports fans and Tiane, who, as a teacher of mathematics, seemed to believe they held the secret of everything.

He liked the cemetery wall though. The carvings intrigued him. The demons exhibited a profound and untrammelled spite. He took his sketch pad out of his bag and started drawing. Tahoma immediately held up a reproving hand.

'No sketching, Salinger Nash. This is a sacred place.'

Salinger apologized, and put his pencil behind his ear. When Tahoma continued talking, she seemed to be addressing her remarks to Salinger. The mechanical aspect of her voice had given way to a more fluid and engaged tone. For the first time, Salinger felt that Tahoma was interested in what she herself was saying.

'They call this the enchanted mesa. Some visitors have told me that when they come to the pueblo they can see clearly. They see far into the distance of their own lives. Something special in the space or in the air.'

'Right,' muttered Salinger. He wanted her to

turn her back so that he could begin sketching again. But even when she turned to lead the group towards the church, she looked behind her frequently. He had the sense that she was constantly watching him from behind her veil. He decided not to risk it.

The small party made their way into the interior of the church, where there were giant paintings depicting purgatory.

'Both Acoma and Catholic religions are practised here,' said Tahoma, balancing unsteadily on a leather stool. 'There are paintings on buffalo hide. The new church was built on top of the *akivas*, old sacred places. To this day, masses are held by Franciscan monks on Sundays.'

Salinger examined the rainbows painted on walls, festooned with parrots. Tahoma had explained that monks had brought parrots here as it was supposed to encourage rainfall. There was a confessional box, a depiction of the Stations of the Cross and paintings of cornstalks.

'The traditions,' continued Tahoma, 'are always oral traditions, in which dancing, music, art, theology, astrology, philosophy and history are taught. The traditional foods that are planted here are beans, pumpkins, corn, chillies, onions, and fruits like apples, apricots, peaches, plums and cherries. The pueblo was photographed by Ansel Adams in 1941. Posters of that photograph are available in the gift shop.

'The church is forty feet wide and a hundred

and fifty feet long. Thirteen families are still living here in the pueblo. There is no water here, and no electricity.'

'What do they do in the evenings?' asked Carson brightly.

'They go to bed,' said Tahoma flatly.

Outside the light rain was little more than a mist. The tour was over, but the bus was not leaving for a further twenty minutes. The group began to spread out and break up.

Salinger examined the ancient *mica* windows and the *kiva* ladders – wooden, free-standing sacred ladders that were propped against the side of the huts. The rungs ran only halfway up the struts which continued into the sky. The idea was that they would pierce the clouds for rain. Some of the ladders had three struts instead of two. The ladders were also necessary for practical reasons since access to the houses was through a hole in the roof. They could be pulled up for security.

After a while, the group started to congregate once more in order to return to the bus. Salinger felt oddly claustrophobic, and went and stood at the edge of the mesa, looking out towards the west. He immediately felt clean and clear-headed.

A gap opened in a cloud and a lance of sunlight stretched from the sky to the ground. A military aircraft appeared overhead, screaming through the silence. Salinger felt a jolt in his mind. He rocked slightly back on his heels.

A sick, rising panic came upon him. A thought

had arrived out of the blue, out of the silence, out of the light.

An image of the Polaroid photograph came clearly into his mind. He saw it as if for the first time.

He swayed in the wind. The light blinded him. The rain had become heavier. It lashed at his cheeks. The noise of the aircraft faded into the distance. Low chatter from the rest of the tourist group seemed to fall away.

He heard words, but they made no sense. The landscape in front of his eyes fell away. He still saw the picture in his head, abruised, blackened, ruined face. He recognized the face now with perfect certainty.

He felt himself lose balance and teeter. He heard a voice behind him and felt a hand on his arm.

'You OK, Salinger?'

Salinger felt his consciousness flickering. His legs buckled. He became aware of Tahoma standing next to him. He put his weight on her shoulder. She held him up. Light poured into his mind, buckling it.

Tahoma led Salinger back to the bus. Inside, Carson was reading a pocket Bible, half the size of a paperback. Salinger sat next to him. Carson didn't look up. Salinger said nothing.

When they arrived at the visitor centre, Carson tipped Tahoma ten dollars, but Salinger gave nothing. He still felt unsteady on his feet. They made their way out of the heat into the air-conditioned interior. Carson said he was going to the bathroom and to visit the museum and gift shop. There was an exhibition with the unenticing title of 'One Thousand Years of Clay'. Salinger told Carson that he would take a rain check, and ordered himself a coffee.

Salinger sat alone in the café. After a while, most of the party that had been with them on the visit to the mesa drifted off. The café was deserted apart from Salinger and the serving staff, who were clearing crockery from the tables. Salinger felt himself breathing rapidly.

He reached inside his bag and took out the Polaroid from where he kept it in a zipped pocket, and removed it from the protective envelope. He stared at it blankly.

He wondered why anyone – presumably his mother – would have taken a photograph of such a thing in the first place.

He looked up and saw a woman wearing blue jeans, cowboy boots and a Harley Davidson T-shirt walk towards him. It took him a moment or two to figure out that it was Tahoma. She nodded in his direction. He looked away, obscurely ashamed of his collapse at the pueblo. Tahoma, undeterred, came and sat beside him, carrying a bottle of Evian water.

'You OK, Salinger?'

She took a sip of the Evian. Salinger looked up. At close range, her features were truly startling. Her hair was purest black. Her eyes were slanted, the eyelids so low they were barely more than slits. The eyes glittered. Her skin looked as if it had been polished. Her mouth was small and her nose on the large side, but the element of imperfection added to the impact. Salinger could barely look at her.

'What happened up there, Salinger?'

'I don't really want to talk about it.'

Salinger could smell vanilla. He wondered if it was her perfume, or her natural odour.

'It's not the first time I've seen people lose it up there,' said Tahoma, lowering her voice. 'I know you think this is just tourist-guide shit, but there is something weird about the pueblo. Don't know if it's really enchanted. Maybe it's the air. Ozone or something. Some people go a little whacky. They remember things they'd forgotten. They become aware of things that they were never aware of. I've seen it.'

Salinger wanted to be left alone, but he felt unable to ask Tahoma to leave.

'You seem troubled, Salinger.'

'This part of the tour?' Salinger said sharply, sucking down the last of his coffee.

He felt Tahoma's hand on the back of his. It felt so soft he was barely sure that it was touching.

'I have a sister. Lives down by Pecos. Near Marfa, Texas. She can help.'

'I don't need help.'

Tahoma reached into the pocket of her jeans and brought out a small, worn, brown-leather purse. She reached inside and pulled out a crudely printed card which read *Native Indian Healing*. On the flip side of the card was a hand-sketched map.

'Take this anyway.'

'I'm not going in that direction. We're just going as far as Las Cruces. To see my father.'

'Take it all the same. You can never be sure what direction you end up taking.'

Salinger took the card and put it in his pocket. Over Tahoma's shoulder, he could see Carson approaching with a white stone pot, the size of a grapefruit. It was decorated with representations of birds, flowers, and swirling geometric patterns.

'Present for LouLou. Only fifty bucks. Hey, Tahini. You flirting with my brother? He's got a girlfriend already back in London.'

'My name is Tahoma. Tahini is a dip.'

Carson sat down, cradling the pot. Tahoma rose from the chair.

'I would never have guessed you were brothers,' said Tahoma, finishing her water and tossing the bottle into a trashcan.

She began to walk away but turned once more.

'Salinger. Her name is Wakanda. I'm not jazzing you. She has a real gift.'

Tahoma walked away. Carson put the stone jug on the table and fidgeted with Salinger's empty coffee cup.

'Who the hell is Wakanda?' he said, wiping a coffee stain from the table with a paper tissue.

CHAPTER 12

LAS CRUCES

D usk was easing out the last of the day as they reached the outskirts of Las Cruces. They did not speak during the ride except for the point at which Carson pointed out a road-runner, which, to Salinger's disappointment, looked nothing like the cartoon.

It had three long feathers spread out like a fan protruding from the end of its body, a body shorter than the feathers, and a protuberant beak. It was profoundly ugly. Neither was it running, but standing still, staring at them, as if its feelings had been hurt. It had something sticking out of the edge of its beak which Carson claimed was the rear end of a rattlesnake. Snakes were apparently a big part of a roadrunner's diet. It also ate birds, spiders and lizards. According to Carson, it was a member of the cuckoo family. Its call was like that of a pigeon.

Or so Carson claimed. Salinger believed that his fund of useless information was at least half made up. He just liked to think he knew it all. It was a genetic thing – all firstborn children, so far as he could make out, lived under the same illusion.

They came in on the I–25, which traced a geological sink, the Jornada del Muerto. The heat showered from the skies and then rose up from the road to meet itself. They watched antelope grazing – Las Cruces was built on the corona of fertile ground that surrounded the Rio Grande. You could see the tree line stop on either side and then give way to desert again. But where the antelope fed, the grass was thick and rich.

Salinger, as they came towards the outskirts, felt vaguely disoriented by the sheer lowness, the spreadoutness of it all, the relentlessness of the commercial messages, of pleas, demands, invocations, offers and promises. At the edge of his vision, strange pink and orange adobe houses dotted the outer suburbs, punctuating the *arroyos*.

When they arrived at the Hotel Encanto, Carson steered the bike into the parking lot. As soon as he had switched the engine off his cell phone rang. He picked up while Salinger busied himself with unloading his side of the pannier. Salinger fumbled with the metal catch, snicking his finger as he unpicked it. He felt sweaty and tired. His legs ached from the ride.

The journey had numbed him slightly. The landscape was so unchanging – mesa, desert, sky, thunderheads, straggled clouds – and the roads were so cruelly straight. In the distance he could see a great hunk of rock topped with a ragged skyline of the Organ Mountains, now splashed red with the setting sun, looming over the uninflected flatness.

Carson yanked off his helmet and beckoned excitedly to Salinger.

'Guess who this is?'

'Is it Jesus?'

'He wants to know if I'm talking to the idiot.'

'The patrolman? What does he want? Did he decide to arrest me on charges of criminal incompetence?'

'He says "Tell the idiot that we found the car that he lost."'

Salinger stopped unloading the pannier. Two pairs of underpants and a white T-shirt dangled from his hands.

'They really did it, Sal. The cops found the car,' said Carson, grinning from ear to ear.

Carson returned to his conversation with Wendell Valentine as Salinger stuffed the clothes back into the pannier and fumbled for cigarettes and matches in his shoulder bag. The return of the Lexus seemed to call for celebratory fire.

Behind the hotel the stars were just starting to come out. Salinger could smell sand, and cooking grease from the hotel kitchens.

Carson clicked off the phone. Salinger offered him a cigarette, but Carson waved it away. His eyes were sparkling with excitement.

'*Knew* they would find that car. Just knew it.'

'No – you didn't.'

'After I prayed, I did know it. Now I won't have

to stall with LouLou any more. Jesus, what a relief.'

'Isn't that blasphemous?'

'Christ almighty, who cares?'

'Is it OK? Is it in good condition?'

'Not a single fricking scratch. And our luggage is completely intact. Five pieces.'

'Now I get why you believe in miracles.'

'You said it, bro.'

'Makes the Resurrection look like something David Blaine would cook up. A whole different order of improbability.'

'No, listen though. It gets better still. Wendell is driving it out here for us. That's right! Be here sometime tomorrow. He's got friends in Cruces, knows the bike-shop owner, and he's going to take the bike back to Amarillo with him.'

'You're fucking with me now.'

'Only in America, bro. Only in America.'

Salinger threw his cigarette to the ground and stamped on it. He held up his hand for Carson to give him a high five. Carson slapped his palm and gave a whoop and a skip.

They made their way happily into the hotel lobby, each clutching a pannier bag. Despite Carson's promise that it was 'boutique-y' it was little different from a Holiday Inn – bland and impersonal, with floral-print soft furnishings, veneer on the woodwork and cladding on the walls. The look was standard corporate. In its determination to offend no one, Salinger found

it tiresome. But his buoyant mood was indestructible.

'Nice place,' said Carson. 'Told you you'd like
it.'

He went to the check-in, whistling 'The Yellow
Rose of Texas' to himself.

'I half wish I'd told LouLou about having the
car stolen now, if only so I could tell her that I
got it back,' he said over his shoulder, as the clerk
handed him a pen.

After check-in, they both took a shower, then
went downstairs to the bar to order a drink. The
bar had a low ceiling, and was furnished in dark-
brown wood with carriage lamps on the pillars.
So many American bars were designed to embrace
gloom. He supposed they mistook it for cosiness.
There were two inset mirrored arches in front of
which the spirits were displayed. They studied the
exotically unfamiliar liquors on sale – Blue Agave
Tequila, Black Star Farms Grappa, Basil Hayden's
Bourbon – then inspected the cocktail menu. They
both ordered margaritas. Carson still seemed zippy
with excitement. He slapped Salinger on the back,
nearly spilling the crushed ice that slopped about
in the frosty brackish liquid.

'Everything's working out so *good*, Sally. If the
car hadn't got stolen, we'd never have taken this
cycle ride. So . . .'

'So you can never tell how things are going to
shake out, I guess.'

'Right! I *said* everything has a purpose! And now

we're going to see Dad! Together! I can hardly get my head round it.'

Salinger stirred the slurry of ice with a swizzle stick. The end that protruded from the glass featured an orange plastic flamingo.

'I don't want to piss on your Popeye's fried chicken, Carzy. But seeing Dad might not be so great. You should think about managing expect-ations.'

Carson took a swig from his margarita, still smiling relentlessly.

'You're so *negative*, bro. Come on! We've having the journey of a lifetime, we've become good friends – haven't we? And now we're going to meet our long-lost dad – the old rogue. It's going to be great, I just know it.'

Carson started nodding furiously. Salinger stared at the football game that was stopping more than it was starting on the giant TV in the corner of the bar.

'I just don't want you to get hurt, Carson.'

'Me? I'm a pretty tough guy. I don't do all that boo-hoo stuff. That's your department – the sensi-tive artist, right? I know whatever Dad throws at me, it'll be OK. He's had his reasons. But he loves us both. How can you not love your own children? Hell, mine isn't even born yet and I love him more than . . . more than . . . I don't know . . .'

He paused for a moment. When he spoke again, his voice had moved down several registers, from ebullience to measured, deadly seriousness.

'More than my life, Sally. I love Henry Jnr more than my life.'

He looked at Salinger meaningfully.

'Carzy . . .'

Carson brushed aside Salinger with a wave of his hand. His voice lifted again.

'Hey, let's have another margarita. These are pretty good margaritas, ain't they? Hey . . .'

His eyes scanned the name tag of the bar waiter.

'Hey, Duane. How about another couple of these cocktails? They are pretty good. No salt for me for though, this time.'

'Yes, sir.'

The bartender began mixing the drinks. Salinger picked up some cocktail biscuits from the bar and started crunching them. They were stale. The pulp stuck between his teeth, stubborn as wallpaper paste.

'I just think maybe you're getting your hopes up a little high, Carson. He didn't even give us his address. What does that tell you?'

'It's just a game – a little test to make sure that we really want to find him.'

'Maybe he doesn't want us to find him.'

Salinger took a sip of the drink, felt grateful for the kick.

'Can I say something?'

'You gonna give me some *insight*, bro?'

Carson kicked at the bar lazily with the tip of his shoe. His eyes were slightly glazed. The margarita seemed to have blurred him from the inside.

'Yeah, I'm going to give you an insight. I

think you have a lot of trouble with being honest about your feelings.'

'All righty!'

'You never really like to show vulnerability. Never like to show – never will acknowledge – that anything might hurt you.'

'Man, here we go. Another one of Salinger's half-baked dime-store psychiatrist theories.'

Carson said this entirely amiably as the bartender delivered the fresh drinks.

'Just because the theories are mine doesn't mean they're wrong.'

Carson took a sip of the cocktail.

'It's an intriguing thought, Doctor Salinger. But I really don't want to go there.'

'Why not?'

'Because it just leads to conflict. Because the past is gone. Because I think your theory of psychology has more holes than a warehouseful of big Swiss cheeses. A warehouse with a big hole in the floor.'

'What is my "theory of psychology"?'

'Either people are reacting against something or copying it. That's what it all amounts to. So I ran to America to be like Dad, you became an artist to not be like me, or to be like Dad, Dad ran to America to not be like his father – you can explain anything at all that way. It don't explain *zip*.'

'It's a bit of a coincidence that Dad moved out here, fell in love and married someone and you did the same, though.'

'You're always looking for *meanings*.'

He spat the word like a scrap of peanut shell.

'I just happened to fall in love with someone when I moved out here, not to "be like Dad", or to pursue him. I liked the weather. I fell in love with a woman. I had nothing in England to keep me there. It was pure circumstance – simple as that.'

'So what's your explanation then?'

'Of what?'

'Of the way people are? Of the way they turn out?'

'There is no explanation. Things just are.'

Salinger frowned. Carson pulled at his drink and swayed on his stool slightly. His eyelids were beginning to droop.

'Why are you always discontented, Sal?'

'The usual reasons.'

'Those being?'

'Those being that everyone's alone and nothing makes sense and death makes everything small.'

Carson stared blearily at Salinger's reflection in the bar mirror.

'Yeah – but apart from that.'

'Apart from that?'

Salinger squeezed his eyes together and tried to think. The drink was clouding his mind.

'It's because I can't find a story that fits, I guess.'

'That fits *what*?'

'That fits the facts. That fits my life.'

Carson shrugged, turned away from the bar mirror and looked into his glass.

'I don't get it. Story. Facts. What's the difference?'

'That question is the difference between you and me.'

'It's the difference between you and most normal people.'

'At last, you're being honest about it. You think I'm a loony. A nutjob . . .'

'I didn't mean that. Anyway, not everyone is such a big fan of honesty as you are.'

Carson had started rearranging a matchbox on the counter, balancing it on one side, then another, then a third.

'After all, you're so honest that you snooped on my computer.'

Carson stared straight at Salinger. He no longer seemed drunk. Salinger felt the colour in his cheeks begin to bloom. He hoped the low light would not make the blush obvious.

'What are you talking about?'

'You don't know what I'm talking about?'

'No.'

'Salinger Nash – the truth-teller. The keeper of the flame. That's a double bust. You snooped and now you're denying being a snoop. On the day we left New Orleans, you used my computer without telling me.'

'Oh *that*. So? That's not a criminal act, is it?'

'Seems strange not to mention it.'

'It didn't seem important.'

'That you hacked into my password?'

'I didn't think you would mind.'

'Struck me as kind of sneaky.'

Carson paused, took a sip of the margarita.

'Find anything interesting on there?'

'I just checked my emails.'

'And that's the truth too – is it?'

Carson was looking unblinkingly into Salinger's eyes. Salinger looked directly back at them.

He wished now he'd looked in the hidden folders, and been hanged for a sheep as much as a lamb. The trouble with virtue, he thought to himself, was that it was always so disappointing compared with the unlimited possibility of sin. All that mattered, finally, was whether you were found out or not.

'That's the truth,' Salinger lied.

The next morning they rose early. It was a Monday. Salinger had been in America for a week. Already commuters were jammed down the highway heading for the long, existentially indispensable American workday.

Both Salinger and Carson had kept back a clean set of clothes ready for the visit to Henry. Carson was whistling to himself and carefully ironing a pair of jeans and a T-shirt. Salinger was searching in vain for his one remaining clean pair of under-shorts. Eventually he gave up and hauled out the pair he'd worn the day before.

'You're a pretty unsanitary guy,' said Carson idly, holding up his T-shirt to inspect it critically.

Unsatisfied, he replaced it on the ironing board and attacked a small wrinkle by the hem.

'I'm just an average Limey soap dodger. We just don't have the same anxiety about germs as Yanks. We kind of accept them as part of life.'

'This some new liberal poster campaign? "I Heart Bacteria"?'

'We just don't think that every tiny thing is out to kill us. So anyway. Where are we going to start looking for Dad?'

'Last time I visited him there was this café he and I went to.'

'This was after he told you he wasn't interested in keeping in contact?'

'No, before. It was at the café he broke the news.'

'Were you upset?'

'I sort of accepted it, I guess. Can't quite remember what the place was called – hell, it was, what? Twenty years ago? – but I remember roughly where it was. It was in a sort of bohemian part of town. This isn't that big a place. Someone in that café will know where he is. So . . .'

'What if he's not here?'

'I haven't really considered that possibility, Sal. Why wouldn't he be here?'

'Because he's the kind of person who just disappears.'

'You got a lot of negative energy poppin' around inside your dome.'

'It's like bad hygiene. Just an English thing. It means we can avoid disappointment.'

'By having no hope. That's sucks as a trade-off. Henry will be there. Don't worry about it. First, though, we have to meet up with Wendell.'

'He's here already?'

'Drove through the night. Said he would meet us for breakfast and then we can switch keys.'

'I don't like that he calls me the idiot.'

'Just don't be rude to him. The guy brought the Lexus all the way over here from Amarillo. He's taking the bike back for us. He's being nice. Americans are like that. They're pathologically nice until you piss them off, and then they shoot you. So just try and act American for a half-hour, will you? It's easy. Just smile and act dumb.'

Wendell was returning from the breakfast buffet when they came down to the hotel café. His gaze fell on Salinger, his bullfrog eyes giving a single blink.

'Hey, idiot. How ya doing?'

'Fine, thank you, officer.'

'Listen, idiot, call me Wendell.'

'Fine, thanks, Wendell.'

Wendell held out a hand, which first Salinger shook, then Carson.

'Food here is pretty terrible. Sure ain't the Big Texan in terms of quality.'

Wendell sat back down again and picked at a stack of pancakes with his fork.

'Did you have a good journey?' said Carson, sitting on the chair opposite. There were paper napkins on the table and a jug of tepid water with lemon slices in it.

'Pretty good. I got eyes that can see in the dark. Like a cat.'

He widened his lids, making his bulbous eyes appear to stick out further.

'Mind if I have some of this coffee?' said Salinger, taking the third seat and pouring himself a cup without waiting for a response.

'That's a nice car your brother's got there. Drives like a beauty. What kind of car you drive back in jolly old London, idiot?'

'I don't have a car.'

Wendell looked genuinely puzzled by this.

'You shitting me, English?'

'You don't really need one when you live in London. Anyway, they damage the environment.'

'Should have thought of that before you flew three thousand miles here. And back again, I guess, if you can find your way to the goddamn airport.'

'How did you find the car?' said Carson.

Wendell rocked back in the chair, balancing it on the two rear legs. A button in his shirt popped just at the top of his belly. Small, wiry hairs sprang out of the gap.

'Now this took me by surprise, but seems there's more than one idiot in the world. Some dumb Mexicano tried to just go right ahead and unload it at a used-car lot out in the 'burbs. The salesman takes one look at this guy with his dime-store shirt and paisano's hands, and asks himself the obvious question. How come this wetback got a solid gold-plated whitebread wheels? Then the salesman made like he had a good offer to throw him, but he had to check with the supervisor. Made a phone call to us instead. Not exactly original, but that's the great thing about dummies. You don't *have* to be original. The salesman kept stalling him. Gave him a cigarette, talked about the ball game, told him how much he admired his fucking hat and his stupid moustache. Ten minutes later we turned up, arrested idiot number two and took back the car.'

Wendell's disapproval of the pancakes didn't seem to be acting as a check on his appetite. He rocked the chair forward again, wolfed down the sixth and final pancake in the stack, and licked his lips with a tongue that, Salinger noted, carried a thick coat of grey-white fur.

'There's really no damage?'

'Hell no. They actually polished the thing so they might get a better price. Damn well near *valeted* the sucker. Idiot number two gave up his address after we took him to the rest room and threatened to waterboard him with some tap water and a hand towel. So we went back to his house and found all your luggage – the clothes, toiletries, the lot. They're in the trunk. These pancakes suck dick. Taste like chalk and toffee with ground-up indigestion tablets. You two going to eat?'

'Guess I'll have some more pancakes. Just can't seem to shake off this hunger today.'

He beckoned for the waitress. A gargantuan white middle-aged woman staggered to their table wearing a hotel uniform – a tight, knee-length orange skirt and polyester mustard-coloured blouse that she could only just squeeze into – and took his order. Salinger and Carson asked for coffee and toast. The waitress waddled back to the kitchen.

'Worked up an appetite on that drive and I'm going to need some food inside me for the cycle ride back. Looking forward to that. Just like *Easy Rider*, right?'

'Except that you're a cop.'

'Yeah, 'cept for that.'

He chuckled, and picked up a spoon to scoop from the pool of maple syrup.

'How long you in town for?'

'I'm staying for the night with a buddy. We're going to go out drinking, drink ourselves into a damn stupor, fall over, make ourselves *real* sick, and then we're going to get up in the morning and regret it all over the place. And then I'm going to have to drive the three hundred and fifty damn miles back to Rillo. It'll sweep the cobwebs off. That's a nice bike. Rick always does nice bikes, good clean machines. You messed it up at all?'

'Not a scratch on it.'

'You been driving it, idiot, or did you leave it all to big brother here?'

Wendell's second order of pancakes arrived and he set about demolishing them with a metronomic efficiency. Syrup . . . cut . . . stuff . . . swallow . . . syrup . . . cut . . . stuff . . . swallow.

'Wendell,' said Salinger finally. 'You know I thought it was pretty funny when you started calling me idiot. But – well – don't you think the joke has worn off a little bit?'

'Not for me, amigo.'

'It *is* kind of amusing,' said Carson.

'After all, man, you are a pretty big goddamn idiot, wouldn't you agree, Salinger old chap, wot wot?'

Wendell's teeth showed through as he ripped his face with an enormous grin. They were yellow and scraps of pancake and syrup were stuck between the gaps.

'Yes, I'm an idiot. I acknowledge it. But can't you think of it as a sort of disability? You wouldn't laugh at a cripple, would you? Or call them cripple?'

'Guess not.'

'So I'd appreciate it if you'd just call me Salinger.'

'Man, you artists are real sensitive, ain't he, Carson? That's what it says on your passport, right? Artist?'

'That's right.'

Wendell regarded Salinger carefully. Then he put down his knife and fork and cleared his throat.

'OK, OK, Sally boy. I'll stop busting your balls. But you're still a goddamn idiot. And don't you forget it.'

'I've never really been allowed to.'

'Well why the hell don't you do something about it?'

'I've tried.'

'Has he tried, big brother?'

Now Wendell was slooching at a huge mug of coffee.

'He's tried. He's always tried. He can't help it.'

'You got a real good big brother there, Sally. Can I ask you two something? What the hell are you doing driving across Texas anyway? I thought you two was faggots.'

'Not the first time someone has made that mistake,' said Salinger.

'We're looking for our father,' said Carson.

'You lost your father?'

'He lost himself. Left home in England thirty years ago to come to America, and we never saw him again.'

'Except that Carson did,' said Salinger.

'Just for a day. Back in '88.'

Wendell looked puzzled.

'So he didn't want to see you? Your own father?'

Salinger and Carson both nodded, accidentally in perfect synchronization.

'Man, you guys look like two of them Chinese cats they sell in dime stores. Hell, though, that's hard about your pop. So why you out looking for him now? Still haven't given up – right?'

'That's right. Also he's ill.'

'Might be your last chance, that right?'

'I guess.'

Wendell nodded ruminatively. He picked a fragment of pancake from his trousers.

'I don't want to rain on your parade or anything. But – I'm just saying this for your own good, mind – don't expect too much.'

'I don't. Carson does,' said Salinger.

'I think it'll be OK,' said Carson calmly.

'I'm telling you, Carzy – Carzy, is that what your brother calls you, right?'

Carson nodded.

'I'm telling you, Carzy. My own father left us long ago, me and my own idiot brother, when we was boys. I went looking for him, just like you. Found him too. Found him in a gutter in Tucson, lying in his own puke. He didn't even recognize me. Or maybe he did, I don't know. Didn't show any sign of it if he did. That's how I remember him now. That's the face I can remember. Red and broken blood vessels everywhere. The puke.'

'Did you talk to him?' said Salinger.

'Yeah, I took out my badge and told him to move along. He didn't recognize me. He got up to go. I told him to clear up his puke before he went. He wiped it up with his blanket, then walked off carrying the blanket. Guess he slept under it that night.'

'You sorry you found him?'

'Sure I'm sorry. This is what I'm trying to tell you. If I hadn't looked for him, I would have at least remembered him differently. How you remember someone matters. In my case, as a person instead of a piece of street trash. That's just my experience. All I'm saying is, Carzy, watch out for yourself. People can hurt you when you don't think you can be hurt no more. They don't even have to try. They don't even have to know who you are.'

He swilled back the last of the coffee and stood up.

'OK, lecture con-cluded. Carzy, show me the cycle. And here's your keys. Or shall I leave them with your darling brother? Who ain't an idiot whatsoever, right?'

Wendell threw the car keys over to Carson who deftly caught them.

'One more thing. You know what I think. But if you have trouble finding him and all, you have my cell number. I might be able to help. I don't know why, but I like you boys in a funny kind of way. Sometimes I'm a natural fool like that.'

Wendell shook Carson's hand, then Salinger's. His grip was bruising.

The three of them made their way out into the car lot. Wendell put on Carson's rented motorcycle helmet and kicked the bike off the stand.

'Don't forget. Call me if there's any need, now.'

'OK, Wendell,' said Salinger.

'I wasn't talking to you, idiot,' said Wendell.

He revved the engine, which issued a mighty roar. Then the exhaust coughed and made a noise like a gunshot. Wendell raised a hand in farewell and cruised out of the lot, heading in the direction of the mountains.

Carson and Salinger spent the morning visiting haunts that Carson imagined Henry might frequent. They focused on what was as close to a town centre as a suburban spread like Las Cruces possessed, Mesilla Plaza. A stone plaque announced that Mesilla Park was where the Butterland Overland Trail stopped. The legend explained that this was an early rival to the Pony Express. The green itself was a square bordered by nineteenth-century houses and shops and dotted with pecan trees.

On one corner, a sign announced, was the court-house where Billy the Kid was tried, later to be hanged. Which was confusing, because Salinger had always thought that Billy the Kid was shot by Pat Garrett. It was now a souvenir shop, selling Hopi kachinas, authentic Indian headdresses, chilli posters. There was a Billy the Kid fortune-teller machine. Salinger put in a quarter. The card that came out was blank. He considered asking for a refund then just threw the card in a trashcan.

Outside there was a bandstand where, according to Carson, mariachi bands played at the weekends and during festival times. Painted signs outside red-brick buildings trumpeted that they dated back as far as 1860. A T-shirt advertised twelve reasons why handguns were better than women. A Catholic church on one side of the square sounded pre-recorded digital bells on the hour. All around there were agave cacti and ocotillo and azalea bushes.

'In spring it all bursts into colour,' said Carson. 'That's when I last came here, in spring. Hey! I think the café Dad and I went to was over here.'

He pointed to the west of the square then started striding purposefully towards it. Salinger followed him. The café was located down a side alley. It seemed to have no name and made no attempt to advertise itself. The entrance was a plain doorway with a faded sign above it that simply had the letter M on it.

'I guess it stands for Mesilla,' said Carson.

'Or Macguffin,' said Salinger.

'No, it would be Mesilla,' said Carson flatly.

They entered the dark and unpromising doorway. The place inside was small, and the tables and chairs were old and rickety. There was a young woman with dirty straw-blonde hair and a very large mole the colour of a raspberry on her bottom lip standing behind the counter, mopping at it listlessly with a dirty cloth. She wore a stained gingham apron. It seemed that they were the only customers and that she was the only member of staff. There was a sepulchral atmosphere. They found themselves lowering their voices.

'It's different from how I remember it,' whispered Carson. 'You couldn't get a table last time. The place was heaving. We could hardly hear ourselves talk.'

'Maybe it's the wrong time of day,' said Salinger.

'Can I help you gentlemen?' said the woman, not looking up from the scratched melamine surface that she was wiping down with a soiled rag.

'Well hi!' said Carson, flashing her one of his bright, generic, invitational smiles. The woman made no response. 'How are ya!'

The woman simply nodded and continued to dab at the counter.

'I was wondering . . . It's a bit strange, I know, but we're looking for someone. An old man, well, not old, he's sixty-four years old. About five foot ten, got a slight stoop, ears stick out a little like this.'

He pushed his ears forward then let them flap back.

'English accent. Used to live here, maybe twenty years ago, came back a little while ago. This used to be his favourite café. I just thought you might know where I could find him.'

'I doubt that this was his favourite café,' said the woman sourly. She finally raised her head. She looked profoundly indifferent to everything. 'You want to order something?'

'Well, we would like some coffee, yes,' said Carson. 'It's just this man is our father, and we very much need to find him. If he doesn't come here any more, I just thought you might have some kind of an idea what sort of place he might go, where someone like that might, if you will, frequent. An artist, I mean. A writer.'

'What kind of coffee you want?'

'What you got?'

'Ordinary drip. Caf and decaf.'

'OK. Two cups of ordinary drip.'

'Caf or decaf?'

'Caf, right? Caf.'

'Anything to eat?'

Carson examined the glass counter containing dried-out-looking cookies and a few apologetic pastries.

'No thanks. As I was just saying, I was just wondering, do you know a café where, you know, an artist – a writer – might go to hang out around here?'

'I doubt it.'

The woman turned her back and began pouring the coffee into two grimy-looking but enormous mugs. She reached out and hit a button. Loud music began to reverberate, something by a bad country rock singer. Garth Brooks, Salinger speculated, but then that was the only modern country singer he'd heard of, other than Billy Ray Cyrus, whom he had only discovered in Crawford.

Carson and Salinger sipped once at the dishwater weakness of their coffees, threw a few dollars on the counter and left. They stood outside squinting at the sunlight. Carson put his sunglasses on, aviator-style Ray-Bans, and stuck his hands against his hips.

'So now what?' said Salinger.

'We look at all the other coffee joints around

this place. One of them Henry's got to be hanging at. People would remember him. He hasn't lost his accent like I have. Leastways not last time I spoke to him. We'll stay on his trail. It'll be fine.'

They spent the morning trekking from one café to another. Most of them suffered the opposite problem of the M café – they were cheery, bright and dull. They simply weren't the sort of places that Henry would hang out in.

Eventually, they located two places around half a mile from the Plaza itself. Each of them was filled with people wearing European-style clothes, or reading the *New York Times*, or poring through books with literary-looking covers. None of them, however, remembered having seen a sixty-four-year-old Englishman.

'How long since he actually arrived back here?' asked Salinger, as they made their way to the eighteenth coffee house of the day.

'I don't know,' said Carson. 'I only know when I got the letter. She didn't say how long it was they'd been back in Cruces.'

'How the hell are we going to find him?'

'We'll find him,' said Carson. But his grin had faded.

They spent the rest of the day checking the local newspaper files, the library, the local telephone directory, the few small gallery spaces in the city. There was nothing. As night crowded in, even Carson started looking dispirited.

'He's got to be here somewhere, man. I mean, the old guy wouldn't just play a practical joke on us, would he? So . . .'

'He's a strange person, Carson. Like Wendell said, some people just like to disappear.'

'But he must want to see us. He must. He just must.'

Carson was staring out the window of the bar they were sitting in, trying to console themselves with whiskey sours. Salinger scrutinized Carson's face carefully. There was frustration there, but no pain, he thought. Carson didn't do pain. It was one of those American lifestyle choices.

'You ring LouLou today?'

'Yeah. She didn't answer.'

'Think something's wrong?'

'Nah. I'll call her tomorrow. She's probably just left her phone somewhere. She does that sometimes. Come on, Sally. You live off your imaginings. Where is Henry? What do you think?'

'I don't know, Carzy. I'm not even sure that he's here.'

'We can't wander the streets for ever looking for him.'

'I don't see what other choice we have if we want to find him.'

'Think, Sally. *Think*.' Carson stared at his whiskey sour, which he hadn't touched.

A police car siren sounded outside. Momentarily the room was filled with blue light, which then faded. Salinger smiled.

'There is one obvious avenue which we seem to have overlooked.'

'There is?'

'Wendell.'

'Wendell? Wendell! Of course.'

Carson immediately took his cell phone out of his pocket and hit the speed dial button. Carson's face lit up as Wendell answered.

'Wendell! How are you?'

Carson nodded as he listened. He brought his free hand to his mouth and tilted it back in a gesture – thumb to mouth, fingers twisting back – implying that Wendell was seriously drunk.

'Listen, Wendell, I'm glad you're having a good time. Sounds like it's a real party. No, it's a terrific town. Yes. Well, OK, it's not that terrific. But look, you said you might be able to help us find our father. Yes. Does that offer still hold? Great. His name. Henry Neville Nash. Hmm? He's sixty-four years old. Born 8 May 1944. Correct. Great. Well, we'll wait to hear from you.'

Carson clicked off.

'Absolutely no chance. I don't even think he knew what he was saying. He sounded completely unhinged.'

Salinger felt his spirits slump.

'I guess we might as well just go back to the hotel.'

'I guess.'

'I hate the place.'

'Yeah, I shoulda stuck to the Holiday Inns.'

They lapsed into a mournful silence.

'Wanna go out and look at the stars?' said Carson quietly.

'The stars?' said Salinger.

'Last time I came out here, I took a drive out into the desert to look at the stars. The air is very clear out here. You can see the sky go almost milky white. Can't really do it from inside the city limits, but if you take a twenty-minute drive, it's an awesome sight.'

'Sure. Got nothing better to do. Anyway, I like stars.'

'Who doesn't?'

Carson drained the whiskey sour. The Lexus was parked outside. They climbed in and Carson set a course due east. He put on a Grateful Dead track, 'Dark Star'.

'You like this?'

'It's a little schematic.'

'Pardon?'

'Just keep driving.'

They carried on listening to the track in silence as they headed out of town. It was eleven minutes long. Just as it was fading away, Carson turned the car into a side road, and then after another mile pulled the car over and shut the engine and the lights.

'Wanna burn one?'

They got out of the car and Carson lit them both a cigarette. Salinger looked up. He rocked back on his heels slightly.

He actually felt slightly frightened. The sky seemed truly immense. The stars turned the black night into tinted milk. The universe seemed immensely *present* – here and now to a hallucinogenic degree.

'I've never seen a starscape like that, Carzy.'

'Pretty neat, huh?'

Carson was smiling his all-purpose Carson smile, the same for ordering coffee or contemplating the wonders of the universe.

'All those dead stars. You know that we're seeing them years after they really are? That the light takes that long to get here?'

'I wish you wouldn't spoil things by trying to be intelligent, Carzy. Yeah, it's all in the past. The stars died long ago. Yada yada.'

'You know that, huh?'

'It's widely known.'

'Not in Louisiana it ain't.'

'It is in Tokyngton. And most of Brent, I imagine.'

Carson and Salinger carried on staring up at the heavens. Every thirty seconds or so, they could see a shooting star trace a belt in the sky.

'You know what I don't get, though?'

'What don't you get, Carson?'

'If we're seeing those stars as they used to be, then if there was people living on those stars, then they would see us as we used to be. Right?'

'But there aren't people on the stars.'

'Yeah, I know. They're too hot. I get that it ain't fairy dust. No, that's not the point. Anyway, who's to say who is where in the universe. The thing is, if you were far enough away and you were looking back at the earth, if you had a really *really* powerful telescope then you could see things from the past, because the light, it would be old light, correct?'

'I suppose.'

'So if you had a good enough telescope and you pointed it at our bedroom from – I don't know – that red star up there.'

'I think that's Mars,' said Salinger.

'Whatever, it doesn't *matter*. Just so long as it's far. Then if you pointed that telescope, you would be able to see you and me as kids, in our house back by the cemetery. Because that light is just out there, it doesn't disappear. It's indestructible. And if you could get far enough away and had a really really *really* good telescope, you could see the kings and queens of the old days and the cavemen and the dinosaurs and everything just like they were still alive.'

'That can't be true.'

'Sounds true to me. Miracles, see. Wherever you look.'

They both finished their cigarettes and continued staring at the sky.

'Do you remember when we were children there was patterned paper on the ceiling? You know – it was midnight blue, and it had pictures of silver stars all across it,' said Carson.

'I couldn't see it quite as well as you could

because I got the bottom bunk and you got the top one,' said Salinger.

'You never forgave me for that, did you?'

'No one who got the bottom bunk ever forgives.'

'I used to stare up at those paper stars. I used to think that we were floating in space and just looking at the stars. Me and you.'

'The both of us?'

Carson tilted his head another ten degrees towards the skies. When he spoke again, he spoke so softly Salinger could barely hear him.

'It would be lonely there without you, Sal.'

Salinger glanced at him sharply.

'Would it?'

Carson ignored him and kept his eyes on the heavens.

'All those nights I spent staring at the stars with my brother, and now here I am again. Only these are the real stars.'

'And we're not children any more.'

'You know something, Sal?'

Carson looked down and turned to him. The blandness of his face had suddenly ripped, like a paper bag. It seemed to Salinger to be tinged with pain and longing and regret.

Just then his cell phone rang.

'Leave it,' said Salinger.

But the moment had broken. Carson fumbled in his pocket and brought the phone to his ear.

'Wendell? Yep. Yep. Hold on. Let me get a piece of paper.'

Carson fumbled in his pocket for paper and pen. He covered the mouthpiece of his cell.

'He's found him, Sal! He's got an address! We can go there right now. Hey – turn round so I can rest this on your back.'

Carson wrote on the scrap of paper while Wendell talked.

'Thanks, Wendell. You're a really good guy. And hey – the idiot sends his love.'

'I do,' said Salinger. 'I really do.'

Carson clicked the phone off.

'We did it, Salinger. We found Dad. He lives in a place called Angel Fire Court. Few miles from here.'

They started to laugh. Carson put his arms around Salinger and hugged. Salinger held him tight, right back. They danced slowly together, shuffling, kicking up dust beneath their feet.

High above, the stars pumped dead light, emanating colossal indifference, dark radiation.

CHAPTER 13

ON ANGEL FIRE COURT

Salinger and Carson were ten minutes from the house on Angel Fire Court, but the drive to Henry's house was going to have to wait a little longer. Minutes after Carson had finished his conversation with Wendell, LouLou had phoned.

Carson had wandered off into the near distance as he talked to her in a half-whisper. Apparently the content of the conversation was more intimate than usual. Salinger walked off into the desert in the opposite direction to empty his bladder and smoke a cigarette.

When he returned to the car, Carson was standing outside it with his hands limp by his sides. As Salinger approached he didn't look up.

'Are you OK, Carzy?'

Carson seemed to be slowly emerging from a deep trance. He examined Salinger as if he didn't recognize him. Slowly, the familiar default smile slipped back into place. But it seemed slightly out of register, as if it didn't quite fit his mouth.

'You look a bit weird. Something happen?'

Carson didn't respond. Then he bent over and

threw up. Salinger waited until he had recovered himself.

'What's the matter?'

'Shouldn't have necked that whiskey sour,' said Carson. He took a fresh paper handkerchief out of his pocket and carefully wiped his mouth.

He looked at the sky for a long time, until Salinger became uncomfortable. Then he abruptly climbed back into the car. Salinger paused, then climbed in the other side. Carson immediately started the engine and pulled off the roadside, spinning the wheels. Instead of the normal slow, controlled acceleration, within seconds they were travelling at 60 mph.

The windows of the Lexus were open, the air conditioning was switched off. Warm air buffeted the inside of the car.

Gales were everywhere, thought Salinger, blind hurricanes of genes, circumstance, history, the unconscious.

'Carson, are you OK?'

'Can you smell that?' said Carson softly.

Salinger tried to work out what it was that he was meant to be trying to smell. There was a trace of something in the outside air. It held a faint sense-memory for him, some scrap from childhood. It was woody and dark, and it suggested enclosure of some kind. But he couldn't place it.

'From the creosote bushes,' said Carson. He was still speaking barely above a whisper. 'Come spring they will be covered in yellow flowers. It's a beautiful sight.'

Salinger decided not to press Carson about the phone call any further. The noisy intoxication that had overcome them after Wendell's phone call had unaccountably decayed into an anxious, fraught silence.

After a few more minutes, the Lexus slowed. Salinger saw a sign ahead for Angel Fire Court. Carson made a right turn onto the wide avenue. The surface was cracked as if with black lightning. The houses were softly rounded, pastel orange-coloured, single-storeyed.

It took another five minutes of slow cruising to reach 4230. The house itself was a peculiar shape, with the double garage appearing larger than the bulk of the house. Two windows, making a sideways L, adorned the façade. A chimney protruded from the roof. Some kind of ivy hybrid crept over the wall that connected the garage to the main house. The front yard was tidily kept. There were blinds pulled down and lights on inside.

Carson switched off the engine.

'Here we are then,' said Carson.

The moon perched atop the house, a pale-red beacon.

'That's right,' said Salinger.

'Who's going to do it?'

'We both are.'

Salinger could hear a faint noise in Carson's throat. It sounded like he was gulping for air.

'What are we going to say?'

'It's not the sort of thing you can plan,' said Salinger.

Carson's face was stretched and anxious. The all-purpose camouflage smile had disappeared. Salinger wished he could draw his brother right at that moment. He had never seen Carson's face so naked. And yet he couldn't say what it was he was seeing. The emotions that flickered across Carson's features, although no longer hidden, were complex, obscure.

Salinger got out of the car. Carson didn't move. Salinger went round to the other side of the car and opened the door. Leadenly, Carson put one leg outside, then the other. With agonizing slowness, he swung his body out of the car as if underwater. Then he moved round to the offside of the Lexus and stood there, perfectly still. He didn't even glance towards the house.

'Shall we have a cigarette first?' said Salinger, taking a pack out of his pocket.

Salinger handed Carson a cigarette and lit it for him, then lit his own. They smoked the cigarettes to the stub before either spoke again.

'Will he be pleased to see us?' said Carson.

'He hasn't exactly gone out of his way to stay in contact,' said Salinger.

Carson flicked his cigarette furiously on the ground and stamped on it repeatedly, finally grinding it into the concrete with his heel.

'Then why are we *doing* this? What's the *point*?'

'You're the one who suggested it.'

'There's no need to get *smart*.'

'Calm down, Carzy.'

'I don't need to calm down. I'm not angry.'

He shifted his weight from the left foot to the right, then right to left. He scratched the back of his neck fiercely, raking it brutally with his fingernails.

'Your smart mouth. Same when you were a kid. You just can't hold it, can you? I've had enough of it. Hell to you.'

For a moment Salinger got the impression that Carson was actually going to get back into the car and drive away. But he seemed pressed into a tight box of confining space, the walls of which seemed unbreachable. He had been rooted to the same spot since leaving the car, his back to the house, stiff and immobile.

'We've got to go through with this, Carson.'

Carson's mouth was thin and tight. He nodded once. Then he spun on his heel, and took a step towards the path that led to the door. Then he stopped dead. Then, haltingly, he took another step. Salinger took up position beside him.

They walked, almost in step, to the front door. There was the rattle of pebbles beneath their feet. Again, the smell of the creosote bushes.

The front door was elaborately carved with representations of birds and flowers. It was painted a glossy purple. A bell push had a white paper sticker under it which read *Birdy and Hank*. In a

270

smaller space underneath the words scribbled in ballpoint pen *bell broke knock on door.*

Salinger knocked. Another light flicked on inside. Footsteps could be heard echoing on wooden boards. Salinger put his hand on Carson's shoulder. It was rigid, as if the flesh under the shirt had been picked off, leaving only bone.

A woman's voice came from the other side of the door.

'Who is this?'

'Is Henry Nash at home?' said Carson. His voice sounded unnatural, too loud, yanked out of shape.

'Who is this?'

'I'm Henry's son, Carson. I have with me my brother, Salinger Nash.'

There was a pause.

'He's Henry's son too.'

A few more moments passed. Salinger found himself trying to suppress an urgent need to laugh. He coughed to try and disguise it.

'What's so fricking funny?' hissed Carson, turning angrily.

'Isn't that a given?'

'What is?'

'That I'm his son too. I mean, if you're my brother.'

The door suddenly opened. Inside there was a tiny, wizened Hispanic woman in a shawl who looked puzzled and defiant. Five feet behind her stood an equally shrivelled man, who was leaning on a carved wooden walking stick.

'What you want? Who the hell are you?' said the woman.

Salinger was still fighting his urge to laugh. He couldn't speak, only concentrate on keeping his face straight. A few seconds passed. The old man tapped his stick on the ground making a faint tattoo.

'Christ, you've not aged well, Dad,' said Salinger.

Now the old man stepped forward.

'You crazy! We call the police.'

The old man reached for the phone, while the woman began to shut the door.

'No, no!' said Carson, regaining control of himself. He jammed his foot into the door. 'We're Henry Nash's sons. I promise. I can prove it.'

The door opened again to reveal that the old woman was holding a huge pistol, something like the size of a .44 Magnum. She could barely support its weight. Salinger again fought the impulse to burst out laughing. She looked like a dwarf with a bazooka. Carson very slowly reached for his pocket.

'Easy now, ma'am. I just want to show you some ID.'

'Don't fuck with me,' the woman said. 'Hank never said nothing about no sons.'

The old man continued to watch them both intently, balancing on his stick. A small line of spittle was visible at the side of his mouth. Salinger watched, fascinated, as it started to descend with plumb-line straightness to the ground.

Carson pulled his wallet out of his pocket. He took out his driving licence and held it up for the woman to inspect. She squinted at it through the gloom.

'Don't mean nothing. You just got the same name.'

'Why don't you just get Henry out here and ask him?'

'Hank ain't here. He gone away. Him and Mrs Birdy together.'

Salinger looked at Carson. He got the impression that he had shrunk. Salinger found his passport from his pocket. His arm felt indescribably heavy as he held it up towards the woman.

'We really *are* his sons,' said Salinger, his voice suddenly thin and tired. The disappointment that Henry wasn't there gripped sharply at his chest.

The English accent seemed to finally convince the woman. She lowered the gun, then put it on the table at her side.

'Don't work anyway. Jus' to scare people.'

There was a lengthy silence before the woman spoke again.

'So Henry got sons, huh?'

'Yes,' said Salinger. 'Henry got sons.'

The woman, apparently convinced at last, suddenly became theatrically friendly, insisting that they both come in for a cup of *horchata* – which, Carson informed him, was Mexican rice tea. Salinger and Carson crossed the threshold and entered the hallway of the house.

The woman explained in a non-stop stream of only partially comprehensible English that Henry and Ladybird had left for a hotel in Marfa, Texas, two days previously. They had taken very little luggage. They had asked the housekeeper and her husband to stay in the house for security's sake while they were away. Mrs Ladybird had said they would be back in a week or so.

She led Salinger and Carson into a large, low-ceilinged front room. It was not expensively decorated, but it was clean and elegant. All the furniture appeared to be custom- or hand-made. The floor was polished wood and there were paintings of desert landscapes on the wall. The woman noticed Salinger inspecting them.

'Mrs Birdy's pictures. She paint them.'

'Very nice,' said Salinger. Carson nodded in vague agreement.

On shelves, vivid ceramics and books that stretched from ceiling to floor. A large fireplace contained artfully arranged pine logs.

'I phone Mr and Mrs Hank to tell them you are here. Got the number for the Hotel Paisano here somewhere.'

'I'd rather you didn't,' said Salinger.

Salinger spent several minutes convincing the housekeeper and her husband not to phone Henry and Ladybird. He wanted to keep it as a surprise, he said. It only occurred to him after he said it that this was true. He wanted to see shock on Henry's face as they emerged like spectres out of the past. He wanted to leave no time for him to dissemble or prepare.

It was two hundred and eleven miles from Las Cruces to Marfa. The housekeeper seemed to have no idea why the couple had gone there with barely enough luggage to see them through any kind of holiday. Instructions had been scant – to keep the house tidy and clean, and to await their return.

Carson and Salinger spent twenty minutes in the house, fighting to maintain a conversation, which was hampered anyway both by the housekeeper's poor grasp of English and by the spectacle of her silent husband refusing to sit down but continuing to eye them warily, fingering his cane as if it were a cudgel. He was not prepared to believe that they meant no harm.

By the time they returned to the Hotel Encanto it was close on midnight. Carson started quietly folding clothes. Since having his luggage returned by Wendell, he had unpacked the whole suitcase, and ironed the contents.

Carson seemed to have only temporarily overcome his fit of nerves. During the drive home he had seemed peaceful. Now Salinger could sense a tension building in him again.

'We going to drive to Marfa tomorrow?' said Carson.

'We'll get up early, do some sightseeing on the way,' said Salinger. It's only four or five hours. Let's enjoy it. We shouldn't let Henry ruin our holiday. I want to see the McDonald Observatory. Says in the guidebook that it's located at the darkest place in the whole United States. And I thought that was George Bush's arsehole.'

'Let's just go to sleep and see how we feel about it in the morning.'

'What might we feel other than, "Let's go to Marfa and see Dad?"'

Carson looked at Salinger blearily.

'Don't be combative, for once, Sal. Let's just go to sleep. We'll talk in the morning.'

He was in his Brooks Brothers blue-drill pyjamas. As usual, Carson had effected the transformation from fully dressed to nightwear without any interim stage being observable.

'Are you OK, Carzy?'

'I'm fine. I'm just very, very, *very* tired.'

Carson climbed into bed, shut his eyes and closed off the bedside lamp. Salinger got undressed, leaving his clothes in a pile on the floor. He didn't bother setting an alarm, knowing that Carson would wake him up at 7 a.m. sharp, as he had almost every morning since Salinger had arrived.

Salinger climbed into his own bed and turned towards Carson, watching him silently. He could see that his eyes were shifting frenetically underneath the lids, dreaming, or searching for something in the dark.

When Salinger awoke, he could see by the bedside clock that it was just past nine o'clock. There was no sign of Carson. He had made his bed, as he had in every hotel in which they had stayed, even though he knew perfectly well that the maid would just remake it anyway.

It wasn't like Carson to behave so unpredictably. On the other hand, thought Salinger, they were more than a week into the trip and he still didn't really have the faintest idea of who Carson really was.

Salinger got out of bed, kicked the clothes on the floor out of the way and went to the bathroom. The thing that had worried him most about the luggage being taken was that he had been deprived of his Prozac. He was frightened of not being able to get a prescription and, as a result, fall back into a state of chemical depression. He had resolved that if the car didn't turn up in three days he would go to an American doctor in the hope that he could get fresh supplies. But now he examined the pack, he thought that maybe he could do without them after all.

As quickly as the idea came, it dissolved. He tore open the plastic of the blister pack and swallowed the pill. It tasted of nothing. Perhaps it was nothing. There was a carload of quacks who believed Prozac was a placebo, no better than a sugar pill.

He had showered and dressed before he noticed the note on the table in the corner of the room. *Didn't want to wake you. Needed some air. See you downstairs for breakfast around nine thirty? C.*

Salinger duly made his way to the anonymous café where the same gargantuan waitress who had brought Wendell his pancakes was lumbering grimly from table to table. He beckoned to her. She deliberately turned her gaze in the opposite direction.

It occurred to him that he probably hadn't left sufficient tip the previous morning. In fact he might not have left a tip at all. He could never quite take on board the required size of the American gratuity, and the constant requirement that it be dispensed. To reduce hospitality to a purely commercial transaction struck him as one of the least attractive of all American customs.

He was still waiting for service five minutes later when Carson walked into the lobby, looking fresh and well rested. He smiled mildly when he saw Salinger and came and sat down at the table.

'What's occurring?'

'I can't get Ganesh the elephant woman to take any notice of me.'

'Did you tip her yesterday?'

'Not enough, apparently. Or possibly not at all.'

'I did though.'

Salinger lifted his eyes to the waitress. She nodded in acknowledgement and made her way over to the table. He thought that he could smell her. Something powdery, something citrus, something else dark and bloody.

'Two coffees, please, and don't spit in his.'

'Excuse *me*?'

The woman looked as if she were capable of crushing the both of them with a sweep of her pale, bloated forearm. But Carson gave one of his most charming smiles, and touched the woman on the wrist.

'Just kidding. He's English, he doesn't understand the way we do things here. Can I have a big fat stack of buttermilk pancakes?'

The woman summoned a corporate smile.

'Sure.'

She turned to walk away.

'And could my brother order something?'

She checked herself and slowly hefted her weight back towards Salinger. She licked her pencil and held up her order pad.

'Sir?'

Salinger was struck, not for the first time, at how adept the Americans were at converting this simple expression of polite deference into a devastating slur, simply by a slight modulation of the tone and a jink of the smile.

'I'll just have a cheese omelette, please.'

'Monterey Jack or Cheddar?' She sucked her teeth.

'I'm not sure that Monterey Jack really qualifies as a cheese.'

'Excuse me?'

'Cheddar. A Cheddar cheese omelette, please. And some toast.'

The waitress scribbled on her pad, turned her back and lumbered towards the kitchen.

'You just have to make things worse, don't you, Sally?'

Carson sighed and sniffed the air.

'It's a good morning. It's a good day.'

'Where have you been, Carzy?'

'I've been to church. I've been praying to the Lord.'

Salinger searched Carson's face in vain for any trace of self-mockery.

'And what does the *Lawd* say?'

'He says I got to see this thing through.'

'You were thinking of not seeing it through?'

'It did occur to me that maybe I was – we were – just wasting our time, trying to rake up things that were dead. I don't know. Suddenly, after last night, it just all seemed so pointless. After all – what's going to happen?'

'We don't know.'

'We don't know. And when I talked to Jesus today, He said that same thing. We don't know what's going to happen. Even God doesn't know what's going to happen. You know what Jesus said to me? He said that God traded in being all-powerful so that He could experience surprise. That's what makes life interesting, right? Even for Him. So I got to go ahead.'

'You're going to meet Henry.'

'Yes.'

'Good on Jesus, good on God, and good on you.'

Salinger glanced at his watch. He didn't expect the waitress to return any time soon.

'Listen, mate, I thought we were going to make an early start.'

'Thought that there was no point unless I got my head on straight first.'

'Is it on straight now?'

'Straight as a plumb line in a ruler factory. I also checked the website for the McDonald Observatory. You can see a live feed of the sun. Imagine that. You can look right at the sun.'

'From the darkest place on earth.'

'I was thinking about that. The website said you could go star watching there after dark. We could find a hotel nearby and go back in the evening and look through the telescopes.'

'You're not trying to put off this visit, are you?'

'Just like the idea of getting a good night's sleep before we get to see the old man. It's only twenty-one miles from the big telescopes to Marfa. We could be there at the Hotel Paisano right after breakfast.'

Salinger's omelette arrived with some soggy toast and a tea bag soaking in insufficiently hot water.

'Can I get some coffee instead?' asked Salinger.

The waitress grimaced. She placed Carson's stack of pancakes in front of him. They were accompanied by a hillock of streaky bacon, sweating grease.

'You know, you've been very understanding towards me on this trip, Sal,' said Carson, picking up a stick of bacon and crunching on it. 'Because you know, always, in the past, I thought you were a little bit of a . . . I don't know what.'

Carson moved his head in circles as if exercising his neck muscles.

'Got a bit of a crick last night.'

'You were saying. That I was a little bit of a you don't know what.'

'Well – let's just say we haven't always seen eye to eye, have we? But I wouldn't have imagined that you and I could have got on as well as we have done on this journey. I thought we might not even make it through the first night. We're pretty different, you and me.'

'Shit and Shinola. Whatever Shinola is.'

'What I'm trying to say is . . .'

Carson paused and scratched the back of his neck.

'Ah – it doesn't matter. I don't know what I'm trying to say.'

A cup of coffee was placed, too firmly, on the table in front of Salinger. Drops spilled onto the tabletop. The big woman didn't bother to apologize or mop them up. She waddled away without another word.

'She smells of air freshener. The kind that covers up toilet smells.'

He took a sip of his coffee.

'She spit in it?'

'Don't think so. It's about 30 per cent piss though.'

'Hey – have you heard anything yet from Tiane?' said Carson.

Salinger had checked his emails the night before.

There had been a short reply from Tiane, but it explained nothing. She apologized for not having got in touch sooner. She had been working very hard at the school. There was an Ofsted inspection approaching. They could have a good talk when he got back.

He considered using Carson's cell phone to call her direct, but he didn't like to show need to Tiane. His mounting panic was something he felt compelled to suppress. Also, he didn't want to be told something he didn't want to hear a few hours before he would be seeing his father again. As with Tiane, he was determined to show Henry no hint of weakness.

'Everything's fine,' said Salinger firmly. 'Everything is just tickety-boo.'

The journey to the McDonald Observatory, just south of Fort Davis on the I–10, was a five-hour drive. Salinger was happy to be back in the Lexus again. It was cool and comfortable. Salinger continued with *East of Eden* as they drove. Towards the end of the journey, Salinger started to read out loud.

'"*Two stories have haunted us and followed us from our beginning,*" says Samuel.'

'I find it difficult to concentrate when people read out loud to me,' muttered Carson.

'It's only a few paragraphs.'

'Who's Samuel anyway?' said Carson.

'Never mind. He's just a character. Listen to the

story. *"Two stories have haunted us and followed us from our beginning. We carry them along with us like invisible tails. The story of original sin and the story of Cain and Abel. I don't understand them at all. But I feel them. Here we are . . . this oldest story. If it troubles us it must be that we find the trouble in ourselves . . . it's such a little story to make so deep a wound."* Now Lee says . . .'

'Who's Lee?' said Carson.

'It doesn't *matter* who Lee is. He's another character. He's Chinese. Based on some guy who used to live with Steinbeck when he was growing up in Salinas.'

'Chinese, OK. Wisdom of the East. I got it.'

'And Lee says, *"We gather our arms full of guilt as though it were precious stuff. It must be that we want it that way."*

'"We are Cain's children," answers Samuel. And then Lee says, *"It is the symbol story of the human soul."'*

'What is?' said Carson.

'The Cain and Abel story, of course. Are you trying deliberately to be obtuse? Just listen. Lee says, *"It is everybody's story . . . the greatest terror a child can have is that he is not loved, and rejection is the hell he fears . . . And with rejection comes anger, and with anger some kind of crime in revenge for the rejection, and with the crime, guilt – and there is the story of mankind."'*

Carson yawned.

'"If rejection could be amputated the human would

not be what he is," continued Salinger, speeding up his reading as the words became more urgent. "*One child, refused the love he craves, kicks the cat and hides his secret guilt. Another steals so that money will make him loved. And a third conquers the world and always the guilt . . . and revenge and more guilt . . . this old and terrible story is important because it is a chart of the soul, the secret, rejected, guilty soul.*'"

'Right,' said Carson indifferently.

'Doesn't the story *say* anything to you, Carson?'

'Yeah, it tells me that you think I'm full of a sense of rejection and I'm angry and I'm going to commit crimes because I'm so angry and then I'm going to get guilty and then I'm going to kick the cat and then I guess the cat gets guilty, et cetera et cetera, blah blah.'

'It's a biblical story. The Bible, you know. The good news. The truth.'

'I don't believe everything in the Bible and I can't swallow your interpretation of it.'

'It's not mine, it's Steinbeck's.'

'Listen, Salinger. You ever heard of the rubber ducky explanation? It's a Hollywood thing. I was reading this interview in *People* magazine with this big shot director and he said that the worst screenplays always had this moment when you explained the bad behaviour of the villain or the hero by cutting back to the moment when he had his rubber ducky taken away from him as a kid. It's pat. It's not convincing. No one knows why people behave like they do.'

'Except God.'

They came to a turn from the I–10 marked *University of Texas McDonald Observatory*. The signpost also gave the distances for Fort Stockton and Pecos. Salinger blinked at the sign and started fumbling in his bag.

'Can we do the Observatory some other time?'

'What?'

'Just pull over a moment.'

Carson slowed the car and pulled it onto the dirt at the side of the road and left it idling while Salinger produced from his bag a small cream-coloured business card.

'Pecos. Thought I had heard the name before.'

'Pecos,' said Carson. 'What's the big deal about Pecos?'

'Tahoma gave it to me. Her sister is a Native American healer.'

'Who's Tahoma?'

'She showed us around the pueblo. You thought she was foxy.'

'Oh yeah, the guide. So what?'

Salinger considered for a moment.

'I'd like to pay her a visit. It's very near here.'

'Where?'

'Outside Pecos.'

'That's not "very near". It's fifty miles. Anyway, why would you want to go and see some damn witch doctor?'

'Look, here's a map.'

He flipped the card over.

'*Native American Healing. Half-mile outside Pecos, TX.*'

'Is there a phone number?'

'No.'

'So you're just meant to turn up? What kind of business is that?'

'Maybe it's not a business.'

'What about the Observatory?'

'It's just big telescopes.'

'I wanted to see it. We're almost there.'

'I may not get another chance to do this, Carson. It feels important to me. Sort of Karmic. We can go to the Observatory after we've seen Dad.'

Carson shook his head.

'We've got a big day tomorrow, Salinger. I'm not really into having a Red Indian dancing round my head with a fricking tomahawk. The hotel is booked in Fort Davis. That's going to be another seventy-five-mile drive at the end of the day.'

'So find somewhere nearer. You don't have to do anything, Carson. I'm sure your soul doesn't need rebalancing. Just drop me off and pick me up later. It's no big deal. Look, she probably won't be there anyway, or she'll have another appointment.'

'You're being freaky. What did that tourist guide at the pueblo say to you?'

'She just said it was something I should try.'

'It throws the schedule out of whack.'

'Throwing the schedule out of whack is what this whole trip is about. At least in my mind. It's about doing things you don't normally do. Trying things we don't normally try. So far we've buried a dog, had a car stolen and crossed from Texas to New Mexico on a Triumph America motorbike. It's adventure, this is *adventure* – being open to it all. This woman, Tahoma, told me I should go and see her sister. I told her that we weren't going that far, and now we're just a few miles away from Pecos. Everything has a purpose, right?'

'I wish you'd stop throwing that back in my face. OK, I admit it. Not *every* fricking thing has a purpose. And it's not a few miles, it's fifty.'

'I just want to see if there's anything here. I want to see if her sister will see me.'

'Is this a sexual thing? You think she might be as hot as Tahoma?'

'No, it's not a sexual thing. I don't know what it is. I just have an impulse.'

'You just have an impulse.'

'That's right.'

Carson paused, then slowly pulled the car back onto the road, heading back towards the sign for Pecos.

'I don't know why I'm indulging you.'

'Because I'm your little brother. That's what big brothers are meant to do.'

CHAPTER 14

PECOS

T he drive to Pecos took an hour. It was Carson who spotted the sign by the side of the road – a weather-stained, painted piece of bare wood nailed crudely to a wavering plank that stood at a forty-five-degree angle to the road.

Native American Healing 1m was all it said. There was a childishly painted black arrow pointing eastwards.

'I can't imagine that sorry piece of crap is going to attract much in the way of passing trade,' said Carson.

'You think a flashing neon light would be more fitting?'

'What kind of set-up sells itself with a sign like that?'

They took the small dirt road that the sign indicated.

'It's four thirty, Sally. She's probably closed up shop for the day.'

'Then we've wasted about an hour of our time. Does it matter?'

The wind was gathering force. Low blankets of

dust spread across the plain. They had driven more than a mile. There was nothing in view.

'Stop,' Salinger called out, pointing a finger.

'I didn't see anything.'

'Just back there, you just passed it. Another sign.'

'I don't think there was, Sally.'

'Just turn back. It's only a few yards.'

Carson sucked his teeth and turned the Lexus around. Fifty yards back there was another sign. It had been easy to miss, since it was nailed to the trunk of what Carson claimed was a bur oak tree, and overhung with branches. It proved to be slightly more expansive than the first sign, *Native American Healing This Way, ¼ mile, Open.* The arrow indicated another, even narrower dirt road.

'This is beginning to feel like some sort of sting. We're going to get carjacked or something,' muttered Carson.

'I can see something over there. A sort of tent.'

Carson squinted into the rising dust.

'I don't see nothing.'

'Just drive down the road. It's not far.'

Carson pulled the car down the dirt track. Sure enough, a few hundred yards along the track stood a single mud-coloured tipi. It was decorated with a series of faded yellow suns stretching round the base of the material. Out of the top, support struts were exposed. They intersected and spread outwards like the crest of a bird. The tipi was large, the base maybe fifteen feet in diameter.

As they pulled up to it, a third version of the sign

was visible lying loose against the tipi – *Native American Healing Here*. There was nothing else in sight – no cars, no other buildings, no visible means of transport. There was just the cone of the tent. In the half-light, Salinger could see that the thin membrane of the cloth – or hide, or whatever it happened to be – was faintly illuminated from the inside, making the tipi glow faintly.

'There's not going to be anyone here,' said Carson.

But, peering through the rising dust, Salinger thought he could see a shadow move inside the tipi. Carson and Salinger got out of the car. The bustling of the wind made it hard to hear one another. A piece of grit lodged in Salinger's eye and he rubbed at it furiously. They both covered their faces with their hands to protect themselves.

No opening in the tipi was visible. Salinger walked around the other side where he found a small, triangular, unsecured flap with ragged cloth ties hanging from the edge of the material.

'Do we knock?' said Carson. 'I feel vaguely ridiculous.'

He pulled out a cigarette and lit it, cupping his hand against the wind.

'Nothing to knock on,' said Salinger. 'I guess we just better shout.'

Salinger put his mouth close to the tent entrance.

'Hello! Anyone there?'

The flap flew open, although nobody had visibly touched it. Before it flapped closed again, Salinger could just make out a candle burning inside and the outline of a slight figure. Salinger lifted the flap and called out again.

'Anyone there?'

Hearing no reply again, Salinger entered. A young woman – Salinger guessed she was in her early twenties – was sitting on what looked like a three-legged milking stool. In front of her was a long, ramshackle, unvarnished wooden table with a hole cut into it at one end. There was a bottle of water, and a small bag on the floor. Next to the bag was an enormous, and very sharp-looking, hunting knife with a handle in the shape of a bear.

The woman was staring straight in front of her with her eyes wide open, completely still. She did not react in the slightest to Salinger entering. Salinger spoke a little more loudly this time.

'Hello?'

Still nothing. Salinger took another step forward and put a finger gently on her arm. At his touch, the woman jumped, so suddenly it made Salinger recoil with surprise.

'Huh? Wha'? *Shit.*'

The voice was small, girlish, puzzled. The woman seemed to be shaking herself awake. She seemed unsure where she was. Salinger was alone with her in the tent – Carson was still hanging back, embarrassed, or possibly frightened.

'Hello? Sorry. Hello? Are you open?'

The woman seemed faintly panicked and still

struggling to come out of a sleep, or a trance. Salinger wondered momentarily if she might be blind.

'Sorry, I was somewhere else. I was . . . yes. I was elsewhere.'

'I'm sorry to disturb you. Wake you. Whatever. Are you Wakanda? Your sister, Tahoma, sent me.'

'Tahoma?'

The girl stood up. He saw now that she was wearing a battered straw hat, and faded-denim bib-and-tucker overalls. Her skin was light, and her hair long and braided. She had freckles on her face. She looked nothing like his image of a Native American and nothing like Tahoma. She was more like a character from *Huckleberry Finn* or a small-town schoolteacher in a Norman Rockwell painting.

She opened her eyes wide and smiled unexpectedly. It was a great, gorgeous, generous smile. Now she looked about fifteen. She had plastic braces on her teeth, coloured red. Her eyes were enormous. Salinger found it hard to take his gaze away from them. There was something yellow in them and something green. They glittered, even in the dusk.

The girl, despite seeming half asleep, appeared unsurprised by the arrival of visitors. Without comment, she started to pour from the bottle of water into a plastic cup. Salinger became aware of a vague smell of eggs, and of potato chips. There were a few pieces of pottery strewn about the floor.

'Acoma pottery?' said Salinger.

'Walmart,' said the girl, who held out her hand. 'Wakanda isn't my real name.'

Salinger took her hand, which was tiny, like the paw of a small animal.

'My real name is unpronounceable. Acoma Indian names can go on for ever. Tahoma's real name means "woman who touches the sky with her hands and brings gold from the clouds". My name's even stupider. Tis-see-woo-na-tis. It means "she who bathes with her knees".'

'"She who bathes with her knees"? What the hell does that mean?'

'Hell, I don't know. That my parents had a sense of humour, I suppose. It's not even an Acoma name, it's Cherokee. In fact, I'm not even sure that it's Cherokee. Anyway. I just use Wakanda.'

'Why Wakanda?'

'I just sort of like it.'

'Wakanda – I'm Salinger Nash.'

'Like in J.D.?'

'That's right.'

'Aren't you going to ask your friend to come in?'

'He's just finishing a cigarette.'

Wakanda suddenly and noisily broke wind. At that moment, Carson pushed his way into the gloomy space, still exhaling tobacco smoke. It was already stuffy. The hot breeze pushed at the frail structure. It felt like it would give way at any moment. Carson looked faintly nervous.

'Smells bad in here,' said Carson, waving his hand in front of his face.

'Carson, meet Wakanda.'

'Pleased to meet you.'

'Hey.'

'Unusual set-up you've got here,' said Carson.

'It's the way we've always done it. You guys want some coffee?'

Carson shook his head. Salinger nodded. Wakanda poured from a vacuum flask into a plastic cup, and gave it to Salinger.

'Don't you get scared out here on your own?' said Carson.

'No, but I get the shit bored out of me. Still, this is what we do. This is what we have always done. OK, so who's first? I close up pretty soon.' She checked her watch, which was cheap pink plastic with a digital display.

'No, no, not me,' said Carson. 'I'm just dropping my brother off. Your sister seemed to think it would be good for him to see you.'

'You're brothers?' Wakanda seemed puzzled.

'Yes, we're brothers,' said Salinger. 'He's four years older.'

'You don't *seem* like brothers,' said Wakanda.

'Yeah, Tahoma said something similar,' said Salinger.

She took some oil out of a small jar and began rubbing it into her hands.

'Have you two been estranged or something?'

'We've been apart for the last twenty years,' said Salinger.

'Listen,' said Carson, who seemed to be sweating

295

and appeared deeply uncomfortable. 'I need to go. I want to get a shower, freshen up a little.'

'This place make you nervous?'

Wakanda focused her enormous eyes on Carson's face through the gloom.

'Not in the least.'

'You sure you don't want to stay? You might find it interesting. You're a Christian, right?'

'How did you know *that*?'

Wakanda shrugged.

'That would be the crucifix round your neck, I guess.'

Carson automatically put his hand up to his neck. He blushed slightly.

'Thing is, you find God in the funniest places. Right?' said Wakanda.

Carson took a step backwards.

'This really isn't for me. I don't do this type of thing. My brother – he's more open-minded. He likes to experiment. I'm a real stick-in-the-mud. Everybody says so.'

'That so?' said Wakanda. She turned and spat into a small cracked enamel jug. ''scuse my manners. Dust gets everywhere.'

She turned away from Carson to Salinger.

'Salinger, could you lie down on this table. Face up. Keep your clothes on. I'll get to it.'

'There's no preamble?'

'Preamble?'

'Incense, wind chimes, floaty music, a few prayers to the deity. That sort of thing? Brushing the air with burning sage. A few words about what you're going to do. Where you're going to take me. What disciplines you follow.'

'Just do what I do. Don't know where I'm going to take you. You want to do it or not? Because to be honest I'd be just as happy knocking back a few cold ones back in town.'

'Is it reiki? Or chakras? Or reflexology? What do you do?'

'It don't really have a name. You still here, Carson?'

Salinger looked round at Carson, who was fidgeting with his cigarette pack.

'Pick me up in . . . what?' said Salinger.

He looked enquiringly at Wakanda, who shrugged.

'Could be an hour, could be three. I don't know. Depends how fucked up you are.'

'Three hours!'

'It's not a fucking dental appointment,' said Wakanda, taking a swig of water. She gargled and spat it out on the floor.

'Leave it at least two,' said Salinger. 'If she's not finished, you can wait outside, smoke cigarettes and shoot the shit with Jesus.'

'I'm getting kind of tired of the Jesus jokes.'

'Then stop being one,' said Salinger.

Carson paused, then turned and lifted the tipi flap.

'You be careful, Salinger.'

Carson glanced in the direction of the hunting knife, then slipped out through the flap. Salinger looked at Wakanda, who was now adjusting the table slightly. She looked up again.

'You OK, J.D.?'

Salinger felt nervous. He considered for an instant Carson's theory that the woman might be deranged. A comic-book image of the cartoon character Little Plum from the *Beano* setting about his head with a tomahawk came into his mind. Yet another part of him felt extraordinarily relaxed and comfortable.

'I'm fine.'

'Let's roll, then. Lie down and close your eyes. Take off your shoes and socks. Try not to open your eyes at any time. Do what I tell you. If I hurt you, it's because I have to. You can make as loud a noise as you want. There's no one around here anyway. Don't get scared. It's all fine.'

'That's meant to reassure me? What do you mean, if you hurt me?'

'Don't really matter. The result is the same anyway. Not sure what's going to happen though. Shame your brother couldn't stay. Is he a fag, by the way?'

'Not so far as I'm aware.'

Wakanda made a snorting noise, and swatted a fly by clapping her hands, then flicking the remains into the air. In his attempts to alleviate his mood swings, Salinger had visited a number of alternative therapists and healers. None of them ever swore. None of them warned you that they were going to hurt you, or spat or broke wind. Also,

298

none of them had ever had the slightest effect on him.

'Lie down, and if you don't mind, keep your mouth shut until I tell you. Important to stay silent.'

Salinger removed his shoes and lay down on his back on the rickety table, which seemed slightly unstable. When Wakanda touched it, it rocked slightly. The moment he closed his eyes, Wakanda began to gently manipulate his toes. When she touched them, he felt something like a mild electric charge. When she spoke again, her voice had changed. It was very low. Salinger could barely hear it.

'Breathe in. Deep breath.'

Salinger took a deep breath.

'Then out – and now in again.'

Salinger tried to take another deep breath even though he had hardly exhaled.

'You have to breathe in more than you breathe out. Get it, J.D.?'

Salinger nodded. He started to breathe in deeply, then out slightly, then in again. It wasn't easy. His chest started to hurt. He began to snort when he lost the rhythm, and felt breathless. But he continued trying. Minutes passed. He felt cool and relaxed, even though the tent had a moment ago seemed hot and stuffy.

Wakanda did nothing except gently manipulate his toes one by one. His breathing now became laboured, but every time he slackened his efforts a whisper in his ear urged him to keep the breathing going.

The experience was uncomfortable and seemed to go on for a very long time. After what he guessed was around twenty minutes, his breathing pattern changed slightly. This did not feel like a decision he was consciously making. It was as if he was inwardly watching the rhythm of his own breathing regulate itself.

Then he began to almost hyperventilate, breathing in fast and barely breathing out at all. His head felt light. He noticed, as if it were happening at a great distance, that Wakanda was now manipulating a single point just below his kneecaps.

Another ten minutes passed. He was beginning to feel bored and uncomfortable, when he felt a tiny point of heat behind his left ear, as if it were a node of electricity. A few minutes later, he felt another behind his right ear.

'And breathe . . . follow your breath . . . breathe . . . IN and out, IN and out.' Wakanda's voice had become musical, remote, like a distant chant.

The feeling of electrical charge grew and spread. Now the skin behind his ears was like a superheated pad. A sensation of heat spread to his chest, then his stomach and after a while to his entire body. Then the feeling changed imperceptibly from heat to vibration. He felt as if he were a tuning fork, humming gently. Every time he breathed out, the sensation intensified slightly.

The awareness of a slight electrification, a low buzz, stayed with him for some time. He could no longer tell how long. He had lost his sense of time. Then he began to notice colours appear under his eyelids. At first there was a corona of red, then blue. The colours pulsated, expanding from a tiny circle to a glowing orb that filled his inner vision, then disappeared, then reappeared. Every so often in the distance, he heard improbable sounds. Water running, a drum, the call of an animal he could not recognize.

'Breathe – and exhaaale – and breathe . . .'

He calmly decided that he had been somehow hypnotized. He was both fully conscious and yet far away. The electrical, vibrating sensation was fading now. He suddenly felt that he was coming down, returning to a sense of boring normality. Outside, he heard the slap of rain against the tent. His mind reflected on how odd this was, since the skies had been clear when he had entered the tipi. He heard what he thought might be a rumble of thunder. A light, which he assumed was lightning, illuminated the space around his closed eyes momentarily. There was a sense of wind passing across his skin. The table rocked slightly.

A sense of ennui suddenly incubated. He felt that he had had enough. He wanted to sit up and have a cup of tea. But he could still hear Wakanda's voice distantly telling him to breathe – and let go, breathe – and let go. And breathe.

Without warning, he felt a sharp pain in his

stomach. Wakanda had made her way up to a small scar he had been left with after an operation during his infancy. It had been something to do with the leukaemia. She was pressing on it. It hurt intensely. He was aware, as if from a great distance, of his own voice pleading.

'Please stop.'

Wakanda dug her fingers more deeply into the scar. The pain, already scarcely bearable, intensified. Salinger felt on the point of pushing himself off the table with his elbows. But Wakanda seemed immensely strong – or was it that he had been somehow enfeebled? He vaguely intuited again that he had been put into a hypnotic state.

Now he became aware that Wakanda was actually sitting on top of him pinning his body down. She had the full force of her fingers, and the body behind them, pressed into his operation scar. He was aware that he had started making a low yowling of pain, coming from deep inside his abdomen. He had chanted once in India; the groan was like the 'om' sound, a deep vibration, but full of some unidentifiable agony.

Wakanda's hand felt as if it was bent into a bow now, and was digging away at the scar with the tips of her clenched fingers. He felt as if she was actually going to rip the wound open. Salinger felt his groaning transmute into a cry of panic and despair. It was as if the pain was jumping a gap, like a spark, and somewhere within that gap being reprocessed from physical to emotional pain.

302

He heard a second voice in the tipi. He was distantly aware that Wakanda was moaning, crying, shouting along with him, producing a mangled harmony.

Wakanda relaxed her fingers and the pain immediately ceased. He could hear Wakanda's voice once more urging him to breathe. A strong smell of creosote penetrated the tipi, then something else which he remembered, but could not recognize. He identified it as the metallic smell of the bed he had slept in as a child.

He felt Wakanda shifting herself further up his body. It seemed that she was on the table too though he couldn't imagine how the rickety table could support both their bodies. It felt vaguely erotic. Without embarrassment, he felt himself harden under his boxer shorts. Then he felt a point of pressure on his chest. Wakanda was pushing down on his sternum with the point of her elbow. She had her whole weight behind it. She pushed down, and into, it felt, the chest cavity.

'Christ!' gasped Salinger.

He felt that his breastbone was about to crack. But Wakanda simply pushed harder. He began crying. Quietly, over the sound of his own weeping, he heard Wakanda speak in a voice so low it was barely audible. He couldn't make out the words.

The pain had not lessened. It was stronger than ever. Salinger felt himself squirming to get out of the way of the point of her elbow, but the more he moved, the more she seemed to find a gap and push herself further down onto the bone. Again, the strange sensation of physical pain morphing into emotional pain came over him. He was choked with sobs.

'Stop. Please stop.'

But he didn't want her to stop.

The words came again.

Salinger let out a full-throated scream, and Wakanda joined in, screeching with him. It sounded like a symphony of pain. Then Wakanda started muttering again. This time he heard the words clearly.

I'm sorry, Mother.

Wakanda gave another twist of the elbow and drove it downwards again. The pain was unendurable, but the weight of Wakanda on his chest made it impossible for him to shift. A thought flashed across Salinger's mind. *It was like being fucked, right to the heart of his being.*

His weeping intensified. He had no sense of time.

He felt a cool breeze blowing along his back and the table moving again. There was a rustle in the distance. A voice drifted distantly into focus. The voice was angry.

'What the hell do you think you're doing?'

Salinger's eyes flickered open. Carson was standing at the entrance to the tipi. Salinger felt as if he was drugged. He could barely rouse himself to speak. Wakanda removed her elbow from his chest.

'Go outside.' Wakanda's voice was like an arrow tip.

Salinger managed to offer a feeble nod to Carson. 'It's OK.'

Carson looked uncertain and confused.

'You sure?'

'Go back to the car. Get out.'

Carson retreated slowly outside the flap. Vaguely, Salinger worked out that if Carson had come back he must have been on the table for at least two hours. It had seemed like thirty minutes.

He felt Wakanda climb from the table. There was a pause of several minutes. Then he felt her small hands in his hair, stroking it like he was a child. He could feel that his face was wet with tears.

'It's OK, Salinger.'

Salinger let her stroke his head. His chest felt bruised.

He wanted to stay there for ever.

Salinger had no idea how much time passed before Wakanda spoke again.

'You're OK now.'

He slowly opened his eyes. Wakanda was standing in the half-light with a ceramic cup filled with a steaming liquid.

'It's herbal tea.'

Unsteadily, Salinger sat up and took the cup. His hands shook. He looked up at Wakanda. Her eyes were monstrous with compassion, vast, frightening sanctuaries.

He drank the tea. It tasted like nettles and honey and earth.

'What did you do?'

His voice sounded thin and high, like a child's voice.

'I don't know what I do. I don't know what happens. I don't know what I say.'

Salinger swung his legs over the side of the table.

'You said, "I'm sorry, Mother." Why did you say that?'

'I don't remember.'

'You must.'

She began stroking his head again.

'Who was speaking, Wakanda? Who was asking for forgiveness? Was it you speaking to your mother?'

'Me?' said Wakanda. 'Why would I ask forgiveness? My mother was a bitch. Look, hombre, I'm not a fucking mind reader. I just do the work.'

Salinger felt again the bruising on his chest. He sipped at the tea.

'It hurt like hell when you worked on my operation scar.'

'You have an operation scar?'

'You must have known that.'

'How would I know that? You were wearing your clothes.'

Salinger didn't answer.

'When did you have the operation?'

'I was born very ill. I had leukaemia.'

'They operate on you for leukaemia?'

Salinger paused, momentarily confused.

'They must do.'

'I thought they treated it with chemicals and shit.'

'Not with me, apparently.'

Salinger tried to shake his head clear.

'What time is it?'

'Around eight o'clock, I guess.' She checked her watch. 'Cheap piece of shit is broke. Present from my boyfriend. Pretty classy guy.'

He had been under for almost three hours. Perhaps spellbound was a better word. He wondered if she had slipped something into the coffee.

'You can stay here as long as you want, until you feel ready to go. But I think your brother is waiting for you outside. I get the impression he's feeling anxious.'

'Can I just ask something?'

He felt himself crying again. Once more Wakanda began to stroke his head.

'Sometimes I just feel so fucked up, such a *mess*. Sometimes I think I'm mad. Sometimes I think I shall go mad.'

'You're OK. Or if you're not OK, you probably won't get any worse.'

'Thanks,' said Salinger. He meant to tinge the word with sarcasm, but it came out sincere.

Wakanda stopped stroking his hair and started putting items into a Gap plastic bag – a white towel, a few smooth pebbles and a bottle of oil.

'Yeah, you'll do fine. But I'm not so sure about your brother.'

Back in the Lexus, driving south down the 285, Salinger felt lightheaded – as if he shed ten pounds, or had had a malignant lump removed. He gabbled at Carson.

'It was incredible, Carzy. You should try it, mate. I've never experienced anything like it. That girl had a natural genius, some kind of weird voodoo fucking gift.'

Carson concentrated on the road ahead. As usual, the speedometer pointed to a spot two miles under the speed limit.

'She hurt me – properly hurt me. My chest hurts like a bitch.'

'Drove all the way to Fort Stockton and back just to keep myself amused while you were getting the crap beaten out of you. I rang the hotel in Fort Davis to say we'd be late, but they didn't have any record of our booking. They were full. So I found us a room in Stockton. It's nearer anyway.'

'See what I said? It was meant to be. If we'd gone to Davis we'd have been stuffed.'

'We wouldn't have been stuffed. We'd have found another hotel. Heck, when did you get so New Agey all of a sudden?'

Salinger pulled up his shirt. There was a blooming brown-black discoloration.

'Something *came out*, Carzy. I don't know what it was. I don't believe in this stuff, Carzy, I've never been interested in all that New Age crap. But this was real.'

'How much did she charge you?'

'Why does that matter?'

'You ever heard of cognitive dissonance? The more she charges you, the more likely you are to believe it had an effect. Sounded like she was just damn torturing you. Maybe you converted it into a "good experience" to stop yourself feeling foolish. So how much did she charge you?'

'I gave her two hundred dollars.'

Carson let out a long low whistle.

'I guess you'd feel pretty stupid if you'd paid out two hundred dollars and it didn't have any effect.'

'I didn't pay her till the end and she said to give her whatever I thought it was worth.'

'Even smarter psychology. What was with the breathing? She got you *breathing* in some way, right?'

'It's an Indian technique. To raise the life force, she said.'

'So what did you have to do?'

'I simply breathed in a lot more than I breathed out.'

Carson nodded and twiddled a dial on the CD player for no apparent reason.

'That's called "inducing hypoxia". Kids do it for a kick. It's a purely physiological process.'

'It took me somewhere.'

'She probably knows a thing or two about hypnosis as well.'

'It doesn't matter, Carzy. It *affected me.*'

'I'm not mocking. I hear you. So what did you find out?'

Salinger slumped back in his seat.

'I don't know. I don't know what it all meant.'

'What did she say it meant?'

'She didn't say much. All she said was that I was all right, that I would be all right.'

'That all?'

'She said she was worried about you.'

Carson gave a dry, faintly unpleasant laugh.

'She doesn't know squat about me.'

'She didn't know squat about me either, but I cried my eyes dry.'

'You're always crying your damn eyes dry.'

'I don't know how come a born-again Christian gets to be so sceptical about spiritual experiences.'

'I'm just saying it may not be all that it seems.'

'I want to go back again. After we've seen Dad, I want to go back and do another session.'

'Sure, why not. Obviously, you've got dollars to burn.'

'It *helped* me, Carzy. It's helping me to face Dad. It feels easier to see him tomorrow. I'm not so frightened.'

'Why are you frightened?'

'I might as well ask you why you were frightened when we went to the house.'

'Frightened? I wasn't frightened.'

Salinger frowned.

'Angel Fire Court. The house. You didn't want to go in.'

'I was a little nervous, sure. But *frightened*? Not at all. That's your imagination again.'

'You wouldn't go in!'

'I went in. It was me that knocked, remember?'

'Why are you pretending that you weren't afraid?'

'Because I wasn't. You're just reading into it stuff that ain't there. Here we are.'

Carson pulled the car into the driveway that led to the Fort Stockton Motel parking lot.

'You're right. I'm sure you're right, Carzy. You know how you feel, right?'

'Sure. Doesn't everybody?'

CHAPTER 15

FORT STOCKTON – MARFA

They rose the next morning early. There was no wind, not the faintest webbing of cloud. Opposite the motel there was what the online site for Fort Stockton described as the world's largest statue of a roadrunner. It was – the website proudly announced – eleven feet tall and twenty-two feet long.

'I wonder where the second largest statue of a roadrunner is,' said Salinger.

'Or the smallest,' said Carson. 'Come on, let's catch some pixels.'

Carson, dressed in pale-cream chinos, spanking-white deck shoes and a pale-pink Ralph Lauren polo shirt, started gesturing for Salinger to pose in front of the statue.

'This is what America is all about.'

'Pointless tributes to widely disliked species?' Salinger tousled his hair so it would look elegantly distressed.

'I don't think they're so widely disliked.'

'So what is it that America is all about?'

'Stupid fun. We're great at stupid fun.'

Underneath the statue was the legend *Welcome to Fort Stockton.*

'His name is Paisano Pete,' said Carson.

'Hey, Pete,' said Salinger. He struck a pose, thoughtful, 'artistic' in front of the bird while Carson snapped.

'OK, I'm bored now,' said Salinger after Carson had shot maybe a dozen times.

'Shall we go and get a coffee?' said Carson, putting the camera in his pocket.

'We just had a cup. Are you trying to stall?'

'Why? Because I'm "frightened". Forget the coffee. Let's get on the road. Sooner we hook up with the old man the better.'

The Lexus as usual was immaculate. The daily detritus that Salinger left behind him – candy wrappers, cigarette packs, used Kleenex – was cleared meticulously every morning by Carson. He utilized a hand-held portable vacuum cleaner with six separate attachments, all of which he employed. It was around eighty miles to Marfa. As they set off along the I–67 Salinger noticed that Carson was driving slightly further below the speed limit than usual.

'You heard from Tiane?' he said.

Salinger pulled a stick of Big Red cinnamon chewing gum from the packet. He offered one to Carson, who shook his head.

'Not as such.'

'So you and Tiane don't want children, right?'

'She's never shown much sign of it. As for me, I've not had the urge.'

'Not good to leave it too late. Risk gets worse. Miscarriages. Defects. You don't want to go through that. Believe me.'

Salinger chewed slowly on the gum. He didn't really like cinnamon much. He'd just admired the design of the packet.

'I'm happy for you, Carson. I know how much you've wanted children, and it's great that it's all worked out. I just don't have the same impulse.'

'In case you end up like Dad.'

'Meaning?'

'You're scared of having children in case you end up like Dad. Trapped, and then having to run away.'

'That's a rubber ducky story. I don't want to have children because I don't want to have children. Simple as.'

'OK, if you say so.'

Carson adjusted the mirror slightly and rubbed a spot of dirt from the windscreen with his finger.

'Must be nice driving the Lexus.'

'I do enjoy it.'

'I've never driven on an American highway.'

'I dare say.'

'It must feel good.'

'Are you trying to tell me something?'

'I'm trying to ask you something.'

Carson looked puzzled, then started to laugh.

'Absolutely not. No. No way. Forget it, Salinger.'

314

'Why not? I've got my licence. I've been driving for twenty years.'

'You ain't insured.'

'Just give me a chance to drive this beautiful car of yours. Just for a few minutes.'

'You'll total it.'

'At least I won't run over any fucking dogs.'

'Screw you.'

'Come on, Carson. Give me a break. Show me that you trust your little brother.'

'I don't trust my little brother.'

'Pretend that you do. Look, if I hurt the car, I'll pay for it out of my own pocket. I swear it. It's just the last twenty minutes. I've never driven a car in America. And I've never driven a car as nice as this.'

'I don't *think* so.'

'Oh come *on*. Don't make me blackmail you again.'

'How you going to blackmail me?'

'I'll think of something. Tell LouLou you were screwing Ganesh at the Hotel Encanto.'

'I don't respond to threats.'

'You rented the motorcycle.'

'Not because of threats.'

'Sure it was because of threats. OK, fair enough. No threats. Please, Carson. Let me drive the car for a while. Please.'

'Stop it. You're embarrassing me.'

'Don't make me beg.'

'You're already begging.'

'It's humiliating.'

'Oh for God's *sake*.'

Carson pulled abruptly over to the side of the road.

'Ten minutes is all. Then you give it right back to me, OK?'

'Outstanding. You're a mate. No. You're a brother.'

Salinger took over the wheel. He drove the rest of the way to Marfa with Carson sitting stiff-backed in his seat. But there were no mishaps. Salinger drove strictly at 50 mph. He contemplated briefly slamming his foot down on the gas pedal just to see Carson's reaction, but decided that the thought was probably more amusing than the actuality would be.

Salinger was still driving as they penetrated the skirts of the town. On practically every street block there was a church. The avenues felt as widely spaced as in Rome. Carson was photographing the lonely spindle of the water tower as they drove past.

'Where's the hotel?'

'On North Highland. Hey, Sal, have you heard of Marfa Lights?'

'I don't think so. What are they? Cigarettes?'

'People have been seeing them here since the last century. They're these weird lights in the sky. They come down and hover around you and then dash off. Or you can see them dancing in the distance sometimes.'

'Like UFOs?'

'Some say. There's a Marfa Lights viewing centre a few miles outside town. And a Marfa Lights festival.'

'Don't need much excuse for a festival here, do you? Or a tourist attraction. Some nutcase thinks he sees a couple of lights in the sky and suddenly it's one of the wonders of the world.'

Fifty yards in front of them Salinger saw a long pink-and-cream two-storey building with blue-striped awnings over the windows. He began to decelerate.

'You know that that old Rock Hudson flick was filmed here. *Giant*,' said Carson.

'The James Dean movie?'

'They all stayed at the Hotel Paisano. The cast, the crew, everyone.'

The car came to a halt in front of the hotel.

'So this is where Dad is,' said Carson.

'According to the crazy housekeeper with the bazooka.'

They got out of the car and hauled the luggage out of the trunk. A bellhop helped them carry it into the lobby. There were wooden beams supporting the ceiling and flagstones on the floor. There was no piped music. It felt cool and quiet, almost sepulchral. Just outside the lobby, a small concession was selling James Dean and movie memorabilia.

Past the shop was the reception desk. There was a huge buffalo head attached to a wall to the left of the desk. An old-fashioned silver bell ring was on the polished wooden surface. A small man with thin, slicked-back hair was inspecting a piece of paper behind the desk. A rangy, elegantly dressed woman with long grey hair who looked about sixty was standing in front of the desk tapping the end of a pen on a blotter. The bellhop, who was wizened and grey-haired, stood by, panting slightly from the exertion of carrying the luggage.

'I help you gentlemen?' said the clerk with the slicked-back hair, barely glancing up from a computer screen in front of him.

'We have a reservation for a twin room in the name of Nash.'

'An embarrassment of Nashes,' said the clerk, turning towards the tall woman. 'You two related?'

Carson and Salinger followed his gaze.

'Sort of,' said the woman, looking up.

'Ladybird,' said Carson. 'I didn't recognize you.'

'I got older,' said Ladybird.

'Me too,' said Carson.

'You must be Salinger,' said Ladybird.

'Hey, Mum,' said Salinger, recoiling slightly. He was surprised at the bitter sarcasm in his voice. Ladybird gave a smile like a wisp of smoke.

'You found us. Henry never thought you would. But I had a hunch you'd track us down.'

The three continued to regard one another as if each was a fascinating mannequin in a museum of curiosities. Ladybird maintained a street-mime stillness, detached and very faintly amused. Salinger found that he was staring at the floor. Carson was grinning manically, as if he had just walked in front of the cameras as a guest on a chat show.

Ladybird broke the impasse by taking a step forward and embracing Carson with long, slender arms. Carson kept grinning. Salinger watched as if this was some kind of mysterious trick of 3D projection. Carson, still in the embrace, didn't seem to know what to do with his arms. They stuck out loosely at an angle behind Ladybird's back.

'I'm glad to see you again, Carson. After all these years.'

Carson did nothing. He stayed attached to Ladybird as if letting go would mean he would slide to the floor. Ladybird eventually freed herself and took a small step towards Salinger, her arms extended. Salinger held his palm up to stop her.

'Of course. I understand completely. I'm sorry.'

Ladybird let her hands drop to her sides. Salinger realized that he had picked up his luggage. He put it down again. He looked at Carson, who had stopped smiling. His face now wore a stupefied expression.

'Would you like me to have the bellhop look after that?' said the desk clerk.

'Sure,' said Salinger. His eyes were back on Ladybird. The ancient bellhop picked up the bags.

'Room 15,' said the desk clerk. The bellhop, panting, began dragging the suitcases towards the stairs.

'Shall we sit down?' said Ladybird. She indicated

a table just beyond the reception desk with a sofa and two chairs around it.

They each sat down at the table, Ladybird on the sofa, Carson and Salinger in the chairs.

'You've had a long journey,' said Ladybird.

Her voice was light and warm. Salinger inspected her face. There was a slight horsiness to it, with cheekbones long and angular and the teeth marginally protruding. She was not an attractive woman, but held herself as if she were one. Salinger supposed it was what was meant by poise. She was tall. Even sitting down, the upper part of her frame put her above Salinger.

'Where's our father?' said Salinger, again surprised – this time at his own formality, his urgency, his need.

'He's asleep.'

'How is he?'

'He's dying, I'm afraid.'

Salinger had once gone on a fishing trip off the coast of East Africa. He had bought the trip on impulse, after seeing a scrawled chalkboard sign leaning against the harbour wall offering an afternoon hunting swordfish for what amounted to little more than thirty dollars. He had never fished before, but the promise that the grinning, gesturing, importuning fisherman had made was that he would, without doubt, be able to catch a swordfish with ease. He could more or less guarantee it. There was heavy tackle and a restraining seat on the deck. He had been excited at the possibility of manfully struggling to bring in a six-foot pronged fish. It struck some primal, predatory chord.

Salinger and the fisherman had travelled out onto the Indian Ocean. They fed the water with meat scraps and blood. In two hours they caught nothing at all. Eventually, the fisherman shrugged and apologized and turned the boat back towards home. The money had been paid. There was no question of a refund. Salinger had resigned himself to the fact of having fallen victim to a scam – or simply having suffered bad luck, as the fisherman monotonously and repeatedly claimed.

Just as they were approaching the harbour again, Salinger felt a tug on the line. The tug was light. It couldn't possibly be a swordfish. Helped by the fisherman, he reeled in the catch. Sure enough, it was a small fish, not much larger than a sea bass. But as the line shortened and the fish came clearly into view, suspended above the waterline now, Salinger was struck with amazement.

The fisherman looked unimpressed, as he picked the fish off the end of the hook. Clearly it was not an uncommon species. Typically for a tropical fish, it was brightly coloured. The remarkable thing about it was that the colours were not fixed, as it were, in a static design. It was spangled with an iridescent array of shades and hues. The entire prism of colours, changing and transforming, was splashed across the writhing, slipping envelope of scales, as the lowering red sun captured the fish with its rays.

It was more vibrant than a bird of paradise. Salinger thought it was spectacular – he had never seen anything like it. But the fisherman just ripped the hook out of its mouth and threw it on the deck in disgust. He apologized, then returned to steer the boat into the harbour. Salinger had watched the fish as it lay on the deck of the boat and flicked its tail more and more slowly.

Then, in front of Salinger's eyes, the colours on the scales began to flicker out, one by one. It was like watching a colour Polaroid photograph of the light cast by a prism develop in reverse, going from something charged and luminescent into a state of mere absence. The purples disappeared, the reds, the oranges, the greens, the electric blues. In a few seconds, what was left on the deck was a grey piece of fishmeat. He had stared at the dead fish for minutes on end. Eventually, just as they arrived back at the harbour, the fisherman had simply picked up the carcass and flung it over the edge.

Salinger glanced up at Carson. His face had turned the colour of the grits he had fed him in New Orleans.

Ladybird was nodding determinedly and repeatedly, as if she wanted both Carson and Salinger to be entirely clear about the non-negotiable quality of mortality.

'Henry came here to die. Marfa was where it

all began for him. He saw *Giant* at the Kilburn Gaumont State Cinema when he was ten years old. With Rock Hudson and Elizabeth Taylor and James Dean. He always told me he fell in love with America that day. He said that it made him think it was a country where loneliness had grandeur. That was the phrase he used.'

'He's dying,' said Salinger, turning the phrase around in his mind and examining it for meaning, for resonance.

'That's right,' said Ladybird. 'He's very close to the edge now.'

The desk clerk looked over from behind the desk. 'You want some coffee?'

'Decaf. Skimmed milk,' said Ladybird crisply.

Salinger nodded. The clerk looked at Carson, but Carson did not move or show that he had heard anything. The clerk picked up the phone and ordered two coffees.

Salinger looked at Ladybird, as if convinced that either he had misheard or she was grotesquely misinformed.

'He has prostate cancer. He's got a couple of days left. Maybe a week.'

'That's very exact,' said Salinger. He felt that he was speaking from very far away.

'He's got his own schedule which he means to stick by.'

'His own schedule?' said Salinger.

Instead of elaborating further, Ladybird turned to Carson.

'Are you still a Christian, Carson?'

Ladybird looked across the table at Carson. Carson said nothing. Salinger reached over and patted the back of Carson's hand.

'I can't really take all this in,' said Salinger.

'I understand,' said Ladybird. 'It must come as a bit of a shock.'

The coffee arrived. There was silence while the waitress distributed the cups and placed the pot down. Ladybird handed her a five-dollar bill.

'I hope you're not expecting too much of Henry,' said Ladybird after she had poured.

'Is he lucid?' said Salinger.

'Completely. He's in some pain, and he's tired, and he's very thin. But he's got morphine to help him. He's self-medicating. When the time comes, he will fully self-medicate.'

There was a pause as Salinger took this in.

'He's going to kill himself. Why don't you just come out and say it?' said Salinger.

The desk clerk looked up sharply.

'He'll leave life as he lived it,' said Ladybird. 'On his own terms.'

'I want to go to my room now.'

Both Salinger and Ladybird turned to Carson. It was the first time he had spoken since they had sat down together. His voice sounded petulant and impatient.

'Yes. You must be tired,' said Ladybird. 'Take a shower. Have some lunch. We can meet again later.'

'When do we get to see Dad?' said Salinger.

'I'll talk to him,' said Ladybird.

'Expect he can barely wait,' said Salinger, bitter again.

'He's very tired most of the time. The early evening is best. You've waited all these years, a few more hours isn't too much to ask.'

'I want to go to my room,' said Carson again. This time, his voice was completely toneless.

In room 15, Carson and Salinger lay on their separate beds staring at the ceiling. The afternoon sun was making patterns there, moving matrixes of yellow light. Carson still seemed unable to speak. Salinger mentally shifted words about, trying to find a sentence that wasn't too small for the situation.

A cloud passed across the sun. The room fell into shadow and Carson finally spoke.

'I wish I had never come. It was a stupid, stupid mistake.'

'I'm not so sure.'

Carson swung his legs over the side of the bed and looked at Salinger, who was still stretched out.

'What are you feeling, Sal?'

'What am I feeling? I'm feeling that I want to give the old bastard a piece of my mind before he pegs out. He abandoned us, ignored us, disowned us. Now he leads us on a wild goose chase, so he can enjoy the narcissistic glory of having his sons there to watch him die. Well, fuck him.'

'No, no, no, no, no. He's our father. You mustn't say that.'

'He's a prick.'

'Sal – stop it.'

'He's always been a prick.'

'So why come all this way to see him?'

'So I could be absolutely one hundred per cent sure what he was.'

'Thinking that way – it's not going to get you anywhere.'

'I'm not a Christian like you. I don't have to go around forgiving every fucking prick in the universe.'

'So what are you going to do? Settle accounts on his deathbed?'

'Why not?'

Carson fell back into silence. He got up and inspected his face in the wall mirror.

'I look ten years older than I did when I started this journey.'

'You still look younger than me.'

There was a faint knock at the door. Salinger rose and opened it. It was Ladybird. Salinger invited her in, but she remained in the corridor.

'I just want to say that Henry is strong enough to see you this afternoon.'

'Good of him,' said Salinger.

'Not for long. Maybe ten minutes. He's weak.'

'Only ten minutes?'

'I guess since he's dying, he gets to call the shots.'

Ladybird peered inside the door.

'That OK with you, Carson?'

Once again, at the sight of Ladybird, Carson appeared struck dumb.

Ladybird nodded once.

'So – you staying here? Or you going to have a walk around town?'

'We're not sure,' said Salinger.

'So listen – maybe be in your room about four o'clock? I'll come and get you. OK?'

Ladybird withdrew. Carson started to pace nervously up and down the floor.

'He's dying, so he's all-powerful,' said Salinger. 'He's rubbing our noses in it.'

'I don't know if I can face going in there,' said Carson.

'You did it before.'

'He wasn't dying then.'

There was the sound of motorbikes outside, and a faint police siren. When they faded, there was birdsong. Outside, in the sky, Salinger could see large hovering silhouettes that Carson had identified as vultures.

'I'll pray. It'll be OK.'

'Even if it's not OK, it will be over soon. What's the worst that can happen?'

'The worst that can happen has already happened.'

'What's that?'

Carson's eyes were wide and desperate.

'He's *dying*, Salinger. We'll never see him again.'

'We never saw him again anyway.'

'But this is different. It's the last chance.'

'The last chance for what?'

There was the chiming of bells in the distance. Salinger wondered if, like the church bells in Mesilla Plaza Green, the sound was recorded, and then wondered if it mattered. The sound was the same, he supposed.

Later, Salinger decided to take a walk into the town. Carson was asleep, or had his eyes closed at least and wasn't responding to questions.

There was nothing much to be seen. Churches, houses, empty streets. The sole art museum, the Chinati Foundation, was closed. He felt simultaneously bored and tense.

After half an hour, he started to walk back towards the hotel. Three blocks before the hotel, he saw a second-hand bookshop that he hadn't noticed on the outward journey. As much to get out of the heat as anything he went inside. There didn't seem to be anybody serving. He browsed the books.

After a few minutes' rummaging, he heard a woman's voice drift from the other side of the room.

'Looking for anything in particular?'

'I'm just trying to get out of the heat.'

'You don't like books?'

Salinger looked up. A woman was standing behind the counter. She was fully made up with dyed red hair and wearing a tight-fitting dress. She looked like she ought to be in a nightclub.

'Up to a point.'

'Then you're in the right place.'

'I just don't read many of them.'

'What kind of books *do* you like?'

'Textbooks. Reference books. Comic books. Those novelty books you put in the bathroom.'

'Come on. I don't believe you. You look smart.'

'There's a few authors I still think worthwhile, I guess.'

'Who do you prefer? English or American? You are English, right?'

'I don't read many American novels.'

'How come?'

'A deep and ineradicable childhood scar.'

'I thought the English were meant to be stoic.'

'English stoicism went out of fashion sometime in 1956.'

'Good books are *really* good though, aren't they? When you find them.'

'I guess.'

Salinger's eye lighted on an old, cloth-covered novel. He slid it out from the shelf. It was marked *$3*.

'This is one of the good ones.'

He held it up to the woman behind the desk.

She licked her lips. It was as if she actually found the thing sexy.

'One of the great ones. You want me to wrap it?'

Salinger got back to the hotel room at around three thirty. Carson was awake and blankly watching Jerry Springer on the TV.

329

'Rehearsing for the meeting with Dad? "Father Abandoned Sons for Romantic Vision of Distant Country and Now Wants to Kill Himself."'

Carson ignored him. Salinger picked up the remote and switched off the TV. Carson didn't react. He continued staring at the blank screen.

'I got you a present.'

Salinger handed the parcel to Carson. He lethargically tore at the paper, then stared at the cover.

'Thanks.'

'You must have a copy already, I suppose.'

'Must I?'

'Come on.'

Carson put *The Ballad of the Sad Café* down on the bed. Salinger had liked the edition, which was entirely typographic except for a strip down the left-hand side which displayed an illustration in browns and reds of Carson McCullers, her fringe cut to within half an inch of her brows, her slightly bulbous nose, her undistinguished mouth.

'What are you talking about?'

'What are *you* talking about?'

'Who's . . .'

He picked up the book and studied the spine.

'Who's Carson McCullers?'

'You're kidding me.'

'What?'

'You were *named* after her.'

Carson laughed.

'That's bull! Carson's a man's name. I was named after Kit Carson. You know, the frontiersman.'

'Who told you that?'

'What does it matter who told me? Hell, I don't remember.'

Salinger sat down on the bed.

'You were named after Carson McCullers. Carson McCullers is a woman. You can ask Dad yourself.'

Carson started to turn the book over in his hand.

'Surely you knew that, really, Carzy. How can you forget something like that?'

'I guess you forget what you need to.'

'I'd rather be named after Carson McCullers than Kit Carson. She was a genius.'

'She was also a fricking girl. I'm sticking with the Kit Carson story. He had a gun and everything.'

'A coonskin hat.'

'Or was that Davy Crockett?'

Carson stared at the book.

'Thanks for this anyway. I might even read it.'

'I wrote inside.'

Carson opened the book to the title page. Inside there was a pencil line drawing of Carson and Salinger in the car looking out onto the highway. There was a roadrunner crossing the road in front of them, and a dog running away, a terrified expression on its face. A thought bubble emanating from its skull contained an exclamation mark.

Carson was depicted behind the wheel with his eyes fixed on a sign announcing the speed limit. Salinger was sitting next to him, dangling a set of keys precariously out of the window. A dangerous-looking Mexican with a cartoon moustache was running by the side of the road ready to catch the keys when they dropped. Behind them was Wendell in a tiny police car brandishing a pistol which he was pointing at the Mexican.

The inscription read *Carson and his idiot kid brother, USA, summer 2008. With love, Salinger*

He patted Salinger tenderly on the arm. Salinger covered Carson's big, ham-like hand with his delicate, long fingers. He squeezed Carson's hand very slightly. Carson did not try and take it away. Salinger felt the warmth of the skin pressed against his own.

Eventually, after several seconds had passed, Carson slid his hand out from under Salinger's and picked up the book again and studied it.

'It's real nice, Salinger. Artistic as hell,' he said very softly. 'Thank you.'

'You're welcome.'

Then his voice racked up to the normal level again, as he put the book away in his briefcase.

'Still think I'm named after Kit Carson though.'

The knock came at exactly four o'clock. Salinger answered. It was Ladybird, who had changed into floaty layers of what appeared to be yellow and cream silk. She was barefoot. Her toenails were painted midnight blue.

None of them spoke. Salinger and Carson followed Ladybird down the hall, up a single flight of stairs, and to the furthermost end of a long corridor. Ladybird knocked on a door. Something between a growl and a mutter emerged from the other side.

Ladybird put her key card in the door and pushed. Inside, the curtains were closed and the light was low. Salinger and Carson were forced to squint through the gloom.

Henry was sitting in a wheelchair by the window with his back to them. There was a table by the chair with a half-full bottle of Scotch and a tea mug. Salinger could hear the rasp of Henry's breathing. He did not turn as they entered, or show any sign that he was aware that they were present.

There were two empty upright wooden chairs behind him. Salinger and Carson approached slowly, while Ladybird held back. She retreated into an opposite corner of the room, where she sat in a third chair, watching the scene intently, as if to moderate.

Salinger and Carson took up position next to the chairs behind Henry. He did not look away from the window. The three of them stayed frozen in this posture for ten or fifteen seconds. Then Henry slowly manoeuvred his chair round to face them.

Salinger tried to make his gaze bore into his father's face. Henry didn't flinch. His eyes were watery, red and blue, faded, angry. Rough white bristles forested his skin, which was laced with broken blood vessels. A plastic tube penetrated his right nostril. He stared up at his sons silently. His lips were pursed into white cables. They glistened with spittle.

'Hello, Henry,' said Salinger. He had planned to be blithe, but his voice was graver than he had intended.

Henry nodded. Salinger felt the presence of Carson next to him. He could hear intakes of rapid breath.

'Hello, Dad.'

Henry nodded again. Salinger could see that his right arm was trembling slightly. His face showed no expression. His mouth was slightly turned down at either end. He raised his left arm and gestured towards the chairs in front of him. Salinger and Carson sat.

Henry held them both in his gaze. Salinger could see that, for all his physical weakness, he was still strong. There was the power of will in his eyes. His lids fell slightly in the dusk. His hands were bony, and were flecked by light-grey hairs.

'You came.'

His voice was surprisingly powerful, grave and defiant.

'Yes, Dad, we're here,' said Carson. He reached across to grab hold of Henry's hand, but Henry pulled it sharply away.

'I'm sick. I'm not an invalid. You don't have to treat me like a cripple.'

'Dad, I wasn't,' said Carson.

The room fell back into silence.

334

Salinger felt aloof and distant, separate from the proceedings. The old man in front of him meant nothing to him. He was a near-carcass, an irrelevant detail, a rainbow fish mustering its strength for a final flip.

Henry's gaze moved slowly from one son to the other.

'You sure you want to have this meeting? Not too late to drive away again. You've seen me now. Mission accomplished.'

'Of course we want to see you, Dad,' said Carson. 'Salinger's come thousands of miles.'

Henry began coughing, then, with great difficulty, seemed to haul himself under control. He took a drink from the tea mug. It had the *Hotel Paisano* logo on one side and a picture of James Dean in a cowboy hat on the other.

'If you're hoping I'm going to ask you both for forgiveness, you should turn round right now.'

Another fit of coughing overtook him, but then his eyes cleared. There was nothing in those eyes that Salinger could read.

'How are you, Dad?' said Carson.

'I'm dying. How the hell do you think I am?'

Carson suddenly, shockingly, began to cry. His chest heaved, and he gave way to great racking sobs. His shoulders shook. His face was turned to the floor. Salinger had never seen Carson cry in his life.

He was surprised at how satisfying it felt.

'You look pretty good to me, Pops,' said Salinger, ignoring Carson. 'For someone at death's door.'

Henry wheezed. Salinger realized it was laughter.

'What made you such a mean old motherfucker?' said Salinger.

Carson abruptly brought his sobbing under control.

'Sal . . . don't . . .' he muttered.

Henry continued his wheezing laughter.

'That's it, Salinger! You tell it like it is. How's things back in that rinky dink little shithole of a country you live in? At least Carson had the guts to get out.'

Carson looked pathetically grateful for this remark. Salinger scratched calmly at a small mole on the back of his hand.

'So how are you really, Henry? Considering, as you say, that you're nearly dead.'

'Pretty good, considering that vital caveat. Hey, boy.'

He was looking at Carson.

'You got a cigarette?'

Carson had a pack of Lucky Strikes crammed into his top pocket. He fumbled for them and handed one to Henry with a lighter. Henry lit it and took a deep, appreciative breath.

'I don't think you're supposed to smoke in here,' said Carson.

'What they going to do to me?' said Henry. 'Kill me?'

'So how have you been for the last thirty

336

or so years? You know – since you left us,' said Salinger.

'Happy. *Damned* happy, I would say. Until I started dying.'

'Well, that's great, Dad. I'm really tremendously pleased,' said Salinger.

'So when did you two suddenly become such great friends?' said Henry, his lids drooping, hooding his eyes, as he switched his gaze once again from one to the other.

'No responsibilities, that kind of thing,' continued Salinger, ignoring Henry. 'That must feel good.'

Henry pulled at the cigarette. Salinger had a sudden vision of the smoke as Henry's departing spirit.

'Always the angry one. Determined to exact his tithe of repentance. You're wasting your breath, kid. Sorry.'

'We don't appear to be living up to your expectations.'

'You're living up to my expectations precisely.'

Henry stretched and relaxed. To Salinger's surprise, he got up out of the wheelchair, holding his drip bottle in his hand, and began to pace slowly around the room.

'Don't get me wrong. You weren't bad kids. Weren't that good either. But I did what I did. It's kind of lame chasing me halfway across a continent to wag a finger at me – isn't it?'

He turned his gaze to Carson.

'Or to put me up on some kind of ridiculous pedestal. You're men now. Be men.'

Salinger scanned his father's features again. The yellowed skin, the white hair, the burst of beard, the out-of-control eyebrows, the slight trace of wetness at the corners of his mouth. He might have been looking at a perfect stranger. He did not recognize him at all. The face did not chime with his memory. Neither did he bear any resemblance to the young man in the photographs that Salinger had brought over for Carson.

'But, Dad, we . . .'

Henry cut Carson off simply by raising his hand.

'You know why I was happy, Carson?'

Other than asking him for a cigarette, it was the first time that Henry had addressed Carson directly.

'I was happy because I was free. You ever known what it feels like to be free?'

'I don't know, Dad, I guess I . . .'

Henry turned and gazed out at the falling light.

'Your breath tastes different in your mouth, in your lungs. More of it. Your world opens up. Your mind has windows. You're not hedged in. You can see the sky. My God, it's a fine feeling. I never knew what it felt like till I came to America. Till I met my darling Birdy.'

He turned to look across the room at Ladybird, and smiled.

'Then it was like a great rush. A goldrush. A landslide of possibility.'

'High price,' said Salinger.

'Hell – not for me,' said Henry, pulling on the

cigarette, and letting the ash drop carelessly on the floor.

He seemed to be building himself up into some kind of frenzy. He feebly punched at the air with a trembling arm.

'Freedom, see. This is what I'm saying. What this country is all about. The *feeling* of freedom. Do you even remember what that's like? With your CCTV and your DNA profiling and your health and your safety and your safety and your health. Fuck that. I need another drink.'

He took a swig from the mug and topped it up from the bottle of Scotch.

'I had the guts to go out and take it. Birdy helped me to do it, but mainly I did it for myself. People talk about being proud of bringing up their kids, but it's bullshit. It's just something they say. Bringing up kids is the price you pay for keeping the loneliness at bay, for paying off the fear of doing something different, of *being* someone different.

'Yeah, I had some happy times with you two and even poor old Evelyn. But not that many. Not that many. And in the end, it kills you, it destroys you, it sucks you dry. I wasn't going to let that happen. I didn't let that happen. That I'm proud of. Yes.'

He fell into silence, simply contenting himself with a series of affirmatory nods.

'Is this all you have to say?' said Salinger, reaching into his inside pocket. 'This is the best you can do?'

'What do you *want*? You're in my past. I'm in

yours. Let's face facts. Yeah, from your point of view I'm a lousy, selfish old shit. So what follows from that? Nothing. It is what it is. There is no restitution.'

'Come on, Dad,' said Carson pleadingly. 'Don't be that way.'

'Don't you have any guilt?' said Salinger. 'Any shame? Any *explanation*?'

Henry laughed, a sound that was almost indistinguishable from his coughing.

'You want a manifesto? You want my *philosophy*?'

He nodded, sat back down in the wheelchair, and stubbed his cigarette out in an ashtray made of tinfoil.

'Let me state it plainly. Let me go on the record. Write it down. Get it framed, if you like.'

Ladybird stepped forward from the shadows in the corner of the room.

'I think Henry's tired now. Perhaps we should carry on with this tomorrow.'

Henry waved her away. She hesitated, and opened her mouth to say something. Then she seemed to think better of it, and melted once more, silently, into the background.

Henry was slurring his words slightly now. Salinger wondered what effect a mixture of Scotch and morphine would have on your mind.

'I gave you pain. Yes, I did. But you can *do* something with pain.'

He fixed his eyes on Salinger, and pointed a long bony finger.

340

'It made you a good artist, Salinger. I gave you this. I gave you the desperation, the passion to *understand*. Otherwise what would you be? Where would you be? In some nuthouse somewhere. You'd stink of spaghetti hoops and spend your day making baskets. Because you've been cracked since you were a kid.'

Now Henry turned to Carson.

'And you – I gave you a new life, because you came to America instead of pushing paper in some grisly, grinding office, like the place I spent the first fifteen years of *my* life before I left, draining the blood out of me, day by day. Didn't matter that it was just so you could be on the same continent as Daddy. The thing is, you made the switch. You took a risk.

'But that's just hindsight, that's just chance. We don't know about *outcomes*. It isn't *given* to us. You just do what you must, or what you're brave enough to do. You can't be good and happy – you have to choose. In the year of 1978, I finally figured it out. I was good for the first part of my life. And for the second part, I was happy. You want me to regret that? I can't. I won't. Fuck regret. Regret stops you being free.

'Now – sure – I'm unhappy again. Dying isn't a stroll in the park. It scares the shit out of you. But don't fool yourself I'm unhappy because I think I made a mistake. I never made a mistake. So don't unload all your need for restitution on me. I don't need it and I don't want it. You're

341

not here to see me. You're here for revenge. You're here because you didn't get your bill paid, you didn't get your *due*. But I didn't do anything *criminal*. And I'm the one who's dying. Me. Me. Me.'

Henry shook his head, wheezing again.

'Are we done?' said Henry, spluttering so hard that Salinger thought for a moment he was going to expire there and then.

'You cold-hearted, selfish fuck,' said Salinger. 'You monster. You failure.'

'That's the spirit, Sal. That's my boy,' said Henry, regaining his breath.

'You're going to be a grandfather, Dad,' said Carson softly.

Carson for the first time met Henry's gaze. His eyes were red-rimmed, his cheeks stained with dirt and water.

'LouLou – my wife, LouLou – is pregnant. She's due in three months. Less.'

'Congratulations,' said Henry flatly.

'I wish he would have known his grandfather, Dad.'

'Why the hell would you want that? Salinger's just said what I am. He's got my number. He's dead right.'

Salinger watched Henry carefully. Some chink had appeared behind his eyes. Salinger could see it. He hadn't expected the part about the grandson. It had caught him off guard.

Salinger suddenly felt that a space had opened

up, a space in which he could get to Henry. In which he could hurt him. He felt in his inside pocket.

'So. No regrets,' said Salinger, pulling out the Polaroid photograph.

'Regrets are stupid. They're what stops you—'

'Stops you doing what?'

'Stops you being free. I just told you. Why the hell don't you listen?'

'What about this? You got any regrets for this?'

He handed the photograph to Henry, who reached tremulously for a pair of wire-rimmed glasses that lay on the edge of the table next to his chair. He looked towards Carson, who was staring at Salinger with wide, frightened eyes. He hissed at Salinger, as if trying to camouflage the words.

'You told me that you wouldn't . . . you *promised*. On the life of Henry Jnr.'

'He has to face up to *something*. I won't let him go from this world without it. Anyway the photograph isn't what you said. It isn't Henry at all. It's me, Carson. It's me.'

Henry was inspecting the photo through his glasses now.

'I know who it is, Salinger,' said Carson, his voice heavy and sad.

Salinger turned sharply in Carson's direction.

'You *knew* what he did? You knew what Henry did to me, and you never told me?'

'No, it's not what you . . .'

'What you got to say about that, Daddy?' said Salinger, turning back to Henry, cutting Carson short.

'What do you want me to say?' said Henry levelly, handing the photograph back to Salinger.

Salinger's sense of distance collapsed. He felt a rush of awful, world-destroying rage. He wanted to grab the sick old man. He wanted to punch him in the face until his face was that of the child, that of Salinger himself.

'Look what you did to me. Look what you did to me. You didn't just leave me. You did *that*. What did you use? Your fists? Some kind of weapon? Was it just once? Did you do it whenever you were drunk?'

Henry was wheezing again, and shaking his head.

'I believe it was a cricket bat,' he said calmly. 'And I was never drunk.'

Salinger could barely take in the words now.

'My whole *life*. My whole life has been depression, and hurt, and sadness, and anger, and mental wards, and guilt, guilt, guilt. I never understood why, Henry, I never understood it. But you hurt me. You did it to me. I was four years old, for God's sake. I can't be more than four years old.'

Henry stretched his neck, and said nothing.

Suddenly, without warning, Carson snatched the photograph out of Salinger's hand. Salinger snatched it back and held it out of Carson's reach. Carson looked like he had gone wild, like he was about to jump on Salinger and fight for it.

'The fuck, Carson!'

'You said you wouldn't do that, Sal.'

'You know why Carson told you not to do that, Sal?' said Henry in a low, tapering voice.

He took another sip of whiskey. Salinger sensed that Henry's self-possession had finally deserted him. Henry was staring at Carson, but Carson wouldn't meet his gaze.

Salinger felt a bolt of confusion. There was some charge of knowledge passing between Carson and Henry that he didn't understand.

'Stop it, Dad,' said Carson. 'Please stop it.'

Henry said nothing. Then Carson, to Salinger's amazement, abruptly turned and started pacing swiftly towards the door.

'Carson!'

Carson said something. Salinger couldn't make the words out. Then Carson was gone, leaving the door swinging open behind him.

'What did he say?' said Salinger. 'I couldn't hear him.'

'He said, "I'm sorry, Daddy,"' said Ladybird, stepping once more out of the shadows.

CHAPTER 16

MAY 1972

Carson had saved for the Airfix kit of the Focke-Wulf FW 189 'Flying Eye' reconnaissance plane with his own pocket money and it had taken him an entire week's worth of spare time to assemble it. The final result had justified the effort. The glued seams showed no trace of seepage. It had taken painstaking application of eleven kinds of paint to complete the livery on the unique twin-boom design. The MG 15 machine gun in the rear cone looked excitingly poised for action. The transfers had taken perfectly – blue, white and red German crosses on the wings and tailfin, with yellow 'Eastern Front' markings on the wing tips.

On the morning of his father's birthday, he had presented it to Dad, just before he left for work, as he was hurriedly finishing his breakfast of Rice Crispies and marmalade toast. His father had taken the unwrapped gift from Carson's small, eager hands, which were still sticky with glue, and he had smiled and said thank you politely. He examined the model plane for a moment, from several angles.

Very nice, he had said. *Very nice.*

Then he put the plane on the kitchen windowsill, checked his watch and left for work.

When it remained there, unclaimed and unremarked upon by his father for a further week, Carson took it to his room and with a small hammer that he had taken from his father's tool kit, smashed it to pieces and threw it in the dustbin. His father never said anything about the disappearance of his gift.

Salinger's offering had been received differently. The gift was nothing much – a drawing with wax crayons that he had completed in ten minutes or so. Carson had watched him do it, the day after Dad's birthday (Salinger had forgotten and had to be reminded by Mum).

It was a pathetic drawing, thought Carson – some squiggles that were meant to be party balloons, some cartoon hearts, and a picture of a cowboy holding a lasso with the word 'Dad' scrawled on his ten-gallon hat. His father had hugged Salinger when he received it. He had hugged him long and close. Then he had secured the picture with drawing pins to the wall of his bedroom, above the chest of drawers that faced the bed.

Now his father had left on a work trip. He would be gone for two weeks, his mother told him, over his breakfast of Golden Nuggets and orange juice. He had left without saying goodbye to Carson, because, his mother said, he had thought Carson was asleep. But Carson had not been asleep. He had been lying in bed, listening to his father zipping closed his holdall, removing his keys from the hook in the hall and bidding a long farewell to Mum and Salinger, who had woken early because he had been having a bad dream. Salinger was always having bad dreams.

Later that day, Carson returned from school, and was playing with his magnetic robot game, while his mother was downstairs doing the ironing. He watched the robot spin to point the answer to the questions on the board. He was amazed by magnetism – the attraction, the repulsion, these powerful, invisible forces.

Now he decided to return to work on the British Supermarine Spitfire MK1 that he was making for his father. His father simply didn't like German aircraft, that was all. It had not occurred to him that the Germans were the enemy. He just thought the Focke-Wulf looked beautiful and dramatic, but he had been very stupid to think that his father could like a gift that was flown by Huns and squareheads.

But he would like the Spitfire. Carson was sure of it. He'd never met anyone who didn't like Spitfires. The blunted wings decorated with the concentric circles of the bull's eye, the dragon's teeth beneath the nosecone, the khaki paintwork. He was just affixing the propeller to the front. It was nearly finished now. It had been a present from Granny Moll for his eighth birthday and he had been saving it up for himself, to put on his shelf next to his GI Joe and his collection of *Sgt Rock* comics. Now it would be his father's, and this time he would like it enough to put it in his bedroom, perhaps on the chest of drawers beneath Salinger's picture. Salinger's picture would eventually fade and peel from the wall, whereas the Spitfire was durable. There was no reason why it couldn't remain there for ever.

As he worked on the Spitfire, he wondered momentarily where Salinger was. He wasn't crying or making a fuss for once. He was drawing, probably. Salinger was always drawing, or reading some stupid book.

From downstairs, he could hear the faint sound of his mother singing a song to herself. *Carry on* . . . she sang. *Carry on* . . .

After a few minutes, Salinger appeared at the door of the small, cold room that they shared at the front of the house, overlooking the road. Carson didn't look up. Gluing the propeller on was tricky, a delicate operation which required maximum concentration. Also, he was nearly out of adhesive because Salinger had stolen it the previous day in order to glue some cardboard together to make a model house.

Salinger picked up a toy mouth organ from the floor where it lay and started playing it tunelessly. Carson stretched out, snatched the mouth organ from his hand and put it on a shelf out of his reach. Salinger started crying.

Carson told him to stop crying. Salinger cried louder.

Mum came in and told Carson off. Carson stared as words firecrackered out of her thin red mouth. She picked up Salinger and held him. She didn't pick up Carson much any more. She said he was too heavy. He didn't care. He didn't like her touching him. He hadn't since she had come back from hospital, years ago, with the complaining bundle of flesh and flannel that had now turned into this present, unceasing provocation. She stood now by the door, clucking over Salinger like a stupid hen.

He was relieved when Mum took Salinger downstairs with her. It meant that he could concentrate on his work. He had reached a crucial moment – the attachment of the tail section, after which he could start applying the decals of the plane's livery. He traced a thin trickle of glue across the open edge of the frame of the body of the plane. It smelled sweet and toxic, like cherries and sulphur.

There was a noise at the door. He looked up and saw Salinger again. Salinger stuck his tongue out at Carson. Carson ignored him and returned to the plane. He pressed the edges of the tail section against the main body of the fuselage. After holding it there for several seconds, he carefully let go. It held, but he knew it would be fragile until the glue set.

Salinger began noisily playing with Meccano, banging the pieces against one another. Carson told him to shut up. Salinger said that he wouldn't. Carson got up from where he was sitting and took the Meccano from Salinger. Salinger began to scream. Carson told him to shut up again.

Once again, Mum arrived. She was now wearing a pinafore with small red roses on it. Her hands were dusted with flour and she was wearing a scarf around her head. Salinger was complaining that Carson had taken the Meccano from him. Mother turned to Carson and slapped his leg, telling him to leave Salinger be. Carson didn't cry. He just looked at Salinger and his mother blankly and then turned and started to apply the decals to the fuselage.

Salinger and his mother went downstairs, but once again, five minutes later, Salinger returned. He kicked the wall and sat on his bed, staring into space while Carson worked silently. Salinger picked up a picture book, glanced at a few of the pages, then threw it across the room. It hit Carson on the leg with the corner. It hurt him, but Carson ignored it. He concentrated on the aircraft. He was pleased. He imagined the soft glue in the tail slowly hardening into something solid and unbreakable.

Salinger found a toy wooden cricket bat, and was bouncing a tennis ball up and down on the flat side. Carson told him to be careful with it. Salinger stuck his tongue out again. Carson continued to work on the Spitfire. It had taken him even longer than the Focke-Wulf to make. He would finish it today. There was only one colour of enamel paint left to apply, the Brunswick Green. He reached for his paintbrush, leaving the model balanced on the floor.

When the tennis ball smashed into the Spitfire, Carson felt oddly cold. It was as if someone had opened the window and let in arctic air, although it was warm outside. He looked up, and inspected the expression on his brother's face. He was hiding his pleasure by pretending to be frightened. Salinger started to scream. Without moving, Carson looked out of the window. His mother was leaving the house holding an empty cup. Sometimes she went to neighbours' houses to borrow flour or sugar.

Salinger was still gripping the cricket bat. Carson went over to Salinger to wrestle it out of his hands. To his surprise, since Carson was so much older and stronger, Salinger fought back.

As Carson got Salinger into an armlock, he looked across the room at the wreckage of the Spitfire. It was obviously irreparable. Salinger started screaming again as Carson tried to get the cricket bat from him. Salinger leaned across and bit Carson's arm through the material of his thin cotton shirt. The pain shocked him, but he remained calm.

Carson finally forced the cricket bat out of Salinger's hands. He drew it carefully back and brought it down in an arc into his brother's face. Salinger, instead of crying out, fell silent. Carson liked the silence, and the way the blow felt. He thought that nothing had ever felt so complete or satisfying. He struck him again, then a third time. He only stopped when he saw the blood coming out of his brother's nose, and when Salinger fell still on the floor. It was then that Carson decided he ought to start crying.

When his mother returned, with the neighbour from whom she had been borrowing sugar, she turned white and ran from the room to where the telephone was. He ran after her, calling,

It wasn't my fault. I'm sorry. I didn't meant to do it.
I'm sorry, Mother.
I'm sorry, Mother.

As his mother came back up the stairs, having phoned someone, she attended to Salinger whose eyes had now flickered open. Carson begged his mother not to tell his father. He was very scared that his father might find out what he had done. His mother didn't reply, which he hoped meant that she might keep it as a secret.

Then everything went blank, because there was so much noise and activity. He knew that things were important when an ambulance arrived. He started to worry seriously when his mother didn't punish him. She just ignored him, concentrating entirely on Salinger. Salinger and his mother went to the hospital together, leaving Carson alone except for the neighbour, a virtual stranger.

He had the odd sensation that he had experienced something like this before, long ago.

★　　★　　★

The ladies from the council came the following day. Or Mum had said they were from the council. Carson wasn't sure what a council was. The council apparently had Suspicions.

Salinger had returned home. His face was bruised and stitched. The worst scar was in front of his right ear. The ladies from the council talked with Evelyn, who they called Mrs Nash, and took Polaroid photographs of Salinger's face. One of them didn't work properly. Mum watched as the social worker threw it in the bin.

When the lady from the council took Carson into a separate room and asked him about why he had hurt Salinger, he could only answer that it was because he broke his aeroplane. He said that he was very very sorry. The lady from the council smiled, but it wasn't a happy smile.

The lady from the council asked other questions – about his father, about his mother, about what he could remember about things that had happened a long time ago. Most of them he was unable to answer. She asked him if he would ever do such a thing again. He shook his head. She asked him if he had ever done such a thing before. He shook his head again, but he didn't think the lady believed him. She had probably been talking to Mum.

After a while, he said that he wanted to see his father. The lady told him what he already knew – that his father was away. Eventually the lady thanked him, patted him on the shoulder, gave him a liquorice Black Jack and left him alone.

Then he could hear his mother and the ladies from the council talking in the next room. Their voices were soft, but his mother's voice was urgent. Still no punishment came. He returned to his room and started picking up fragments of the Spitfire, which he had left there since the day before. Salinger was in the room. Salinger didn't look at him and didn't say a word to him. Carson liked it that way. Carson said very little to Salinger after that day. Salinger didn't bother him so much, either.

The punishment he had thought inevitable never came. More people came from the council and talked to him, and asked him the same questions as the first lady, but no one even smacked him. He had thought that the people from the council might take him away, but that didn't happen. Nothing happened. In ten days Salinger's face, with the bruising gone down, almost looked normal again. He hoped when his father saw it he wouldn't notice anything.

Eventually his father returned. Carson burst into the kitchen to greet him. His father looked up at him, and his face registered nothing at all. He said nothing. Then he turned and started talking to Mum again. Carson noticed a photograph on the table. Carson wondered if his mother had betrayed him. He decided that she must have done.

Carson turned away and went back upstairs. Shortly afterwards his father came into the room. Carson tried to hug him, but his father pushed him away. He told Carson to sit down, and explained to him that he was very angry about what Carson had done to Salinger. Carson said he was sorry and he would never do it again, but that Salinger had made him very angry.

Carson had kept all the pieces of the broken plane. He showed them to his father and told him how he had been making it for him, and that Salinger had broken it. He tried to put the pieces of the broken plane in his father's hand but his father wouldn't take them.

His father told him that, if Carson ever hurt Salinger again, Carson would no longer be able to live with them, and would have to go and live in a horrible place where none of the children had mothers or fathers. He made him promise.

His father said some other things that he didn't understand. Then he went downstairs again.

As soon as he had gone, Carson started working on the plane, trying to put the shattered pieces back together. He was determined that his father would accept his gift. He didn't care if it took for ever.

CHAPTER 17

MARFA – LONDON

Salinger woke late. He had been dreaming that he was strafing Piccadilly Circus from a Second World War fighter plane. Strangers scattered, screaming. The statue of Eros exploded into fragments under machine-gun fire. His brother, sitting in the back seat of the plane, told him in a calm, unemotional voice that what he was doing was unfair. Salinger was weary of his complaining. He had pressed an ejector-seat button which had catapulted Carson out of the plane. He found it pleasant to watch Carson tumbling towards the ground. Carson's parachute opened, but it was the size of a child's T-shirt. It could not possibly save him.

Carson had still not returned. Salinger tried repeatedly to phone him, unsure what he would say to him if he managed to make a connection, but there had been no response. He had phoned LouLou in New Orleans who had told him – as, it turned out, she had told Carson, when she had phoned him in Las Cruces, as Salinger and Carson looked at the stars – about the test results she had received for Henry Jnr.

The chances of Down's syndrome were one in five. This was what had prompted Carson to throw up by the side of the road – not the fear of meeting Henry. Or not only that fear.

LouLou was frightened. When she had told Carson, he had told LouLou to put her faith in the Lord. LouLou had told Carson, for the first time in their marriage, to fuck off. Then she had hung up the phone. She hadn't spoken to Carson since. Salinger reassured her that he was likely to arrive home any time now. She told him she was sorry the trip hadn't worked out. He said he was sorry about Henry Jnr and hoped it would be all right.

Still under the bedcovers, Salinger switched on the TV. John McCain and Barack Obama had both been summoned to Washington for an emergency meeting. The financial crisis was now spiralling out of control towards some kind of apocalyptic conclusion. Some part of him was enjoying the spectacle.

He was looking forward to speaking to Henry again. Ladybird said that she would come to the room when he was ready. He was not frightened of Henry in the way that Carson had been. He could see that Henry was scared of death and this made him smaller. Salinger's safe emotional distance from Henry had re-established itself.

When Henry told him the truth about the photograph, Salinger had been careful not to react. He would not give Henry that satisfaction. Besides, he didn't know what to feel.

He ordered room service, lay naked and drank coffee. He ate an omelette looking out of the window at the space where the Lexus had been parked. As he finished a glass of orange juice, there was a knock on the door.

Salinger slipped on a dressing gown and opened it. It was Ladybird, fully dressed in a pure white Indian-style thobe and sandals. She wore no make-up.

'Can I come in?'

Ladybird entered the room. There was nothing of her. She was stretched, thin and tired.

'Henry died.'

'What do you mean?' said Salinger.

'Around three in the morning.'

'I don't understand.'

Ladybird touched his arm.

Salinger turned to look out of the window. Pale sunlight was illuminating the side of his face. He looked down at his shoelaces. One of them was frayed.

The knowledge worked itself far enough inside him for Ladybird's words to begin to register. A single thought drifted into the slipstream of his understanding, bobbing and diving in the buffeting currents.

'Did he do it to himself?'

'No, Salinger. He just died. He died in his sleep. He died in my arms.'

Salinger blinked. He expected to start crying, but he felt nothing, not even surprise. The discomfort he felt was purely a matter of manners. He wasn't sure how to behave with Ladybird.

He examined her carefully. Then he held out his arms to her. She allowed herself to be enclosed by them, but it was awkward. She was too tall. He guided her towards a chair. Ladybird sat down, trembling slightly.

'I'm sorry I'm not crying,' said Salinger.

'Do you want to see him?' said Ladybird.

A plastic *Do Not Disturb* sign hung on the handle of the door. Inside the room, it was flooded with morning sunlight. On the king-sized bed, Henry was stretched out.

Ladybird had dressed him in plain white cotton pyjamas. For some reason, she had put his spectacles on. With the white beard, he looked like a sleeping prophet. She had combed his hair. His eyes were closed. His arms were crossed over his chest.

Salinger approached cautiously as if Henry was going to jump up and grab him by the neck. Ladybird withdrew a pace or two behind.

'Do you mind if I draw him?' said Salinger.

He took a pad and a pencil from his shoulder bag. Ladybird said nothing, so he began to sketch. He had never seen a dead body before.

'Maybe seeing you two was what he was waiting for,' said Ladybird.

'I'd like to say that he looks peaceful,' said Salinger. 'But he looks angry.'

His mouth was stretched slightly, and turned downward. His brows frowned. There was grey hair in his ears and his nose.

'He was angry at having to die,' said Ladybird.

Salinger's pencil moved back and forth across the paper, capturing the compactness, the wistfulness, the clear but intangible distinction that held death apart from sleep. He sketched the small, stiff feet, the wired hairs on the chest and the back of the hands. He felt a determination to capture every detail.

Henry was so still. He had never seen anything so still. He remembered how even with the little life that was left in him the previous day, Henry had been suffused with spirit. It raged, it was tormented, it was afraid, but it was burning. Now there was nothing. The span of the nothingness was immense.

'I don't feel well,' said Ladybird.

'Let me just finish this,' said Salinger.

Ladybird collapsed onto the floor. Salinger put down his pad and guided her gently to her feet. Her eyes were flickering. Salinger helped her to a chair.

'Could I have a glass of water?'

She straightened up on the chair, then stood up, only to sit down again. Her eyes were dazed, foggy. Salinger went to the minibar and brought out a bottle of water.

'Who are you, Ladybird?' said Salinger.

She drank from the bottle, draining half of it.

She put it down on the table and stared directly at Salinger.

'I'm the woman who loved your father. Nothing more.'

'You cost us so much,' said Salinger.

'Everybody pays the bill for goods they never received,' said Ladybird.

She looked defiant for a moment. Then her eyes fell back into a cloudy grief.

Salinger felt sure that Ladybird would fade away soon, and that she wouldn't mind the fading.

Salinger resumed the sketch, then finished it with a last pencil stroke. He looked at Ladybird. It seemed that she was barely breathing. He took a step over to her, briefly considered putting an arm around her again, then found himself unable to do it.

He held the drawing out to her.

'Would you like it?'

She nodded, and took it from him as if she had always owned it.

'I'd like to be alone with Henry now.'

'I understand.'

Salinger took one last look around the room. Ladybird balanced on her frail arm, her hand supporting her face. Henry in his pyjamas, eyes closed, face tilted towards the ceiling. The room falling into darkness. Two soiled cups of coffee on the bedside table, the milk beginning to sour. He left her there with Henry and went back to his room.

He had left the TV on. There was a special news bulletin being broadcast. A reporter was explaining what President Bush had said about the prospects for the global financial system. He had been uncharacteristically downbeat.

'This sucker,' he had said, 'could go down.'

Shortly afterwards, the Treasury Secretary knelt before the Speaker of the House and begged her for mercy. He had begged her to save the world from itself.

But the world would not be saved. That which strained against the leaden boundaries of self could be felt everywhere – in every house, in every temple, in every shop, in every bank. It was famished, insatiable. And in its wake would soon come the flood.

Salinger flew back from Las Cruces to New Orleans for his connection to London. He had made no further attempt to contact Carson. Neither had Carson phoned or sent an email. On the flight back to London, despite being seated next to a griping baby, he slept in perfect peace.

Tiane was not there to meet him at the airport. He had sent her the flight details and she had acknowledged receipt, but sent no message in return. Salinger knew without doubt now that something serious had happened.

As he made his way through the airport labyrinth that would lead him to passport control, the baggage carousel and customs – international airlocks leading back to the English world – he found himself staring at a plate-glass window adjacent to a moving walkway. The window reflected the travellers on the concourse.

His eyes shifted range to focus on the reflections behind the window. There were refracted figures moving in processions in both directions. Shadows moving in one direction and another, human forms, double images.

He tried to locate himself among the army of shadows, but he was indistinguishable from the mass. He was one among many, an unreachable ghost. Nothing solid, only a process, glimpsed indirectly, impossible to bring into focus.

People could not be grasped – they were barely there at all. And yet at the same time, there was nothing more real.

He decided to treat himself to a cab back to the flat. The return to Tokyngton took forty minutes. He observed, once again, the crammed acres of English suburbia. He was struck how green and small and primped it seemed after Texas and New Mexico.

'Been anywhere nice?' asked the taxi driver. He was a black man in his fifties with a lurid red burn scar on his neck and a corona of white hair that had receded to make a horseshoe pattern on his scalp.

'America,' said Salinger.

'Where?'

'Texas, mainly.'

'Just a holiday, was it?'

'Visiting relatives.'

'Not quite the same thing, is it?'

'What?'

'Visiting relatives. Not quite the same thing as a holiday.'

Salinger said nothing, and turned his attention back to the view outside the window. The sky itself seemed crushed. He opened the window of the cab, and mild, bland air blew into his face.

He breathed in England and felt an unexpected pang of love for it. Its smallness, its oddness, its banality, its quiet kindness, its proud philistinism.

Eventually, the taxi pulled into the familiar terrace in Tokyngton. The trees looked faltering and disappointing. Salinger looked for a sign of Tiane's car, but it was nowhere to be seen. The taxi driver drew up outside their house. Salinger paid him, and declined a fistful of blank receipts.

Salinger hauled his bags up to the front door and felt in his pocket for his keys. Before he could reach them, the door opened.

'Hello, Sal.'

'Hello, Tea.'

Something was different about her. He couldn't work out what it was. Then he understood that Tiane was wearing make-up. It was subtle, but unmistakable. She was wearing blusher and foundation and eyeliner and even lipstick. For once it was properly and carefully applied.

More than the emails she had never written,

365

more than the scene at the airport when he had left, it made him feel frightened.

Tiane held out her arms. Automatically, he moved into the space that they offered. They held one another stiffly, then Salinger took a step backwards. Tiane relieved him of his bag and they walked through to the kitchen.

'You want a cup of something?'

Salinger nodded.

'How was the trip?'

'If you'd answered any of my emails you would know that already.'

'Did you hate it?'

His mind flashed back. He saw the great open spaces. He saw Wakanda and Tahoma, he saw Wendell Valentine and the Mexican housekeeper brandishing the giant gun. He smelled the creosote, he tasted the brisket roll. He saw Gloria laughing as he dropped the coins and notes on the diner floor. He thought of the elation of the gliding motorcycle, the tilting loom of the Organ Mountains, the stars in the sky over Las Cruces.

'No,' he said firmly. 'I liked it a lot.'

Tiane scratched her nose. Salinger noticed that her fingernails, which were always bitten and unvarnished, had been manicured. They were painted red.

'I'm sorry about Henry.'

'Are you?'

They were still standing awkwardly, facing one another.

'Let's sit down,' said Tiane.

Salinger sat at the kitchen table while Tiane began to fumble with the tea bags, sugar and boiling water. He picked at a knot of wood in the table's surface, until a cup of red, steaming liquid was placed in front of him.

'Raspberry and vanilla,' said Tiane.

Tiane sat down directly opposite him. She was wearing a simple white cotton smock, leggings and no shoes.

'I brought you a gift,' said Salinger.

He reached into the bag and brought out the milagro cross he had bought for Tiane in Austin.

'Gifts are for people who deserve reward,' said Tiane.

'It's magical. It has powers to soothe spirits and calm waters.'

'Maybe you should have it then.'

'That sounds ominous.'

'Salinger . . .'

As he looked into her face, he knew clearly that he loved her, and he knew with certainty that he had lost her.

He felt the tears begin to come, and brushed them angrily away.

'Who is he? Why are you still here?'

'What makes you think there's a "he"?'

'Because I'm not an idiot.'

'No. That would be me.'

'Meaning?'

'Meaning I did something stupid.'

Salinger moved silently in his chair as if trying to dislodge the sensation of icy water in his bowels. The enjoyable feeling of invulnerability he had felt after the death of his father had evaporated.

'Tell me.'

Tiane spoke in a long tumble of words. There was nothing random about them. They had been meticulously rehearsed.

Never had Salinger listened to a voice so absolutely. Usually words sprinkled themselves on his surface, leaving the slightest sensation, then fell away like drops of moisture. These buried themselves under his skin, pellets of phosphorous, working their way to his core.

The man was a teacher at her school. His name was William Tarbox. He was married and had a child. They had been good friends for a long time. Salinger had met him once. He was unremarkable. He was from Northumberland, a steady, serious, practical man. He had propositioned Tiane the week before Salinger had left for America. He had not merely wanted to sleep with her, he had wanted to marry her. To have children with her. She had turned him down, but the offer had nagged at her, worried at something that had previously been secret within her.

'I think I was going a little bit mad that weekend before you went away,' said Tiane. 'I looked in the mirror and my eyes weren't mine. I started to believe in signs. It seemed such a coincidence that you were going to America just a matter of days after William had put this awful question to me. It seemed as if the world was speaking to me.

'I became overwhelmed with the idea of *finding out*. Finding out who I was – who I really was, underneath all the pretence about who I thought I was. After all, it seemed that I could be utterly surprised. Because William – the life that he offered me – it was calling out to me, so loud and clear. He wanted to have three children with me. Three.'

This number seemed to hold a special significance for Tiane. She fell silent. Salinger sat still, waiting for her to continue. Her eyes shimmered with tears. Eventually, she spoke again.

'I knew I loved you. But this noise in my ears. It drowned everything. I couldn't hear the sound of my life any more. So I decided to set you a test. I knew that you would fail the test. I knew that it wasn't fair. But it seemed at least to introduce an element of choice. Once I started to believe that the world was speaking to me, I thought I could give it a chance to make a comment, if you like. To nudge the future in one direction or another.

'So I told you to trust me. To trust me, and cancel the trip. It seemed to give you a chance. It seemed to take the burden of responsibility from my shoulders a little. It seemed to implicate you, just a little, in what I felt was about to happen. It asked something of you that I knew you would not give me, and which William had offered. That thing was absolute, unquestioning trust. And the stakes were so high for him. He said if I refused him he would leave his wife and child anyway. Loving me made his marriage impossible. He would give up his job, because to be around me if I refused him would be unbearable.'

Salinger felt a wave of sickness overwhelm him. He hooked the litter bin with his foot and brought it towards him, just in case, then held himself in check. But he could taste bile in his throat.

'I needed to find out, Salinger. So I took the opportunity.'

'You took it the night I left.'

'Yes.'

'You slept with William.'

'Yes.'

The silence that followed seemed to spread way deep from the past into the future. Eventually, Salinger could bear it no more. He wondered if, in some remote, abstract sense, he was dying. If this was what it felt like to be extinguished as a person, if not as a body.

'What happened after you slept with him?'

He tried to keep his voice even and unemotional. It was difficult. It kept vibrating, falling out of register.

'Everything was clarified.'

'Clear that you and I couldn't carry on.'

She leaned forwards towards Salinger. Her face filled his field of vision. He could only avoid her eyes by looking at her mouth. He watched it move as she spoke.

'I told him the next morning that the entire thing had been . . . The words I used were *ill-fated*. It was something I needed to do to understand what . . . what I now understand.'

'What is it that you've found out? What is it that you've *understood*?'

'William loved me. Loves me. He didn't want to fuck me. He didn't even want to date me. He didn't want to be my friend. He wanted me to have his children and spend my life with him. Do you understand?

'He wanted that passionately. He was prepared to destroy his life for that. I knew when you were away he would try and take me away from you. That's why I didn't want you to go away. Because I knew I would be weak.'

Salinger shifted his eyes to a small patch of discoloration on the table in front of him.

'Did he make you come?'

'Shut up, Sal.'

'How many times? Did he have a big cock?'

'Men. Always with the cocks.'

She risked a smile. Salinger found somewhere within himself an answering smile, bitter.

'Listen, Salinger. Listen to me. It doesn't matter. I only love you, Sal. That's the thing. That's what I found out. That's the information. Even if I never can have kids. I'll get over it. I'll get over it somehow. Being with you is more important to me than having children. Do you hear what I'm telling you?'

Salinger felt himself reeling, even as he sat, losing balance. He had prepared himself for Tiane's farewell speech. He had ripped himself open to make space to take it in. He had prepared himself for the conclusion, he had prepared himself for the slow walk along the hall.

'I want children, yes I do. I would love them, to tell you the truth. I didn't know that until William asked me. Then the feeling of it, the *possibility* of it, the potential of it – overwhelmed me. But we're strong enough to survive this.'

'What is it that we're surviving?'

'Not having children. I love you enough not to have children.'

'What about me surviving you sleeping with someone else?'

'That's for you to say.'

'You haven't said that you're sorry.'

'I'm not sorry. That's the terrible thing. I had to find out, Salinger. Otherwise it would have poisoned us all our lives.'

'Poisoned you.'

'Poisoned me, and therefore you.'

Salinger smashed his fist down on the table. The cup of herbal tea that he hadn't touched fell to the tiles on the floor. Inexplicably, it didn't break, although the tea was spilled onto the white tiles, leaving a spreading red pool.

'Can't you just *say* you're sorry? It's just – I

thought I might have earned an apology. Just a little apology. For going out and fucking someone else.'

'OK then. I'm sorry.'

'But you don't mean it.'

'I'm sorry that I hurt you. And I'm desperately sorry, if it means we can't be together. But I'm not sorry I did what I did. It took me to somewhere new. Where we can be stronger.'

'So you just said. But I have no understanding of your idea of strength.'

Salinger, defeated now, rose from the chair and started half-heartedly mopping at the tea with a cloth.

'Leave that. I'll do it later.'

Salinger continued with the mopping. He just seemed to be spreading the liquid wider and wider across the floor.

'What happened to this man?' said Salinger, crouched on the floor. 'This . . . William.'

'He was as good as his word. He left his wife. He misses his child desperately. He said it was the worst thing that had ever happened to him.'

Salinger considered this.

'Good.'

'He has no job. He's alone.'

'You've been cruel to everybody, then.'

'I'm not a cruel person.'

'You might not like being cruel. But you're prepared to be.'

'Maybe that's a sort of strength.'

'Maybe you're just a cunt.'

At last the tears came that Salinger had been holding back. He was not sure who they were for – Tiane, himself, Henry, Carson. Tiane did not move or speak.

'Did you use contraception?' said Salinger finally, when the tears had dried.

'Yes. I'm still on the pill.'

'That's thoughtful. Thank you, Tiane. Now can I ask you a question?'

'Of course.'

'Will you just fuck off now?'

Tiane didn't move.

'I mean now. Right now.'

Tiane nodded. Without another word, she picked up her coat and walked out of the door.

Salinger, to his surprise, slept well that night, despite his body clock being out of sync.

He rose in the morning, took the paper from the mat downstairs, and made himself a cup of coffee and toast. It was the first really good cup of coffee he'd had in weeks, and the first decent toast. The bread was sourdough. He scraped it with Marmite and savoured each bite.

He liked it, being alone in the kitchen. He imagined what it would be like here with Tiane moved out. He knew that he didn't need her. The only question left was whether he wanted her. And, of course, whether or not he could accept her story.

Life was entirely made out of stories. Everything

hinged on which ones you caught hold of – or which ones you couldn't unhitch yourself from.

The toast caught in his windpipe. He found himself struggling for breath.

All the stories, all the rationalizations, pressed in on him.

I was only a child, Salinger.

Regret is what stops you being free, Salinger.

I had to find out, Salinger.

He put on Radio Four and listened to the tumbling burble of daily events. Earthquake in China, an unimaginable number dead. A mother stabbed in a post office with a meat skewer by a teenager. Somebody fiddled their expenses. Some food that was once thought healthy was now harmful. Poor people were suffering. Good people were suffering. Everyone was suffering.

Most importantly of all, he was suffering.

After he had finished breakfast, he picked up the phone and dialled Tiane. She answered after a single ring.

'Come over. Let's settle things.'

He put the phone down, wondering what it was that he felt.

He was much clearer on what he thought.

CHAPTER 18

NOVEMBER 2008, PROVINCETOWN, MASSACHUSETTS

The drive from Boston Airport to Provincetown took three hours, first south then north along the spine of Massachusetts Bay. Here, English roots still pushed through into the American present – Salinger saw signs for Weymouth, Plymouth, Bridgewater and Yarmouth.

Once more, there was a hurricane coming. It wasn't just the Southern states that got battered by weather. America's extremity extended from coast to coast. As Salinger drove, he fought to keep control of the Chevrolet Aveo that he had rented from the airport. Sheets of water obscured the windscreen. Puddles were so deep he frequently found himself in danger of sliding off the road even travelling at 10 mph.

It wasn't for some time that the rain eased, and he could see clearly out of the window. A giant poster by the side of the road showed a mono-chrome shot of Barack Obama against the red and white of the American stripes. Salinger had punched the air for joy when the result of the election had been announced, two days earlier.

The mood stayed with him for an entire day, and even now, the world felt like a more lucent, hopeful place.

It was twenty-four hours until Henry's funeral. There had been a protracted inquest after his death in Marfa. The desk clerk had overheard the conversation after Salinger and Carson had arrived, when Ladybird hinted at Henry's intention to end his own life. Like Carson, the clerk was a strict Christian. He objected passionately to euthanasia.

But Ladybird, it turned out, had been telling the truth. The post-mortem showed that Henry had died of a seizure in the middle of the night brought on by pneumonia. The quantity of morphine Henry used was at the normal level for pain relief and was unlikely to have proved fatal.

By the time Salinger reached Provincetown, the storm had cleared. He drove through the narrow streets. The painted clapboard houses gave the town a cheerful, almost celebratory feel.

He drove into the small town centre. To his left the Atlantic Ocean swelled, the soft greenish grey of the English seaside. Driftwood signs advertised whaling tours. A pier stretched out into the bay. Clam chowder was peddled from plain, authentic-looking restaurants. Salinger liked the names – the Crowne Pointe Historic Inn, Bubala's by the Bay, Ciro and Sal's. He could see no children. The population seemed mostly male and middle-aged. There appeared to be a surprisingly large population of dogs.

There were coffee stores and pizza parlours and a Marc Jacobs clothes outlet. A few tourists scuttled through the streets, ducking the sea spray, remnants of the summer. Cool winds whipped in from the bay.

Salinger checked his map and realized that he'd overshot the house. He looped round behind the town again. He drove past the Province Lands, acres of sand dunes hidden behind a stretch of woodland. Branching off to Howland Street, he drove slowly until he found the house. It was about half a mile east of the town centre, on the road that flanked the bay, Commercial Street. The house was nearly opposite the small art museum that provided an exhibition space for many of the local painters and sculptors. He pulled the car into the small lot outside, and clambered out, stretching his legs, which were stiff after the long journey. The air was crisp, briny, pure.

He knocked on the door. Ladybird answered, wearing a fur jacket and ripped jeans. She embraced him, speaking just his name, then ushered him in.

Inside it was all rickety plain wooden furniture and flaking blue paint. There was wickerwork and there were standard lamps and antique cushions, and a pot-bellied iron stove. Native art was on the walls and the floor was painted white. Light from the sea flooded into windows facing onto the beach. Everything seemed artfully weather-beaten.

'So this was the love nest,' said Salinger. 'That's what my mother always called it. "Daddy is with his fancy woman in their love nest," she used to say.'

'It's not a bad description,' said Ladybird. 'Did your mother hate us very much?'

'Not Henry,' said Salinger. 'Just you.'

'Did she ever get over it?'

'I don't think she ever stopped hating. No.'

'It was bad luck for her,' said Ladybird.

'Henry got all the luck,' said Salinger.

'Luck runs out when you're dead,' said a voice from the corner of the room.

He looked over to see Carson, rising to stand, dressed in black trousers, immaculate white trainers, and a blue open-necked shirt. He was holding a brown paper parcel in his hand.

'I wasn't sure that you would come,' said Salinger.

'I wasn't sure that you would want to see me,' said Carson.

'It's Henry's funeral,' said Salinger. 'This has nothing to do with whether I want to see you or not.'

Over coffee that Ladybird had boiled in an Italian stove-top Moka pot, Carson apologized. He apologized for running away from Marfa and driving back to New Orleans without Salinger. He apologized for not being in touch since they had parted. He apologized for not having been there during their mother's final illness. He apologized for leaving Evelyn's funeral so peremptorily. He had come to make offerings at Salinger's feet.

Salinger listened, sipping at his coffee, and said nothing.

'Anything else?' said Salinger to Carson, who seemed finally to have run out of steam.

'You know,' said Carson. 'You know there is.'

Carson simply sat dumbly, holding onto the parcel. Salinger turned towards Ladybird, whose lined, leathery face wore an expression of remorseless, intractable neutrality.

Carson leaned sideways against the back window that faced onto the restless grey sea. He looked so young; younger than Salinger. Like Dorian Gray, except that it was Salinger's face on the painting. Violence, bullying, cruelty – they didn't corrode the soul, they protected you against corrosion, thought Salinger. They made you feel better about yourself.

Salinger batted the thought away before it could root itself and grow tendrils into the loam of his understanding. *No.* They had both just been part of the cycle of shit – agony falling down the generations, like fluorosulphuric acid, so powerful it would eat through the glass bottle that held it, then through the floor of a house into the room below and the room beyond. Nothing you could do to stop it.

'What's in the parcel?' said Salinger to Carson, who had fallen silent and left his coffee cup untouched. He was still holding the paper parcel tight.

Carson very slowly unfolded the lip of the parcel

and brought out what appeared to be a small scrap of cloth. He handled it with infinite care. Salinger held his hand out to take it, but Carson did not hand it over. He laid a clean blanket on the floor, then spread the cloth out on top.

It was a child's T-shirt, ragged and torn, somewhat stained. The neck was frayed and the body shape was saggy. On the front, a faded transfer of Captain Marvel could still be made out.

'Ladybird gave it to me,' said Carson. 'Dad kept it all this time.'

'May I?' said Salinger.

Somewhat reluctantly, Carson picked up the T-shirt and passed it gingerly to Salinger. Salinger turned it over in his hands, inspecting it carefully. He raised it, and buried his face in it.

'It smells of something lost,' said Salinger, taking the shirt away from his face. 'Old and lost.'

'I don't think he washed it in case it fell apart,' said Carson.

Salinger handed it back. Carson carefully folded it and returned it to the paper parcel. He continued holding the parcel close to his body.

'He did care,' said Carson. 'He must have.' Carson's eyes glistened.

'Yes,' said Salinger. 'Yes.' He touched Carson on the shoulder. Carson stared back at him helplessly.

Salinger looked across at Ladybird. She appeared drawn, but less drained than at the hotel room in Marfa. He broke away from Carson, suddenly embarrassed at the show of emotion.

'How are the arrangements coming along?'

'All in place. I had plenty of time. I'm glad I can finally put him in the ground.'

'Many people coming?'

'Maybe two hundred.'

'There aren't even two hundred people living in this town – are there?'

'He was popular.'

'Apparently.'

'The way you saw him – he wasn't like that. Dying made him bitter. Something else. He didn't want you to like him. He thought it would just make it more difficult for you. He wanted you to think that you weren't missing anything by not having him there. Then you could think he was a terrible old bastard and that you were well rid of him. But the truth is, he suffered to be the way he was with you. Strange as it seems, he was doing it for you.'

'Maybe it's just that guilt makes you cruel,' said Salinger.

Ladybird shrugged. 'That happens too.'

'And if what you say is true, then you're welching on him,' said Salinger.

Ladybird seemed to consider this carefully.

'It's a betrayal of sorts. But he also trusted me to do what I thought was best. This is what I think is best. It was a bad call, to treat you both like that. He often did make bad calls. Thing is, he didn't care about being wrong. He took responsibility for what he did, then he moved on. He said that every day was filled with mistakes. They can't be escaped. The point is not to let them dent your courage. Henry was brave. He was brave to be a dutiful father for the first part of his life, and brave to live for himself at the end.'

'He didn't always seem like a very nice person,' said Carson.

Ladybird started clearing their coffee cups away, before they had finished, making loud clattering noises. She seemed suddenly furious.

'Henry wasn't nice. He was good. There's a difference. I'm trying to tell you that he was a good man. Henry didn't really understand that you needed to know that. What I think is that this knowledge will help you.'

'You were his partner. Naturally, you thought he was a good man,' said Salinger.

'I guess it's all a question of perspective,' said Carson.

Carson's blandness was annoying Salinger again, after less than an hour together. Ladybird held her hand up to pacify him, as if noticing his impatience.

'It's not my opinion. He was good in an object-ive way. Talk to some of the mourners tomorrow. See what they say about Henry.'

'Everyone talks well of dead people,' said Salinger. 'It's the only good thing about being dead.'

'If you can't come to this ceremony with a spirit of generosity then you ought not to have come.'

Salinger was surprised to hear that it was Carson

who was talking. He was looking at Salinger, his eyes brittle, flinty.

The funeral was scheduled for 2 p.m. the next day. That night, Carson and Salinger slept in separate rooms, both overlooking the ocean, while Ladybird took the room facing the road. Ladybird could no longer bear to sleep in the bed that she had shared with Henry, so Salinger took it. It felt indecent occupying the same space as his father. He found out which side Henry slept on, and then confined himself to the opposite one.

Salinger felt surprised that Ladybird had asked them to stay with her. She barely knew them, after all, and he didn't doubt that many other visitors would have wished to share the house the night before the ceremony. But it was just Salinger, Carson and Ladybird in the house.

In the morning, Ladybird made them breakfast, despite Salinger's insistence that she had enough to do. Hot cakes, eggs, Tabasco, coffee, home-made jam. Salinger could see deep grooves on her forehead that had not been visible in Marfa. Grief and time were gouging at her face.

A fog had rolled in from the sea. Outside the window, the street was obscured by a damp, grey, clinging haze. It seemed to muffle sound as well as light. The cars and trucks that passed outside were barely audible.

The three of them sat down to eat. Ladybird was staring out of the window towards the road.

A flat bed truck pulling a small rowing boat was just about visible through the murk.

'What are you thinking, Ladybird?' said Salinger.

She spoke without turning her head. A branch moved in the breeze outside, mottling the light and putting part of her face into shadow.

'That people don't know what's important any more. That the old words have lost their meaning.'

She stopped to examine the backs of her hands. Salinger followed her gaze. Blue veins stood out like pencil leads.

'And I'm thinking what's wrong with everything. That's what I'm thinking.'

'Most things are wrong,' said Salinger. 'Nothing's working properly.'

'I'm talking of something specific. I'm talking about pride,' she said.

'You mean – being proud? Like . . . I don't know . . . Gay Pride?' said Carson.

'I'm talking of spiritual pride. Biblical pride, the old sort. The only unforgivable sin. It demands everything. It gives back nothing. It destroys the world.'

She swivelled away from the window and turned her gaze on Carson and Salinger.

'Henry did not have it. In your father, it was entirely absent. Henry was the most humble person I ever met.'

Salinger's gaze was caught by a large photograph of Henry above the mantel. It looked like it had been taken maybe fifteen years ago. Henry looked somehow grim, intimidating and profoundly at ease all at the same time. He was wearing a white rough-knit polo-neck sweater. His stubble was white. His eyes were gazing at something far off. He looked like an idealist, like a romantic hero.

'Another old word is gratitude,' said Ladybird. 'Something else we don't understand any more.'

Salinger turned his eyes from the photograph and studied Ladybird's face. He saw at that moment how perfectly beautiful she was – despite her age and the oddness of her looks. Her crooked nose, her pointed chin, her ungenerous lips, combined with the cheekbones, lent her a strange, unsettling majesty.

'I was so grateful for what we had,' said Ladybird. 'We both were. For this house, for each other, for this town, for our world, for our lives.

'People aren't grateful any more. They're out of control. They want everything. You can't have everything. One choice always destroys another.'

'And not only for yourself,' said Salinger.

'No. For everyone else, all the time,' said Ladybird.

Mourners began to arrive at the house at around midday. By one o'clock the house was full and people were spilling out onto the small patch of grass in front of the house and onto the wooden deck behind. The fog had still not dispersed. People shivered in thin, formal clothes.

'Looking forward to having a chat with Jesus

about Henry, Carson? Before Henry gets planted,'
said Salinger, offering Carson a cigarette.

'I don't really do that stuff so much any more.'

'You mean Jesus stuff? Or tobacco?'

'Neither of them.'

'You're telling me that you're backslidden? Isn't
that the word?'

'I don't know. I still go to church. Still read the
Bible. Still say my prayers. I just feel like I'm sort
of going through the motions nowadays.'

'Maybe your faith is being put to the test.'

'Not sure it's a test that I'm going to pass.'

'How does LouLou feel about that?'

'I haven't mentioned it. I'm hoping it'll all come
back.'

'I'd have thought it would be a relief to be rid
of it.'

'I don't know, Salinger. I kind of miss it. But
maybe you don't have a choice about this kind of
thing. Jesus is there or He's not. Right now, He's
far away. I can't hear Him. I can't feel Him.'

'Is this to do with Henry Jnr? LouLou told me.
About the possibility of . . . you know. I'm sorry.
It's a tough break.'

'Maybe. I don't know what it's to do with. All
sorts of stuff mixed up in my head.'

'Is he going to be OK? I mean, healthy?'

'We're still not sure. I guess it's just a matter of
luck.'

'I guess you're praying for him, right?'

'I just don't think they're going anywhere. I don't

know if there's anywhere for them to go. I used to feel that they went up. Way up. Now they sort of fall into the dirt. There's no breath in them. No wind behind them.'

Ladybird interrupted them, holding two trays of food and drink, and a pile of paper plates.

'Put yourself about, would you? You're family. That means you get to do shitwork.'

Carson took his tray and began moving among the crowd. Salinger stayed with Ladybird for a moment until Carson was out of earshot.

'Thanks for doing the T-shirt thing, Ladybird,' said Salinger, now taking his tray.

'It was a kind thing for you to do,' said Ladybird. 'Especially since . . .' She left the thought unfinished.

'I don't know. There's something so sad about Carson sometimes. Even being so solid.'

'It's the solidity that's sad. Some hollowness gives life space to resonate. Was it hard to find?'

'It wasn't so difficult. I searched eBay and maybe five or six vintage clothes sites. When I found one that looked a bit right, I got hold of it, then screwed it up, ripped it in the right places and left it somewhere damp for a week. In the end, it looked pretty authentic. Anyway, you believe what you want to believe, right?'

'Right. It could have had a Walmart price tag on and Carson would still have bought the story.'

Salinger smiled. He took his tray, turned away from Ladybird and headed after Carson into the crowd. The mourners were a mixed bunch, mainly men, mostly over forty, many in their fifties and sixties. Salinger found himself unavoidably drawn into conversations as he distributed spucadella bread rolls with lobster mayonnaise, potato chips and Samuel Adams beer.

'Tireless, tireless,' said one lumpish six-footer with fading white hair and a foggy, distracted smile, pulling on the neck of a beer. He was wearing weather-beaten brown lace-up boots with his black mourning suit. 'Henry never stopped. "I will not cease from mental fight." Could have been his motto. Blake, right? When I was ill a few years back, he came over every day, rain or shine. *Every day*. It was for three months. Think about that. I didn't even know him that well. I don't think I might have made it without him.'

'How did you know him?' said the man. 'Those spuckies are good.' He helped himself to another roll.

'I really didn't know him that well. I'm just helping out here,' said Salinger.

Salinger moved on to a woman, small, perky, mid-fifties, with a sour-looking mouth and a gingham dress that looked twenty years too young for her. She took a single potato chip, broke it in half, and ate one of the halves. She said her name was Jane. She was extremely thin. Before Salinger had a chance to move on, she grabbed his arm.

'Friend? Relative?'

'Just a well-wisher.'

'I know everybody says good things about people after they die, but Henry was something else. Do you know about the kitchen?'

Salinger looked towards the kitchen.

'Not that kitchen. Henry set up a kitchen here for the homeless. Did it more or less by himself. Ran it for what? Five years. A nice place. Treated people with respect. For what they had lost. Some of those people he helped, they're here. There . . . and there . . . and there . . .'

She jabbed her finger vaguely around the room. She wore black-lace gloves with open fingers. Salinger looked around for signs of anyone looking itinerant or poor, but everyone seemed well dressed and fed, apart from Jane, who looked like she would rattle when she walked.

He moved on to serve a very tall young black man whose head bobbed at least six inches above the rest of the crowd. The man refused any food, but was standing alone with no one else to talk to, so Salinger asked him how he knew Henry.

'I didn't meet Henry exactly. He found me.'

'I guess you would be hard to miss.'

'Less so when I'm flat on my back. Which is what I was, right by the roadside, maybe half a mile from here. Outside the old town hall. I was so down, I couldn't see no up. I didn't know what to do. Forgotten what it was really to do anything at all. I was messed up with drugs, robbing people, didn't care none about myself. Henry found me sitting there. It was late in the night.

'I was about to rob him for whatever money he had, but instead of being scared of me he sat down beside me and started talking to me. You know, nothing preachy or anything. Just, how you doing, talking about the weather and shit. Had this real nice British accent. Before I knew where I was, I found myself crying like a kid. I hadn't cried for many years. Many years.

'You could hear the whales sing that night. Least I could, I believe. Sounded like a creaking door. I asked Henry if he could hear the whales, and he said that he believed he could. We sat and listened together for a long time.

'Then he took me into his house, this man, he gave me a bed for two weeks, him and Mrs Nash. He showed me that a stranger could care for a nobody. I can't tell you what I owe that man. I have my own business now, I fix storm drains. I have two lovely children. Sounds like Disney, don't it? Sounds like Cindyrella. But I would be in jail or dead otherwise but for Henry Nash.'

The stories went on and on. Henry as a volunteer literacy teacher, Henry as an AIDS counsellor, Henry the friend and comfort to everyone he met.

At around one forty-five the hearse bearing Henry's coffin pulled up outside. The vehicle was a black 58 Chevy Impala station wagon. It was decorated with coloured paper, silk ribbons and silver stars. Woven twigs of driftwood spelt the name *Henry Nash*.

Salinger went outside to join Carson in the crowd of mourners. He guessed there were around a hundred people here now.

'Henry wasn't who I thought he was,' said Carson.

'No one is, I guess,' said Salinger.

'You heard the story about the night he went out on his boat to help rescue a tourist boat in a storm?'

'Didn't hear that one. Ladybird was right. Our lousy piece of shit good-for-nothing father was a fucking saint. Don't know if it makes me feel better or worse. Maybe Henry was right. Maybe it would have been better to have remembered him the way he wanted us to remember him.'

It was no more than half a mile to the church. The cortège set off at walking pace behind the hearse, with the mourners, some dressed in bright colours rather than mourning black, following behind. Three men wore top hats, many sported ebony armbands. Ladybird was at the head of the procession. She wore an elegant, expensive-looking pure white dress, trailing lace on the ground. It was by Balmain, a gift from her father many years ago. It still fitted her perfectly. She said she would always be married to Henry and wanted to wear it to say goodbye. She wore a garland of flowers in her long salt-and-pepper hair, which fell halfway down her back.

Tourists watched the procession pass, locals were lining the side of Commercial Street to watch the funeral move forward. Some took photographs. Every now and then someone joined the followers from the roadside. Occasionally Salinger would hear an anguished wail, or somebody weeping. The fog still clung to everything but the smell of the Atlantic Ocean came clear and fresh, reminding Salinger again of the English seaside. They turned right towards Town Hill and the Pilgrim Monument.

The church was just a hundred yards behind the Monument Tower, which marked the first landing point of the Mayflower. Salinger looked up. Gargoyles stared distantly down from the crenulated summit.

At the church – a wooden-framed building, entered through an arch supported by four Palladian columns – Salinger and Carson joined two other pallbearers, the hefty white-haired man with the beaten trainers, and another much smaller, much younger man who was lightly built and wearing a T-shirt under the black jacket of his suit.

Inside the church it was draughty and cold – even colder than outside. There was a slight haze, as if the fog had worked its way into the air. They carried the cedarwood box to the front of the church. The coffin felt extremely light. Salinger worried that he was not taking his share of his father's weight. They laid the coffin on a bier, which stood at waist-height, to the left of the lectern and in front of the chancel that led to the altar.

After three prayers and two hymns, members of

the congregation began to be called up to the lectern to make brief statements about Henry, mostly repeating or echoing the tributes that Salinger and Carson had heard at the house. Ladybird had elected not to speak, but she had asked if Salinger or Carson had wanted to say a few words. Carson had declined. Salinger, because he had the impression that Ladybird desired it, agreed to say something. He didn't know what, though. He hadn't made any preparation and was beginning to regret his offer.

When the pastor beckoned Salinger to come up to the pulpit in front of the congregation, he shook his head to decline, but Carson nudged him. Somehow the gesture contained enough force to raise him from his seat and up the steps to the lectern.

He gazed out at the crowd of faces. His mouth felt dry. He looked out at Ladybird in her wedding gown. Her eyes were elsewhere, raised towards the stained-glass window behind Salinger.

Salinger put his hands on the lectern, not to steady himself so much as to lend his presence, which felt insubstantial, more weight. He suddenly felt he had no right to be there. The silence grew. He was aware that a number of the people in the congregation had begun to fidget and cough.

He finally spoke, surprised at how clear and strong his voice sounded.

'I am Salinger, Henry Nash's son.'

There was a murmur from the congregation.

Salinger knew from talking to the mourners at Ladybird's house that most had not been aware that Henry had sons.

'Over there,' he nodded towards Carson, 'is my older brother, Carson.'

Heads turned towards Carson, who shifted uncomfortably and looked at the floor.

Salinger cleared his throat. Someone had left a glass of water on the lectern. He took a sip. It tasted warm and slightly tainted with bacteria.

'We didn't see much of Henry in the last thirty or so years,' said Salinger. 'In fact, we didn't see anything of him at all. He left England in . . . sometime in the 1970s. He never returned. I was ten years old and Carson was fourteen. He had a wife, Evelyn. She was our mother. She died two years ago. Henry didn't attend the funeral.'

He felt himself stall. He couldn't think what else to say. He looked desperately at Carson.

Carson. The sound of his name in Salinger's head gave birth to a further thought.

'Henry named my brother Carson after Carson McCullers. He named me after J.D. Salinger. What did those two great Americans write about? They wrote about loneliness. Henry named Carson and me after his loneliness. I think by coming to America, he shrugged off that loneliness.'

Salinger took another swig of the water, spilling a few drops onto his shirt cuff.

'I met my father for the first time in more than thirty years only a few weeks ago. He was close to death. Carson and I went to the room he was staying in at a small hotel in Texas. We didn't know what we wanted from that meeting and we don't know what we took away. Henry wasn't particularly welcoming to us. That's for sure.'

Salinger wondered momentarily if that was the end of his speech. It didn't feel like a good ending. He looked again at Carson, who had his head in his hands. A few places further along the row, Ladybird sat still and composed. Then Salinger's eyelids flickered. He licked his lips, and stared down at the congregation.

'I have this memory,' said Salinger. 'I've just had this memory. It's from when Carson and I were little kids.'

Salinger saw it all, in vivid colour, in his mind. It blotted out the church and the congregation. He closed his eyes, then opened them again.

'Our house used to back onto a cemetery. Huge old Victorian place, like a park. Except for the dead people, of course. Hardly anyone ever went there. We would use it like a playground, sometimes. Running between the stones. Henry would come with us. We might kick a ball, or have a picnic.

'One time, Henry bought us a kite. It was shaped like a butterfly. Its wings were orange, like the sun. It had blue eyes.

'On a windy day, we took it over to the cemetery. It was so gusty, we thought it would be easy. But the kite wouldn't go up. We held it this way and that, while Henry played out the line. Sometimes the wind would catch the kite and carry it up, sometimes as much as maybe ten or twenty feet. But then it would crash down to the ground again.

'Henry got annoyed with us. He yelled at us. He thought we weren't launching it properly. So then he held the kite while me or Carson held the line. Still it wouldn't go up. After a while, it got cold. Carson and me said we wanted to go home. Henry was so obsessed by the kite, by getting it up to the sky, he didn't even hear us. We just walked home by ourselves.

'It was getting dark. When I got back to the house, I looked out of the window. And I could see Dad running among the gravestones. Running like crazy, I mean, full speed. He had got the kite up maybe twenty feet, and he was trying to stop it falling. The momentum of the running kept the kite up there, see. The wind, though, kept rising and then dropping to nothing. But the kite wouldn't stay up. It just wouldn't stay up there.

'He ran as fast as he could, but in the end, he stumbled and fell, and it just crashed to the ground again. I saw him just sit down on a gravestone. I got the impression that he was crying, I don't know. He had his head in his hands.

'When he came home that night, he said that the kite had got stuck in a tree. He never mentioned it again.'

Salinger paused.

'I can't quite work out why I'm telling that story. It just came to me. Maybe Henry put it in there.'

He waited for his own tears to come. But they would not. Salinger was aware of his voice weakening.

'I guess in the end, what I'm trying to say is . . . I don't know.'

Salinger looked across at Ladybird, who he saw was crying for the first time.

'I can't blame a man for wanting to fly a kite, I guess.'

There was a long silence. Salinger stared at the faces in the congregation. Some of them were nodding, others were staring at the floor, others were weeping. He looked up. He saw that there were birds in the roof of the church, perched on one of the rafters. One of them took flight. The light caught it underneath, as if supporting the bird.

He stepped down from the lectern, then down more steps to rejoin the congregation. Before returning to his pew, Salinger stared down at the coffin. He touched the coffin with one finger. Then he walked unsteadily back to his seat next to Carson. On the way, hands reached out to shake his. He shook each one of them in return.

He felt nothing. He was glad that he felt nothing. But also, feeling nothing was the worst feeling of all.

★　　★　　★

Watching Henry's coffin having the earth packed on top of it – so much earth, packed so tight, Salinger felt he was good and fucking *buried* – left Salinger with a feeling of satisfaction. Henry was dead while he – Salinger – was alive. It was a triumph of some sort.

The congregation, now close on two hundred strong, retired back to a small hall near the town centre for the wake. There was a great deal of drink, tables creaking with seafood, meat and fish. People were talking loudly. The atmosphere was turning to one of celebration.

Salinger couldn't bring himself to do much more socializing. Mostly he stood next to Carson, making small talk – the resemblance of Provincetown to the English coast, the progress of his latest artwork. They talked about the road trip they had taken. It had already taken on the buffed and sanitized texture of nostalgia. The disturbing story about the dead dog had become comedy. The comedic story about the housekeeper and the gun had become high drama. The theft of the car had been an amusing episode of slapstick.

Then Carson thanked Salinger for forgiving him.

'What for?' said Salinger.

'Everything,' said Carson.

At that moment, Ladybird took Carson by the arm and led him away to meet the pastor who had conducted the service. The pastor was enthusiastic about meeting a true believer. He was of the opinion Provincetown was a pretty Godless place.

'What makes you think I forgive you?' said Salinger quietly, as Carson walked away, arm in arm with Ladybird.

CHAPTER 19

DECEMBER 2008, TOKYNGTON, LONDON

The phone rang. Salinger picked up. All he could hear was crying. Then:

'Salinger. He's born. He's born. Early. Ten minutes ago. He put up such a fight. LouLou was in there for fourteen hours. I'm so proud of her, Salinger.'

Then the crying again.

'Carson?'

'Salinger . . . I . . . Salinger . . . the boy.'

'Is he OK? Is he OK, Carson? Is Henry Jnr well?'

The weeping died away. Salinger waited, unbreathing, dazzled at how much he cared.

'He's perfect, Salinger. He's perfect in every way. He's my son. He's so beautiful. You're an uncle, Salinger. You're the first person I called.'

Salinger felt a slow smile spread across his face.

'I'm so happy for you, Carson. And for Henry Jnr.'

'No. No, Salinger. We're not going to call him Henry Jnr any more. That's all done with. No.

401

Salinger. After what we went through. Our journey. I've changed my mind. No. LouLou agrees.'

'What are you saying?'

'We're going to name the baby, Salinger. We're going to name the baby . . .'

'You're going to name the baby Salinger? Carson. I can't believe that you would . . .'

Salinger felt the choke of a sob in his throat.

'I'm so proud. I'm truly honoured, Carson. No one has done anything like that for me before. A nephew. That's such a thing. And LouLou agreed? I can't quite . . . Carson?'

He was aware that Carson had gone very quiet. He let his end of the line fall silent in unison. Eventually, Carson spoke.

'No. No, sorry, Sal. I'm all garbled up. I'm saying, we're going to name the . . . we're not going to name him Salinger. Sorry, if you . . . I just put it wrong.'

'Oh.'

'No – listen though. It's better than that. You'll love it. It's my tribute. Listen.'

'I'm listening.'

'The baby is called Wendell. Wendell Valentine Nash.'

Salinger heard himself laughing.

It was perfect.

He could hear Tiane moving around downstairs. She would be leaving for work in ten minutes. He could hear the briskness in her movements, clack,

clack, shuffle, thud. It was geometrical, the way she retrieved her keys, packed her bag, zipped the inner sector where she kept her wallet, the simple, regular tattoo of her shoes as she marched towards the door.

Things had been on a strangely even keel since he had invited Tiane to come back to live with him. They barely discussed either the American trip or Tiane's infidelity any more. It wasn't for fear that picking at the past would inflame the present. It felt more as if it was no longer relevant.

Some kinds of past had resonance, retained an inner force, for good or ill. Other events had no slipstream. They just died away. As each day passed, Tiane's night with William Tarbox had seemed to matter less and less. The betrayal was erased by the commitment she had made to Salinger. He had no illusions about the magnitude of that sacrifice.

He was still wondering if he forgave Carson for the damage. The Captain Marvel T-shirt was evidence that he had. The truth was, though, he still felt angry. Perhaps forgiveness was not a choice. Perhaps it was something that happened to you. Or failed to happen to you, whichever was the case.

He had decided to give Franklin De Freitas his paintings to exhibit. Damage was nothing to be ashamed of. Everybody had it. Artists were there to share it. If condemnation came, then at least he had shown courage. Courage was more important than being good. Henry had taught him that.

He was also working on an installation called, simply, *Reject*. He had written to a number of key public figures to send him letters, emails, or notifications of failure, rejections slips, letters refusing an offer of marriage, failed exam results. He isolated film stills where a character was being rejected by another character, and blew up their expressions to poster size. He made paintings of decree nisis and decree absolutes, he photographed forms for admission into foster homes. Patched into the corner of the installation was the black-and-white Polaroid photograph of himself, bruised and bloodied. It would not be noticed there. That was the point.

Rejection was the central human fact. People were made out of rejection. He lived with it every day. Everybody lived with it, every day. And no one noticed – no one on the outside, at least.

He continued to design greetings cards and accepted commissions for illustrations and cartoons. He did it now without self-hatred, or a sense of failure. Commitment wasn't everything after all. Life lived according to absolutes held too much power – for creation, but also destruction. Salinger would do what almost everybody else did. He would be normal. He would compromise.

He opened the bathroom cabinet and searched for the aspirin box that contained blister pack of

Prozac with his fingers. He found it and examined the capsules through their cellophane coat.

He looked down at the bin. He ran his finger up and down the packet. He found himself pressing with his foot on the lever that opened the lid.

He thought of Carson and Henry and the harm. He thought of the love. He thought of the idea of forgiveness. He thought of expiation. But there was no expiation. Discovering the root of your wound did not cure it. The tide would always come and go. The shore would never be finally clean.

His foot slipped off the pedal to let the bin lid close. He opened the foil wrapper, took out the capsule and swallowed.

He put the packet back into the cupboard. As he did so, his hand brushed against another blister pack. Salinger picked it up and examined it. It held Tiane's contraceptive pills, marked out in days. She had already taken that morning's dose. The edges of the cellophane blister were ragged. He rubbed at the edges absently with his fingers.

Holding the plastic sleeve in his hand, he suddenly felt the thrust and the weight of his life behind him. At the same instant, he felt all the possibility of the future in front of him. He was aware of everything narrowing down to this second, this inescapable, indestructible instant.

In the end, it all came down to now. It always did come down to now.

The sun came from behind a cloud. Sunshine flooded through the bathroom window, making everything appear momentarily changed. He pulled the blinds closed.

He stared at the bin and then examined the contraceptive pills in the palm of his hand. They felt weightless – weightless as time passing. The moment opened as if it were a bud. In his mind, he saw a horizon, and he saw space, and he moved towards them both, suddenly sure of his own momentum.

His foot pressed on the pedal once more, and the steel lips yawned, both swallowing and reflecting light.